52
FRIDAYS

52 FRIDAYS

A Polyamorous, Queer, Kinky, Tantric Love Story

KamalaDevi McClure

Published in the United States by Cleis Press, an imprint of Start Midnight, LLC, 221 River Street, Ninth Floor, Hoboken, NJ 07030.

Printed in the United States.
Cover design: Allyson Fields
Cover photograph: Adobe Stock
Text design: Frank Wiedemann
First Edition.
10 9 8 7 6 5 4 3 2 1

Trade paper ISBN: 978-1-62778-300-2
E-book ISBN: 978-1-62778-513-6

Art for Book of Shadows "Violet's Submission" reproduced with permission from the artist. All rights reserved to Mila, Sharmila Graefer.

*To all those
who love so freely,
they don't require sexual exclusivity.*

Contents

Ethical Disclaimer

This book is a work of fiction. All names, characters, places, locations, and events are the products of my imagination. It is a wildly falsified projection of my intimate network. As such, I invite you to enjoy the story and not to assume, project, or infer anything about any of my family, past or present.

Any conclusions drawn about the private lives of my partners are entirely inaccurate.

The views, thoughts, and opinions expressed in this story belong solely to the author and not necessarily to any associated individuals or groups.

As a tribute to my mentors, I asked permission to use their real names in order to honor Annie Sprinkle and Charles Muir as larger-than-life archetypes in the world of sacred sex. Since they granted dramatic license, it is important to note that their likenesses and the actions of their characters also are fictionalized from my imagination.

I believe fantasy play is fundamentally different from physical behavior.

This book reveals a series of fantasies that contain explicit sexual acts, graphic details, and objectionable language. Certain scenes include various acts of BDSM and group sex. I do not endorse any form of nonconsensual physical behavior.

Consent includes mature discernment. I do not approve of sex with anyone who does not have the critical faculty to make responsible and empowered decisions regarding sexuality.

I advocate the yogic principle of "Ahimsa," or nonviolence toward all living things. The directive to "Do No Harm" is critical for ethical power play and the safe exploration of intense sensations.

I wish to make an essential distinction between hurt and harm. Hurt is often involved in the process of growth, whereas harm indicates injury or damage. Consider the example of going to the gym: it hurts to stretch and grow new muscles, and overdoing it may result in harm, such as ripped muscles or torn tendons.

Hurt and harm can both be psychological as well as physical. Psychological trauma is a form of harm and can result when there is insufficient emotional and mental safety, violations of trust, or poor discernment.

I do not condone any sexual acts that damage the body, mind, or spirit, or that jeopardize relationship integrity.

This story is told to shine a light into the shadow of our collective psyche. Although these 52 scenarios are seemingly idiosyncratic, we believe they are expressions of universal emotions, desires, and primal impulses. I hope that by exploring our personal psyches, others might feel less isolated, and have new possibilities for how they can ethically relate with their own shadows.

Speaking openly about power and violence removes the shame and social stigma, allowing us to behave more rationally and responsibly when dark fantasies arise. By making the unconscious more conscious, I am raising awareness and empowering readers to explore their inner libidinal landscapes.

This material is intended for healing, education, art, and entertainment. This is not an instructional guide or manual. If you are seeking more information on the topics of polyamory, kink, and queer identity, please visit kamaladevi.com for recommended readings and resources.

ACT I

SUBTEXT

Sub·text /ˈsəb-tekst/

Noun

1. the unspoken motivations that are played out by actors

2. an underlying theme in a conversation or script

3. a tool playwrights use to make psychologically complex characters

The Other Woman

66 "This is awkward," Damien declares.

Raven pinches his thigh and protests, "It's only awkward because you keep saying that."

They are sitting beside each other on this couch, anxiously awaiting Violet's arrival. "They have sat together on this couch countless times before, but frequently they were half naked, with candles lit, enraptured in conscious touch or conversation. It's only been a month since they broke up and now Raven is about to meet the woman Damien wants to spend the rest of his life with.

"Actually, this is legitimately awkward. I understand now why monogamous people don't introduce their exes to their new lovers," Damien insists.

"Ex? Is that how you think of me?" Raven says, half teasing, half hurt.

"Would you prefer 'former lover'? That doesn't fit. My love hasn't stopped. You know that. There are no words for what we are." Damien's hazel eyes reveal deep compassion from beneath his large brow and shaggy red hair. Raven lets out a sigh and melts into a familiar sideways hug. She is a natural beauty who doesn't usually wear makeup, but has a hint of eyeshadow glistening around her dark eyes tonight.

Damien's right. There are no words. They've spent hours musing on how language is insufficient to express the essence of embodied love. They marveled on the unpredictable nature of life. And now, life has delivered an unimaginable opportunity for growth, named Violet.

At the first knock, Damien springs to the door. Raven stands slightly behind, observing their intimate embrace while holding her breath. Violet enters with a giant jug of honey under her arm. She's a curvy blonde in a short silky dress. Totally opposite of what Raven had pictured. Violet's bright, warm smile is positively authentic as she presents Damien with the honey pot, throws her arms around Raven with the enthusiasm of a golden retriever, hugging a little too tightly, and says, "Damien talks about you all the time. He thinks the world of you."

Raven looks over her shoulder at Damien's handsome freckled face and censors the impulse to say, "So this is the woman that has taken my place?" Instead, she forces herself to politely say, "I hope I can live up to all that you've heard."

"What is this?" Damien says, unscrewing the massive jug.

"Sorry I kept you waiting, I searched the farmers market for the perfect gift. Then I met a local beekeeper who harvests raw organic honey. There's plenty to share. Raven, you've got to taste this."

Violet pokes her finger into the jar and holds it up to drizzle off the excess. "Open wide."

It takes Raven a second to realize Violet's serious. She brings her lips close enough to be fed by Violet's sticky-sweet index finger. Once the syrup has touched her tongue Raven realizes the only graceful way to conclude this exchange is by sucking this woman's pointer.

"Your turn, Damien." Violet dips another finger into the pot.

"No thanks," he says, and Violet slowly slips the second finger into her own mouth instead.

"Mmm . . ." She makes a big show, licking both fingers. "Who needs a spoon? This is so good. . . . You know honey never spoils?"

Damien ushers both women to the couch, shaking his head and saying, "You're one of a kind, Vi."

Violet is determined to break the top layer of ice with small talk. "So, Damien tells me that you're an art teacher?"

"Performance art, mostly. Right now, I'm leading a class on monologues. In fact, I'm teaching right after this. But most of my creative energy is going into my one-woman show."

Damien adds, "She runs an experimental theater company. She's writing a piece about sacred prostitution. Some of her radical performances are online. One, in particular, I want you to see." He leaps up to grab his laptop.

Raven turns to Violet, but speaks loudly enough for Damien to hear, "He's nervous about our meeting. He thinks escaping into the computer screen will somehow make this go smoother."

Damien defends himself: "Aren't we all a little nervous?"

"Instead of talking shop," Raven proposes, "how about we have a little heart-to-heart, first?"

Violet sinks back in the couch and says, "I'm in! Where would you normally have a heart-to-heart? I mean, if I weren't here. If it were just the two of you. Would you normally connect here, or in the bedroom?"

Raven speaks slowly, trying to calm everyone down,

especially herself. "Anywhere. The place doesn't matter. I just want to hear about your hopes and fears."

"Sounds great," Violet says. "As long as we still get to watch your videos."

Damien kneels on the floor in front of Violet and pivots his broad shoulders so he can face them both. "If I'm nervous, it's only because I care about you both and I don't want to see either of you get hurt. I especially don't want to be the cause of that hurt. I wouldn't have gathered us together like this if Raven didn't insist it would ease the pain from our . . . I don't want to call it a breakup, I'd rather reframe it as a phase transition. Also, it's obvious to me that you both have medicine for each other, I just hope you get time together to discover what that is."

Raven closes her eyes to take it all in. Upon opening them, she sees the other two staring at her, so she clears her throat and tries not to sound too rehearsed. "I've wanted to meet you since the moment Damien said he found his primary partner. Anyone who captured his heart must be extraordinary themselves. I hoped I could continue dating him while you two established your foundation, but I understand that is too much to ask, since you are new to all this. So, in the end, I'm left with a choice. I could surrender to my jealous programming, and resent you for taking Damien from me, or I could turn this around and embrace Damien's new love and be part of your new life together."

Violet squeezes both of their hands, looking directly at Raven. "Damien always talks so sweetly about your Monday nights. It sounds so romantic to have a weekly rendezvous. Like it was something stable, something sacred. And I'm sorry Damien had to break it off on my account. I can imagine how painful that is."

Raven is taken aback by Violet's candor, and her aim. It was a direct hit to a fresh wound. "Yes. I'm still heartbroken, but I have a husband and other lovers to help me through this."

Raven tries to deflect the attention to Damien, hoping Violet doesn't notice she is teetering on the edge of tears. "Did he tell you about my husband and my son?"

Violet reassures Raven with her big blue eyes, "He tells me everything. We have an open relationship."

"But not open enough to share him." Raven catches the sharpness in her own tone but isn't able to dial it down.

"I tried to accept your connection," Violet says, "but when he would come back from his weekly dates with you, I felt so conflicted, so unsure, so turned on and yet so turned off all at the same time. I just fell apart. But that was before I met you."

Despite Raven's irrational impulse to flip the coffee table over and run out the door, she leans in. "What do you mean 'fall apart'?"

"I cried buckets, for weeks," Violet says.

"Damien never told me." Raven shoots him a look, only to find he's frozen in some kind of suspended animation.

Violet continues, "I mostly hid it from him, until it got unbearable and I stopped wanting sex. That's when he decided to break it off with you. I'm really sorry. I just don't know how to share him, yet. I still don't understand how it all works."

"Well, you've picked the world's best teacher. I'm sure he'll help you figure it out," Raven says, attempting to help Damien defrost.

Damien thaws enough to offer, "I used to think open relating was an abstract concept, good on paper, not in practice, until I started dating Raven and saw how she was with Nick. Their open marriage embodied my deepest values of truth and freedom. If love doesn't include that, it's not real. It's just possessiveness and neediness masquerading as love."

Raven looks at Violet, who is beaming at her. "I'm genuinely excited about learning." Violet speaks with a childlike enthusiasm. "I'm not just opening to make it work with Damien, I've always been attracted to a lot of different people and I'm a terrible liar. I want to learn from both of you."

Damien measures his words carefully before resuming. "I transitioned out of my romantic relationship with you, Raven because I couldn't keep hurting Violet. A love like ours isn't defined by romance or sex, it's deeper than that. By slowing down, I can nurture a more secure attachment with Violet. Eventually, we'll have a strong enough foundation to explore other lovers. And I've told Violet that there's no foreseeable future in which I go back to being monogamous. That would be a regression, away from my deepest values."

Violet places her nervous hand on Raven's thigh, and in an attempt to lighten the mood asks, "Do you want to show me your performance now?"

"You can watch YouTube anywhere, anytime. I wonder if there's more ground we can cover before I have to go teach my class?" Raven suggests.

Violet massages Raven's thigh, and with a soft voice suggests, "Maybe there's something that can only be said with body language?"

"Are you serious?" Raven asks.

Violet bats her eyelashes and looks at both of them. "How else am I going to learn?"

Raven turns to Damien. "Is she for real?"

Damien looks like a deer in headlights. "How about those YouTube videos?"

"I've got an idea," Violet perks up. "We can cuddle on your bed and watch them."

Raven surrenders, "I'm always down for cuddling."

They reconvene in Damien's impeccable room and prop themselves against the headboard with designer pillows. Raven is surprised to see that the meditation candle on Damien's dresser is already lit. Lying beside Violet, Raven notices a certain electricity between their bare shoulders.

"Do you have any videos of your one-woman show?" Violet asks, with sincere interest.

"I'm still in rehearsal. But I hope you can come see the show. Live performance is so much better than a video. Besides, something tells me this whole YouTube racket is just a ploy to get us into the bedroom."

The sound of Violet's giggles reminds Raven of coins falling into a wishing well. "Oooh. Busted! You've got me figured out."

Raven can't help but laugh with her.

Damien interrupts to say, "I actually do want Violet to see the one where you tie yourself up and talk about finding sexual liberation through lesbian domination."

Violet can't keep her hands from caressing Raven's soft skin. "I promise to cyberstalk you later, but right now, maybe you could show me how you two would normally connect before I was in the picture?"

"Is she always this flirty?" Raven asks Damien.

"I'm not flirting." Violet winks. "I just want to know if you'd be wearing this much clothing if I weren't here?"

"You're right, you're not flirty, you're downright frothy!" Raven teases.

Damien pumps the emergency break. "I don't think that's a good idea. Remember how upset you got last time Raven and I were sexual?"

Violet argues, "But I didn't know her then. I can see now, she has a heart of gold. She's like a golden girl. She can do no harm."

"Thanks." Raven wonders if she's trembling from being turned on or because she's upset. "As much as I'd love to take off my clothes and roll around with you both, it would be pretty confusing to my system. The de-escalation with Damien has been hard, I hope you understand."

"Of course," Damien says, placing a warm hand on her shoulder.

Violet adds, "I don't want to confuse anything. I just want to nurture you with some touch. If you take off your bra, I can massage your shoulder blades."

Blood rushes to Raven's tender parts, but her olive skin is too tan to blush. "I'm enjoying your touch, but think I better keep my bra on."

Damien appears relieved to not be the only one governing Violet's advances, but seems conflicted about something else. "The real reason I wanted Violet to see your Shibari performance is that I thought maybe you could shine some light on the topic of rough sex."

Raven is mindlessly melting into Violet's deep-tissue massage, and she responds with a relaxed, "Mmmm-hmm." Meanwhile, she's wondering: *How dare he ask me for sex advice for his new lover? How audacious, and yet, how endearingly humble.*

"Violet asked me to dominate her." Damien pauses and lays his hand on Raven, as if testing for a fever. "I'm sorry if this is too much, but it's a real dilemma."

"It's okay," Raven says, leaning into the warmth of his palm.

He continues. "Naturally, I want to help her explore her fantasies, but this is an edge for me. Sometimes when she goes down on me, she takes my hand and pushes it on her head. Which feels disrespectful, but the harder I push, the more turned on she gets. It's irresistible the way she looks up at me and smiles with those big, watery eyes."

As he speaks, Raven's mind drifts to the last time wrapped her own lips around his throbbing cock. She flashes on the ecstasy in his face, then her chest is pierced with longing. She breathes into the growing warmth between her own legs and envisions her etheric cock growing hard and hungry to penetrate.

She imagines herself thrusting forcefully into Violet's face. The thrill of Violet's resistance while she drives into her soft mouth. *Take that, Bitch!*

Her private revelry is interrupted by Violet's curiosity. "Damien says you worked with a professional dominatrix, is it true?"

"It's true," Raven says, overwhelmed with the yearning to defile this innocent woman.

"There's so much I want to ask," Violet presses.

"Another time, maybe," Raven says, scrambling to sit up and sort out her feelings. Is she hurt? Is she jealous? All she knows is that she's turned on. "I think I'd better go."

"What's wrong?" Damien asks.

"It's too soon. The seduction is too strong. If I'm going to keep my vow to do no harm . . ." Raven finds her feet and impulsively pecks Damien on the cheek. ". . . I better leave now."

"Is it something I did?" Violet wonders out loud.

"No. You're intriguing, almost irresistible, and maybe if we met in different circumstances it would be a different story, but I need to take a little break from Damien." Raven leans in to hug Violet, who manages to kiss Raven square on the mouth, the warmth of which lingers on her soft lips long after she darts out the door.

Teacup in the Temple

Violet shows up uninvited and unannounced to an old church in the queer neighborhood of San Diego, where Raven's performance art class is in progress. On the door, directly under a faded rainbow sticker, a brass shingle reads: THE BAREFOOT AND PREGNANT THEATER. The building is in dire need of a paint job, but even with the combined income from benefactors, ticket sales, and acting classes, Raven is barely breaking even.

Violet seamlessly blends in with a couple dozen students who are selecting audition sides and running lines.

From the third row, Raven listens and critiques each student's monologue. She does her best not to look offended when "Big Mike," a longtime student, recites the famous "You complete me" monologue from *Jerry Maguire*.

After the class applauds, Raven confesses her intolerance for the codependent monogamous propaganda. "I would hate to see any of you blow an audition because of poor content selection. Know your audience. Who are you trying to touch? Even if it's just an audition. You don't want to offend a casting director by performing the wrong piece!"

"I was going for dramatic irony," Big Mike says in defense.

Raven softens her tone. "While I celebrate your taking an artistic risk, I'd hate to see it backfire. In any case, there were several sweet moments during your delivery where I felt raw emotion. I want more of that." His body relaxes as the class applauds and he steps offstage.

Raven sighs as she pinches the bridge of her nose and then addresses the class. "I'm sorry. The monologue struck a personal chord." She composes herself for the next monologue by crossing her legs and announcing, "I'll try not to let my own biases color my critiques. Who's next?"

Violet steps onstage. It takes Raven a moment to realize the stunning young woman in a short blue skirt is Damien's new partner. Raven strains to maintain her professionalism as she calls out from the front row, "Welcome. State your name."

"My name is Violet West," she says, visibly nervous.

"Great. Show us what you've got." Raven clears her throat in an attempt to discharge her unexpected but undeniable attraction.

"I'll be reading a poem by Sandra Cisneros, entitled: 'Down There.'"

Without hesitation, Violet launches into a classic piece about menstrual blood written by one of Raven's feminist idols. While listening, Raven can't help but wonder whether Violet is bleeding, and if so, whether her panties are cotton or lace. When the selection ends, the audience is stunned. Violet doesn't know how to bow. The delayed applause includes catcalls from a few of the lesbians in Raven's troupe.

Since Violet is new, Raven spares the critique and says: "Nice work." Then adds, "I want to see more from you."

"Is that it?" Violet exhales as if she were bracing for criticism.

"For now," Raven says sternly.

"Can I talk to you after class?" Violet presses.

"Fine," Raven responds, suppressing her teacher's-pet fantasy. "Let's hear it for Violet."

On the second applause, Violet steps offstage.

After the final performance, Raven closes the class with director's notes. "After memorizing the text, you can add layers by using subtle body language and vocal intonations to convey what is not being said. I want everyone 'off book' next week so we can really start performing." She glances at her trusty tomboy watch, then offers to preview a teaser from her upcoming show, for students who are willing to stay after class. The room erupts into enthusiastic applause.

Raven steps center stage and says, "I know I tell you not to disclaim your work, but the teacher doesn't always follow her own rules. As you know, my show is called *The Sacred Slut Series*. It's a collection of personal narratives that culminate in a tribute piece to Annie Sprinkle's work, *The Legend of the Sacred Prostitute,* from her historic show *Post Porn Modernist,* which toured internationally for five years and is controversial because the final scene had a sex-magic ritual that included self-pleasuring. I'll give you a glimpse of the prelude I wrote leading up to the climactic scene."

After a few breaths, Raven's smile becomes bigger, her voice becomes higher, and she somehow grows taller as she plays Annie Sprinkle:

"Did I have a real orgasm? That's what everyone wants to know. Did I fake my orgasm? Why people are so hung up on this point is rather amusing. It is not about orgasm. The ritual is about re-creating the feel of the ancient temples, entering a state of ecstasy to bring prayers to the Divine.

"Let me address the orgasm question once and for all. I see no point in faking an orgasm, and I never did. Keep in mind I have a more expanded concept of orgasm than most folks. With the use of the cool crystal dildo, I almost always had a vaginal, cervical, or G-spot orgasm. I also usually had some kind of breath or energy orgasm. About half the time, I had a clitoral orgasm, and a third of the time I had a clitoral climax. For me the two are different. I experience clitoral orgasms as smallish orgasms that radiate through the pelvis, and clitoral climaxes are much more intense, starting in the clit, radiating throughout the pelvis, then shooting through the entire torso and out the top of my head. Usually, it results in moans or screams. On approximately a dozen occasions, I'd have what I call a full-body-mega-kundalinigasm, where ecstasy-electricity streamed through my entire body for several minutes. Let me tell you, nothing makes a girl feel more like a real Goddess than a mega-kundalinigasm!

"Sometimes my orgasms were subtle, and sometimes my battery was empty and I had no orgasm at all. Those times were an important part of the whole and made the performances all the more interesting and challenging."

Raven steps to the edge of the stage, drops her smile, and lowers her voice. "Isn't that what great art is? Finding something that touches your heart, but confronts you to the core? It stretches your limited sense of self so you're forced to grow.

"So I'd ask myself, what do I need to do to be ready for this ritual? What do I need to let go of? Then I realized, I just need to step out of my own way."

Raven slowly reaches up her skirt and with a single movement pulls her panties down her thighs, stepping out of them one leg at a time. She bows. The room is silent as the church it once was.

Her students are shocked but supportive. She picks up her panties, bows again, and announces, "Please take flyers to pass out and post in public places. The show is a month away, and only running for a week!"

As Raven makes her way offstage, Violet corners her. "Do you have a minute?"

"What did you want to talk about?" Raven says, gazing into Violet's eyes, momentarily lost in a cloudless sky.

"Nothing in particular." Violet plays coy. "I just wanted a little attention from you. I watched your YouTube videos, all of them. I didn't want to stop," Violet says, casting herself in the role of teacher's pet from Raven's fantasy.

Raven forces herself to look away and stacks her flyers. "What are you really doing here?" Raven asks.

"I want to get to know you. I wonder what our connection would be without Damien," Violet admits.

After a deep breath, Raven says, "Sorry to leave so abruptly last week."

Violet drapes the sensual curves of her body against the end of the stage. "Me too. I didn't want it to end on that note, so I came here tonight to make it right."

The old double doors in the back squeal and slam every time a student exits. Suddenly they become starkly aware that the last student has left. They're in the theater alone, together.

"I was thinking about how hard it must be for you to not be seeing Damien on Monday nights anymore."

"Pause right there." Raven winces and instinctively pivots away from Violet. "Give me a moment..." She finds herself facing the concession stand, staring at the cups, and blurts: "Want tea?"

"Yes, please," Violet says.

Raven manages to escape her emotional storm by washing two clay mugs in the theater sink.

"I heard what you said to the class about the 'You complete me' speech. I can only imagine what you're going through."

Raven pauses her dishwashing when she feels a piercing ache in her low back. She remembers Damien's promise that his love would never stop, it would just run underground, like groundwater.

"He's been one of the great loves of my life," Raven says. She dries the mugs, pours the hot tea, and delivers a cup to Violet in the first row, where they both sit quietly blowing on their tea.

"What's happening with your lower back?"

Raven realizes that she's been fussing with her left hip while waiting for her tea to cool.

"It's nothing; I overextended my sacrum during rehearsal, but I have to keep rehearsing, so it's becoming chronic." She doesn't know how long she can remain polite.

Violet lays her hand on Raven's hip, gently. "I do massage, you know?"

"I remember. And yoga. and pole dancing. Damien is very lucky to have found you."

"He adores you too."

Violet invites Raven to lie across the stage so she can work on her sacrum, reassuring her, "It's a purely professional offer."

"It better be." Raven lies with her face pressed in a mat, in front of an empty audience, ruminating: *Why is this woman so persistent? I should be mad at her. Why does she smell like strawberries? If her fingers weren't so damn skilled, I would kick her out of my theater, right now.*

While Violet works the tender ridge of Raven's ass, Raven surveys her set design. There is an eight-foot flat painted with the Taj Mahal, a full-length mirror on wheels, and a makeup table covered with wigs. In the far corner of the stage, there is a massive altar with a golden Buddha surrounded by a variety of exotic sex toys. For Raven, the theater is a special space; a sort of sacred temple. Her eyes linger on the futon in the corner, imagining how Violet's naked body would feel against it.

"Is this the set for *The Sacred Slut Show*?" Violet asks.

"Mmm-hmmm . . ." Raven says, enjoying the perfect pressure on her bottom.

"Your temple is so familiar, yet so foreign. It reminds me of a yoga cult I used to teach at, except the guru didn't have your erotic twist."

After several long strokes, Violet digs in. "When we met, I thought I'd feel competitive, but I don't feel that at all. I have a strange feeling that you can do no harm, you're glorious, like this golden Buddha."

Violet suddenly spies an eight-inch phallus prominently displayed in the center of the altar.

"Is that the cool crystal cock you talked about in your monologue? Is it real crystal? Is that what you'll use to masturbate onstage?"

Raven nods to each of Violet's questions.

Violet's touch seems to have become intimate, and is now filling Raven with arousal.

"Do you want to flip over so I can work on your pelvis?" Violet asks innocently, which somehow overloads Raven's circuit breaker, firing up her defense system. She rolls over swiftly and lands a firm hand on Violet's upper thigh.

"No. I better get back to rehearsing," Raven says sharply, pushing herself up. "You've got amazing hands, but it's late. I've got a lot to do."

"Did I do something wrong?" Violet asks.

Raven doesn't answer.

Violet backs off. "Okay. I understand. But I want to keep coming. I've always wanted to take acting lessons. Is that okay?"

"You could use direction," Raven blurts. "I mean, you have potential. As long as we can keep our roles clear."

Violet is ecstatic at the prospect of continuing her connection with Raven and exclaims, "You're the teacher. When I'm in class, I'll follow your direction."

Raven smiles and walks Violet to the door. They fall into a good-bye hug, which melts, then lingers. Neither wants to pull away. Violet's hand slides down Raven's back to her hips.

"How's your sacrum now?" Violet asks.

"Better."

"I'd be happy to get my hands on you, anytime, Mistress Raven."

Raven releases a breath. "I've got work to do."

"Are you going to rehearse the self-pleasuring scene?"

"Good night, Violet." She opens the squeaky door and watches Violet walk out into the cool dark night.

Raven walks dreamily through her theater, picking up papers and props from the class. She dims the house until only the ghost light is left. Ritualistically, Raven begins lighting each meditation candle at Buddha's feet while reciting a Pagan prayer: "By the North which is her body, by the East which is her breath, by the South which is the bright light of her spirit, and the West which holds the waters of her womb . . ."

Raven breathes deeply and envisions a full audience. She runs her hands up the length of her torso, lingering on her breasts. She imagines a drummer, as she moves energy up her spine and pumps her pelvis to the rhythm of her breath.

With eyes closed, she remembers the feel of Violet's hands massaging her inner thighs. Then she flashes on Violet's short skirt and thinks how easy it would be to lift the blue fabric and reveal more of her mystery.

Raven returns to her lines while rubbing coconut oil on her

sacred crystal cock. Her mind becomes a salad of images: Violet's adept fingers, blonde hair, and heart-shaped lips.

Raven is simultaneously aware of how she longs for Damien's embrace. The loss of his warmth overwhelms her with sobs. She cups the crystal wand, holds it to her heart, and surrenders to her grief.

At that moment, the door swings open and Violet calls, "Raven? Oh, Mistress Raven."

Raven stops crying and quickly sets the crystal dildo down.

Violet makes her way down the aisle of the dark house to say, "I'm sorry. I would've called, but I don't have your number."

Raven has already dried her tears, but her voice breaks when she says, "It's okay, what did you forget?"

"Your teacup. I left it on the stage."

"You came back for a stupid teacup?"

"I didn't want you to think I'm a slob. I wouldn't have been able to sleep. Let me wash it." At this point, Violet notices Raven's swollen eyes and the buoyancy drains from her voice.

"Have you been crying?"

Trembling, Raven struggles to hold back a stream of tears, but Violet's comforting caresses are already all over Raven's body.

"I just miss him."

"Of course you do," Violet says, comforting her new friend as they sit silently in the glow of the candlelight. "Are you mad at me?"

"Not anymore. I used to be, but that was before we met. You're so sweet. Who could stay mad at you?"

"I wish I could do something to make you feel better. I mean, it's my fault."

Raven goes for sarcasm. "Yeah, but what am I going to do, punish you?"

"If that would make you feel better. I'd do anything to help you, right now." Violet looks directly into Raven's eyes and says tenderly, "Maybe I deserve to be punished."

Raven tries to laugh it off but knows she's not kidding.

"You can take it out on my ass. I mean it." Violet pleads.

Raven sobers up. "Really? Are you up for a little spanking?"

"It's the least I can do, after taking your boyfriend," Violet urges.

Raven situates herself on the futon and directs Violet to drape her body across her lap, so that their crotches are close together, but not touching. "Lie here. Facedown."

Raven rolls up her sleeves and rubs her hands together while saying, "Look, we've never done this before, so you have my full permission to say Yellow, if you need me to slow down, or Red, if you need me to stop. Okay?"

"What about Green—if I want more?"

"Smart-ass!" Raven is smiling as she peels up Violet's skirt and is delighted to find a matching blue thong wedged in the crack of her developed gluteus muscles. Raven begins by rubbing her warm hands against Violet's cool bubble butt.

"I'm ready," says Violet.

In a deep voice Raven teases, "So, this is going to hurt you more than it hurts me," and she starts with little rhythmic taps to bring blood to the surface.

"I have a high threshold for pain," Violet says, encouraging Raven to hit harder.

"Good. You're going to need it." Raven lightly tickles Violet's asscheeks and notices little goose bumps forming on the surface.

Slap! Slap! "This is for taking my boyfriend."

Slap! Slap! "This is for being so fucking cute."

Slap! Slap! "And young."

Violet giggles.

SLAP! SLAP! "This is for not knowing how to share."

SLAP! SLAP! "I had a good thing going with Damien, and then you showed up with your short skirts and unbelievable ass, and you pulled us apart."

SLAP! SLAP! "You knew that he was dating two other women when he met you. He dropped them when he started seeing you."

SLAP! SLAP! "You probably loved getting him all to yourself."

Violet protests, "No. Actually, I didn't."

SLAP! SLAP! "Who said you could talk back?"

SLAP! SLAP! SLAP! SLAP!

Spanking has an impact like penetration. Each shock is a thrust of Raven's sexual power. Violet undulates her pelvis and wordlessly begs for more.

"This is for pretending to be all innocent when you are clearly enjoying this." *SLAP! SLAP!*

"This is not for anything you did, but because you are a great little whipping girl." *SLAP! SLAP!*

Raven strokes her rosy ass and savors how vital and ecstatic she feels. The pocket of space between the two women's crotches seems to shrink in size.

Raven vigorously rubs Violet's ass to distribute the sensation. "Did I hurt you?"

"Yes, Mistress," Violet says with obvious pleasure in her voice. "And I loved it."

"You want more?"

"Yes, please," Violet confesses breathlessly.

"Good." *SLAP! SLAP! SLAP!*

"That's for enjoying yourself." *SLAP! SLAP!*

With every slap, Raven's hand grows hotter, and the blood rushes between her legs as if she's growing an erection.

Violet reaches around to massage Raven's thighs. Raven stops spanking and removes Violet's hands.

SLAP! SLAP! "That's for grabbing at me like a bitch in heat."

Violet explodes with more giggles. Raven realizes how deeply willing she is. There is nothing stopping Raven from rolling Violet over and fucking her on the stage. In order to resist her impulse to grab the crystal cock from the altar and use it on Violet, now, Raven decides to busy her hands with a continued rhythm of vigorous spanking.

SLAP! SLAP! "And this is for showing up to my class uninvited."

SLAP! SLAP! "And seducing me with that sexy poem."

Raven slows her spanking and lightly caresses Violet's sensitive behind.

"There. Now I feel so much better. I'm going to put your bottom away and you're going to leave here without any aftercare!"

Violet slowly adjusts herself as she stands up. "Can I kiss you?" Violet asks as she moves toward a hug.

"No. You don't even deserve a hug. I hope you're satisfied with yourself. I expect to see you next Friday." Raven pulls away. "And take your damn teacup."

FRIDAY #3

On Neutral Grounds

There's a gay-owned café a block from the Barefoot and Pregnant Theater. Violet arrives in a formfitting black dress and a strand of pearls. She savors the smell of burnt coffee beans, admires the decadent collection of cupcakes in the display case, and wishes she knew what Raven likes so she could have it waiting when she arrives.

She finds a table near the window and peers at the faint reflection of her hair arranged in a French twist. She's wearing heavy eyeliner that turns up in the corners like the eyes of a feral cat. She carries a clutch handbag containing silk gloves to wear during her monologue, later. At 5:00 p.m. she wonders if Raven has changed her mind about coming. Violet laughs at the irony of being stood up in her femme fatale costume.

At 5:08 Raven turns the corner and greets one of the store

owners before seeing Violet, who stands to plant a European kiss on both cheeks. Raven tolerates the formality.

"Your greeting goes with the costume."

"You mean this old thing?" Violet says, patting her hairdo. "I thought it would add subtext to my feminist poem."

"You look like a high-class Parisian hooker."

"Even better."

Smiling, Raven shakes her head. "You look stunning, like a seductress." Violet swoons and they indulge in a moment of mutual adoration.

In a flash, it's gone. Raven seems clouded by the weight of what she has come to say. She clears her throat and leans forward, getting down to business. "Thanks for meeting before class."

"I'm surprised you invited me out, in public no less. It tells me you aren't ashamed of what you did to me last week."

"Oh, I meant to ask, was your ass sore?"

"Yes, but it was worth it. You can go harder on me next time." Violet winks and simultaneously shoots a finger gun.

Raven heads her off at the pass. "Look, about next time, I've been thinking there's a lot at stake and . . ."

A waiter with red suspenders interrupts to ask Raven if she wants her "usual." Violet takes note that Raven ordered a dirty chai latte.

Raven continues, "I've got a big show coming up and my hands are full. I can't have new distractions right now. I'm sorry."

Violet's smile doesn't waver. She shrugs and says, "No problem, I'm not interested in distracting you. I want to be an inspiration. Your show is about the Sacred Slut, right? Even a Sacred Slut needs a little study break."

Raven upturns her head with closed eyes, releasing an audible breath. "Look, it was hot, and I'll admit in a twisted way, it shifted how I feel about Damien. It healed something, but you're his girlfriend now, and I can't rebound from him to you."

"I talked to him about our chemistry and the spanking scene. He thinks you're good for me. He says there are things you can teach me that he can't. Not just because you're a woman, but because you're you."

Raven shakes her head. "It's too complicated. This can't continue."

Violet feels like something precious is being ripped out of her grasp. "So that's it? You're ending it before it starts? You asked me out to this cute little café so that you can break up with me on our first date?"

Raven softens her tone. "This isn't meant to be a date, I just wanted to meet you on neutral ground, so we would keep our hands off each other. Otherwise, I don't think I could see the situation rationally."

Violet approaches from a new angle. "You don't need to be rational, I know you're still heartbroken. I just want to ease your loss while getting to know you better." She places her arm on Raven's arm and feels the warmth between them. "Maybe if we got together for a few hours each week, you could cry on my shoulder until you don't miss him anymore."

"Tempting, but things could get complicated real quick. I want to be clear, not cruel, and the truth is, I don't have the bandwidth to take on any new projects. If it weren't for my show, believe me, I'd love to take you on, but I have no business dating a monogamous, straight woman."

"See that's where you're wrong. I may be new to polyamory, but I'm not straight."

Raven is clearly taken aback. "I just assumed that when you said you were new to all this, you meant . . ."

"I came out as bi when I was sixteen. My big brother used to hang out with the neighborhood tomboy. She was rather butch. She wore camouflage pants and combat boots and shaved the back of her head. She pulled her hair into a ponytail just to show it off. I'm not sure if I had a crush on her, or if I wanted to be her.

"One night, we stayed up late watching TV. My brother fell asleep, so I asked her to tuck me in. When we got to my room, I undressed and jumped between the sheets and asked her to kiss me good night."

Raven leans in, her palm naturally moving to Violet's thigh. "Did she?"

"I kissed her, open mouth, giving her permission to kiss me everywhere. She planted one on each nipple and a quick peck on my pussy. I asked if I could do the same to her. She pulled her pants halfway down and pushed her pussy into my face. I just stuck my tongue between her legs.

"Afterward, I told her it was my first time and she said, 'Yeah I can tell,' then left.

"But I couldn't sleep . . . my ego was bruised. Later that week, I got up the courage to ask for a do-over. I knew her parents were out, so I went over to her house when she was already in bed, and I flung the covers off and found her wearing white cotton panties. I said, 'I want you to teach me how to go down on you.' She said, 'I'm sleeping,' but I was determined. I pulled off her panties and threw them on the ground. She was like, 'Go slow.' She taught me to put my hand on her clit as I slowly sipped my finger inside her.

"She started grinding on my hand and the next thing I knew she was cumming. I was shocked at how fast it was. I thought, *this is what it must feel like for guys.*"

"Then what happened?" Raven pleaded.

"I wanted to tell the world. I came home and told my mom, 'I'm bisexual,' and she said, 'No you're not.' And I'm like, 'Yes, I am. I can prove it,' and I showed her my new hicky, and she's like, 'I don't like anyone doing that to you, whether it's a guy or a girl.' Then I announced to my girlfriends: 'I'm bi.' But I didn't get down with any girls for a long time afterward. I've always wanted to be with a more experienced woman, like you." Violet squeezes Raven's thigh. "So you're not going to get rid of me that easily."

Raven can't hide her smile as she announces, "And with that, I'm going to the powder room."

Violet sits for a moment with her legs crossed . . . bouncing . . . feeling the pressure on her engorged clit. . . . Unsatisfied, she follows Raven to the bathroom.

For a gay-owned coffee shop, the decorations are unremarkable. It has one sink, two stalls, and it smells like cheap disinfectant. At least it's clean. It has a high ceiling with a little skylight where you can see a single branch with one little leaf waving in the breeze.

"Raven?"

"I'm peeing."

"Don't mind me. I didn't follow you in here, or anything," Violet lies. She turns on the water and watches the branch whip around like a flag.

Raven steps out, pants still unzipped, to find Violet rubbing her hands under the water. Raven approaches the sink, but Violet makes no attempt to move out of the way. Raven presses her body against Violet's curvy back, reaching around and adding her hands to the flowing stream. Watching over Violet's shoulder, she plays with the webbing of Violet's fingers. Violet marvels at the sensation of touch under water, then turns her face to question Raven, feeling like captive prey, before they melt into their first kiss. Raven pins Violet against the wall, a leg between her thighs. They are kissing, the water is still running, and they are still in a second-rate bathroom.

"It feels sorta dirty, doesn't it?" Violet whispers in a trance.

Raven laughs. "I was too turned on to pee." Raven breaks the embrace and returns to the stall.

Violet finally turns off the faucet and says, "Don't mind me, it's not like I'm listening." She takes a brown paper towel from the dispenser and makes a production of drying her damp hands.

"Don't distract me," Raven says, but her laughter betrays her.

"Are you pee-shy?"

Then, Violet hears Raven's urine and visualizes a golden stream spraying into the bowl from between her nether lips. She reaches into her clutch and pulls out the satin gloves.

"I brought gloves for tonight's class." She stuffs her slender fingers into one of them, smoothing it up to her elbow, then reaches under the door to wave to Raven. "Do you think they're too much?"

"Go away," Raven insists.

Violet pulls her other glove on. The peeing stops. She drops to her belly and pokes her head up into the stall . . .

"Crazy woman, what are you doing?" Raven exclaims through an undeniable smile. Violet slithers in her low-cut dress under the door. Her pearl necklace is a surreal contrast with the bathroom tiles.

"Get in here before someone sees you." Raven moves out of Violet's way and helps her stand up.

"Who's going to see me? We have total privacy."

They kiss again, and the walls of the bathroom dissolve. Raven hikes Violet's dress up and guides her onto the toilet seat. Her fingers are blocked by Violet's hosiery. "Seriously, woman, what are you wearing?"

Raven scrapes her teeth against Violet's thigh until she has a hole large enough to rip with her finger. She can't seem to get to her pussy fast enough. Her kissing becomes sloppy as she struggles to get under Violet's panties, but as soon as she touches her tunnel . . . time stops. There is silence inside.

Violet utterly surrenders to Raven's touch, moving to the rhythm that makes the world go round. Raven's fingers feel timeless, filled with light and consciousness. A massive wave overtakes them both, then somehow delivers them safely to shore.

Suddenly, they are back in the bathroom, and Raven slowly withdraws her hand. Violet holds Raven's head to her heart and strokes her hair. She thinks she hears Raven weeping but doesn't need to know what it means.

Eventually, their bodies separate, but there is no real separation.

Raven says, "I'll get the door, unless you want to go out the way you came in?"

They giggle like schoolgirls spilling into the once-cramped bathroom, now transformed into something monumental.

"Do you think my ripped panty hose will add subtext to my monologue?"

"You better behave during my class tonight."

"I'll save my flirtations for when we're alone. How's next Friday?"

"It's a date," Raven says with a kiss.

FRIDAY #4

Raven's Nest

Nervous about Violet's visit, Raven rushes around, picking up laundry, toys, and other landmines left by her six-year-old. She's not ashamed of the mess but wants to make a good impression on her new lover. Having already straightened the pillows and props in the playroom, she tidies the entrance until the doorbell rings.

Violet plants a kiss on Raven's lips before slipping off her shoes. Raven admires her white knee-high stockings, which compliment her short pink sundress.

"I thought we'd hang out in my playroom, around back."

"Oooh, playroom." Violet raises an eyebrow.

"Don't get excited, it's not a dungeon or anything. Nick converted the garage into a rehearsal space before we had the theater. Now I use it to work on the show."

"Can I get a private performance?"

"I was hoping to get a little break from all things show related," Raven says, running her hand through her hair.

Violet takes her eyes off Raven long enough to look around the house. "Is your husband home?"

"You want to meet Nick? He's doing his own rehearsing right now."

Violet raises her eyebrows. "What does he do?"

"He's a multi-instrumentalist, but I think I hear his guitar." Raven leads Violet through a hallway toward the muffled music. She cracks the door. "Honey . . . Violet's here." She swings it wide to reveal a muscular man perched on the bed, arms wrapped around an acoustic axe, straining his voice into a falsetto. He finishes the chorus before he stops strumming and smiles at the two women.

"Great voice," Violet exclaims.

"It's a new song, I'm working out the kinks."

Raven greets her man with a casual peck on his forehead. "This is the woman I've been telling you about."

"Uh-oh. What exactly has she told you?" Violet flirts.

Nick offers his hand from the guitar. "I hear you're the teacher's pet."

"I had so much fun in the last two classes . . ." Violet says, smiling.

"And out of class . . ." Raven adds suggestively.

"Any big plans today?" Nick asks.

"I need a little rehearsal break, we'll be in the playroom," Raven says.

"And that, ladies and gentlemen, is why I wish I were gay..." Nick strums his guitar for emphasis as if he were making a joke onstage.

Violet takes the bait. "You mean you wish you were a lesbian?"

"No, dating women is too complicated. I wish I could go to

a gay gym and see someone for a few seconds, and take them to the sauna for sex. I'm just not into guys."

"Imagine how out of shape you'd be if you were always having sex instead of working out," Raven teases.

Nick lowers his voice like he's telling Violet a secret. "The truth is, the gym is just an excuse to check out chicks. Having sex is how I actually keep my body in shape."

Violet is charmed by the whole exchange. "It's great to see you two so open with each other."

"After ten years of living with this Sacred Slut, you kind of have to be," Nick jokes. Raven playfully squeezes Nick's pectorals, and he takes it as the cue that they're leaving. "Tell Damien I miss seeing him on Mondays."

Violet says, "Oh, I almost forgot, he sends his love to you too."

"Tell him he's always welcome."

Raven interrupts, "Sorry, Nick. It's probably going to be a while before I'm ready to see him."

"That's cool. I just thought when you're ready, we could double date... Anyway, tell him I miss him."

Violet nods and follows Raven through the backyard, crunching dry leaves as they walk across the lawn to a separate building behind the house.

Inside, the walls of the playroom are painted like a sunset. The room is filled with colorful pillows and movable furniture. There is a bean bag, several blocks, a night table, and a chaise lounge that looks like a therapy couch. Violet's attention is drawn directly to the futon. After surveying the space for the most suitable place to recline, Violet doesn't just sit on the futon, her body becomes one with it.

"Your hubby is lovely. It's refreshing to hear how he supports you. I guess most men would be stoked about their wives being bisexual, but they would probably ask, 'Can I watch?'"

Raven closes the door to the outside world and says, "My sexuality is not some performance for anyone else's pleasure, and he knows it."

"Says the woman who is about to masturbate onstage," Violet teases.

"It's NOT masturbation!" Raven's tone is sharper than she intended. "That's been a trigger." She rubs the bridge of her nose and slows down to say, "*The Legend of the Ancient Sacred Prostitute* is actually a deeply devotional piece. Whether anyone gets it or not...my intention is to transmit a prayer."

Violet pats the mattress beside her. "Lie here. Let me help you relax."

Raven collapses with a big exhale, grateful for the safety and comfort of this strange creature's touch.

"I'm sorry, this show is all I've been eating, sleeping, and dreaming for months."

Violet repositions her body so she can reach under Raven's shoulders, trace her hands along her neck, and cradle her head.

"I've seen too many self-indulgent one-woman shows. I don't want to turn myself inside out and have people walking out scratching their heads wondering: 'what the fuck was that?' This is not just a show, it's a ritual. I want people to go into a trance, using breath, movement, and sound, so they can access their own ecstasy."

Violet listens quietly and continues with the therapeutic massage.

"If this ritual is performed properly, it's not just for the audience, but for our ancestors. I'm doing this show for all the sexual outcasts, for all the perverts and pioneers. I'm doing it for men and women that were branded as witches and devil worshipers. I'm also doing it for the sad housewives who don't know how not to go numb in their girl parts. I'm doing it for the collective."

Violet's expert hands are rocking Raven's body. It feels shamanic—like she's shaking off lifetimes of trauma.

"I want to surrender to the Goddess and let her perform through me."

Suddenly, Violet's lips are on Raven's mouth. Raven is startled and she gasps. They're holding still, lips locked, breathing into each other's mouths.

Violet pulls away, saying, "I couldn't help it, I find you crazy attractive. Like a turbulent river, and I want to dive in."

Raven throws Violet down in a move that sharply says: *You've had your hands on me long enough.* Raven drags her flat palms over the length of Violet's body. Slowly slipping Violet's stockings off, Raven kneels between her ankles and parts her legs wide. Violet props her head on the pillow to watch Raven massaging up her legs. Raven is kneading, pinching, and rolling Violet's soft inner thighs, which are undulating from pure pleasure. A confused little sound escapes Violet's lips, but Raven cuts her off. "Don't speak."

Raven lifts up the bottom half of Violet's dress, revealing lacy white panties. She exposes Violet's breasts by pulling her dress all the way up, tucking the skirt under Violet's armpits as if securing her with rope. "Don't move . . ."

Slowly she slides her palms to cup Violet's tender breasts, strategically trapping a nipple between her index and middle finger. Gradually, she increases the pressure until Violet squeals loudly.

"Careful, they're sensitive."

Raven continues down to the top of Violet's underwear, which she slides skillfully off. Raven positions her face a few inches from Violet's sex. Her pussy is bare, and the skin is lighter than the rest of her body.

"I want to look at your yoni."

"Yoni?"

"What do you call it?"

"My flower?"

"Well then, I want to adore your flower."

Raven's face is so close she can smell the nectar. She wants to press her face closer but maintains distance—even when Violet thrusts her hips toward Raven's mouth, Raven pulls away to increase the anticipation. After a moment, she sucks her first two fingers slowly and strokes Violet's outer lips with a light tickling, teasing touch. After repeated strokes, Violet's lower lips begin to open. Raven is in rapture watching her lover's petals unfurl.

"Haven't you seen enough?"

"Keep breathing . . . I want to smell you."

"This is uncomfortable," Violet says, revealing her insecurity.

"Relax," Raven whispers. "You're beautiful."

Both women deepen their breath, and Raven notices Violet's yoni transform slowly under her gaze. Eventually, the color darkens as the blood rushes in. She is particularly curious about Violet's long hood and orchid-like folds . . .

"Come kiss me, already!"

"I'm hypnotized by your beauty," Raven says.

"I mean it," Violet insists.

"Fine, but I'm not done here." Raven slowly hovers over Violet's body and teases her mouth a few times before surrendering to a kiss. As they continue, Violet relaxes into an embrace, and Raven sees the sharp contrast: Violet has been tense this whole time.

"Why are you so resistant?" Raven asks.

"It's like there's a little girl inside that wishes she met you years ago."

"Hopefully not too long ago, or this would have been illegal." More kisses.

"I know you want me to relax and enjoy, but it doesn't do it for me."

"It's not for you, it's for me," Raven retorts.

"Well, that makes it a little easier," Violet admits, "but you've touched me so deeply in so many ways. I can't wait to touch you."

Raven withdraws her lips and says, "It's getting late."

Violet pulls her back in. "You've been so generous with my body, I want to thank you somehow."

"The pleasure is mutual. You don't need to thank me. The worst thing we could do at this early stage is start keeping a scoreboard. I take pleasure in pleasing you, but I'm particular about how I like to be touched. We'll get there soon. For now, your job is to let me know your preferences and aversions. Like yoni gazing: thanks for letting me know it isn't your thing. I'll keep exploring other things."

"You want to know what makes me cum?" Violet asks.

Raven's hands become still around Violet's hips. She listens with rapt attention.

"Fantasy. Tell me a story, with juicy details," exclaims Violet.

Raven squints and searches Violet's face. "What kind of stories?"

"Anything, I'm easy. Like tell me about your first time with a girl, since I already told you mine."

"Well..." Raven smiles and walks her first and second fingers down Violet's body as if flipping through the pages of her memory, landing firmly on Violet's mons. "I grew up in a theater family, so gay and lesbian issues were standard talk around the dinner table. I fell in love with my best friend in high school."

Raven pauses to tune into the warmth and wetness of Violet's pussy. Violet lets out a little moan, her body obviously loving the hands-on storytelling.

"One night we were having a sleepover and got buzzed on miniature bottles of Wild Turkey and started fooling around under the covers. She reached over and grabbed my nipple, so I leaned in and kissed her. She got turned on and pulled me on top, and I started poking around to get into her panties. Eventually, she passed out. Looking back, we shouldn't have done it, but I didn't have any context for consent, back then. Neither did she. We woke up when the sky started turning blue. She felt up my boobs, so I shoved my hand down her panties, and this time I found my way inside. She moaned and squeezed her legs around me so hard I thought I was hurting her, but I couldn't stop myself. I felt so powerful penetrating her."

"Mmm-hmmm . . . then what happens?" Violet said, riding Raven's fingers in her own orgasmic trance.

"Even now, when I'm inside you, my heart gets so big, I imagine penetrating you with my desire and watching you become powerless. I feel like a teenage boy with raging hormones. I just want to pin you down and turn you inside out."

Violet is so revved up that she lifts her pelvis off the mattress to increase the rhythm. Raven's hand is playing hide and seek, in and out, peekaboo. The flow between them is effortless, free, fun. They're kids again. Raven hears an echo of children calling out "Olly Olly oxen free" in the neighborhood cul-de-sac... Violet's whole body shudders and lands in stillness, breathing hard in Raven's arms.

Breathless, Violet says, "It's like you were inside my head."

Raven smiles. "Your body language is so clear."

Violet lets out a moan and squeezes Raven with all her strength. "Thank you. I feel so close to you. I want to do something for you."

"There's something you should know. After I was with my best friend, for many years, I used to consider myself a stone butch."

"What's that?"

"A lesbian who is exclusively a top. You know, the one who prefers giving the pleasure. When I was in college I went through a phase where nothing went inside me. I didn't think of my yoni as a place to be penetrated, but that didn't stop me from wanting to penetrate others. There's a stereotype that stone butch women are gender confused because they were hurt or have trauma. But I've never been raped or molested and I love being in a woman's body, although, in my head, I'll admit I see myself as a six-foot Amazonian woman with big bones. Sometimes I'll catch a glimpse of myself in a mirror and I'll think, who the fuck is that?"

"So you don't want me to penetrate you?" Violet checks.

"I'm just telling you this so you know it's sensitive for me. I'm not stone butch anymore, but I still prefer being on top."

"When did it change?"

"When I fell in love with Nick and I wanted to get as close to him as our bodies would allow."

"And Damien?"

"Yes, when I trust someone and when they're really present with me, then my body opens up. That's why this show is so edgy for me. I'm going to allow myself to be penetrated in front of the whole audience. It's symbolic of being able to surrender to the whole universe." Raven looks into Violet's admiring eyes and gently nudges her lips with her own.

They melt into a final kiss that conveys deep gratitude: *Thank you for what you expressed. For getting naked. For baring your beautiful soul. And for another magical Friday date.*

Thank you for being you.

As Raven walks her out, Violet stops at the door and pleads, "Before I leave, can you tell me one thing that I can do for you sexually?"

"You mean, besides letting me penetrate you?"

"Yes," says Violet.

"Mother Nature."

"What do you mean?"

"Getting out into the fresh air and spending time with my feet on the earth. If I can find enough privacy, I like to get naked and feel the warmth of the sun kissing my skin. That's how our bodies were designed: to make love in the wild."

"Well then, what are we doing indoors?"

"Maybe we can go hiking after my show closes."

"After your show? That's three weeks away. I have to see you before then."

"I told you, I'm busy."

"Too busy to have a quickie in nature? C'mon. It'll be like a blessing for your show."

FRIDAY #5

Outdoor Fucking

Raven's hiking boots crunch against the dry leaves as she and Violet follow the trail by the riverbed, which is too narrow to walk down hand in hand. Raven leads until the trail widens and they can stroll side by side, often groping each other.

Raven pauses, in awe of a dragonfly. "Did you know they have some of the most advanced flight engineering? All four of their wings operate independently. Or at least, that's what my son told me. I learn a lot of interesting but irrelevant facts from my six-year-old."

Raven leans her face in close, then presses her parted lips against Violet's and whispers, "Can you imagine making love in midair?"

Violet responds dreamily, "You make me feel like we're flying."

The women wind their way to a clearing under the shade of

a towering oak. Violet rests her foot on a large rock while she reties her ponytail. Raven straddles the trunk of a fallen tree.

"Look, it's a yoni. I love when the scar tissue around a broken branch forms the shape of a bulging vulva."

Violet shakes her head and teases, "You are an ecosexual pervert."

Raven warms her hand on her own thigh. "You know my first orgasm was on a log just like this. When I was a girl, I rocked back and forth and felt so much pleasure all over my body that I didn't even realize it originated from between my legs."

A certain deviant look comes over Raven's face as she pulls a ziplock bag from her back pocket. Its contents: latex gloves.

"Isn't it ironic to be out here in nature using these sterile gloves?" Violet asks, obviously excited.

Raven makes an excessive production out of pulling on the gloves and snapping them on her wrist. "Ironic, or kinky?"

"You want to do it here?" Violet looks around.

"This place is perfect," Raven says, poking at the latex webbing between her fingers.

"It's pretty exposed."

"I thought you'd like the thrill of knowing anyone could walk up that path," Raven says. She lays her sweater on the log for Violet to sit.

She unbuttons Violet's jean shorts and pulls them down her thighs, but not all the way off, in case they have to make a quick getaway.

Raven massages Violet's inner thighs, and with her dominant hand, she lightly strums fingers against her mons. Violet must be surprised by the silky texture of the gloves, because she says, "It's softer than lotion."

Raven marvels at how Violet's innocence seems so easily corrupted. Kneeling, she positions her body between Violet's milky thighs, still facing toward the path, so if anyone walks up she would see them first. Raven stares into Violet's eyes as she sucks on two fingers for lubrication.

"You can just spit on me."

"That's not very classy, is it?" Raven says, coaxing her hidden clit to come out and play.

"But I deserve it."

"But spitting is demeaning. To me, spitting on a yoni is sacrilege. Do you want me to desecrate your temple?"

"When you put it that way, yes, please."

Raven shoots Violet a look, then plunges her two latex-covered fingers deep inside her tunnel. Violet gasps. Raven moves her fingers to the rhythm of Violet's heavy breathing. Violet lifts her hips slightly by pushing against the log, and rocks up and down in Raven's direction.

Violet surrenders into the ride. Raven notices every micro movement; she is listening to every little moan, and pauses when Violet's body tenses suddenly. Raven feels a block in the flow. Intuitively, she knows this is not the tension of pleasure.

"What was that?" Raven inquires.

"Nothing. Keep going," Violet says, trying to relax.

"But you went away for a moment." Raven's hand stills. "Where did you go?"

"I'm right here."

"And so am I. We were connected on a cloud, then you suddenly fell off. Was it a fantasy?"

"I wish it were a fantasy."

"Take me with you."

"This was not a place you want to go," Violet resists.

"It feels like your shame body got activated. Do you want me to pull out?" Raven asks.

"Stay," Violet whispers. "If I ignore it, sometimes I can find the pleasure again."

Raven starts moving her hand slowly. "I'm not going to ig-nore it. I want to bring pleasure into your shame body."

"What do you mean?" Violet asks.

"When I was new to kissing girls, I'd be kissing someone, and then suddenly the whole world would stop, and I'd be like, 'whoa.' A strange feeling of shame would come over me, but that made the kiss even hotter."

"I wish it were that simple. I'm haunted by Sodom and Go-morrah."

Raven slowly extracts her fingers but lightly cups Violet's outer lips.

"You mean like fire and brimstone?"

"Worse, it's like I'm flooded by images of debauchery, sin-ful orgies, with penises and vaginas everywhere. My pussy is all used up, completely destroyed. It's like a curse where people are squirting jizz and juices all over."

"Oh that old story." Raven smirks and shakes her head.

"When I say it out loud, it sounds kinda hot, but sometimes when I see it in my head, it grosses me out. The worst part is my dad will show up and look disapproving, and all these highly spiritual people will say, "Look at how unevolved you are for rubbing your genitals everywhere. Don't you know it's unclean to put other people's genitals in your mouth?"

Raven gestures with her moist hand in the air. "Have you actually read the story of Sodom and Gomorrah?"

Violet shakes her head, "That's all I know about it, but my parents could probably recite it to you."

"It's a funny story, actually—ironic. Want to hear it?"

"I'm not sure I do," Violet protests.

"So, Sodom and Gomorrah were twin cities that really knew how to party. God decides to send two angels down to earth to clean it up, you know, to do his dirty work. So when the angels arrived at the city gate, a man named Lot welcomed them and invited them to dinner. Then a sex-crazed mob came to his door demanding to sodomize the new visitors. Lot tried to protect his house guests by offering his own virgin daughters in trade. Lot instructed them to serve the townsfolk however they desired."

"No way!"

Raven nods. "So, the angels decide to strike everyone blind except Lot and his family. They planned to scorch both cities, even the plants and innocent animals, and promised to spare Lot and his family on the condition that they run away and never look back. Everyone knows what happened to Lot's wife... she's the one that turned into a pillar of salt, for having second thoughts."

"Did you learn this story in Catholic Sunday School?"

"I was never raised religious, as a kid. And I always felt I was missing out, so I majored in divinity and minored in women's studies. I wrote my thesis on how ancient goddess cultures used performance in their ritual services."

"Is that how you got into theater?"

"No, I was born into theater, my father's a playwright. I tried to get away from the family trade, but somehow, I'm always drawn back."

"Like a criminal to the scene of the crime." Violet surprises Raven with a quick kiss, explaining, "You are so damn hot right now."

"Do you want to hear what happened to Lot's daughters?"

"There's more?"

"Oh, it gets worse."

"Will you keep fingering me? Hand sex makes learning bible stories so much more fun."

"Yes. This will definitely re-script your shame body." She slowly slips inside Violet's velvet temple as she continues.

"Lot and his two daughters spent the rest of their days exiled to a dark cave. The older daughter got the urge to procreate but noticed there were no men around except her dad, so she decides to get him drunk with wine and takes advantage of him. And as if that's not enough, she forces her little sister to do it too."

"Seriously?"

"Seriously! They both got pregnant, and the bible hails them as saints for carrying on the family line."

An erotic trance has taken over Violet. Raven feels the passion against her hand and asks, "You like that?"

"Yes, tell me more," Violet says as she undulates her hips.

"I'm imagining we were Sodomites during those times. During the heyday of homosexuality, when adultery and orgies were rampant. I would pull you into one of their dimly lit salt caves, where people were fornicating. I would fondle your body in the dark until you opened to me, then I'd penetrate you, slowly, so you could feel the full scope of my desire. I'd have my way with you, in every orifice, anytime I wanted, in front of whoever happened to be there."

More heavy breathing. The two women are way past the point of caring about judgment or damnation. And then Violet's body gets tense. It's a good tension, the kind that is followed by spasms of pleasure and falling . . . drifting . . . down out of the clouds to a place where the earth is alive, and sexuality and sodomy are not crimes against nature.

FRIDAY #6

No Picnic

Violet knows how much Raven yearns to continue exploring every hidden nook of her body; however, Raven can't do it at the expense of her art. Raven has explained to Violet that if they are going to cultivate a healthy, long-term, sustainable secondary relationship, they need to practice some basic impulse control. Even though they're only physically together once a week, they seem to be growing inseparable on the psychic plane. It's become a bit of an obsession, for both of them. So Raven asks for a dark night (that's what they call it, in theater, when there is no show).

Logically, Violet understands why Raven wants to take a Friday off. Her show opens in seven days. Privately though, she feels tortured, like Raven is punishing her, and not in a good way. Violet finds herself daydreaming about sexy schemes to seduce Raven away from her rehearsal. One such elaborate plot involves taking her to the pier for a quick picnic on the beach. Instead of food, the basket would be filled with sex toys. Oh, the fun they would have, hungry and horny, exploring each other, out of view, under the boardwalk but within earshot of the tan young lifeguard.

In reality, Violet knows this is a serious test of their relationship's sustainability, and she doesn't want to fuck it up. Instigating this hot fantasy scene could cost her everything. Violet can't help but wonder if she has a long history of scaring people away with her love. It's not that she's needy, or pushy, she just has a huge open heart. This scares the shit out of most mortals. When she confesses her concerns to Damien, he reminds her that she and Raven are both love-drunk on dopamine, and that having some space will at least slow her down enough to see the bigger picture.

He's right.

She realizes she might be overdoing it with a basket of sex toys, but a basket of fruit? It's classy, healthy, organic, and most importantly, sensual. Soft peaches, mangos, figs, and obviously bananas. Violet has a glorious time at the farmers market carefully sniffing and selecting each mouthwatering piece.

She drives the overstuffed basket to Raven's house and sits in her car for a moment. She yearns to rush in and steal a quick hug but knows how quickly it would melt into more, and how painful it would be to pull away. Instead, her mission is to drop off the basket, with a special note on the porch, and then drive away. That's it. She hesitates for a moment. To ring the doorbell or not? She decides not to risk Raven catching her.

Returning to her car and turning on the ignition, Violet's mind goes into overdrive with anxiety. What if Raven never discovers her gift? What if someone else takes it? What if animals get it, or fruit flies? Violet pulls over on a random suburban street and sends a text.

* * *

Raven pauses packing her costumes when she hears the bamboo bell notification. A text! Since it's Friday, she knows it must be Violet, and she steals a look at her phone, justifying that she earned this quick distraction.

Violet West
Look on your doorstep.

Raven gasps, hoping Violet might be there. How she yearns to grab her by the hips and pull her close and smell the pheromones on her neck. When she opens the door, Violet isn't there. Her heart sinks as she lowers her eyes to the basket of fruit at her feet.

She looks down the street for Violet's car—nothing.

She stoops to collect the basket and notices the pile of exotic fruit is crowned by a ripe banana. It has something written, in ink, directly on the peel. How clever. It's a banana note. She cradles the banana against her breast and collapses on the couch to read:

I handpicked these juicy treats especially for you, and this banana made me think of you!
Yours,
Vi.
P.S. Eat me.

Raven smiles to herself before responding.

Raven Turner
You came all the way here and denied me the pleasure of your touch.

Violet West

I didn't want to interrupt your work, but you need to stay nourished.

Raven Turner

You interrupted me anyway, you need to be punished!

Violet West

Forgive me, Mistress. How do you plan to punish me?

Raven Turner

With the banana.

Violet West

Oooh! You're making my mouth water.

Both women pause to swoon over their phones, and after a moment of musing, Violet adds:

Violet West

Seriously though, bananas have lots of stress-reducing nutrients, so be sure to eat it.

And that's precisely what Raven does.

FRIDAY #7
Opening Night

Nick hovers around the ticket booth in a vintage blue tux, welcoming guests as they enter. Violet arrives in a tight crimson dress and sniffs the theater's hallway. The usual hint of dust and sweat is masked by burning sage. She hugs Nick and asks him to take an orchid to Raven before the show.

"She's in the greenroom, you can bring it yourself."

Raven pulls Violet into the dressing room and plants a kiss on her parted lips.

Violet stands in awe of Raven's striking figure, framed by an embroidered gown. "You look stunning, my queen!" Smiling, she bows before Raven and presents her with the potted plant.

Raven smells the flowers and exclaims, "Lady slippers! How'd you know?"

"It's from Damien, he told me to remind you, sometimes a cigar is just a cigar, but an orchid is always a vagina."

Raven smirks and says, "Please thank him for all the space he's been giving me. Sorry I wasn't ready to see him, tonight."

"He understands. How are you?"

"Well, I'm past the stage where I wanted to throw up."

"Do you need anything?"

"Just for you to sit in the front row. I reserved a seat, house left. That's where I do the climactic scene, and I want to look out and feel you there."

"I'm honored. I'll go there now." Raven grabs Violet's arm and tugs her in for a hard kiss on the mouth. "If I suck tonight, I'll take it out on your ass."

"And if you rock, you can punish me even harder."

Before leaving, Violet looks back at Raven and says, "I love you." It just sort of slips out. It's less of a revelation than a fact. It feels as if Violet simply stated: "The sun is hot."

Raven's smile says, *I know.*

Violet finds her special seat in the front row and watches nearly two hundred friends, students, and community members file into their seats. Violet smiles to herself, knowing they have all come to watch her queen.

The music stops, lights flicker, and eventually, the chatter slows. Nick steps onstage with his guitar and says, "Consider me the fluffer. I'm here to warm you up with an original number. For those who don't know, I'm Nick, Raven's partner. If she's the Sacred Slut, I'm her patron saint. I wrote this little piece about the decriminalization of prostitution. You laugh now, but you have no idea how hard it is to find words that rhyme with 'victimless crimes' and 'consenting adults' so, please bear with me...."

Violet giggles through Nick's musical comedy set, then nearly jumps to her feet when her queen floats onstage in her royal gown. She carries herself as if wearing heels, but is clearly barefoot with toenails painted like lilacs. She centers herself in the spotlight and waits for the applause to subside before opening with an invocation.

"I dedicate this show to the Sacred Sluts of the world. We are a subversive band of men and women doing holy work in hotel rooms, yoga studios, private homes, and occasionally temples. We are temple priestesses, heaven's harlots, holy whores, and sacred prostitutes. Call us whatever name you choose. We may or may not use labels, we may or may not have sex with our seekers, we may or may not accept money for our work, but we all serve the Goddess."

As Raven kneels at the altar, Violet feels tingles as she recognizes the basket of fruit alongside Raven's crystal cock.

Violet is aroused by the intoxicating sound of Raven's voice, or is it her graceful movement? She feels her own flower blossom against the cushion of her seat. She is hypnotized as Raven shape-shifts into a variety of different forms using body language, vocal intonation, and wigs. Violet's favorite line happens when Raven wears a wavy blonde wig to play the modern courtesan, Veronica Monet:

"And the world was telling me that prostitutes are dirty, and that our pussies would get loose and saggy if we had too much sex, but it was all a lie. My girlfriend, who taught me the business, had the tightest, sweetest, cleanest, most beautiful pussy I'd ever seen. It was easy for me to get over the idea that women who work in this industry are nasty hoes, or undesirable. It was like, oh my God! She's so hot, and you're so wrong. I don't care what you're all saying, you're wrong. My vagina is a muscle, not some orifice that's going to get stretched out of shape if I use it too much. You cannot defile me. I'm a muscle and the more you use me, the more powerful I become."

The show culminated in an indescribable ecstatic sacred ritual wherein Raven's prayers merged so fully with Violet that she lost all sense of time and space. Afterward, Raven tenderly gathered herself in a rocking chair, in the dim downstage light, talking directly to the audience about the dharma of the sacred prostitute: "For centuries, she's been the one whose job it is to take the war out of our warriors…"

After Raven receives an explosive standing ovation, she dashes backstage.

Violet, still in awe, slips behind the concession stand to make a cup of hot tea. She eavesdrops on the excited chatter of the adoring audience on her way to her queen's greenroom.

Violet finds Raven crumpled against a cushion sobbing, her silk robe loosely fastened around her lithe body. She sets the tea down and kneels at Raven's feet, lightly holding her leg. Violet observes Raven's sobbing, pretending not to notice that one of Raven's boobs is peeking out of her robe. She yearns to touch her nipple, but intuits there is a time for inappropriate perverted behavior, and this is not it.

Eventually, Nick pops his head in the door to see Raven's body heaving in her girlfriend's arms. "Do you need anything from the crew?"

"Just to be held. We can circle for notes in like ten minutes." He joins them on the couch with an awkward attempt at encouragement. "It was ten thousand times better than the dress rehearsal."

Violet, who had been unsure about what to say until now, takes his cue. "You blew everyone away, especially me."

"Thank you."

"I'm not just saying that because you're my queen, I actually learned a lot."

Raven slowly sits up, wipes her wet face on her robe, and says, "I love you." She turns to her husband and hugs him. "Both of you."

"Want tea?" Violet offers.

Raven nods and says, "I really went for it. I feel well-used."

Nick asks, "Anything else?"

"No."

Nick smiles and exits, saying, "I'll let the crew know we'll meet in here."

"I need to ask, before I go," Violet says.

"What is it?" Raven says, concerned.

"I'll be back tomorrow, and I'll be telling everyone they must see this show, but I don't feel right about Damien missing it. Can he at least come to closing night?"

A slow smile spreads across Raven's face. "You know, I kind of wish he were here right now."

The Real Slut

The audience has doubled, and ambient preshow music is drowned out by the excited buzz of the full house on closing night.

Violet is excited for Damien to finally experience the show for himself. Of course, he already knows a great deal about the script because Violet has been coming home late after the show every night this week, too aroused to fall asleep, and often recounting her favorite parts as foreplay.

The house manager ushers Violet and Damien to the back row and asks, "Why aren't you sitting in the front row tonight?"

Violet leans in to whisper in Shelby's ear, "Damien didn't want to make it awkward for Raven."

"Oh!" Shelby understands, and she continues to snake through the aisles.

Damien has a gift for sensing what others might be feeling.

Violet imagines it must be a burden, always being inside other people's heads. Perhaps that's why he usually avoids crowds. For Violet, on the other hand, the more humans squished in one space, the better. In fact, tonight's crowd is having the effect of an aphrodisiac.

Violet loves people. They are her hobby. She loves the way they look, smell, feel, sound, and sometimes the way they taste. If she thought she could get away with it, she would lick strangers, at least the ones that smell good.

Violet is content knowing there's more anonymity in the back of the theater and it will make it easier for her to try to orgasm while Raven is performing sex magic onstage. Violet has felt envious each night when she's heard from a handful of women in the audience who managed to orgasm. She wishes she could cum so easily, but she's never been quick to climax. She calls herself the "one-shot wonder" because she cums once and then she's done. Under normal circumstances, she'd be proud of her spiking clitoral peaks, but after watching Raven and other women of this community enjoy multiple slow, rolling-energy orgasms, she somehow feels less evolved. It's not that she needs tons of stimulation, like those women who can only cum from vibrators or hard fucking, but she does need a solid fantasy to get her juices flowing. Part of why she's so attracted to Raven is because she is such a masterful storyteller.

The lights go up and Raven steps onstage, opening a portal into another dimension. Her spell isn't broken until intermission. While Damien steps out for fresh air, Violet offers to help the ushers place egg-shaped rattles on each seat. She knows they're stuffed with dried corn kernels, an ancient symbol of fertility.

When Damien returns, Violet resists the urge to ask him what he thinks of the show so far. Instead, she smiles to herself and waits for the lights to go down, so her fingers can find the fly of his jeans. She reaches into her cat shaped purse and pulls out a small vibrator nearly the same size and shape as the rattle. In the darkness, she puts the items into his hands. After a few kisses, their attention returns to the stage.

Onstage, when Raven slowly steps out of her lace underwear, she invites the audience to stand and shake their rattles and move to the drumbeat.

"Breathe in through your heart and out through your genitals." Naked, except for a strand of prayer beads, Raven reverently wraps them around her wrist. Next, she leans over the altar and anoints herself with essential oils while a recording of Annie Sprinkle's voice comes over the speakers:

"I've been inspired by the legends of the anciently sacred prostitutes. These were incredibly powerful women thousands of years ago in exquisite temples in Mesopotamia, Egypt, Sumeria, Greece. When there was a war or plague, if people were sick and dying, if the crops weren't growing right, or they needed a miracle, all the people would come to the temple of the sacred prostitute . . ."

Meanwhile, Raven sets up the altar, using a cordless headset so the audience can hear the subtle texture of her circular breath. After a few rounds, she says, "Visualize a sacred space around this temple, where time ceases to exist, where there is no ego, where emptiness is everything. . . ."

She kneels at Buddha's feet, facing the audience, and arranges seven candles. "I will consecrate these offerings and our highest intentions and supercharge them with our orgasmic energy."

"This first candle, I light for myself, so my body is healthy and vital for serving the Goddess. I pray the universe gives me as much sexual energy, inspiration, and abundance as I am willing to use on her behalf."

She goes on to light a candle with a prayer for each of the following: family, lovers, community, teachers, the Earth, and the highest good of the audience. The dedications are sincere but verbose.

"The penultimate prayer is for the planet. Mamma Earth, I offer you this pomegranate. Bless your crops and the rivers, trees, air, oceans, mountains, and all of your glorious babies, the animals with fur, feathers, fins, and even the creepy crawly ones. Mamma forgive us for our ignorance and greed. Let us recommit to adoring you, taking care of you, and making sweet love to you.

"Finally, this lotus flower is for you, dear audience. It's your turn to add whatever specific desire you want to energize in this ritual."

Violet closes her eyes and knows immediately what she wants to pray for. She wants to love and be loved by Damien and Raven, both! She may not be ready to accept them being lovers without her, and she's learned to accept her limits, but she is in love with Raven now and doesn't want to lose it. *Please God, Goddess, Universe or whatever, help me keep my girlfriend and my boyfriend*, Violet prays with all her might. She knows it's not going to be easy—Raven and Damien haven't even spoken since that first night, and there is still healing that needs to happen between them. Violet hereby dedicates her ecstasy and all of her heart to doing whatever it takes to make these relationships work.

Onstage, Raven continues channeling the legend of the ancient sacred prostitute as she teases the audience by rubbing the life-size crystal cock up her inner thigh. "I invite you to enter into ecstasy with me, experience an orgasm vicariously, energetically, or physically. Move your body, use your voice, clap your hands, stomp your feet, get something for yourselves, an idea, a realization. Whatever happens for you, or doesn't, is perfect. As I offer my body to the divine, my only directive is to 'not force anything and to feel everything.'"

Violet, along with most of the audience, is standing and rat-
tling to the live drummer. Damien is standing beside her, sup-
portively. She exaggerates the movement in her pelvis, grinding
against him. Damien grabs her hips and pulls her crotch against
the bulge in his jeans. Nobody notices because the lights are
focused onstage. He surveys the congregation to find everyone
in the dark chaotic hall overtaken by a mass hypnotic trance.
The two women on their left appear to be absorbed in their own
ritual. The couple in front of them look as if they wouldn't dare
take their eyes off Raven's half-naked undulating body. There is
no one in the aisle or behind them, so Damien lifts Violet's long
cotton skirt and presses himself against the curves of her ass.
She bends over to press closer to him. Damien uses his thumb to
flick her G-string to the side and finger her wetness.

She angles herself and presses against his hand so that his
thumb slips easily into her opening. He wedges his other hand
between the two of them and slowly unzips his own jeans. The
increased movement of Violet's hips to the rhythm of the wild
drumbeat elevates the challenge. Violet shrewdly licks her palm
and reaches back, sliding her saliva against his shaft a few times
before inserting his hardness between her lips. He enters with a
shock of pleasure, and the room narrows into a dark tunnel of
her femininity. The two are joined. She leans forward and grips
the seat back in front of her to optimize the angle.

In Violet's private fantasy, this is her first threesome with
Raven. She is rapt by Raven's erotic movement around the gold-
en Buddha, while feeling wildly responsive to Damien's every
thrust.

Violet imagines that Raven is the one gyrating on Damien's
lap. As Raven seductively teases and worships the crystal cock
at the altar, Violet imagines Damien is morphing into the gold-
en Buddha. Suddenly, she is showered in a glittering light. It's
almost as if Violet's body swaps with Raven's, and now she's the

one onstage writhing under the intoxicating gaze of the audience. Her arousal multiplies as she imagines the audience naked. Every woman in the entire space is orgasmic, while every man stands with dick in hand. She imagines a crowd rushing the stage to suck and fuck her and each other. She envisions people cumming on the fruit and flowers. The offerings are all drenched with cum. Her own body is spread out in full prostration at the feet of Buddha as an offering for anyone to ejaculate on. She imagines women squirting and spraying like animals in heat. Even the women on their periods are dripping blood on her hands and feet.

She feels Damien spasm and spray his warm cum on her backside. Smiling from ear to ear, she uses her skirt to soak it up, certain this fantasy would please her queen. She imagines even Annie Sprinkle would approve. As Damien is hugging her from behind, Violet closes her eyes for a moment and remembers her intention that her two lovers get along so that she may continue to love them both. As she exhales deeply and pulls her skirt down over her cum-splattered legs, Violet becomes aware of the empty void in her womb. Looking onstage, she memorizes the rapturous look on her queen's face. She has never felt closer to Raven than she does at this moment.

After the alchemy of art and activism, Raven rises from her rocking chair and, in her silk robe, takes her final curtain call. She announces that since it's the closing night, she'll be available for hugs, pictures, and/or final questions. Always the healer, she encourages the audience to ground themselves, whether they want to stay and socialize, or they prefer to slip out into the night to process the experience on their own. Violet and Damien embrace, and Violet whispers, "I can't wait to tell Raven!"

Damien tenses and says, "Not just yet. I want to congratulate her, first."

Violet is still in the post-sex stupor. "But I think she'd be stoked!"

"I'm glad you're so excited, but I haven't seen her in a while, and I don't want to complicate things," he insists. Violet doesn't like secrets, not even naughty ones, but agrees to wait to tell her until next Friday.

The crowd that formed around Raven has dispersed, leaving Violet sitting beside her queen, who is adorned in her silk robe, at the edge of the stage.

Damien waits until the women are done kissing to give Raven an extended congratulatory hug. "You surpassed all my expectations."

Violet squeezes Damien's free arm, adding, "I told you, she was amazing!"

Raven sighs. "It wasn't too much?"

Damien jokes, "It was right on the edge, which is your superpower. I loved it." He goes in for another hug that seems to linger.

Raven breaks free to say, "I finally saw you two way back there. I looked for you in the crowd. I wish you would've sat up front."

"I didn't want to distract you," Damien says.

"Every actor has someone in the audience who inspires their performance more than anyone else; usually it's Violet. But tonight, I knew you were here, even if I couldn't see you."

"I've missed you too. Can you guess my favorite part?"

"Uh . . . You liked how I used the crystal cock you gave me?"

Damien shakes his head. "I noticed that, but what I appreciate most is the congruence with which you delivered your message—you seem to embody these teachings in the core of your being. I especially like the line at the end when you spoke about sacred prostitution as a calling, not a career."

"You have no idea how much you've inspired me." Raven steals a glance at Violet, who still looks drunk from the afterglow.

"And I'm happy you and Violet are having such a great time getting to know each other."

Violet is in heaven watching her two loves chatting, secretly questioning how fast her sex spell will start working.

Nick swings by to coordinate the closing circle. He greets Damien with a hug.

"Want to join us for the afterparty?" Raven asks, even though she already knows the answer.

Damien shakes his head. "No, but let's get together again. Soon."

Damien takes Violet's hand, and as they're leaving he says to Raven, "You know love doesn't go away, it just changes forms . . . I learned that from you."

Goddess Worship

Violet answers her door wearing a cream-colored bra-and-panty set, complete with garter belts and hosiery. Raven barely has time to marvel at her beauty before Violet plants a hot kiss on her mouth and hands her a tall lemonade.

"The lemons are from my garden. I picked the rosemary this morning at the park. Ssssh. They don't know. Today, I'm at your service."

As she follows Violet through the immaculately kept house into the backyard, Raven sighs and says, "I have to warn you, I've been weepy lately."

"What about?" Violet asks.

"Since the show closed, I've been questioning everything and don't have the energy to sort it all out," Raven says, standing in front of a massage table in the shade of a fruit orchard that separates Violet's yard from the neighbor's. There is a pebble path to a rose garden and a large trampoline, where Violet sets a platter of berries.

"It's like the Garden of Eden," Raven says.

"No snakes in my apple tree. Actually, this is a crab apple. I keep tasting them, hoping they'll get sweet, but they don't."

"What else do we have here?" Raven picks a leaf and smells it.

"Mostly citrus and several stone fruits." Violet points to a medium-size tree and says, "That's my prize peach."

"Do you tend them yourself?"

"I used to, but Damien hired a gardener. He takes such good care of me."

"I'm glad he came to see the show. It felt like a reality check for me."

"That was the first time I ever had two lovers in the same place, who knew about each other and were cool with it."

"That's a big deal," Raven admits.

Violet smiles like she has a secret. "I can't wait to talk all about your show, but first let me get my hands on your body." Raven leans in for a kiss, but Violet dodges and insists on undressing her slowly. She folds each piece of clothing, carefully stacking them on the trampoline.

Once naked, Raven lays facedown on the massage table and enjoys the light breeze against her bare backside. Violet takes her rings off and rubs her hands with oil.

"Ever trampoline topless?" Raven asks.

"When I bounce, I can see into my neighbors' yards. Although they would probably appreciate a peep show, I try to keep a low profile." Violet runs her flat hands down the length of Raven's torso. "I wish I could massage your entire crew. Everyone did such a great job."

"I can't believe you came back every night." Raven's words are muffled in the face cradle.

"I wasn't planning to, but I didn't want to miss a show. My

favorite part was the monologue about the prostitute's pussy being so tight and clean. It affected me. You remember that first day at your house when you almost went down on me? You were looking at my flower like it was a buttered biscuit. I wouldn't have minded if you ate it, but I couldn't stand you just staring. I was so self-conscious, but now, after hearing your show, it shifted the way I feel about my flower. Even Damien noticed I'm more relaxed when he's going down on me."

"Deep down, you must've known." Raven props herself on her elbow for emphasis. "I imagined your pussy when I delivered those lines."

"Really?" Violet strokes her hair. "Will you let me look at you the way you admired me?"

Raven, humored by Violet's excitement, turns over.

Violet lightly runs her fingers over Raven's front to build anticipation and her own confidence. "I never get to massage genitals, because of my massage license. I can touch side boob, but no nipples, ass, or inner thigh. And definitely no genitals. Every woman is so different, so I don't always feel like I know what I'm doing."

She positions herself on the table between Raven's parted legs and softly pets her overgrown stubble like she's stroking a kitten. "I like your five o'clock shadow."

Raven props herself up to glance at her own pussy. "I haven't shaved since the show closed."

"Your little hairs are cute, like ants marching toward your cunt."

"Such a poet."

Violet brings her hands to prayer. "I feel like a pilgrim at the gates of your temple. May I enter you?"

"Wait. I thought you were going to yoni gaze."

"I did. Now I want to feel you," Violet says, gingerly brushing her pussy lips.

Raven covers herself with her hands and says, "I'll relax more if I can show you how I like it."

Violet squeals. "Yes please, direct me, command me, I'll do anything you want."

"You've been touching like you're afraid of breaking something. Trust your hands, let them tell you what to do."

"Like this?" Violet adds steady pressure to Raven's mons.

"Better. Now massage it like you would any other part of the body, with confidence. Find the pressure points, naturally, like you're giving a foot massage."

"You want me to massage your pussy like a foot?"

"That feels better. Mmm . . . Except, be careful on my urethra."

Violet's eyes grow large, and she cocks her head. "Where's your urethra?"

"You know, my pee hole. Mine is bigger than most, so it tends to be more sensitive."

"I don't know where it is."

Raven sits up. "You don't know where your urethra is?"

"No."

"You have a mirror?"

Violet's smile grows large, and she runs to the house, returning with a hand mirror. She eagerly pulls down her own pants, jumping onto the table beside Raven, sitting naked in the sunlight.

Raven skillfully fingers Violet and says, "See? That little button with the star-shaped opening, that's called the meatus. The urethra is technically the tube inside, but you only need to know that if you're giving someone a catheter."

Violet is smiling ear to ear, excited and embarrassed as if she just discovered her elbow. "I will never forget this moment!"

Eventually, Violet regains enough composure to coax Raven back to a supine position. "I want to explore more. I want to get to know yours, the way you know mine, which seems better than I know it myself."

Violet slides her fingers around Raven's petals. "This is so special. I can't believe you deprived me of this pleasure." Massaging Raven's outer lips, she opens them enough for a slow, wet entry. "I adore you. I want you to feel as good as I feel. Can I tell you a dirty little secret?"

"Always." Raven is breathy.

"I didn't exactly cum during your show, but I tried."

"Really? Do tell."

"Well, I'm not like you. I can't just cum with breath or by rubbing against someone's thigh. Since I knew I needed direct stimulation, I brought a pocket vibrator, you know one of those little bullets? So after the intermission, I held it in one hand against my dress."

Violet continues stroking Raven while talking with increasing energy. "I shook the rattle in the other hand. Nobody noticed, so I danced and watched you as I vibrated. I nearly came with you, but I wasn't sure when you were cumming. It seemed like you went through different waves. I fantasized we were fucking onstage in front of everyone."

"I love it!"

"On the final night, when I was there with Damien, I rubbed myself against him."

"Slow down," Raven pleads.

"Okay." Violet slows her touch, but continues her story. "We both got so turned on that we made love in the audience."

"Hold on." Raven holds Violet's hand still. "You had sex in my theater?"

"Yes!"

Raven tenses her body. "With Damien?"

"Yes, we were in the back. The lights were down, so nobody saw us."

"Can you pull out?" Raven sits up. "Just stop!"

"Are you upset?"

"While I was onstage?" Raven says.

"We were right there with you, making love. I thought you'd appreciate it."

"How could you do that?"

"I'm so sorry. I thought you wanted the audience to participate. Are you jealous? You and Nick have been sharing lovers for so long, I didn't think you'd be hurt. Please don't be mad."

"Why didn't you tell me?" Raven insists.

Violet tries to reassure her, "I wanted to, but Damien said we should wait. He didn't want to upstage your big night."

"So you waited until your fingers were inside me before you decided to talk about it?"

"I thought it would turn you on. I thought you'd like to hear how your performance inspired us. In a million years, I never imagined you'd be upset."

Raven sits up. "Oh, I'm happy for you . . . I just don't see how this is supposed to work out between us. I'm leaving."

"Wait, you're covered in oil, let me run the bath or at least a shower . . ."

Raven looks around and finds the garden hose. "This is fine." Her skin puckers under the cool spout, but she's still fuming inside. Violet stands motionless. Utterly useless, staring at the water pouring down Raven's oily body.

"Can I help you dry off, at least?" Violet mumbles.

Raven rips the towel from Violet's hand and pats herself down. "I'm still raw from the show, not to mention Damien breaking up with me. I'm going to need some time to sort it all out. Do you understand?"

"You're just going to end it like this?" Violet takes the limp hose. "Let's talk about it."

"I need space. Next Friday is off."

FRIDAY #10

The Back Door

Raven reads Mark Twain to Mason and reflects on her own childhood bedtime routine. Her father read from dead playwrights such as Beckett, Brecht, and Ibsen. She wonders how much of her parenting style is compensation for her dad incessantly provoking her existential angst? She wonders what Mason is really learning when Tom Sawyer talks his friends into painting the fence. Is he learning about honesty or clever ways to manipulate people?

Mothering and wifing has always come easier than running a theater company or maintaining multiple lovers. This Friday, Raven has taken the night off teaching to rest and recover from the show. Her stage manager, Shelby, was thrilled to substitute but eager to know how her director was feeling. Raven reassured her that she just needed a little rest, and decided not to mention how carelessly Violet had punctured her heart.

Raven sighs, knowing Nick is particularly skilled at nursing her through such wounds. He has a way of minimizing personal drama. Most of his lovers are long distance. Is it by design? If only her love life were so simple, Raven thinks. If only she were monogamous. Tonight she resolves to have a drama-free date night with her reliable rock of a husband.

After bringing Mason water and lightly tickling his back, she pulls the door shut and rushes to meet Nick in their bedroom.

It's adult time.

As a tenured married couple, they have established a routine. Nick shuts down the blue glow of the computer screen. "I still have some numbers to wrap up, but I'll do it before my meeting tomorrow."

Nick switches on the amber glow of salt lamps on each of the nightstands, as is their routine before "sexy time."

He clicks through his playlist, pulling up their lovemaking set. Raven turns down the bedsheets and pulls lube from a decorative box by the bedside where they keep condoms and her smaller toys.

"Let's just forget everyone else exists, tonight. I want to put all my attention on you. You've been so supportive during my show, and throughout the whole ordeal with Violet."

Nick sets his phone on the charger and casually undresses. "I'd hardly call it an ordeal. Ever since you started seeing her, you've been so giddy and extra hot in bed. I'm grateful we still have so much juice for each other. Can you believe how many couples suffer in a sexless marriage? I'm trying not to judge, but I could never do monogamy."

"Well, polyamory is not exactly the easy path. . . ."

Nick senses the tension in Raven's voice. "Do you need to vent?"

"I know I said I wasn't going to talk about it, but I'm angry.

I still feel hurt and betrayed." Raven catches herself. "But I'm done crying about it."

"As long as you get naked and massage me, you're welcome to process as much as you want."

Raven strips and assumes her position straddling Nick's butt, massaging the tense shoulder muscles alongside his spine. "I don't want to make the whole night about Violet, so after I say a few things, I'm going to shut up and make love to my man."

Nick smiles. "Want me to gag you so you can't talk about it?"

"Before you do, let me just say . . ."

". . . How much you miss Violet," Nick teases.

"No. Actually, I was going to say how awesome you are. I don't think there's another being on the planet that could share me as widely as you do." She kisses the back of his head and continues to dig her thumbs into his shoulders. "It's easy to love someone when they're expanding their love and bringing all that newness back home. But to love someone when they're broken down and sad about someone else, now that's the real deal. You get extra points for that."

"Points? How about blow jobs?"

"We'll get there. You know, one of the most healing things you ever did for me was that night when I told you I couldn't make love because my heart was broken. I was missing Damien so badly. I felt guilty for not being open to you. You held me tight and told me that you loved me. All of me, even the part of me that was heartbroken. You said that you still wanted to make love to me, regardless of who I was thinking about. That was huge, that helped me open my heart even wider. . . ."

Nick rolls over and holds Raven.

"I love being inside you when your heart is open. It's so tender and sweet when you cry. And I love seeing you happy. And the reality is, you were happy with Violet."

"I know," Raven says, and she starts to sob. "But it was all too much. Too fast. It's okay to fool around a bit, but then we fell in love. You don't know what it's like when two women love each other. It's intense. It's insane. I can't just ignore the fact that she goes home to him, every night. Damien doesn't even talk to me anymore!"

"Because you told him not to, and you pushed him away. Now you're pushing Violet away too."

"See what I mean? It's all so complicated. I just want to go back to being a housewife."

"Right. Okay. So you're just going to step away from the woman you love because she lives with the man you madly miss, because you figure if you cut them both out, you'll be content as a housewife. Sounds like a good plan," Nick says sarcastically, then he tries to smooth it over with a few soft kisses on Raven's neck.

Raven turns her head to sob into a pillow, and Nick continues. "You know what this is? This is postpartum depression. This is a classic crash after your biggest performance. You go through this every season. This show was your life. Now you're coming down from the high, and you're looking for someone to blame."

Raven wraps herself around Nick and squeezes tight until the sobbing subsides.

"Why do you have to make everything sound so damn simple?" She kisses him hard with an open mouth.

Between breaths, Nick says, "Somebody's got to counterbalance your tendency to complicate everything."

"Thank you for being my rock."

"I'll show you my rock," Nick jokes, but deep down she feels his desire, and she wants to show her gratitude. This is another one of his gifts—being in his body. It brings her out of her head.

"Are you ready for that blow job?" she says, shifting gears.

"Finally," he laughs, leaning back into the pillows. "I adore you."

She moves slowly at first, admiring his smooth hard shaft, then swallowing the length of his sex. She lifts her head to say, "I am so blessed to have you," relaxing into the erotic flow. Her body is flooded with memories of when they were first in love. "You are my perfect mate."

She flashes on the time he bought her a gold belly chain. It was silly, she'd thought, until she'd worn it during sex and something had come over her. It had glittered with every movement. She'd shape-shifted into a temple dancer.

"You are my king," she says, reminiscing.

It had been the beginning of their role-playing, the first glimpse of the fountain of creativity that flows from sexuality. How each new location, costume, or memory can create an infinite combination of fantasies and orgasms.

"My lord, mmmmm . . . my lover." Their mutual moaning is interrupted by a knock.

"Did you hear that?" Nick asks, breaking the trance.

"What?" Raven murmurs with his cock still in her mouth.

"I think someone's at the front door," Nick says.

She maintains a rhythm of stroking him with her hand so she can use her mouth to announce, "We're busy!"

"That's right, woman, get busy." He closes his eyes, and Raven continues slurping and moaning louder to drown out the obvious knocking at the front door.

"Do you want me to hold it?" he says, which she knows is shorthand for, *I'm close to cumming, so if you want to have sex, speak now, or I'm going to explode.*

Raven slithers up his body and straddles him. This is their most reliable position for a simultaneous orgasm. With a few minor adjustments of her hips, she can usually plug him into her sweet spot, but their concentration is suddenly interrupted when the knocking becomes louder. It's now at the bedroom door, which opens to the side yard.

"Raven? I know you're in there," says a familiar voice.

Nick groans, "Who is that?"

"It's Violet." Raven lowers her body close to Nick and continues her movement.

"Aren't you going to get it?" Nick says, somewhat amused.

"I didn't invite her!" Raven says, focusing on her orgasm.

"Raven, why didn't you come to class, or answer my texts?"

"Go away!" Raven yells, thrusting harder.

Silence. Except for Nick's muffled breath—Raven can't tell if he's turned on or laughing. She rides him harder.

"Please, let me apologize," Violet pleads.

"Maybe she'll join us," Nick jokes.

"I'm still mad at her!"

Violet sounds desperate, "You can't shut me out. I know you said you need space, but that's what you told Damien, and I'm not that patient, it's been too long. . . ."

"What did she do that was so bad?" Nick asks.

"She had sex with Damien in the audience on closing night."

"Sounds hot!" Nick says.

"It's not!" Raven says, picking up the speed. "I've never even had sex with someone in my theater," Raven blurts, her face red.

"Who are you kidding, you energetically fucked everyone in that audience."

"Shut up and fuck me," Raven says, pulling Nick over on top of her. She knows he'll focus more if he has to do the work, and with her feet pressed into the bed, she can lift her hips and guide him toward her cervix.

"I'm willing to wait for you. . . . In fact, I'll wait right here," Violet calls out.

Raven thinks if she can only orgasm, it'll be like a kind of revenge.

"She wants you," Nick protests.

"She's been a bad girl," Raven quips.

Raven's heat is contagious, and it inspires Nick to ask, "So how would you punish her?"

"I'd pin her down, just like you have me, but harder. I'd take her arms over her head."

Nick grabs Raven by the wrists and knows just how to distribute his weight, thrusting from his tailbone.

"And when she was helpless, I'd jerk myself off inside of her."

Nick knows how to take direction. Raven moans from deep in her throat as he continues thrusting and panting, until he nearly collapses with an orgasm. Raven keeps clutching him hard as they slow their breathing together.

"Raven, I'm not going home until you hear me...."

Raven shakes her head in disbelief and signals to Nick with one finger on her lips as they listen.

"I've never let any woman this close to me. It's like you already know me, inside and out. It's like we're shaped for each other. I know there are things I still have to learn, but I'm a quick learner. I'm not afraid of making mistakes. What do I have to do to make it up to you?"

Raven wraps herself in the silk robe from the show and swiftly opens the bedroom door, greeting Violet with a pouty look before returning to the foot of the bed where Nick lies innocently, his wilting erection covered by a thin sheet. Violet enters shyly and offers a dainty wave, scans the room, and after taking off her boots, tenderly sits on the bed beside Raven.

"Thanks for letting me in." She crinkles her nose. "Sorry I interrupted you. I should have known you were . . ."

Nick is quick to accept her apology. "It's okay, Friday is kinda your day, so if anyone should be grateful, it's me."

Both women break into a smile. Then Violet winces, and Raven starts to sob.

"I love you," one of them says, but they're so tightly entangled in a hug, it doesn't matter who.

Raven leans toward Nick and pulls Violet onto the bed. "Come cuddle us."

"It's an honor to join your little love nest," Violet says, while settling into a three-way spoon with her back to Raven's breasts.

"See, I told you we should've invited her in earlier," Nick says.

"Oh, I don't think she's ready for that."

"Group sex?" Violet perks up. "How would that work?"

Nick is quick to answer, "All it takes is consent from everyone involved, including Damien."

"That would be another complicated conversation, and I am definitely not ready for that," Raven says.

"I'll do whatever it takes to make this work," Violet insists.

"Yup. She's a keeper, this one," Nick says.

Violet turns to face Raven with watery eyes and says, "I may not know all the etiquette, but I know what I want. When you were onstage, I made a prayer. I want to keep my boyfriend and my girlfriend, both."

Raven cups Violet's face and presses her lips hard against her soft mouth.

Violet stares at Raven. "Seeing you in this light, with Nick, is so different than whenever we meet in private. You really are someone's wife. Nick, I don't know how you do it."

Nick rouses from near sleep. "There are so many things I can't give her, so I'm stoked if she can get it from you."

Violet says, "I'm glad you two have been doing this for so long and know what you're doing."

Raven chuckles, "Honey. We don't know what we're doing any more than you do. We are all just making it up as we go."

FRIDAY #11

Changing Tides

Black's Beach is among the most breathtaking stretches of Southern California's coastline. Hiking down the caramel-colored cliffs is an ideal setting for three visionary lovers to redesign their relationship. If only they were able to keep up a coherent conversation without being distracted by a dazzling peregrine falcon circling overhead. During the twenty-minute descent to the sand, Raven silently prays for guidance in her evolving connection with all her beloveds.

At the bottom, Raven discovers the sand is surprisingly cool between her painted toes. Since it's a nude beach, she unhitches her sports bra and steps out of her khaki shorts. Violet wraps herself in a Polynesian scarf to protect her light skin from wind and sun.

Damien is standing over a tide pool poking at a sea anemone with his finger. Raven marvels at how easily these fragile creatures could get crushed by a human foot or tumbling rock. Such is life. Everything is temporary. The tide is low, but about to rise.

"Let's find a spot," Raven says, musing on how whatever relationship agreements they come up with are also only temporary. She spots a secluded nook in the rocky cliffs, and the triad settles into the shade.

Fortunately, Damien is not one for small talk. But Raven knows the burden of beginning this difficult conversation is hers. After a few moments of situating their bodies and sharing reassuring touches, Raven commences. "As you know, my connection with Violet is unexpectedly deep, and we want to keep exploring it, but at the same time . . ." Raven sets her hand on Damien's thigh as her eyes grow wet. "I'm still mourning the loss of what we had. I can't keep avoiding you, Damien. I know how important it is to keep all channels open in a web of lovers, so I guess I'm looking for an arrangement that works for everyone."

"I've missed you," Damien states.

Suddenly, Raven is hijacked by sobs. "Really?"

Violet throws her arms around Raven, trying to comfort her girlfriend. "I can't tell you what it means to have my two loves talking again, and how perfect is it that we get to do it here, in this romantic cave." Violet's enthusiasm is contagious. Tears turn to laughter. Violet kisses Raven first, then Damien. Raven can't help but notice the familiarity between their lips and senses a stab in her stomach.

Wiping her wet face, Raven says, "Well, I'm sorry your first experience is so hard, for me."

Raven gazes at Damien's freckled face and thinks it looks like art against the cave wall. Damien rubs her thigh and says, "When I first met Raven, I wanted to learn everything about nonmonogamy, so I asked her for weekly sessions. As we started to fall in love, she asked me to be her boyfriend. But I thought, she's a married woman. What exactly does that mean? Do you remember? You laid it out for me. All you wanted was a regular rendezvous to explore the mysteries of the universe together. You said, 'Look my husband meets all my primary needs, for sex, money, companionship. . . .' You promised never to pressure me to move in together or have kids. So, I thought, it's not a bad proposition. You thought you were 'low maintenance.' But as we deepened, you wanted more emotional support and commitment, then you came to me with tears in your eyes . . ."

"Kinda like I am now?" Raven says, smiling because she knows where the story is going.

"Yes. Like this." Damien continues telling the story to Violet, "And apologized for the false advertising. She realized she was not low maintenance at all."

"I had no idea what I was getting into," Raven tells Violet. "I didn't expect he would turn my world upside down and inside out."

"And I said it's okay that you're not low maintenance, you're, you're a high-performance woman. High-performance systems are never low maintenance. Most guys don't want low maintenance, they want high-performing sports cars. Seriously, who wants a Honda when they can drive a Ferrari? And yes, darlin', you are a Ferrari. We may be in the shop a lot, but when we get back on the road, it's worth it. So, the way I see it, that's what we're doing here: tinkering under the hood a little so we can have a more extraordinary ride."

Raven smiles and breathes more freely. "Why can't extraordinary be easy!"

Damien smiles and rubs Violet's thigh, scanning her sweet face for reassurance. Watching them, Raven is struck by the tenderness of their relationship. She has been so self-indulgent, with all her attention pouring into the show. She hasn't stopped to put herself into Damien's shoes or to consider how much he has at stake. There aren't many men who'd be comfortable supporting their girlfriend having weekly playdates with a dominant lesbian sex activist.

Raven says, "I'm touched and grateful that you've shared your beloved with me on Fridays. We have such a different dynamic than you and I used to. I'm curious what impact this has had on you."

"There are two main things." Damien speaks as if he's given the subject considerable thought. "I want to start by acknowledging you, Violet, for how well you try to include me after every date." He reassures her with a pat. "Your transparency is impeccable, baby." He glances back at Raven. "She can't wait to tell me every detail when she gets home. But I have to admit it's hard to hear at times, since you and I don't have our own connection anymore—it feels a bit imbalanced. Especially if Violet and I are doing something domestic, and not as sexually adventurous that night."

Raven nods with understanding.

Violet is quick to offer, "Well, I'm not as threatened as I was in the beginning. I'd be open, if you two wanted to explore your own connection again."

"I know," Damien says. "But that's not what I'm asking."

"I'm not sure I'm ready for that, either," Raven whispers, and she remembers this conversation is long overdue. "I know there's a second point, and I'd like to hear it."

"My other challenge is around Violet's first-time experiences. Ironically, the whole reason I wanted you two to meet is because I knew you could teach her things I couldn't. But I noticed there are certain experiences she has with you that are hard to celebrate because I haven't had them with her myself."

"Like what?" Violet interrupts.

"Like spanking, yoni gazing, outdoor sex . . . I don't need to introduce her to every first sexual experience, but if I can't be there to witness, I'd at least like to be considered. The first time we try anything can be so formative and bonding, like losing our virginity."

Raven leans toward Damien and impulsively wraps her arms around him. "Of course I want to consider you. You have no idea how much I care. Too much actually. I love you both." Damien squeezes her hard before she pulls away and wipes away more tears. "If I'm honest, it's been hard to accept you as a couple. It's still so surreal, even now that I'm here with you both."

Violet, who's intoxicated by this three-way process, is eager to share. "Maybe that means we just need to spend more time together. I want it to be easy to be together. I mean we're three conscientious adults who all love one another. We can work this out."

Raven blurts, "But the problem is I'm still in love with Damien."

Silence. Damien looks at the sandstone wall, weighing what to say next.

Violet breaks the tension, "Why is that a problem?"

"Don't you get it?" Raven snaps. "The more I open my heart to you, the more hurt and longing I feel for Damien."

"Naturally," Damien says thoughtfully, "the human heart can't open to feel pleasure without also feeling pain. I know what an emotional woman you are. Loving you is a roller coaster, which is why I need to be clear with both of you. I can't be romantic with Raven right now. It's too complex and too risky. Violet is the love of my life, and I don't want anything to jeopardize our partnership. Clearly, being with you makes her happy, and I want to support everything that makes her happy, but for now, I need to support it from a comfortable distance and only within certain parameters. I hope you understand."

"I may not like it, but I agree. I love you both, and I don't want to lose Violet, or jeopardize what you two have."

Violet asks, "What do you mean by certain parameters?"

"Well, when I was dating Raven, she had specific relationship agreements and a clear container around when we'd see each other."

"Sounds so lawyerly," says Violet.

"We need to find a win-win arrangement." Raven squints her eyes.

"You make it sound like I'm property and you're discussing my dowry."

"Aren't you?" Raven teases.

"Okay, maybe a little, go on . . ." Violet props her chin on her fist and assumes an exaggerated listening position.

Raven begins the rally with, "I propose we stick with Fridays. It seemed to happen spontaneously. Let's make it official."

"And I want you to come home to me afterward so we can make love," Damien says.

Raven feels another stab in her belly, but reminds herself that she has her own primary partner. "Nick loves it when I bring all the juice from our dates home to him."

"Oooh. That's hot!" Violet squeals.

"And I want you to send her back to me better than you found her," Damien says playfully.

Raven holds up two fingers like a scout and says, "I promise to keep the campsite clean."

"Since we're doing Friday daytimes, I could change my yoga class to have more time to meet before," Violet says eagerly.

Raven nods. "Since it's difficult for me to be around Damien right now, why don't we meet at my place?"

Damien turns to Violet. "I don't want you to have to do

all the driving, you can use our space when I'm at work on Fridays."

Violet is in awe of the process. "Do you have detailed rules like this with Nick?"

"We haven't even started on the details yet," Raven jokes, and then with a half smile says, "Nick and I used to have a ten-page contract, and one rule was we both had to be naked when we negotiated our agreements."

Damien smiles. "Sexual arousal does make processing easier doesn't it?"

"Maybe, someday we can teach her what it's like to negotiate a threesome?" Raven flirts.

Damien laughs. "I move that we revisit that proposal at a later date." Then dropping into his usual philosophical self, he adds, "Before discussing any more strategies, let's address the underlying values. A strategy is only successful if it solves the underlying issues."

"Well, I heard you say you valued being considered, especially around Violet's firsts."

"That's right," he says, looking into Raven's eyes and smiling.

"What does it look like for us to consider you? Would it work for you if we checked in with you before doing certain things, if she's never done them before?"

"We need a deeper inventory of what exactly she's done and what she hasn't," Damien says thoughtfully. "I'd be happy to work with you on that."

Violet squealed, "Ooooh! I like the sound of that!"

Damien points to the ocean. "The tide is rising. We need to head back soon, or we'll get trapped on this strand."

"Wait. I've heard you say there are certain things you feel I'm uniquely qualified to teach Violet, and I want to be clear about the specifics. I'm assuming you're okay with things like ropes, scissoring, pegging, and other kinky girl-on-girl scenes?"

"Yes, thank you. When Violet comes home, I'm delighted to hear about your adventures, and I see how much she's growing, and that's the real measure of my fulfillment in this partnership."

"Wow, you two are like one big lucid dream," Violet exclaims.

"I feel blessed too." Raven gazes out at the vast blue sea. "Before we hike back, I want to offer myself to the ocean."

"Well, I anticipate this will be an ongoing process that might be challenging for a while," Damien says.

"But we're in it for the extraordinary!" Violet declares, and she pulls her lovers into a three-way hug. She plants a kiss on each of their cheeks and they look at each other with glowing smiles.

Before pulling apart, Raven proposes, "A three-way kiss?"

Damien asks his beloved, "Violet, have you ever had a three-way kiss?"

"Not yet," she says eagerly.

"A first!" Damien declares.

Raven directs, "Start slow, way slower than normal." They all lean in. There are lips upon lips, and for a moment, there is nothing else.

Until Violet squeals, "My heart just exploded!"

"Yes!" Raven exclaims. "Mamma Ocean is calling me. Who's in?"

"I'll watch," Damien says.

"I'll pass," Violet says, snuggling up under Damien's arm.

Raven disrobes and saunters to the edge of the sand, where the land meets the sea. Silently a private prayer forms in her heart:

"Oh great Goddess, cloaked in the ocean's arms." She plunges her body into the depths. "I surrender myself to thee."

She holds her breath and submerges her entire body. "Baptize me." She dunks again. "Wash away all of my attachments." And a third time. "Cleanse me from my suffering."

Then she paddles beyond the break, allowing the salt water to surround her as she floats on her back. Out loud she continues, "Let me love as you love, Mamma Ocean. May I be reborn into this relationship. Cleanse me of this heartache. Wash my memory of ever being hurt. May I trust myself and know that others cannot hurt me. May I love him through my love for her. May I learn to love the whole world through this woman. Thank you."

She glances toward the shore between her floating toes and smiles at the sight of Violet cuddling Damien. He has his phone out, so she knows it's time to go.

She kisses the Goddess good-bye and walks out of the sea like a mermaid regaining her land legs. She is born again. She is herself: a mother, a wife, and a lover of everything good. Her life is a work of art, and it's always changing, like the tides. She is living at the edge.

ACT II

VIOLET'S
BOOK OF SHADOWS

———

FRIDAY #12

Learning the Ropes

Raven told me pagan witches keep records of all their magic spells and potions. They call it their *Book of Shadows*. I want to keep a journal of all Friday fantasies, especially now that we have Damien's blessings.

Today was a monumental initiation into ropework. It feels like Raven is schooling me, not just in kink and polyamory, but all things magical.

Raven likes to start each scene by setting intentions. She calls it "creating the container." Today, she formalized it by lighting a candle and saying a prayer. Her intention was to explore my preferences and aversions. She brought a whole bag of toys to try.

I told her my intention was to surrender.

That pleased her.

When she asked about my boundaries, I told her I didn't

have any. She found that unacceptable. I explained that I trust her implicitly and I'd be willing to try anything.

But that didn't stop her from lecturing me about how she can't trust my "Yes" unless I'm willing to say "No."

"Okay, I don't want to pee in your bed," I said.

She laughed, but I wasn't kidding.

Then she made me kneel obediently in the corner as she unwound the ropes. It was hypnotic, like she was pulling a snake out of a basket.

"This is not necessarily a sexual practice, but it's not NOT sexual either," Raven explained. "The ropes represent the kundalini, and as they wrap the outside of the body, they create more space on the inside for the serpent energy to rise up the spine. When you're fully bound, you can focus on the universe beneath your skin."

She covered my eyes with a soft silk scarf, and it was like a cloud descended over the room. I immediately fell into an erotic trance. I relaxed into the firm embrace of her ropes, and let my body be guided into various positions. She secured my arms behind my back, and crisscrossed my pelvis, putting pressure on all the right places. She moved like a spider, knowing exactly where to step when spinning her web. Every touch vibrated through the hemp lattice, which distributed pleasure throughout my being.

Then she started experimenting with various implements. Lightly at first, she started with feathers, silk, and what felt like the whiskers of a cat. I never knew where she would caress me next. I giggled, moaned, and squealed to let her know what I liked and didn't.

Then she got stern, with little spanks and pinches. Every time she would slap one of the ropes it would reverberate against my sex. She pulled out a flogger and started thumping me everywhere. I wasn't sure what other things she used, but I did not like the riding crop. It stung my back and thighs. I told her she was being downright nasty, and she reminded me that I could use my safe words.

By the time she touched my flower, I was wet and ready. In a way, I felt like my whole body was a giant pussy, everything was so sensitive and hungry. I don't even know which toys she put inside me. I felt her finger at first. She pinched and pulled my lips with her hand, but I wanted more. I thrust my pelvis in her direction and she filled me with something foreign. I even asked, "Please, my Queen, what is inside me?"

"Do you like it?"

"Yes," I said.

"Do you want more?"

"Please," I begged.

"Then it doesn't matter what I put inside you, does it?" She let out a wicked laugh.

"No, my Queen."

"You little slut," Raven commanded. "Tell me you want me to stuff random things into your pussy."

"Yes, please. You can put anything you want inside me."

"You are like a bitch in heat, aren't you?"

And that's when the fantasy took over. I was a lowly maid-servant and she was my powerful queen. She was benevolent and proper in public, but when she came back to the bedchamber, she needed a whipping girl to take out her sexual frustrations. I felt totally devoted.

When she was done, I told her my bladder was full, Raven asked if I had a final request.

I had no words, no notion of what to ask for.

"A kiss?" I heard myself saying, as if I were a million miles away. And then I felt her hot breath between my nipples. I didn't know I was sweating, but I could feel the moisture of her mouth and the slipperiness of my skin as she trailed down toward my nether lips. She kissed my navel and my mons. Finally, she arrived at my clit. Her kiss melted into more. Raven made out with my flower.

Pussy.

Or yoni.

Whatever . . .

Everything escalated to another level of arousal. She read my every breath and movement with precision. Right at the point when I couldn't take any more, Raven said, "I will be unbinding you now."

I didn't even have to tell her.

"Good. I have to pee," I said, and she unbound my arms but didn't remove my blindfold. She held my ropes and guided me like an animal on a leash to the toilet, where she made me pee through the entanglement of hemp. It was humiliating.

Afterward, she stood before me and spoke. "These ropes represent everything that holds you back from your full expression. As I untie you, you are hereby liberated from all of your bondage, physically, psychologically, and in every dimension. Relax and enjoy your return to liberation."

As she spun around my body, untying the ropes knot by knot, I focused on the vibration of the fibers rubbing against each other. I loved every little pull and tug. I felt the breeze on my skin as the ropes fell to the floor along with every artificial limitation that ever burdened me. I was stripped down to the last knot, which Raven held firmly in place at the breastbone. Then she slowly lifted my blindfold so that the first thing I saw was the sparkle of love in the eyes of my queen. She beamed at me with unimaginable tenderness. After a few timeless breaths together, she ceremoniously released the final tie, and I stood naked. I had never felt so free.

She bowed and said, "Thank you for the gift of surrender."

I curled up next to her under a snuggly blanket and nearly

fell asleep in her arms, until she said, "Tell me about your experience."

"I loved it," I mumbled. "I loved every moment. I've never experienced anything like it, and ironically, I feel like I've done it before, centuries ago, and I want to do it again, forever."

She smirked. "I know what you mean."

"How did you learn to do all this?" I asked.

"I had a mistress named Magenta. I once did a whole performance about how she tied me to the shower curtain rod... but I don't want to talk about it now. You can watch it on YouTube."

"Can I see it now?"

"Later. I want to debrief the scene while it's still fresh. I for one learned that your nipples are your most sensitive part." She pointed to them, which made me squirm. "What did you learn?"

"I learned that I love rope. Will you teach me to tie like that please, please, pretty please?"

She not only agreed, but she sent me home with her precious snakes so I could play with them.

Yours,
Vi.

P.S. I also told her my fantasy about being her maidservant. She loved it and told me next time she wants me to speak it out loud while it's happening.

P.P.S. I watched her YouTube performance like ten times: *Liberation through Bondage*. Then I used her ropes to tie myself up.

Monsters and Clowns

Raven arrived with an agenda. She hardly noticed my new designer bra and matching panties that were inspired by a Japanese Shibari master.

I kissed her at the door before she set her stuff down. Then the teapot whistled.

"What's with the clipboard?" I asked as I poured hot water into a clay pot of loose green tea leaves to steep.

"I've started a list of things I know you like and dislike. But I'm going to need more information."

"Well, you already know I love playing with ropes. I was hoping we could do more of that," I admitted.

I set the teapot on a ceremonial Japanese tray and made a big production of kneeling to pour tea for my queen. She seemed pleased.

"What else is on your list?" I tried to steal a peek at her

clipboard, but she pulled it close to her cleavage, stood up, and placed one foot on the coffee table. She towered over me.

"Obviously, I already know you like rope."

"Correction," I said, "I love ropes!"

"And spanking," she said.

"Actually, the spanking is more for you," I said softly.

"But, you couldn't get enough."

"Only because you were enjoying yourself so much."

"Good to know," Raven takes note. "That's exactly the kind of information I want. And . . . you seem to respond well to humiliation."

"What do you mean by humiliation?"

"When I call you my bitch or a filthy slut, it makes you wet!"

"I can't argue with that."

"Arguing with me in general is not a good idea," Raven said in a saucy tone. "So, now I want to know about your self-pleasuring practice."

"Are you going to make me masturbate for you? Because Damien already made me do that," I blurted, without thinking.

Silence.

Damn it. I should have been more sensitive. She told me she was tender when she heard we were moving in together.

"Did he, now?" she said with a smirk. If she was hurt, she covered it up, but that didn't stop me from groveling at her feet. I kissed her toes and said, "I'm sorry, Mistress," looking up at her and batting my eyelashes.

She crossed her legs and pushed her foot into my lap. "Let's discuss your masturbatory material, shall we? And while you're down there, you can work on my feet. I want to know what you fantasize about when you touch yourself."

She asked me to rate each item on a hotness scale of one–ten, as she read from a list:

"Yoga teacher with a private client?"

"Eight."

"Massage therapist molesting a client?"

"Seven."

"Theater director and acting student?"

"Ten definitely."

"Good. And stranger sex?"

"Six."

"How about Hollywood actors?"

"Like who?" I asked.

"Good question, who would you find irresistible at a cast party?" Raven inquired while sipping tea.

"Hmmm . . . Madonna, of course. And Freddie Mercury. Do dead people count? Oh! And who's the guy in that movie about two Irish brothers? He looks like a sex offender, you know, the guy who played the antichrist?"

"Willem Dafoe?" Raven asked with disbelief.

"Yes! That guy. I'd be all over him."

"Okay, moving on . . . How do you rank the porn star fantasy?"

"Five."

"Being filmed?"

"Five."

"Stripping and/or lap dancing?"

"Nine or ten."

"Huh, interesting . . . How about prostitution?"

"Sacred or streetwalking?" I asked.

"Either one."

"Nine. For both." Then I told her how much I loved her one-woman show. I especially liked hearing how the sacred prostitutes treated the untouchables—the hideously ugly, the people society ignored. For as long as I can remember, I always harbored a secret crush on the most "unlovable" person in the room. If they were disabled, or had acne, or were overweight,

I just wanted to be around them. I would secretly wish I could show them I found them beautiful.

Raven dropped her clipboard for a moment, and sort of swooned. She kissed me and said that is the "dakini directive," or the intuition of a sacred sexual healer. Most sexual healers come into the work because they are healing themselves. "Do you have any sexual trauma?" she asked.

"I told you about Terrance, didn't I?"

Raven was quiet. She seemed surprised.

"If I haven't mentioned it, it's because it's ancient history now. I used to babysit for a family in the town where I went to school. I was molested by the little girl's father. He was a well-known college professor and his wife was actually the dean. When I found out that I wasn't the only one he molested, I blew the whistle on him, and he lost his job and his wife."

"Oh, honey." Raven looked pensive.

"It's okay, I've done a ton of work on it, like talk therapy, emotional release, and during my massage training I did primal scream too."

"I didn't know," Raven said flatly.

"I'm happy to talk about it. It just doesn't make for such sexy foreplay. Let's continue."

When Raven resumed her interrogation, her tone had warmed a bit.

"How about doctors and nurses?"

"Five."

"Artist and nude model?"

"Seven."

"Fireman, police, or military?"

"Six."

"The maid or the handyman?"

"Eight."

"Chef and/or food play?"

"Five."

"Anal play, butt sex, ass fucking?"

"Zero."

"Zero?" Raven probes. "What do you have against anal?"

"I'm just not into it. And it's not because of some big trauma, or because I haven't tried it. I have and I know, it's not my thing. It's kind of like sushi. Everyone loves sushi. I don't. I've tried it and everyone says, 'You just haven't ordered the right kind, or had the right chef.' I know what I like, and what I don't. I just don't like anal sex."

"That's unfortunate, but understandable. And good to know—it's why we're doing this." Raven takes a breath and is back to business, "How about voyeurism? More specifically, you getting to watch me?"

"Eight."

"Exhibitionism: me watching you?"

"Eight."

"Reading erotica together?"

"Five."

"Viewing pornography together?"

"Five. Unless you're talking about cartoons," I asserted. "One time, Damien and I watched animated monster porn. It was pretty hot! This redhead was hanging from a pull-up bar trying to get away from a big spiky monster who was dominating her with his huge cock. Realistically, his cock was so big and veiny it would have busted through her organs and killed her, but her vagina magically accommodated it. I got wet from watching it, even though I knew it was impossible. That's why I like animation. It's a lot like my fantasy world."

I asked Raven if she enjoyed porn, and she launched into a rant about the distinction between normal porn and feminist porn, where the stars aren't doing it for money but as an empowered act of pleasure activism.

"Oooh . . ." I said, remembering. "Once I saw clown porn. By accident, actually, but I never forgot it. There was this girl in her twenties and she was blindfolded by these clowns. She was lying facedown on the table with her ass in the air. There were circus freaks holding her arms. She seemed really aroused and, in the distance, you could see more clowns leading this older hairy man into the room. He also wore a blindfold and had a protruding belly. The clowns directed him to start fucking her."

Raven looked at me for a minute, then she set down the clipboard and half-jokingly said, "There are few people whose tastes are kinkier than mine, but monsters and clowns never even made it on my radar."

"It's not the clowns, per se. I think I'm somehow turned on by the taboo. I like the way she was tricked and had no say in the matter. You know, the sexiest thing I've ever seen on the internet was your bondage piece. I'm serious, I want to learn to tie like that. Someday, I'd love for you to give me a live performance."

She smiled and shook her head as if she were saying, *silly child*. She explained: "The *Sacred Slut* was my last performance for a while. I'd rather be behind the scenes. I'm going to be directing a storytelling showcase soon with students from Friday's class. You should audition with a personal narrative."

"But I'm not a writer," I protest.

"You don't have to be, just tell a sexy story from your life."

And all of a sudden, I felt a jolt of electricity surge through my heart, sex, and gut. At that moment I made two decisions. I would learn to tie myself up the way Raven did, and I would surprise her at the audition. I felt like a dirty old man inside my head was saying, "Ssshhh . . . this will be our little secret."

"Will you be filming the auditions?"

"Video can never capture the magic of live performance. Why do you ask? Are you interested in amateur film?"

"A sex tape? No, thanks. The only condition in which I'd let you film me is if you tied me up and forced me," I said, dangerously hinting at my own private joke.

"Remind me to put that on my list." She cupped my face and pulled me into a deep, lingering kiss. Soon her fingers were plucking at the straps of my new designer underpants.

The curiosity was killing me. "You didn't tell me about your likes and dislikes."

Obviously eager to get inside my pants, she quickly rattled off: "I'm into gender play, role-play, fantasy, humiliation, and light pain, both giving and receiving, but no structural damage, no breaking the skin. Personally, I'm okay with blood play as long as it's ritualistic moon blood. And as you already know, my greatest turn-on is getting dirty in nature."

With that, her greedy fingers deftly found their way to my petals, and after a series of sweet strokes outside of my slit, she suddenly stopped.

"Oh! I almost forgot, how you feel about strap-ons?"

Still processing everything she'd said, I fumbled, "Uh. I don't know, I've never tried it."

"Never?" She looked at me with eyes twice as wide as normal. "You've never been pegged?"

"Sorry, but strap-on play seems fake to me."

This really broke the spell. I saw the hurt in her eyes as she said, "Well, maybe you have never been with a woman who knows how to wield her girl dick."

I got the feeling that this was one of those arguments I wasn't going to win.

"Maybe, someday," I said, and I stepped out of my undies. "Right now, I'm done talking about sex and just want to have it." I stretched my body across the couch. Raven straddled my thigh. Her hand, like a heat-seeking missile, honed in on my hot zones and I let out a huge sigh.

Raven increased the rhythm of her pumping while rubbing her wet lips against my thigh. I imagined she was just using my body to get off, which is exactly how I want her to use me. She was panting, stroking, and breathing hard until I felt the contraction of her pussy around my leg. Her hand went stiff inside me, and then she was still. When she resurfaced from her orgasm, I reassured her that I love seeing her get off. And she doesn't need to make me cum.

"No?" She smirked. "I bet you'd cum if I had my red nose and a monster cock."

We laughed so hard it hurt.

We untangled our bodies and she continued, "What if I drove my VW bug over here and had all my clown friends get out so they can gangbang you?"

More giggles.

"Yes, Mistress Jelly Beans, do me. Please, do me!"

"You think I'm joking, do you? You have no idea what I have in store for you."

Yours,
Vi.

P.S. Raven also asked me if there was anything that I've found particularly triggering. I couldn't think of anything. She asked if I was jealous of her other lovers, Jess and Sebastian. I told her I didn't think so. She suggested we keep our discussion of other lovers to a minimum during our precious date time. We agreed that if any poly processing came up during the week, we'd talk by phone during the week so Fridays could be completely concentrated on each other.

FRIDAY #14

Strapping It On

I begged Raven to come over and tie me up with the same rope that she had used in her bondage video, so she sent me this mysterious text response:

Raven Turner
Wear something pink.

After my steamy shower, I rubbed lotion on my legs and slipped into a pink polka-dot bra and matching panties. I waited, twitterpated, wondering what Raven had planned for our afternoon.

She arrived wearing black business casual with a toy bag over her shoulder. I dragged her into the bedroom to show her the pink pillows I'd placed on the bed to honor her request. I asked what was in the bag.

"Have you been practicing with the rope I gave you?"

"Every day," I said.

"Show me what you got. Are you ready to tie me up?"

"Really? I've only ever tied myself up. And my teddy bear." I pulled my fuzzy brown comrade from under the bed. He was bound in a basic harness called a *karada*. "His name is Wet Spot and he's very obedient."

Humored, Raven said, "I actually have a specific tie in mind. And if you treat me right, I might teach it to you."

"What can I do for you, my Queen?"

"You can rub my ass."

"Yes, Mistress. Can I take off your pants?"

"No." Raven lay across the bed. "I want a ten-minute tune-up to help me get into 'top space' before getting naked."

I gently kneaded her tight glutes with my knuckles. "Are you going to tell me why I'm wearing pink?"

She carefully explained, "I plan to introduce you to my cock today. It's pink."

"How cute! Your strap-on is pink?" I clapped my hands.

"Careful now, when it comes to sex, my masculine ego is sensitive."

"So you want me to pretend it's really big?"

"Actually, the size doesn't matter, my girl dick is on the smaller side, so you can take it without bottoming out, but under no circumstance do I consider the word 'cute' a compliment. You have been warned."

"Yes, my Queen."

"And for today's scene, I'd like to be called Daddy."

"Are you supposed to be my daddy or someone else's?"

"Whatever turns you on, Baby Girl." Raven turned over and pulled my hair to draw me close for an open-mouth kiss.

"You turn me on, Daddy." And I meant it.

After our intention-setting ritual, she revealed her pink-

plastic member from her magic bag, along with thirty feet of
pink cotton rope.

I was delighted about the rope, but the dildo, not so much.
"Why is it lumpy?"

"Shaped for your pleasure."

"I think I prefer real skin or your hands."

She snarled and said, "Do you want me to show you how to
tie a rope harness or not?"

"Yes, please."

"The goal is to hold my cock in place so that I can be hands
free when I penetrate you, understand?" Then she proceeded to
direct me.

The midpoint of the rope is called the "bite," and you start
by folding the rope in half. We wrapped it around her like a
belt buckle, intertwining the long U-shaped loops. We pulled
the rope through each new loop we made, running it up her
butt like a G-string. I was surprised by how turned on I got by
the sight of my queen, I mean, daddy, with rope around her, I
mean, his crotch, not to mention the way the fibers of the rope
felt running through my fingers. After several back-and-forth
movements with what is called the "running end" of the rope,
we created a loop to actually hold the base of the dildo steady
against her pelvis. Raven adjusted her cock over her clitoris for
extra stimulation, and then secured it with a more intricate
macramé knot. She added a few straps to the side for support. I
noticed how careful she was to always keep it symmetrical, for
the artistic effect. Finally, she showed me how to wrap the end
of the rope, creating a polished finish.

"I love how it frames your ass. So cute, I mean handsome.
So handsome, Daddy." I started to play hard to get by crawling
away from her and onto the bed. She darted after me, caught
and kissed me. With her dick in hand, she pressed it firmly
against my inner thigh, which made me gasp.

"I'm not sure how you're going to fit that big thing inside me."

"Listen, Bitch. It's not a dildo or a dong, so you better call it my cock. This is an extension of me. You are going to take it in your mouth just as you would a bio-cock."

Raven positioned herself at the side of the bed and commanded me to turn onto my belly.

"Yes, my Queen."

"That's Daddy to you."

I opened my mouth and sunk the plastic thing past my lips.

She directed me: "Good start, but I want you to beg for it." She pulled out.

"Please, Daddy, can I suck your cock?"

"That's right." She pulled my hair back and held my head. I closed my eyes and imagined a strange man forcing me to suck his pulsing member. I glanced up to see if she was enjoying it, and I caught her looking down at me with intense power and tender care. I continued. She moaned and bucked her hips, obviously aroused.

"That's a good bitch. Get me hard so I can fuck you right. Would you like that?"

"Yes, Daddy," I slurred with the cock depressing my tongue. I suspected this was part of the humiliation, and clearly, it worked for her.

"Now I want you on the bed. Legs spread."

I scrambled to get into position. I started taking down my panties, but she/he stopped me.

"Let Daddy do that. I want your legs nice and wide, like I taught you."

Raven rolled a condom on the cock, while I was waiting there at the peak of my humiliation. I asked, "What's the condom for, Daddy?"

She looked at me and smirked. "I'm going to cum inside

you, of course." Raven thumped the outside of my flower with her cock.

It took a while to find a rhythm because I couldn't relax, being poked with a plastic prick. Raven was obviously into it, so I started imagining she was punishing me for being such a flirt. I flirt with everyone, even the mechanic who fixed my Prius last week. I remembered the way the guy on the floor of the garage looked up at me with his greasy hands.

I imagined saying, "I don't know how all this rigging works." I imagined him saying, "I'll show you . . ." and taking me into the back, throwing me over the hood of some broken pile of junk, and pushing his weight against me. I'm spread against the grill, and he starts grunting while Raven is moaning. I spread my legs even wider as I imagined Raven as the mechanic, grabbing at my breasts with his big dirty hands. He was pumping and panting and all of a sudden he started spasming. Then there was stillness. I heard Raven breathing on top of me.

"Did you just cum inside me?"

"Sure did," Raven said, pushing herself up.

"I think I felt it," I said, reaching between my legs as she slowly pulled out.

"I should hope so," Raven said, smiling.

"No. I mean, I actually felt your sticky white spirit cum squirt inside me."

Raven placed one hand at the base of her cock and used the other to pull the condom off.

"I had a fantasy that you were some other guy."

"I want details," she said.

I told her everything. Right down to the hair on the guy's knuckles.

"I wish you would've told me while it was happening, because I was having a similar fantasy. What did you think of the strap-on?"

"It was interesting, but I fucking loved playing with rope."

"The way I see it, you've got to try everything at least twice. If you didn't like the strap-on the first time, it's probably because you didn't do it right."

"Again? Already? You want to do it now?" I asked.

"This time, I want you to strap it on. I want you to feel how powerful it is to fully fuck a woman when your hands are free. It'll make it more exciting for you the next time you receive."

"Really, you'd let me do that to you?" I swoon.

Raven looked into my eyes and we shared a moment of silent understanding of what a big surrender this was for her. Then Raven reached into her bag and pulled out a hot-pink harness. She wanted me to wear it since factory-made harnesses are easier to wield than homemade Shibari. It seemed almost equally complex, I thought, as she helped rig me up by adjusting the straps.

"This is quite a contraption," I said.

"You get used to it."

Then the most intimate and perverse thing happened. Raven grabbed her pink cock and expertly twisted and unplugged it from our handmade Shibari tie. Then she deftly inserted it into my harness, thus sharing her detachable penis with me. I was officially endowed with the power of my first "girl dick."

"I feel like such a deviant," I said as I started stroking myself and exaggerating my heavy breathing.

"That's because you are," Raven stated flatly.

"What do I need to know about wielding this thing?"

She told me that the main difference between a strap-on and a bio-cock is it's not self-lubricating, and since plastic dries out fast, extra lubrication is essential. Since you can't exactly feel what's happening, you've got to take it slow and read your partner's body language. The best part is that it has more endurance than a bio-cock—the erection won't wane and there's no refractory period.

Raven bragged, "I could've cum inside you, and kept going until I made you cum, but I decided against it."

"That's quite an advantage. Are you ready?" I said, feeling the horsepower in my hand.

We started off in missionary, since that's the easiest position to see what's happening. I felt sort of clumsy at first. I needed a lot of reassurance, but she kept saying that I was doing fine. Raven helped guide me in and set the pace. Then we got lost kissing, and I'd forget to thrust, but Raven didn't seem to mind. Eventually, she rolled on top of me and started riding me, and it felt like she was doing me. We both ended up laughing because the whole thing felt sort of forced.

"Clearly, this is not the direction of our circuitry. My energy body wants to penetrate you, not the other way around."

It never felt like my penis, it was more like a plastic circuit breaker with no electrical current. So I asked her if she had any last requests before I unplugged.

As we lay in each other's arms, I told her it reminded me of Sissy Training. "When you humiliate a guy by making him wear women's clothing, except it was all backward and inside out. Truthfully, it felt much better when you were penetrating me."

"Well, I'm glad we won't be arguing about who's on top," Raven said.

I buried my laughter in her arms and then told her the thing I'd been thinking since the day we met.

"Even if the strap-on didn't fit me, you do. I mean you are my perfect fit."

Yours,
Vi.

Tantric Tease

My moon came early and hard this month. I had to cancel whatever kinky scene Raven was planning because I felt like a heavy magnet in my uterus was pulling me to the couch. Raven insisted on coming to cuddle me while I curled up with a heating pad.

I felt miraculously better the moment she walked in. She found me all sprawled out in a skimpy camisole and cotton panties, covered by a fuzzy blanket. She kissed me on the forehead. I offered to make her mint tea.

"I can make it myself," she said.

I called to her as she walked into the kitchen, "But serving you is one of my great pleasures. I'm bummed I had to cancel our sexy time, our relationship is too new for 'lesbian bed-death!'"

"Silly woman." Raven returned and pounced on me. "'Lesbian bed-death' only happens to women who live together and rely on each other to meet all their primary needs. We see each other once a week for a fun playdate, hardly enough to argue over whose turn it is to do the dishes. I promise I won't lose interest just because you don't put out this week."

"Thank God! I like having sex during my moon time, I just don't always feel so sexy. Damien usually has to do all the work. I've been wondering, if you didn't practice BDSM with Damien, what did you do on your dates?"

"We'd talk, a lot."

"About what?" I asked, trying to sound casual.

"Everything. You know Damien. I remember musing on consciousness as the interior experience of the universe expressing itself through each individual and how the more we wake up, the more we participate in our own evolution."

"He said you used to practice tantra together. That's something I want to try," I said.

Raven instantly morphed into teacher mode. Her whole posture changed when she asked, "Is there a particular practice you want to explore?"

"I'm open to anything you want to teach me."

"How about we save the teacher/student scene for when you don't have cramps?"

"I can rally."

"I'm sure you can," she says sternly, "but you're always in service. It's so rare that I get to meet your brokenness. I want to embrace your authenticity, maybe try some sexual healing."

Beaming, I pulled her into the bedroom. Raven told me to empty my bladder and asked for a towel. I returned, stark naked, to find she'd peeled my comforter off.

"No fair, I wanted to watch you undress," Raven said.

"I can still undress you," I offered, my hands in prayer. She nodded and I moved in slow motion as I stripped off each layer, down to her sun bronzed skin.

Raven directed me to sit facing her, knee to knee. She said we were going to enter a timeless dimension and should set an alarm clock. I reassured her that Damien wouldn't come home before 4:00 p.m., so I set my timer for 3:45 and flipped the ringer off.

Meanwhile, Raven pulled a red veil out of her little silk bag. She covered the lamp, creating a warm, womb-like glow. She arranged a candle and a quartz crystal on the nightstand.

"I have a particular invocation I want to share. What do you know about tantra?"

"Parvati from my yoga ashram used to say there are people out there doing strange stuff and calling it tantra. She calls it, 'California hot tub tantra.'"

"She has a good point . . . yet the traditionalists are so busy following some ancient lineage that they miss out on the spontaneous awakening that is available in a hot tub. Are you ready?"

"I don't know if I have the energy for a five-hour orgasm."

"People think tantra has to be ecstatic, or long and slow, but it doesn't have to look like anything. Kind of like kink—it's not always pleasurable, and it doesn't always hurt. Tantra says you can't go to great heights unless you dig a deep foundation. The lotus grows from the muck, and sometimes we dig up past wounds for the sake of healing them."

"You're starting to scare me now," I said with a raised eyebrow.

"Let's drop in." After a few deep breaths, she used a simple prayer to invoke Shiva and Shakti, the God and Goddess of all creation and destruction. But she emphasized that they are not out there, in the clouds, they are right here (pointing between her breasts) inside of us. She invited Shiva to look out from the back of our eyes with his all-seeing power of observation. Then she described Shakti as a dancer with many veils and invoked her to animate our bodies and guide the movement in our hips.

After she laid me down and propped my knees with pillows, she asked if I was open to a yoni massage and if I had any boundaries.

"I am a yes to whatever you want to do to me."

"This isn't about doing. I want to worship, the way a pilgrim visits a temple, then I am going to hold still and breathe."

"Are you going to start staring again?"

"It's gazing, not staring, but no, this is different." She massaged my thighs and outer lips, explaining, "I want to enter your inner sanctum and meditate there. All you have to do is breathe, feel, and receive. I know how much you love to please me, but this is for you. There is no pressure for it to even be pleasurable. I welcome whatever comes up."

"So, you want me to just lie there and take it," I teased.

Smiling, she continued in a less serious tone, "If you prefer, you can think of me like your 'service top.' If something comes up you can name it, or give it a sound, or give me directions to help you move through it. When you're ready, I want you to invite me inside."

"Yes please, come in already."

She gazed into my eyes and touched me as slowly as a sloth. I imagined her fingers like a claw with three long toes. That excited me at first, but then she guided me to breathe with her.

"I feel so vulnerable with my legs spread open like this."

"Good. Breathe into the sensation of vulnerability."

She just sat there breathing with her hand between my legs. It was like driving through the desert with no music, no landscape, total flatlands... I wanted a mirage or something. So I asked her if I was allowed to fantasize.

"Don't force or chase anything. Just notice whatever arises, even if it's numbness. It's okay to feel boredom."

I kept breathing, and after what felt like forever, her face started to shape-shift. She looked like an old man, then a young girl, then both at the same time. Next, she started melting into faces of people from my past. I didn't say anything at first, because I didn't want to break the trance. Eventually, I needed to know if she was doing it on purpose, so I asked.

She said, "That's just 'phenomena.' All kinds of experiences can arise during meditation—colors, twitches, visitations—don't let it distract you from your embodied reality."

In the next breath, I started to weep, big elephant tears. I don't know why I cried, but I did.

I must've forgotten to keep my legs open because she had to remind me not to crush her hand. At one point, when she said, "Spread your legs," I got instantly aroused. Raven's whole power dynamic crumbled before my eyes, and I suddenly remembered what I love about this woman.

"You just love spreading me open and stuffing things inside me, don't you?" I blurted.

"The only thing that's inside you right now is my love. No matter how much you beg, I am in service to the Goddess today."

"I feel more like a slut than a Goddess," I said, grinding my hips against her hand.

"You're both. It's the nature of the divine feminine."

And with that, I felt this animal force moving through me. I start grunting, and she encouraged me by growling with me. The animal intensity dissipated when one of us howled and we both started laughing.

I asked to end the session because I felt too much pressure on my bladder.

"You might think you have to pee, but it might be amrita."

I questioned her with my eyes.

"Female ejaculate," Raven said, refusing to pull out.

"No way, I'm not even close to orgasming," I snapped.

"Sometimes after a big breakthrough like this, your body wants to release. I can feel that your G-spot is full inside."

"Because I have to pee," I said, pulling her bloody hand out by the wrist and leaving the room.

On the toilet, I realized that my words came out harsher than I intended. But damn, it felt good to gush into the toilet. I was still high from the whole scene and I couldn't believe it was already almost four o'clock.

When I returned, she had made the bed, put out the candle, and was reclining against the headboard, her arms crossed over her heart. "Why did you say you weren't even close to orgasming?"

"Sorry." I kissed her. "I don't mean to sound ungrateful for the whole experience, it was wonderful, really edgy for me, especially the way you had me spread-eagle. I like being vulnerable with you, it's just if you want to get me off, all you have to do is give me a good fantasy."

"Maybe one day I'll tie you to a spreader bar and force an orgasm."

"I wish we didn't have to wait a whole week."

I placed my head on her chest and she sighed meaningfully.

I would have dozed off in her arms if she hadn't jumped at the sound of keys jingling at the front door. Her muscles tensed when Damien whistled for me. He walked straight back and was surprised to find Raven quickly packing up. A bolt of tension swept through the room, but he navigated it by giving each of us a warm hug. "So good to see you."

My heart accelerated at the sight of my two lovers hugging.

"I was just on my way out," Raven said cordially.

"I don't want to run you off," Damien said.

"We lost track of time," Raven said, squeezing me.

"That means you must've been having fun," Damien teased.

Trying to normalize the situation, I offered, "Actually, I'm still bleeding so we had a slow, tantric healing session."

"Good." Damien pulled Raven in to sit beside him on the bed as he continued. "I've been wanting Violet to experience your Dakini gifts."

"That makes two of us," Raven said stiffly.

I lightened the mood by saying, "I feel like you two are plotting to gang up on me."

"You'd like that wouldn't you?" Raven reached for my nipple, but I dodged her fingers.

Damien asked, "Did she tell you about the strap-on?"

Raven looked at me confused, so I explained, "You know, the pink dildo you sissy trained me with?"

"Yes?"

"Well, you left it here last week. So I sort of used it on Damien."

"As in, you penetrated him, with my cock?"

"Yes, Ma'am," I said.

"She made a whole ritual out of it," Damien bragged.

Raven's eyebrows crinkled as if she had just been slapped, so I tried to explain. "When I told him about our gender play, he wanted to know what it would be like to get pegged... I did just like you taught me, with a ton of lube and—"

"That was my cock!" Raven scrambled to her feet. "And you didn't even ask me!" But instead of fleeing, she started sobbing. "Sorry, I just feel a bit hijacked right now."

"I didn't mean to upset you," Damien said, placing a comforting hand on her back.

"It's just there are certain protocols about sharing toys... and I wouldn't expect you to understand," she sniffed.

"What kind of protocols are you talking about? I need to know where I misstepped," Damien said, pulling her in closer.

Raven softened her tone. "Sharing toys with other lovers is a very intimate act."

"But we share everything else," I retorted.

Raven considered it, then started laughing. "I guess we do."

She wiped her face on Damien's sleeve as he hugged her. "It must be my old monogamous programming. There are a lot of rules in lesbian culture too. Maybe it's my need to have something special, just between us."

"That's understandable," Damien says. "It's not unlike my desire to be part of Violet's first-time experiences. And this was a first for us."

"I hope she pegged you good," Raven laughed.

Smiling, Damien said, "Let's just say, I now have more compassion for my gay brothers."

Relieved to see her smiling again, I said, "Does it help to know I was fantasizing about you when I was pegging him?"

"It depends. Were you fantasizing about pegging me or that I was pegging you?"

"You were on top, of course, going to town on Damien!"

"That works. At least we're clear about who's on top." Raven pulled me into a three-way hug. "I love you." As she stood up to walk out she whispered, "Both of you."

Yours,
Vi.

FRIDAY #16

Doubleheader

I showed up to Raven's playroom bearing gifts. We sat under the canopy of her bed but she didn't make a move. She seemed distracted.

"Damien sends this as a sort of peace offering."

Raven scoffed, "Couldn't he have done that with flowers?"

"He said you don't like cut flowers because they're just going to die anyway."

Raven smiled and unwrapped his gift. It was a strange new purple sex toy. She carefully inspected the odd shape in one hand while reading from the package: "This patented design offers hands-free stimulation for hot, face-to-face sex. This vibrating 'strapless' strap-on is cleverly curved at just the right angle to stay firmly inside the penetrator with each passionate thrust."

"What do you think it means for a man to give me a store-bought cock?"

"He wants us to use it today. He suggested I do the fucking."

"I bet he did. He's trying to top me from a distance."

"I didn't think you'd go for it."

Raven was quiet at first, then barked out directions: "Take off your clothes, except your sexy stockings, and lie facedown."

She pulled off the quilt and prepared the disembodied dick with a condom on each end as I slipped out of my skirt and sleeveless shirt. I buried my face in the pillow and exaggerated lifting my ass into the air. "Come and get me," I teased.

She rolled up her sleeves. "I need to warm up first." She spanked my ass lightly.

"Are you warming me or you?" I asked, my words muffled by the pillow.

Raven hit harder. *Slap! Slap! Slap!*

"This is just to remind you who is in charge." *Slap! Slap! Slap!* "There is giving." *Slap! Slap! Slap!* "And there is receiving." *Slap! Slap! Slap!* "And then there is taking. If I am going to give you my cunt, I am going to take your ass. Do you understand?"

Squealing, I clenched my ass and managed to say, "As long as you mean my butt, not my butt hole."

The spanking felt so good, I might have let her try to slip a finger in, but not that big purple thing.

"Fine," she said. "Now, let me see." I heard her wrestling around with the new toy and slipping off her panties. "If you're the one who's supposed to be fucking me, then I will insert the fatter part inside of you. It's supposed to stay inside without straps. Now flip over."

She poked the thick plastic bulb between my legs. I was wet already, so it slipped right in and filled me up.

"How does that feel?"

"Strange, like a butt plug, except it's in my pussy." I looked between my legs and saw the long purple erection extending from my pelvis.

"Now, I want you to keep your legs closed. Hold still while I ride you in cowgirl position." Raven pushed my shoulders down, forcing me to lie back as she straddled my purple penis. The second she plugged herself onto the cock, I realized both our pussies were wrapped around the same damn thing, and I felt a bolt of excitement shoot through my spine. I grabbed her flexing thighs and watched her cleavage bounce in her push-up bra, her hair flowing over her tan skin. She leaned in to kiss me. I tried to thrust my hips, but it messed up our rhythm.

"The only way this is going to work is if you lie there and let me fuck you," Raven commanded.

Relieved, I surrendered.

Raven changed positions, maneuvering the chubby bulb farther inside me, and said, "Sometimes when I'm having sex with Nick, or any man, I imagine I'm the one penetrating him. Even though his cock is inside me physically, my energy flows out and enters him." She spread my legs wide and gripped the long shaft inside her vagina, then began thrusting so hard the fat bulb plunged in and out. "Can you feel my etheric cock?"

At that moment, I did! I felt her energy extending far beyond the dildo into my stomach. Then, it lit up like a lightsaber, illuminating my entire chest. We began breathing together and gazing into each other's eyes. There was a fluttering in my pelvis. Raven responded by moaning uninhibitedly, loudly and rhythmically, like a car alarm. Grinding and panting, I was covered in her warm breath and wild hair. Raven's energy intensified and erupted like a volcano flowing in all directions. Once she regained her presence, she lifted onto her elbows and shook with embarrassment. "Sorry."

"Why are you sorry?"

"I came so quickly . . ." she said tenderly. "I couldn't hold out any longer."

Raven's face was so soft and misty—I rarely get to see her so vulnerable. I reassured her, "It was beautiful."

"You're not disappointed?"

"It's the hottest strap-on sex I've ever had."

"Thanks, but I imagine it doesn't compare to real penetrative sex."

"What are you talking about? You are my wildest fantasy." I tried kissing her, but she pulled away.

"I just feel inadequate. I don't have a real cock, and as if that isn't bad enough, I came prematurely."

"I love seeing you let loose. It inspires me to want to be more free with my own orgasms. I wish I were that free. It's such a gift to your partner."

"But it feels like my body betrayed me. I'm too orgasmic. I can't even hold out to let you cum first."

"I don't need you to make love to me like a man. You're my queen."

She finally cracked a smile. "You are such an obedient little subject."

And we sealed the session with a long lingering kiss.

Yours,
Vi.

P.S. As she walked me to my car, Raven told me, "Be sure to thank Damien for the double-headed dildo. And let him know if he is, in fact, attempting to dominate me from a distance, we both know who the real boss is."

FRIDAY #17

Casting Couch

I postponed our playdate until after class, so I would be prepared for the big audition. I spent the extra time getting a
pedicure, braiding my hair, and applying false eyelashes while
running my lines. I mean her lines, which after watching the
performance over two hundred times on YouTube, felt like my
lines. I memorized every movement. I just hoped I could coordinate the lines with the ropes without getting tongue-tied, or
literally tangled up.

When I arrived at the theater, Raven was sitting in the center of the house, hunched over her notes. She gave me a quick
kiss on the cheek but didn't mention my kimono or curled hair.
I followed the other performers backstage and waited in the
wings for my turn to audition.

I watched, wide-eyed, from behind the curtain as the guy
before me performed a personal narrative about coming out as

"trans-amorous." He had always been romantically and sexually attracted to transgender people but felt lonely from the lack of support because he wasn't queer himself. I was so engrossed in his story, and Raven's feedback that he should aim to be more vulnerable and less angry, that I almost forgot I was auditioning next.

I crossed slowly to center stage carrying fifty feet of black rope casually slung over shoulder, then spoke my first line:

"You may not be ready for this. It's the story about when I first discovered I was kinky."

I teased the audience by slowly opening my silk robe. "If you have an issue with kink, I suggest you look away. I dare you."

I slipped the robe down my shoulders, carefully hanging it on the upstage chair, and letting the audience admire my crimson lace bra and panties. I untangled the rope and carefully wrapped my body, knot by knot, into the exact full-body harness that Raven did on the video, all while carefully delivering the following monologue:

"When I graduated from college, I already knew I was bisexual. I left my lesbian lover and moved to Hawaii to be with a man. I also knew I was polyamorous because I moved in with him and his lover. We all lived together in an artist commune.

"At the time, I was beginning to explore tantra. A few times a week, the commune's drummers and healers would go out on the land to perform sacred rituals, trance dance, and other spiritual journeys. There was clearly a lot I didn't understand, like shamanic soul retrieval. I thought it was some kind of past life regression where you go into your pain body and relive all your past traumas. I wasn't interested in that.

"I was much more interested in free love and cross dressing. I was the director of Honolulu's annual gay, lesbian, bisexual, transgender pride festival. Though this may sound like a prestigious title, it was just a bunch of drag queens, country line dancers, and lesbians with guitars, but I wanted to direct a variety show.

"I heard there was a dominatrix who lived on the island. She was rumored to be a lesbian, so I called her up. She said, 'I might consider being in your little show, if you give me a ride to my girlfriend's house.'

"I told her that wasn't normally how I ran auditions, but she sounded interesting, so I picked her up at her dungeon and drove her clear across the island. When we arrived at her girlfriend's mansion, she opened these large double doors and greeted us topless with a plate of warm brie. Then she put a glass of merlot in my hand.

"Two or three glasses later, they decided I was kinda cute. They devised an elaborate scene to tie me up and shave me because they said I was too hairy for their taste.

"I have to admit. When they first got out the rope, I was a little nervous. Then when they tied my arms to the shower-curtain rod, I wondered, *What have I gotten myself into?* Next, they lathered me up with warm coconut oil. It smelled so good, I remember thinking, *I'm a yes. I'm in. For anything.* So I didn't hesitate when she pulled out the straight razor.

"She said, 'Do you trust me?'

"Something about the way she moved slowly up my ankle to my thigh made me wet.

"Then she said, 'I think you're enjoying this a little too much.'

"She had this intensity about her that was familiar. She said, 'You've been a naughty girl!'

"At that moment, I was instantly transported back to the day when I lost my virginity. I was sixteen years old and my mother found out and she was raging. 'You're a slut! Everyone is going to find out about this, and they are going to call you the town whore!'

"I felt the guilt and shame I had previously experienced, instantly transformed . . . into arousal."

At this point in the performance, my body was bound and my hands were held high above my head as if I were tied to a curtain rod, and I looked directly at Raven.

"Being tied up, I had nothing to do but enjoy my sexuality. She was shaving away years of repression. I know it's strange to suggest that bondage can lead to liberation, but the body is so much wiser than the mind will ever understand.

"So I ask you, if this is so wrong . . ."

I slowly turned around and glanced over my shoulder, radiating pleasure onto anyone who dared to look.

". . . then why are all of you turned on?"

Big applause. Several classmates actually stood and hollered. I bowed and thanked everyone, then nervously looked at Raven. She was obviously struggling to keep her composure.

"I'm speechless. When I originally wrote this piece, I never envisioned those words coming out of anyone else's mouth. And I certainly never thought anyone could replicate the ropework. It's eerie . . . Have you ever see that '80s movie called *Single White Female*?"

"No," I said, breathless.

"You know, the one where Bridget Fonda's roommate becomes her stalker, gets the same haircut, starts dressing in her clothes and using her things? Never mind. You obviously went the extra mile on your audition tonight."

"You think I'm creepy for stalking you?" I asked.

"Creepy? Yes. Come to think of it, a little bit." Raven ran both hands through her hair and said, "We'll talk more after class. How about another round of applause for Violet?"

I wobbled off stage in a fog. It was like the moment I told Raven I made love to Damien in the audience. I could've sworn she would be happy, not hurt. I headed to the restroom to untie myself, then instead of returning to watch other people's monologues, I stayed and stared into the mirror. My reflection seemed to know I did a good job. I didn't need anyone to tell me so. Regardless of whether she decided to accept me into the showcase or not, I decided, my job was to love her.

I returned in time for closing circle.

"Final decisions will be emailed tomorrow," Raven said as she dismissed the class. All my peers were congratulatory on their way out. Several of them told me they didn't realize it was Raven's story and didn't understand why she was being so weird. People seemed sincerely impressed with my performance.

After everyone left, I helped Shelby put props away and sweep the stage. When finished, I hugged her good-bye, switched on the romantic stage lighting, and arranged several cushions on the floor.

Raven collapsed onto the pillows and extended her arms to hold me. I put my head on her chest and she kissed it in silence. This was one of those times when I knew I needed to let her speak first.

"When I first performed that piece, it bothered me that no-body would ever know how truly difficult it is to tie yourself up while delivering a monologue to an audience. Nobody in the world knows the practice it takes, except you and me."

I didn't plan to cry, but the tears flowed onto both cheeks like a river of relief.

Her face grew serious and she continued, "You are made for the ropes. Not only does your body look delicious all tied up, but I believe you could do a better job with that piece than I ever could."

I wanted to tell her I did it because I loved her. But instead, I said, "So, do I get to be in the show?"

"I don't know. This storytelling showcase only has a

handful of rules and one of them is that it's supposed to be a true personal narrative."

"Which it is."

"It was personal when I performed it, but since you're not the writer, I'll have to think about it."

I squeezed her thigh and asked, "Is there anything I can do to persuade you?"

She pinched my nipple, which made me squeal.

"And that sums up my moral dilemma. The director sets certain parameters for her show. Of course, there are exceptions to every rule, but when an exception is made for the director's girlfriend, it begs the question: is it because it's a worthy performance, or is it because she's the teacher's pet?"

I slowly untied my silk robe. "I trust you'll do the right thing. And if you do decide to cast me in the show, I'm going to need some private coaching. I mean with the ropes, of course."

"Why do you think I ended class early tonight?"

Then we proceeded to make love onstage.

Yours,
Vi.

P.S. Afterward, Raven pointed to the wet spot and said it will mark the spot where I need to stand during my performance in the showcase next month.

FRIDAY #18

Poly Puppet Show

I'd never been so nervous to see Raven before. I told her I wanted to schedule some extra rehearsal time before class, but I didn't tell her exactly what I was working on. I made her sit in the middle of the empty audience and stepped onstage with her ropes. Then I took a big breath and began performing.

"I first read about polyamory in a book. It sounded really interesting, but not having any role models, I had no choice but to continue drinking the monogamy Kool-Aid. I got fully indoctrinated into the idea that one person was supposed to meet all your needs. I was a serial monogamist, having to end one relationship every time I wanted to start another . . . until I met Damien and Raven."

Raven called from her seat, "Wait! Hold on. Can I ask you something?"

"Anything." I said, "You can direct me however you want, that's why I'm here."

Raven stood up and said, "Is this scripted or are you just speaking from your heart?"

I reached into the waistband of my skinny jeans and pulled out a napkin. "I wrote down some ideas. Do you want me to write it all out?"

"Let me see." Raven came to the edge of the stage and took my notes. She unfolded it and read all four sides. "What's your angle?"

"You asked me to tell a story about my sexual awakening and this is it. You and Damien are my guides. If you don't like it, you can change it."

"I like it. I do. But it's so current. It's still happening. It's dangerously close to therapy. And since it's about us, it runs the risk of being self-indulgent. Do you know the difference between art and therapy?"

"Does it have something to do with objectivity?" I guessed.

"And who the performance is for. Are you telling this story for your benefit, or for the audience? It also has a little something to do with skill. Performance is stagecraft, so if we are going to tell this story, it has to have a dramatic element."

"Like the ropes!"

"Exactly. Except we can't use the ropes. That's not original."

"What then? I'm not attached to ropes, not yet anyway." I giggled at my own pun. "Direct me. I'll be your puppet and you can be my puppet master."

"Thank you!" Raven rushed onto the stage and after a few messy kisses she ran behind the curtain and returned with several tattered props. In one hand she held up a stuffed grinder monkey, with a torn vest. In the other, a Día De Los Muertos skeleton with a top hat and tux.

"Okay, let's pretend these are puppets. I want you to give them a voice and personality and let them tell the story for you."

I took the silly figurines into my hands and exaggerated a

deep voice for Damien as the skeleton and an annoyingly high-pitched voice for me as the grinder monkey.

SUGAR SKULL: "Hello, Violet. I noticed your relationship status changed to single."

MONKEY: "Hello, Damien! My boyfriend and I just broke up."

Of course, I needed to narrate the story a bit, so I used my normal voice to explain, "Damien used to be one of my yoga students before we connected on Facebook."

SUGAR SKULL: "I would love to take you on a date and talk all about planetary operating systems or some fascinating philosophy that I'm tackling with my think tank."

MONKEY: "That sounds amazing, but first I have to ask you, are you faithful in your relationships?"

SUGAR SKULL: "I'm currently in a polyamorous relationship with a handful of women who all know about each other and are in full consent."

MONKEY: "So you're one of those guys who likes to worship the Goddess in everyone. You probably run around spreading your polyamorous seed all over town! I don't want anything to do with that. I'm monogamous!"

SUGAR SKULL: "Well, I respect your decision and I make a really good friend." (*Wink, wink.*)

I narrate, "After a week of amazing conversations, Damien started to grow on me."

MONKEY: "Oh, Damien! I wish you weren't so polyamorous!"

SUGAR SKULL: "Have you ever considered polyamory might be the perfect relationship paradigm for you, since you've been a serial monogamist? Instead of dumping your old relationship just to start a new one, you can add and multiply instead of subtracting and dividing. And since you're bisexual, you'd be able to date women and men."

"When Damien and I were first dating, I was terrified of losing him. When he spoke about other women, I had a lot of built-up resentments. I cried buckets of tears and even became less attracted to him."

Raven was so engaged in my storytelling, she spontaneously interjected, "I remember. That's when he decided to break up with me."

"Actually, no. Not at first. I didn't want him to break up with you. I liked what you two had. When he spoke about you, I wanted to hear more, but he did phase out of all his other relationships. Whenever he came back from his Monday night dates with you, I'd give him the third degree. I'd ask him to describe every detail. Show don't tell," Raven prompted.

MONKEY: "Did you kiss her? Did you touch her boobs? Did you have oral sex or penetrative sex? I need to know everything!"

SUGAR SKULL: "Raven and I did make love. It was beautiful. We talked about you and I really missed you."

I explained, "One day, I was so irritated when he came home that I couldn't get out of my head. But I knew if I could drop into my body and have an orgasm, I could literally change the chemistry in my brain so I would be able to hear about you with an open heart."

MONKEY: "Oh, Damien! Why don't we go have sex?"

I add, "But when we first started making love, there was this smell."

MONKEY: (*Sniff. Sniff.*) "What is that smell? It's Raven!"
"I was like, whoa! I really like that smell… And then I started to fantasize."

"Fantasize? About what?" Raven couldn't hide her enthusiasm.
"I imagined Damien was this dangerous gangster guy who barged in the door fresh from his date.

SUGAR SKULL: "Hey. Yo, Baby! I came back from my date with that hot bitch, Raven."

MONKEY: "Oh Damien. I'm so mad at you right now!"

SUGAR SKULL: "I want to have sex with you while I still have her pussy juices all over my face."

MONKEY: "How dare you!"

SUGAR SKULL: "I'm going to make you lick it off and you're going to like it."

MONKEY: "No! Please! I don't want to do that."

SUGAR SKULL: "Come here, Bitch. You're going to take it."

MONKEY: "Oh, No. Oh, Yes. Oh, Yes!"

And then I made the skeleton mount the monkey and pumped their bodies together while I thrust my pelvis against the podium until I nearly orgasmed as retold my fantasy of Damien forcing himself onto me.

SUGAR SKULL: "Oh, yeah baby. Take it like that!"

MONKEY: "Oh, God! Oh yes. I'm cumming!"

I felt Raven equally turned on from just watching me.

I continued to narrate: "When I told Damien every detail of my fantasy, he reassured me he loves every part of me, including my perverted fantasies. He said he wanted to share everything with me, everything including his girlfriend. And that's why, even after Damien had broken up with you, I still had to come to your theater to get to know you!"

Raven interjected, "I think you came to the theater because deep down you are called to perform. I just happen to be able to help you play out your perverted fantasies, but clearly your true calling is puppeteering."

I laughed, not as much from her joke, as from relief that she genuinely liked my story. I glanced at my little napkin to see if I missed anything and concluded with this:

"Unfortunately, it took a few more months of monogamy deprogramming before I got up the guts to finally meet Raven. Although it took Damien breaking up with her for me to feel safe, we've designed a new creative container where we can share everything—our fantasies, our future. We're like family. And our love is based on freedom and wanting for each other's full expression!"

Applause. Raven whistles and cheers. "Wonderful! Would you do something for me?"

"Anything."

"Workshop it in class tonight so we can perform it for the storytelling showcase."

MONKEY: "You bet!"

Then I covered her in kisses.

Raven wrestled her arms around me, firmly pinned my puppets down, and said, "You know, I never realized how much directing has in common with dominating, until today. I felt such a surge of creativity and power to watch you trust and surrender to my direction. I can't imagine how magic it will feel to have this dual relationship with you."

Yours,
Vi.

In the Coat Closet

66**Y**ou walk past the reception desk and nod to the secretary on your way to the empty boardroom. You set your briefcase on a leather chair and sit patiently with your hands folded in your lap, waiting for your boss . . ." Raven spoke as if it were happening in real time.

"What am I wearing? It's important, for my character," I said.

Without missing a beat, Raven continued, "A tailored suit with stern lines that say you mean business, but your plunging neckline suggests something else. If you bend forward, a small slip of a white bra can be seen cupping your breasts—otherwise, every hair is in place. You are the picture of a high-powered executive."

In reality, the only stitch of clothing I was wearing was a blindfold. I sat cross-legged on the bed while Raven unwound her rope, preparing to use it on me. She told me she was taking me on a journey. The only thing that I knew was that she showed up with three different-size dildos. She'd lined them up neatly on the nightstand, beside an open bottle of lube and a pair of rubber gloves, before blindfolding me. She tied the rope around my sternum and continued spinning her story.

"Your boss is rich, Russian, and strangely superstitious. He believes you're his secret weapon. As the CEO, he is feared by most of his employees for his quick and severe decision-making skills. He has zero tolerance for anything less than perfection. His perverted secrets are only vaguely suspected by his long-term employees. Some of the lower-level staff are hired to hide his criminal depravity. They all sign an ironclad NDA.

"His secretary called you in today for a special assignment. You are purposely his first meeting. You're good for business and you know it."

She petted my hair lovingly first, then pulled it back and twisted it into a tight bun.

She whispered into my ear, "When he enters, you stand up. No words are exchanged. He walks behind you. He stands still. You can feel the heat of his breath on your neck. He grabs you by the hips and bends you over, slamming your hands onto the table. He reaches into your suit and squeezes your lace-covered breasts. He presses hard until the underwire of your bra cuts into your skin. You wince, but he doesn't notice. You love this part of your job. His hands drop to the hem of your tight skirt and he mechanically slides it up your thighs. He fingers your lace panties a few times, then orders, 'Take it off,' like he can't be bothered.

"You obey, turning confidently like a model on a runway. You know you're supposed to keep your eyes downcast and not look directly at him. You steal a quick glance at his chiseled face before slipping your panties down your long legs, bending over to slowly step out of them, one high heel at a time."

When I was all tied up, Raven repositioned my body. She laid me down on my back so she could access my flower. My hands were pinned to my sides so I was unable to refuse anything she did to me.

"The ritual you are about to perform has a long history. You've been working for him for over five years, and you repeat it periodically, upon his request, with little or no warning. Are you ready to be fucked in his boardroom?"

I could hear rubber gloves being stretched over her fingers.

"You agree to surrender, partially because of the adventure, and partially because it's good for business. One day spent with him means you don't have to take other clients for months afterward. That is, of course, if you submit to his perversions."

The lubrication felt cold as she rubbed two fingers into my throbbing folds.

"Pantyless, you sit your ass on the shiny black desk and place one heel on each chair. You ceremoniously separate your knees, inviting him inside you. He drops down without looking in your eyes and buries his face in your sex. He uses his hands to grab your lips and hold you in place as he eats you out. He doesn't do much tonguing and fingering because this is about his pleasure, not yours. When he has gotten his fill, he lays you back on his executive desk, unzips his trousers, and unleashes one of the largest cocks you've ever seen. He thumps it against you a few times to emphasize his girth."

Raven covered a huge dildo with gobs of lube and slowly stuffed it inside me.

"You whimper upon his searing entrance, but soon the arousal catches up. He is slow and steady. Every time you thrust your hips even slightly, you can feel pressure against your cervix."

I felt too full. I couldn't stand it. I didn't want to break the scene, but decided to say, "It's too much. It's too big." Then it occurred to me that she might think I was playing along, so I said, "Yellow light, honey, can you use a smaller one?"

"Of course. Thank you for speaking up." Raven slowly pulled out. Relief.

"We'll start with a smaller one, but it's only to stretch you out and prepare you for the big one. Anything else?"

"That's all, and I love you."

"Lie back and take it."

"Anything you say, my Queen."

"So your boss is uncomfortable. He says you're too tight, and that you need to be loosened up. Stretched out."

I giggled. She shushed me, but I couldn't help it, I was enjoying the feeling of this new dildo too much.

"Your boss orders you to fix your clothes and wait for further orders. He wants to have you stretched out and ready for his big cock the next time he sees you. Feeling rejected, you pout as you pull your panties back on and straighten out your skirt. He is watching you. He picks up the phone and presses a button, which rings someone's desk. He says something in Russian.

"A moment later a young mail clerk enters the room. Glancing only at the ground, his glasses nearly slide off his nose as he takes you by the arm. He leads you down the hall, past the executive office with a sweeping view of the city, and along one of those wall-length aquarium with exotic fish.. The whole scene is a designer's wet dream. He continues walking you down the hall until you reach the company coat closet.

"He opens the door to a small room lit with little LED rope lights. As your eyes adjust to the darkness, you catch a glimpse of a queen-size futon with several sex pillows hiding behind a sea of expensive, executive coats. In one corner, there is an open trunk with condoms and other sex toys.

"The man from the mailroom steps inside with you, pulls

the door shut, and produces restraints and a blindfold from the box. He tells you he's been instructed to tie you to the bed frame.

"He mumbles incoherent instructions. The only world you catch is 'naked.' So you smile and think, *He must be new.* You start to strip, but he looks away out of respect, which is a little disappointing. But when he binds your ankles and legs to the bed, he can't help but admire your responsive body as he grazes you with the restraints. Before he leaves, you ask him to prop your hips with a pillow. While he adjusts your position, you hold your ass in the air and rub against him as much as possible before he exits."

Raven suddenly stopped touching me. She pulled everything out. I felt around for her fingers, but they had left.

"When he leaves, you realize you're all alone, you can't even masturbate, you close your eyes and wait. You start to wonder...

"Before you know it, a bear of a man barges in, and with a raspy voice says, 'There you are, you little bitch.'

"He takes your knees and separates them. Then he stuffs himself inside you."

Raven continued speaking as she reinserted the smaller dildo. "He has no concern for your comfort, no interest in you as a person, and doesn't even care about your appearance. To him, you are just another hole, and you love it.

He's one in a long string of men that come to fuck you, to use you, about every half hour. You don't know who these men are, or exactly how they got the duty of keeping you fucked. You suspect that your boss negotiated the terms as some kind of a bonus. Maybe they're used to hiring hookers? Maybe some of them were paid to fuck you?

"Several of them flip you and twist you into their favorite positions, but none of them have any regard for who you are or what you look like. At least, if they do, they don't let on that they care. All except one man: the young guy from the mailroom who brings you water and wet wipes and helps clean you up between fucks. One time you felt him staring at your pretty face. Another time he offered you a chocolate mint, which you could tell was his idea. You know this because the only affection or attention you get from your boss is when he crams his big cock between your legs. Once in a blue moon, after cumming hard inside you, he'll graze your shoulders with a loving stroke or two. It's only a few seconds before he is cold and withdrawn again. His only interest now is to stretch you out so that you'll be ready for whatever he wants . . . whenever he wants you.

"On several occasions throughout the years, you've been lent out to other men, as if you were his property. Your boss is a generous man, but he is also possessive. You were always blindfolded or kept in darkness so they wouldn't fall for your irresistible beauty. He doesn't want to run the risk of losing you to someone else.

"And that's why the unspoken understanding that you have with the mail clerk is so subversive. He sees you. He touches you tenderly. He feeds you. He helps you, not because it's his duty, but because of his genuine humanity. There is a fondness or perhaps a connection between you two. Your boss could never imagine that you would be remotely attracted to a man of no power or status, so he is not perceived as a threat.

"At the end of the day, when all the deals are closed and the other executives have gone home, your boss sends for you. The mailroom guy helps you slip into a silk robe and leads you into your master's private suite for your final fuck. You are told to wait on the leather couch, but before the mail guy leaves, he squeezes your hand and leans in to kiss your cheek. You wonder if you'll ever meet again, besides of course, in your fantasy.

"You're left alone in this large modern office with the glowing aquarium and cityscape.

"'Are you ready?' His voice enters the room before he does. 'I don't want any whimpering from you.'

"You bite your lip as he slides toward your cervix."

I whimpered as Raven plunged the jumbo cock inside of me again. This time it felt welcomed, as if it belonged there. It was almost like I couldn't get enough of it. I seemed to have totally morphed into the woman in the story, and I was finally ready to explode.

Raven mounted me and pumped her hips against me vigorously as she whispered, "This is your last job for the evening." She seemed to shape-shift between the Russian pervert and the narrator as she continued, "Your pussy is sorely bruised from all of the abuse, but knowing this is the final fuck makes it easier to surrender to his fat throbbing cock. He pushes your head to the side so that you're forced to look at the end table. Under the lamp, there is a thick envelope with your name on it. You know it's filled with cash. A thick stack of unmarked hundreds. This is his way of showing you that he owns you."

An orgasm came hard and kept rolling as I writhed against my ropes, quivering and moaning. Raven exhaled long and loud. Her body stayed close to mine as I finally floated down to the bed. She tenderly stroked me back into my body, which was still bound by nylon knots.

"Afterward, you know his secretary will schedule you a spa treatment at a resort. You'll be able to get your beauty rest and be luxuriously pampered before your next assignment. You are his good-luck charm. You keep yourself conditioned for whenever he needs you: to celebrate closing a big deal or to help him relieve stress. No matter what his reasons, he owns you. No matter who else you let inside you, he is always bigger. There will always be an emptiness that doesn't go away because he is the only one that can truly fill you."

Yours,
Vi.

P.S. I couldn't stop wondering what happened to the poor soul from the mailroom!

FRIDAY #20

Medical Supplies

Before going on an afternoon hike in the wilderness, Raven mentioned she had run out of gloves, so we made a quick stop at a local medical supply store. It was a small store. I suspect the silver-haired woman working in the pharmacy was the owner and the chubby redheaded kid at the register was her son.

Ever since I started working on the storytelling showcase, I see the whole world as one big puppet show. I imagine myself in an episode of *The Muppets,* where Raven and I are real, but everyone else is played by oversized puppets.

I'm going to name the overweight kid "Big Red" and his mom "Silver Lady."

BIG RED: "Can I help you?"

ME: "Hey there! Where are your latex gloves?"

BIG RED: "In the back."

ME: "Thanks!"

As we strolled through all three aisles of equipment, Raven said this was a good place to get safety scissors. "Now that you're learning to play with ropes, you might want to keep a pair on hand."

I looked around for other kinky supplies. "Oooh . . . there's a bedpan. In case I ever let you tie me up and make me pee."

We laughed and she kissed me hard right in the middle of the shop. She pointed to the blue plastic pads and said, "Even though the hospitals use these to soak up blood and urine, they also work great for squirters." I fondled a stack of adult diapers and joked about how we could get kinky with Depends.

When we arrived at the aisle with the rubber gloves, I was blown away by all the options. They had three different colors of latex: black, clear, and pink. Non-latex nitrile only came in blue, but there was a choice between powdered or non-pow-dered, both of which were available in small, medium, and large. Raven said she wished her fingers weren't so petite. She grabbed my ass and squeezed hard. She leaned in and whispered, "But small hands are advantageous for fisting."

"Ow!" I said, but felt strangely turned on.

We settled on a box to keep at each of our homes, and a pair of safety scissors. The mother-and-son team were both behind the counter by the time we were ready.

BIG RED: "So are you two nurses?"

ME: "No, we're lesbians."

SILVER LADY: "Well, that's certainly more fun than being a nurse."

BIG RED: "Pardon my ignorance, but what do you use the gloves for?"

ME: "Hiking."

Big Red looked bewildered.

ME: "It's not easy to wash your hands when you're hiking, and if you're going to have sex, you've got to plan ahead. Nobody wants to stuff dirt and twigs inside their girlfriend's vagina."

BIG RED: "Oh. Got it."
He blushes through his smile and waves good-bye.

Yours,
Vi.

P.S. Later, Raven finger-fucked me under the shade of a sycamore tree while I fantasized she was fucking me in the middle of the store while the clerk and his mom watched and couldn't help themselves and had to jerk off behind the counter.
P.P.S. Sorry this entry is so short. I was tired out from all the hiking, and the sex, but didn't want to miss a week.

Shower Scene

I woke up with a mild case of stage fright. Meanwhile, Raven was so busy preparing before the big showcase that she tried to cancel our date. I drove by her house on my way home from the gym. I caught her standing in her driveway, still wearing pajamas, talking on the phone, while loading stage lights into her pickup truck.

I shouted out the window as I parked, "I know you said you didn't have time, but my muscle memory drove me here anyway." She hung up on Shelby to give me a quick greeting. I pressed my sweaty breasts against her braless flannel top. She compulsively grabbed my ass through my spandex shorts.

"I don't even have time for a quickie."

"How about if I pick up a couple of wraps. You've gotta have lunch, it might as well be with me."

"Okay." She sighed like she was frustrated, but I could tell she was grateful. "Would you be willing to swing by the store and pick up some zip ties while I jump in the shower?"

"Of course. What else is a bitch for?" I winked and left her to her multitasking. She has no idea what a tremendous pleasure it is for me to serve her.

When I returned, she hadn't showered or finished loading the truck. I helped her with the boxes and she said, "Remind me to reward you for being a good little bitch."

I told her if she wanted to put me to work, she should let me scrub her body in the shower.

"Maybe after lunch."

Between bites, Raven was distracted by all the details on her director's clipboard. I was impressed by how many itty-bitty details go into each production, even though she always has an eye on the big picture. She was just starting to brainstorm her preshow pep talk when she glanced at her watch. "Damn. Look at the time!"

I unbuttoned her flannel in the bathroom while we waited for the water to get warm. She handed me a seafoam sponge and instructed me to be quick. I started at her feet and rubbed her in circles as if polishing a statue. She didn't notice. She was busy lathering her hair. I'd only gotten to her knees by the time she was ready to rinse and condition. She clearly was not interested in the special treatment I yearned to lavish on her flower.

"Look, I'm all about hygiene right now. We can fool around later." She took the sponge and rinsed her own vagina swiftly but thoroughly. She let me lather her armpits as she conditioned her hair. I felt disappointed and decided to work on my own body instead. When I got to my labia, I noticed she was watching me. Her eyes started to narrow and she had that smile that says she's thinking something naughty. So I exaggerated my washing by lifting a leg on the rim of the tub. I stretched my lips like an open butterfly and let the water run into my folds.

"Can I borrow your hand?" Without waiting for a response, I took her wet fingers and plunged them inside me, deep. She squinted in disgust and retracted her hand.

"What is it?" I asked, giving my flower a final rinse.

"You raped my fingers," she said, her nose still crinkled up.

"It was purely for hygiene. But I thought you'd like it if I used you."

She was silent.

I laughed, "Don't you ever just feel like cramming something up there real quick to clean it out?"

"No," she said, and I could tell something had shifted.

"Are you upset?"

"I feel violated."

"I'm sorry." I pleaded with her, "But it's not like I penetrated you."

She crossed her arms over her chest, which looked extra stern because her hair was slicked back. "So, is this where you're at, now? You think you can just use me sexually anytime you have an itch?"

"No, my Queen." I didn't know whether she was playing or not, but I was dead serious. "I meant no disrespect."

"On your knees," she said as she forced me down on the hard porcelain and pressed my face against her pussy. Warm water was still running everywhere. I strained to push between her lips with my tongue. She pressed her pelvic bone hard against my face. The bridge of my nose bent against her. I kept my mouth open so I could breathe and pressed my teeth against my own lips to maximize her sensation. I was blinded by my desire to please her. She pushed me away and said, "That's enough!"

Rejected, I look up at her and pleaded, "Is there anything I can do to make it up to you?"

Her eyes glimmered with a perverse power. "I feel like pissing on you. To remind you you're my bitch."

"As you wish my Queen," I said, and bowed.

"Get back over here." She pulled me into position. Squinting from the shower, I sat obediently beneath her and opened my mouth.

"Ew. Close your mouth. No."

Not wanting her to be disgusted, I said, "It's actually fairly sanitary. Have you ever heard of uropathy?"

"Shut up, I'm trying to concentrate."

"Sorry," I said while trying to hold still. After a while, I looked up. She laughed first, then I followed. She told me she was feeling pee-shy, so I patiently waited some more. My neck started to cramp and the water was running cold.

Finally, it came dribbling out. I hoped she was enjoying herself since it didn't do much for me. I tried to imagine it came straight from her sex as her pee was now warmer than the shower.

"There. That should teach you to ask permission next time you want to cram something up your cunt, especially if it's my fingers." She pulled me up to standing so that we were equals again, and ran the soapy sponge over me before rinsing. She turned off the water and toweled me off, and it felt like the whole power trip dried out.

As we dressed, we talked casually like girlfriends in a locker room. Before she kicked me out, she kissed me and told me to break a leg at my first official dress rehearsal. In theater, you don't say good luck. Since it's such a cliché, she told me the cast and crew of Barefoot and Pregnant Theater have a special saying: "Break a labia." But since this is my first performance, she wants me to "Break a hymen."

Yours,
Vi.

P.S. Raven asked me to tell Damien she would save a seat reserved for him in the front row beside her and Nick. I told her Damien prefers the back of the house and he planned to bring a date.

"Oh. Anyone I know?"

"Autumn."

"Shawn's little sister, Autumn?"

"Yeah. She's not a kid anymore. She works at my yoga studio now."

Raven seemed surprised but didn't ask for details.

"Just be sure to tell him he's not allowed to have sex in my theater ever again unless it's with me."

P.P.S. The show was so fucking fun, there are no words to describe how much I loved it.

ACT III

DEEP ECOLOGY

Deep e·col·o·gy /dēp / ēˈkäləjē/
Noun

    1. A philosophy and en-
vironmental movement that
regards human life as just one
of many equal components of a
global ecosystem.

Public Flogging

Of all the exotic events Raven hosts, her annual Winter Solstice Sex Party has earned a reputation as the best party of the year in the poly community.

When Raven's living room is filled with people cuddling and conversing on floor cushions, Nick gathers everyone's attention in front of the large bay window so he can co-officiate the opening ceremony with Raven.

"Special thanks to everyone who dressed for the occasion!" Raven says, flaunting a skintight PVC nun's habit with a plunging neckline that shows her cleavage. "You can call me Mother Superior and this is my cohost, Father Nicholai."

Nick is dressed as a priest, complete with a clerical collar. He says, "Come to me if you want to confess your sins tonight." He dramatically dips Raven and kisses her square on the mouth. The crowd hollers.

She makes a show of wiping her lipstick off his face, then straightens her skirt before continuing. "Since the cast from the sexy storytelling showcase is here, tonight's solstice play party doubles as a cast party! Special thanks to our team of naked butlers who will be serving finger foods and other sweet niblets."

Violet stands between two naked men wearing only bow ties and cuffs. She twirls to show off her see-through French maid costume. Her bare ass is framed by lace apron strings and white garter belts.

Nick distributes tea lights to the crowd, while Raven lifts a candelabra and says, "Solstice is a dark but potent time to set intentions for next year. Let's be impeccable with the seeds we plant tonight."

After a group prayer, everyone lights their own candle and makes a private wish before arranging them on the altar against the window sill.

Nick sits before the candlelit crowd to review the social agreements that give structure to the self-directed play party. After the guidelines are in place, the room is permeated with a sense of connection and permission that only comes from a shared understanding of consent.

Raven sinks into an overstuffed chair in the corner to admire what she's cocreated. The nearly naked butlers circulate with delightful desserts and nonalcoholic beverages, as layers of bright Christmas costumes are slowly stripped off.

Raven's attention wanders toward Damien and the new girl, Autumn. Currently, she's lying at Damien's side engaging in what looks like deep conversation. Her elfin appearance is so convincing she might have been born inside a tree hollow overgrown by mushrooms. Raven's touched to see Damien enjoying himself in this social setting, but has mixed feelings about how cozy he seems with Autumn. Violet describes their connection as "fun and easy." But what that translates to in Raven's head is, *She's young and carefree compared to how much drama it is to be with you.* Still, Raven is happy to see Damien shine and knows (in theory) how valuable it is for Damien and Violet to have a variety of poly experiences, beyond what she can offer. She accepts that if she wants their nonconventional arrangement to be sustainable, she is going to have to learn to share.

Raven's ruminations are interrupted when Violet playfully lands in her lap with a chocolate-covered berry poised in her lips. Raven's tongue squishes the red juice into Violet's mouth, and the rest of the party dissolves. Violet says she likes the feel of Raven's vinyl costume against her bare skin. Raven cups her bouncy breasts and draws her in for another passionate kiss, breaking away only to say, "I've decided I want to flog you tonight."

"Here? In front of everyone?"

"Why not? I can't keep my little bitch all to myself forever."

"Oh dear!" Violet plays coy.

"Of course, since Damien's here, we'll have to check in with him first." Raven grabs Violet by the wrist and marches her through the crowded room to where Damien is lip-locked with Autumn. Raven crouches nearby to catch his eye, then interrupts them with, "I would like to request permission to do a public scene with your woman."

He smiles warmly at Raven. "How considerate of you to ask."

Autumn looks embarrassed at first, but with a smile says, "Great event, Raven!"

"Thank you. I'm glad you could make it." Raven offers a quick kiss to Autumn's cheek.

"It's Friday," he says. "So technically, she's all yours tonight."

Raven squints her eyes and scans Damien's freckled face to

see if there's anything more to his statement. "What's that supposed to mean?"

"I'm just pointing out that you've routinely carved this night out to be exclusive." Damien smirks, and his tone is mocking. "And if you have a sudden urge to include everyone, that's your prerogative."

"Sarcasm doesn't suit you. If you have a problem, just come out and say it."

"I don't have a problem. I think it's healthy to integrate your private perversions into the larger ecosystem."

Violet chimes in, "She wants to give me a public flogging! I want you two to be there."

Raven double-checks with Damien, "Are you sure you're comfortable with this?"

"Wouldn't miss it for the world," he says. Raven takes both of Violet's wrists in one hand and leads her toward the entrance.

Autumn follows them to the foyer, calling, "I want a front-row seat!" She sits close to Raven's feet.

Raven pivots Violet's face toward the wall with arms apart over her head. Raven spreads Violet's fingers like a starfish, then lightly kicks the inside of her feet to guide them apart. She pulls on Violet's hips and commands, "Ass out." Her bare buttocks are displayed for the audience to admire. There are over thirty guests in the entrance area alone. Raven unclips the vinyl flog from the belt on her nun habit and warms Violet with a gentle dusting motion. She leans in toward the back of Violet's hair and whispers, "Mother Superior thinks you've been disobedient in your duties as maidservant."

She steps back and swats Violet a dozen times. She looks around and meets Autumn's wide eyes. Raven uses her chin to point toward the overstuffed chair and tells her, "Scoot back. I'm going to need more clearance for my back swing."

"Of course," Autumn says, and she slinks her elfin body

into Damien's lap without taking her eyes off Violet for a second. Raven picks up the pace. Violet starts to moan and undulate her hips.

"You like that?"

Raven continues administering a steady flogging to Violet's quivering thighs.

"More please."

Raven reaches between Violet's legs, feeling the dampness of her vulva, then swats her hard a few times between the thighs. She uses her peripheral vision to locate Nick. She squeezes Violet's lower lips together while leaning to whisper in Nick's ear. He dashes to retrieve her other flogger. Before returning her attention to Violet, she notices Damien is watching with a slack jaw.

Raven resumes slapping Violet's rear until it is good and red. When Nick produces an identical flogger, she starts in with an overhanded double-dutch motion, lashing Violet's backside with both floggers simultaneously. The moment Raven breaks a sweat, she decides it's time to check in with her maidservant. "Remember, you can always use your colors."

Violet turns her flushed face toward Raven and calls, "Green."

Raven squeezes Violet's left tit and says, "You asked for it." Stepping back to use her full force, Raven lands a series of steady hard blows on Violet's left and right flanks. Each swing lands with a dull thud. Violet starts to giggle and cry out, but Raven doesn't slow. She builds, faster and harder, until Violet's laugh turns into a whimper.

Raven leans in for the final time. "Grab your ankles," Raven commands.

"But I'm not wearing panties," Violet exclaims.

"Do it," Raven says, and swats her ass.

Violet bends over, exposing her sex to the room. Autumn gasps.

Raven delivers her final flourish on a concentrated area. Each hit produces a high-pitched squeal from her target. After about a dozen squeals, she throws the floggers to the floor and embraces her bitch. Violet turns, her eyes glowing, as Raven holds her tight against the entrance wall.

The applause sounds like distant rain. Eventually Nick slips into their little bubble to offer a glass of water, and says, "You warmed up the whole room."

Raven asks, "And how was it for you?"

"So good," Violet says between sips. "Did Damien see us?"

"I'm pretty sure everyone saw us," Raven says with a smile. "What do you need for aftercare?"

"I'm good, I just want to know how Damien is."

Raven leads Violet to Damien who is cuddling with Autumn in a vast horizontal puppy pile. Nick is lying nearby, limbs intertwined with Jess, Sebastian, and other lovers.

Autumn stammers, "Damien was just helping me understand it all."

"What's to understand?" Violet asks, kissing Damien as she pulls Raven down to join the sea of bodies.

Autumn continues, "It looked like it hurt, but you sounded like you were having fun."

Raven reaches across to touch Autumn's bare shoulder as she asks, "What did your body feel when you were watching?"

"Confused," Autumn admits, looking visibly turned on. "I'm curious how it felt for you, Violet?"

"I felt intimate with everyone watching. Especially you, Damien. I'm happy you were there."

"Me too, little one." He caresses her face.

"I feel like an alien in a whole new dimension," Autumn says with eager innocence.

Smirking, Raven says, "Maybe you should ask Damien to do a scene with you. Violet tells me he's become quite the dom, and I know how much he loves giving women first-time experiences."

"I would love that!" Autumn swoons.

Damien looks up from his world of thoughts and says, "Thank you, Raven."

Raven lifts her head to scan the room, and although everyone seems to be enjoying themselves, she feels guilty for favoring Violet.

"What is it?" Damien asks.

"I'm feeling obliged to flutter around and sprinkle my attention on other lovers," Raven admits.

"You can start with me," he says, pulling her in closer. Violet rolls over toward Autumn, swapping places to allow Damien to lie face to face, belly to belly with Raven. Damien props his head on his elbow so that they are gazing into each other's eyes. There's something about the way Damien fixes his hazel eyes on her, or anyone, that renders all other concerns meaningless.

After a disorienting squeeze, Raven finally asks, "So how was it for you?"

"It was surprisingly sexy to watch," Damien sighs. "Outside this context, I can't imagine being comfortable witnessing an arcane torture apparatus like that being used on another human being. But I trust your ability to curate a mature audience who understands it's an empowering reenactment of involuntary servitude."

"Do you feel I've been overly punitive?" Raven asks, playfully testing Damien.

"Punitive? No."

Raven sighs. Damien sighs deeper. Then she brushes the red hair off his brow. Sensing something wrong she asks, "Is there something bothering you?"

"I'm concerned about you two becoming overly dyadic. You've seemed to dive so deep into your own universe on Fridays."

"That's the magic of tonight's ritual!" Raven sits up and begins massaging Damien. "It actually felt a little like 'coming out,' or a public love declaration. I don't want to hide our D/s dynamic. Not that I have been actively hiding anything, but you're right, there has been something private about our play-dates."

"It seems so out of character for you. I'm remembering one of your teachings about how maintaining multiple relationships is like tending to a permaculture garden." Raven laughs as Damien teases, "I imagine you like a gardener, tending to your various relationships as if they were plant people; trimming and training them to share your sunshine."

"Yes," Raven replies, "which is exactly why I feel the need to schedule the regular dates. It's like setting up an automatic watering system."

"I respect your schedule—the more complex the system the more structure is necessary. But ever since we've been seeing Autumn, I began to appreciate the importance of inclusion of other lovers."

Raven's hands freeze on Damien's chest when she realizes he's expressing his tender truth. She responds, "I would want to include you, of course, I just don't know how that would look, given our history."

"When either Violet and I go on a date with Autumn, we have an open door policy. Even though we mostly go on separate dates, Violet can always join in at any time, and vice versa. We don't necessarily take advantage of that invitation, but there is a strong sense of inclusion between the three of us. Whereas, you and Violet seem to have a private affair on Fridays, and I don't always felt welcomed."

Raven feels nauseous at the thought of being compared to Autumn, and even worse for hurting Damien. "I didn't know you felt that way."

Damien softens. "I recognize that in the beginning, I was the one that pulled back from engaging with you—I didn't want to risk making Violet jealous again, and then I started making sacrifices to give you two space. But it's been harder than I expected, and things are shifting now."

Raven nuzzles Damien's face and in a low tone says, "I am so sorry. Is there anything I can do?"

"Let me think about it and get back to you. I don't want to pull you into heavy processing, this is a party!" Damien leans in as if to kiss Raven, but she dodges him and buries her face in his neck.

In a playful tone, Raven says, "And don't forget, you're here on a date!"

Damien looks into Raven's face and smiles. "I appreciate Autumn for many reasons, and one of them is that she has helped me see what a gift you are in my life. It's increasingly obvious how deeply all our relationships affect each other."

Raven smiles back. "I guess I ought to spend some time getting to know her then. Tell me, what do you see in her?"

"She's actually a lot like you. She's creative, poetic, and mystical…"

"And a good decade younger."

"Don't be ageist! I think you two have something to learn from each other."

"That's what you said about Violet. But I must admit—you have wonderful taste in women!"

FRIDAY #23

Office Whores

Their naked bodies are entwined as they lie on the lawn in Violet's backyard, sunning themselves in the dead of winter. Violet runs her fingers lightly across Raven's ribs and asks, "What are you feeling?"

"At peace, I suppose. I'm relieved to be done with the showcase and solstice. How about you?"

"I'm slightly aroused."

"That's nothing new, you're like a bitch in heat."

"I can't help it. There's been so much sexual energy in my house lately, with Autumn always coming over to see Damien."

"Oh, really. Have they had sex yet?"

"Not yet, but we're talking about it. We're taking it slow. You know she's new to poly, and she's apprenticing at my yoga studio."

"Well, I guess it's sort of sweet how she offers you something I can't. I'm just not the young innocent type."

"So you're not jealous?"

"I didn't say that. I just said, I can understand the attraction. Tell me, do you fantasize about her?"

"Mmm-hmm."

Raven repositions herself to look Violet in the eyes. Holding her shoulders sternly, she says, "I may not be able to physically possess you at all times"—Raven reaches between Violet's legs, grabs a fistful of her labia, and squeezes—"but I want full access to whatever is happening in your fantasy world. Do you understand?"

"Yes, my Queen."

Raven rolls over onto Violet and plunges two fingers into Violet's already wet sex with nearly no foreplay. "What do you want to do to her? Spare no detail."

Violet swallows hard and starts speaking. "I saw her at the reception desk, wearing a tight sports bra with an oversized zipper in the front. It was unzipped a little, revealing the top of one of her nipples. I pointed it out. Without apology, like a reflex, she shrugged and zipped it up, which made her boobies bunch up. She was so casual about it, like we were in the locker room. Then I went into the yoga studio and tried to meditate before class, but I couldn't concentrate. I just kept seeing her in my head, zipping her cleavage up and down, making her boobies bounce. I got turned on, and then I felt angry, like *How dare she greet our yoga students like that.* Then I imagined what you would do if you were her boss."

"And what do you imagine I would do?" Raven says, sliding her mouth slowly down Violet's warm skin, toward her wet slit, making it wetter by outlining her lips with the length of her tongue.

"Well, I imagined we worked in a real office, you know, with a copy room. And you were a high-powered executive..."

Raven is delighted by the imagery and lifts her head to ask, "Is there a coat closet in this office?"

"Wrong fantasy. In this one, you have a strict dress code and she's violating it! So I report her, and you decide it's time to teach her a lesson. You open the top drawer of your file cabinet and it's full of sex toys and dildos. You kiss me to thank me for helping you enforce the company policy. You command me to take off my underwear. Then you pull up your business skirt and strap on your girl dick. Then you use the intercom to call her in. She comes in, all flustered and innocent like she's reporting to the principal's office, and you say, 'If you want to work here, you're going to need to obey the rules.'

"And she's like, 'Are you talking about this?' She zips her sports bra down and up again, flashing her nipples. You rip the zipper off and her bouncy titties just fly out.

"You grab her by the boobs and say, 'Do you know the punishment for indecency?'

"You order me to sit on your desk, then you spread my legs. I sit there obediently, spread-eagle. Autumn looks shocked and excited—then you grab her by the hair and push her face into my pussy. When her mouth is full, you lift her skirt and tear off her panties. You force her to spread her legs while slapping her cunt and calling her names."

Taking cues from Violet's fantasy, Raven slaps Violet's pussy repeatedly. She shifts her weight so she can grind her clit against Violet's thigh, and though she has to unplug her mouth from the nectar of Violet's flower, she can reach two fingers in deeper to fuck Violet's G-spot.

"Oh yes. When Autumn is smothered by my flower, you lift up your skirt to reveal your big, veiny cock. You stuff it inside her hole, which makes her scream into my crotch. Then you grab a fistful of my hair and pull me in to kiss me hard. We're kissing over her body. It's like you're fucking me through her, until you have a screaming orgasm. You order me to put on a dildo and switch places with you. I grab at her hips and you pull her hair, and I think I'm going to cum."

Raven continues finger-fucking at a steady pace as Violet tenses and shudders and moans. Wordlessly, Violet reaches for Raven's hand to show she is done.

"That's a good girl." Raven holds still while Violet breathes through several aftershocks.

"Want more?"

"No," Violet whispers.

"Want me out?"

"Yes."

Raven slips her hand out and draws her fingers to her mouth, taking a deep inhale of the earthy smell of her lover's orgasm.

"You are so brilliant when you cum."

Violet is speechless and all smiles.

"Have you told Damien or Autumn about your little fantasy?"

"No, silly. I made it up with you, just now. I had some sexy thoughts before, but nothing this detailed. Autumn is so innocent. She's like the neighbor who just comes over to hang out, shop, get coffee, or whatever. Even when she spends the night, it isn't sexual. It's just a fun sleepover."

Raven's glowing mood is pierced. "She spent the night?"

"It was sweet. She slept in the middle between me and Damien."

"I see," Raven says coldly.

"What is it?"

"We've been seeing each other for over three months and we've never shared a pillow, not once."

"Actually, it's been over five months. And you're busy. You've got the theater, your son, your family. Autumn doesn't have anyone at home."

"Why don't you come and have a sleepover with Nick and me?"

"I don't think I could sleep away from Damien. I'm addicted to him. Besides, our relationship dynamic isn't like that."

"I see how it is. You'll let me dominate you, but not domesticate you."

"It's not like that. I just don't think I could satisfy you all night long."

"What if I promised we'd do something totally casual like curling up with a lesbian film?"

"How kinky. You want to role-play having lesbian bed-death. That would be a first! But seriously, I'm addicted to sleeping with Damien. Are you open to sleeping with us? I can talk to him, on the condition that you don't keep me up, and you're not allowed to stare at me while I'm sleeping, cause that's just creepy."

"Call him. Let's see what he says." Raven reaches for Violet's phone from the pile of their clothes. She hands it to Violet and says, "Tell him I'm not expecting a hot threesome or anything. It's purely domestic family time."

"If something more happens, I'd be okay with that." Violet winks.

"We shall see."

FRIDAY #24

Chopsticks

After a light lunch of ramen, Raven returns to the table with a fistful of plastic chopsticks she has swiped from the restaurant's condiment bar on the way out of the bathroom. She flashes the bundle at Violet before stuffing them into her jacket pocket.

"What are you up to?" Violet asks.

"You'll see," Raven says, holding the door open for Violet to exit. They head back to Raven's playroom, which smells of lavender floor cleaner. All the props from the showcase are finally put away. The only thing out of place is a thick-handled hairbrush lying on the bed.

Violet stretches her body out under the canopy as Raven rinses the chopsticks with soap and water.

"What are you planning to do with this hairbrush?" Violet asks, suggestively stroking the handle.

"Take off your clothes," Raven commands, turning on a heater.

"Yes, Ma'am."

Raven opens a condom and places it on a towel alongside a bottle of lube, the hairbrush, and the pile of chopsticks.

Raven runs her fingers through Violet's blonde mane a few times before warming her hands on her silky skin.

Instead of a formal opening, Raven kisses Violet slowly and says a silent prayer into her mouth. Raven asks for inspiration and to be blessed with erotic intuition. When Violet's pelvis begins undulating, Raven knows her prayers have been heard. She lays Violet down for a massage while spinning a new fantasy:

"Someday you long to become a real geisha, but now you're just a lowly apprentice, otherwise known as a *minarai*. It wasn't the most sought-after house, but it had a respectable lineage of geishas and an influential list of clientele. While you're in *maiko* training, your duties include ironing, keeping the closets organized, and making sure the makeup tables are well stocked. Sometimes, when the makeup artist is gone, you get to powder the geishas' faces, or outline their lips. You like to imagine your job is to fluff the geishas in every conceivable way.

"You must stay in the women's quarters where the beds are separated by thin rice-paper screens. Only the geishas are allowed beyond the carved teak doors into the private rooms with tatami mats. That's where the visitors take their tea, and you're definitely not allowed in the special suites where men are entertained.

"At night, when the geishas are out, you fantasize about the day you will be allowed to join them. You long to see the men, to serve them, to pleasure them. You yearn to be like the five geishas who work at your house. Of course, you know it's hard work because you help with all the preparations and you see how exhausted they are when they come home. During their down time, they too want to be pleasured and entertained, and you consider this an honor and your highest duty.

"At night, you sometimes curl up with a geisha and massage her as she tells you about the ways of the trade. You're not so interested in the flower arranging and lute playing, as you already excel at these arts. It's the sexual arts that remain a mystery to you. The geishas often talk about how they entertain the drunk lawyer or busy politician. You listen carefully. You learn how a geisha exposes the nape of her neck when she bends down to help a client slip off his loafers. She is sly about revealing the unpainted skin beneath her loosely draped kimono. Sometimes, you secretly touch yourself as she tells you about his calloused hands or impatient hard-on.

"When you're alone with the lowest ranking geisha, called 'Lucky Sunrise,' she is accustomed to touching you and role-playing. After entertaining, sometimes, when she's sexually frustrated, she might throw you down on the bed and say, 'This is what he did to me.' Your eyes grow wide, because instead of using a penis, she uses the back of a hairbrush. 'He put it in me like this,' she'll say, and you'll spread your legs . . ."

Up until now, Raven's been teasing Violet's vulva with the handle of the hairbrush. She finally slides the spade inside her slippery folds and feels Violet's strong pussy muscles pulse a few times as she finds a rhythm.

"You live for those moments.

"One day, there is a higher-ranking geisha named 'Blessed Dragon' who comes to your room to find you trying on her kimono. She is infuriated. She strips it off your naked body and demands you hang it up immediately. So, there you are, totally exposed, hanging it carefully in her closet, when she orders you to bend over the bed like this."

Raven unplugs the hairbrush Violet's pussy and and

repeatedly spanks Violet with no restraint. "And when your ass is red you plead for more . . ."

Raven is enjoying the rush of power. She takes Violet's hair clip out of her hair and says, "'How dare you use my clip!' Blessed Dragon holds you down and clips it to your nipple and you cry out in genuine pain."

"No, no, anywhere but my nipples," Violet bargains.

"Anywhere? Okay. She spreads your legs like this and reminds you that if you make too much noise the madam will have to take it out of the debt you owe the house. Blessed Dragon takes it on herself to punish you with the hair clip."

Raven carefully tests the clip on Violet's outer lips. And Violet surrenders to Raven's cruel metallic pinches.

"She clips one labia at a time, noticing the noises you make compared with when she fastens both lips together. She glides to the makeup table to retrieve a ceramic jar full of decorative chopsticks. She lowers herself onto her knees before you, peering between your legs, and says, 'I know you can handle a hairbrush, but you need to be wider if you're going to entertain men.' She carefully inserts a couple of chopsticks, stuffing you with just a few at first, but adding more to the center, slowly stretching you out, like this . . ."

Raven repositions Violet so they can maintain eye contact, which also allows Violet to admire her work. She starts by opening Violet's warm wet cave with her left thumb. Next, she gathers half a dozen chopsticks with her right hand, inserting the thin implements no farther than her thumb will reach. She pulls out her finger and moves the chopsticks in a wide circle to massage the soft walls of Violet's vagina.

Violet's eyes are downcast. She has surrendered to her queen.

Raven slowly slides more chopsticks into the center, which presses the original sticks outward, and says, "You're lucky this isn't wood—otherwise you'd get splinters in your pretty peach."

Violet can't help but giggle.

Raven continues, inserting two more at a time. She moves slowly as if it were a meditation.

Excited, Violet blurts, "Okay, just stuff them all in there."

"Quiet! There is an art to what I'm doing. I want you to feel the exact placement of each piece."

Violet imagines all the geisha girls surrounding her and watching, as if they were playing Jenga with her pussy.

Finally, Violet feels full and admits she is at her capacity.

"Breathe deeply and lie back. I'm going to make you take more.

"This is part of your initiation. This is what it takes to become a high-ranking geisha. You will see many men who will desire you, but you will always know that your true place is under the geisha, serving the Goddess."

Raven slowly and steadily adds a final chopstick. Violet holds eye contact with her queen. "There you are. There's the naughty little geisha who couldn't get enough. All the geishas gather to taunt you. Your job is to fluff them. From now on, your job will be to get them wet and ready for their appointments, or if they come home unsatisfied, they will take it out on you."

The pressure is strange, a little irritating, but Violet seems to love it. She lets Raven know with a loud moan. Raven rewards her by circling on her clit with her thumb. This makes Violet squirm. She must writhe carefully—there's no give to the chopsticks inside her. Raven places a flat hand on the outside of Violet's pussy, pinching her hood between two fingers, rubbing hard until she feels a burning in her own clit. Violet's moans grow louder and wilder. She twists her face, expressing painful pleasure. It's disturbing but arousing. Raven encourages her, "The more you moan, the more I'll stroke." The moaning increases in volume, until she's lifting her hips up off the bed in bridge position.

Then Violet blurts, "Hold. Hold . . . oh. Oh . . . OH!" and there is an unmistakable bearing down and spasm of muscles that floods Violet and fills both women with relief, then stillness.

Raven slowly attends to the business of removing the bundle.

As Raven removes the last chopstick, Violet sobs, and Raven holds her. "Give it all to me."

Violet lets herself go, filling the playroom with tears and tenderness.

A reverent tone fills the air after such deep surrender. Raven breaks the silence with the words, "Tell me."

"At first, I contracted because I thought it was all I could handle, but you held me there until I expanded again, and I realized I'm bigger than I thought."

Raven strokes Violet's face and says, "Is there more?"

"It's hard to believe you created this elaborate scene just for me. I didn't feel worthy of all your attention. Then I witnessed how present you were, and it sort of melted my feelings of being unworthy."

"You deserve this, this and so much more. I'd go to any length for your pleasure."

"And I'd do the same for you. It's strange isn't it, the places we go?"

Sleepover

Cuddling naked under Violet's purple comforter, Raven cries silently. Huge teardrops stream down her face during the final scene of *Henry and June*.

Violet shuts the lid of her laptop. "Is it as good as the book?"

Raven sniffles and sighs, "It wasn't based on a book, the movie was made after her uncensored diaries. Anaïs Nin would probably say no book or movie is as good as real life. She journaled incessantly; it was her frantic defense against insanity. But what the movie doesn't accurately depict is how tormented and conflicted she was between her two lovers."

"Anyway, I loved it," Violet says, yawning and massaging Raven's thigh.

"She was obsessed by a lifelong pursuit of beauty."

"Babe, I'm deliriously tired." Violet curls up in Raven's arms. "I want to say good night to Damien. Honey! Can you come in here?" she calls through the closed door while maintaining a firm grip on Raven's bare thigh.

Raven feels a flash of self-consciousness, and she tugs on the sheet to cover her nipples. She stops when she realizes she has nothing to hide. She's done nothing wrong, and Damien's already seen her naked and crying countless times before.

He enters looking distracted from his research. He positions himself diagonally across the edge of the bed.

Having declined the invitation to watch the movie with them, since he'd already seen it with Raven, he asks, "So, what did you think, Little One?"

Violet gives him a peck and says, "It was beautiful. It made me appreciate our poly dynamics. I'm so glad I don't have to choose between my lovers."

"Thanks for sharing your girlfriend with me." Raven nudges Damien's shoulder. It was meant to be playful, but the lightness seems lost on Damien, since he's staring at the floor. Raven knows this look—he's arranging his thoughts.

"I've tried to help Violet comprehend the delicate balance of our relationships."

Raven looks at Violet, clearly confused. "What are you referring to?"

"I didn't want to speak for him." Violet's voice starts to sound defensive. She seems to catch herself and continues in a low tone, "You two need to talk."

"Uh-oh, does this have to do with the chopsticks, or other firsts? I'm sorry, I should've checked in with you," Raven blurts.

"It's none of that. I've been doing better about your firsts. Vi's been diligent about including me."

"What is it, then?" Raven presses.

Damien carefully measures his words. "Look, I know this is your first sleepover. The last thing I want to do is taint it, but I'm just having a hard time getting Violet to understand my perspective."

Raven is struck in the gut with the unbearable thought that she might still be unwittingly hurting Damien. She takes a deep breath and hears the strangest words leap from her mouth. "Tell me." It's the exact tone that Damien has used a million times to pry forth feelings that were hard to articulate.

"As you know, I love you both. I respect your unique connection with Violet. I make a concerted effort to accommodate your weekly time together. In theory I support your exploration. In practice, however, it's challenging to watch my girlfriend have an ongoing relationship with my former lover, when I'm not feeling my needs are being addressed."

Violet exclaims, "But we tried to include you tonight!"

"Now hold on," Damien continues. "You're not hearing me."

Violet interrupts, "It sounds like you're saying that I'm doing something wrong."

Damien glances at Raven then slows down his speech. "Hear me out, you're doing lots of things right. You check in with me before your dates. You spare no detail when you come home. You even bring your sexual creativity back into our bedroom, which of course makes it easy for me to see the benefit of your ongoing connection. But I don't feel like you see how far I've stretched to support your relationship, and if I bring up any of my own concerns, you get defensive and stop listening."

Raven feels like a huge wall is crumbling down around her heart. Although it's painful to feel her defenses dismantled, she's starting to see Damien clearly for the first time in months. Violet is speechless, so Raven takes this opportunity to lean in. "I'm so grateful for what a deep support you've been for me and Vi. You've gone above and beyond to make space for our love, but I see it has come at the expense of your own need to feel welcomed or even heard. If I were you, supporting my beloved weekly to deep-dive with my ex, I can imagine feeling overlooked, and that's gotta hurt." Raven takes another deep breath.

"It's not just the depth that bothers me, but the breadth of things you do together when I don't feel considered. This is a real deal-breaker, honestly. If it were anyone else, I'd say we tried this arrangement and it isn't working for me."

Violet sits up, now fully awake. "What do you mean, a deal-breaker? Are you threatening to veto our relationship?"

Raven lays a reassuring hand on Violet's thigh. "That's not what he's saying. What I hear, Damien, is that you need your feelings to be considered, and that's the bottom line, right?"

"Yes. Thank you. But Violet is so attached to your relationship," Damien says, finally breaking a smile, "it's almost like she's addicted, and any feelings I have seem to threaten her getting her fix."

"Now that's a low blow." Violet giggles and shakes her head.

"He's got a point. I'm pretty addicted myself." Raven leans forward to touch Damien. Her naked body is completely exposed, but she doesn't care. "Listen, I don't want to be a wedge between you two. I only want to enhance your relationship. If I'm creating conflict, the two of us can't continue. You know, my directive has always been to do no harm."

Violet looks hurt and surprised. She tries to lighten things up, saying, "Come on now, harm is the whole basis of our fantasies."

"No." Raven cuts in sternly. "I may hurt you, but that is not the same as harm. There's an important distinction." Violet can tell Raven is not in the mood to be playful. "Unfortunately, it seems I've been harming your relationship."

"To be fair, you've been helping it too," Damien says.

"Damien what do you need me to do?" Violet pleads.

Raven looks at Violet and then Damien. She speaks slowly, "Do you want us to stop?"

"No," Damien says, a knee-jerk reaction.

"To slow down?"

"A little," Damien admits.

"What does that mean?" Violet swallows hard.

Raven offers, "What if we agree that you're always welcome to join us on Fridays, and we stop exploring 'firsts?'"

"Your welcoming me in means a lot. Really. But I don't want you to stop exploring new things," Damien reassures her.

"Do you want me to ask your permission beforehand?" Raven offers.

He shakes his head. "That won't do. Violet must feel free. She can choose to do anything she wants."

Freshly inspired, Violet lights up and chimes in, "I get it. You want my choices to be informed by your feelings!"

"Yes!" Damien says, and nods. "By checking in with each other's feelings, we get a sense of the impact our choices make on each other. Ideally, if you were able to hear me out, without assuming I'm threatening your relationship, then I might be able to give you my blessings. There's a big distinction between permission and blessings."

Violet kisses Damien, almost giddy from the relief of not losing Raven. She chimes in, "But what if I like the idea of asking for your permission? It's kind of kinky. Like please, my Lord, please?"

Damien laughs, "If it brings you pleasure, I guess I could live with it." He looks to be feeling lighter already. He turns to Violet for clarity and reassurance. "I just need to know my feelings matter. And I do like the idea of having an open door policy, where I could come in and give you a kiss. If whatever you're doing is threatening to our relationship, I'd want to know you'll slow things down."

"You mean everything to me. You know that! But my Fridays with Raven have their own energy, it's like a freight train with its own momentum; I don't know how to slow it down."

Raven interjects in a stern voice, "Now hold on, even a train needs an emergency break. When someone calls yellow light in a scene, it's my responsibility to slow down before someone gets hurt. I don't want this to turn into a red light. In truth, I know Violet is not separate from you. I need to find a way to love you both as a couple."

At hearing this, Damien impulsively kisses Raven on the cheek then turns to hug Violet for a few long breaths. Raven thinks she sees him wipe his eyes before releasing her. "It's obvious from this conversation, I should have brought it up sooner."

Raven is touched, but her tears are all used up from the movie. "I may not have been ready for this earlier. It used to hurt to see you two together. But now, it doesn't hurt nearly as much as the thought of losing either of you. I love you both so much."

In that moment, Violet discovers a three-way hug with smiles all around is actually much sweeter than their first three-way kiss at the beach.

Damien wraps up with this: "You know, one of the greatest benefits in 'poly' is three-way processing. I find it so helpful that communication isn't polarized into 'he said/she said.' I've been trying to get Violet to understand my feelings for some time, but she couldn't bear the guilt of hurting me or the thought of losing you, so we just kept hitting the same brick wall. Tonight, I feel we made a real breakthrough."

Violet says, "I'm glad we talked. I'm also exhausted."

In contrast, Raven feels invigorated by the processing and is eager to play. "We still haven't answered one of the hardest questions you'll ever encounter in poly."

Damien takes the bait. "What's that?"

"Who sleeps in the middle?" Raven says with a smile so wide she can't hide her teeth.

"I'm not ready for bed, so I'll let you two figure it out." Damien stands to leave the room.

Raven stands with him. "What are you working on?"

"I'm preparing a paper for a conference."

"Is it theory or application? What's your argument?"

Violet interrupts with a groggy voice, "I love hearing you two geek out, but could you take it into the other room, please?"

"Sweet dreams, Pussy Willow," Damien says, kissing Violet on the forehead. Then he pulls Raven off the bed. She slips into Violet's robe and Damien guides her toward the door. In a groggy voice, Violet calls out a postscript that makes Raven smile. "I would be totally happy for you two if you want to explore anything, sexually, I mean."

In the living room, Raven sinks into the corner of the couch, drapes a leg over Damien's lap, and listens to him talk about his current project. They both seem simultaneously flooded with the familiar flow state that comes from countless nights musing about each other's creative pursuits. Damien stops abruptly in the middle of his animated lecture and stares starkly at Raven's face. She wonders if he's going to kiss her. Instead, he says, "It feels good, doesn't it? To be connecting again."

"You have no idea how much I've missed you," Raven says.

"It wasn't our time, but now maybe we're ready again?"

"Ready for what?"

"Good question." Damien pulls Raven closer. She leans her back against his chest and they breathe in unison.

"You know what I remember most about our time together?" Damien muses.

"Well, I know what I remember, but you first," Raven prods.

"We would get impassioned by our exploration of some topic at the intersection between the unknown and the unknowable, and eventually, we'd reach a point where all words were completely inadequate. Then we'd put our foreheads together and just breathe." Raven shifts her position to look at Damien. "Like this," he says as he slowly leans his brow into hers.

After several moments of stillness, Damien pulls back far enough to see the Eros rising in Raven's eyes.

"Your turn. What do you remember?"

"Well, you heard what Violet said as we were leaving the room. Do you think she meant it?"

"She's told me several times, even before tonight, how happy she would be for us to reconnect, so I know we have her blessing."

"And how would that feel to you?"

Damien pulls Raven in close to his face. She thinks he's going to whisper something, but he just stares at her lips. It's like there's a magnetic field between their mouths. They are irresistibly pulled into a long, slow kiss.

Raven pauses and looks into his eyes. "I have an impulse to put my third eye on your cock."

Damien smiles, exhales deeply, closes his eyes, and nods. As if in an erotic dream, she slides down to her knees between his legs. With reverence, she pulls out his semi hard penis and holds it firm against her brow point. She feels it filling with an erotic current. When she can no longer hold back, she wraps her lips around his shaft. She allows her body wisdom to take over. When Damien is at the edge of orgasm, she turns her mind in the direction of the cosmos and receives an explosion of star stuff in her mouth. After a tender pause, she slowly cups her hand, collects his cum into her hand, then walks outside into the backyard. She holds his seed up above her head as an offering to the moonlight before grounding her hands on the moist Earth. After wiping her hands on the moist grass, she heads inside to meet Damien's warm embrace. Together they float back down into the realm of the ordinary.

Their bodies are intertwined on the couch when Damien

marvels, "I'm grateful for the clearing conversation we had to-night."

"It somehow makes the impossible seem possible again," Raven muses.

"For the record, I fully understand that there is a unique universe that opens in the world between the two of you that doesn't include me at all."

"Thank you. And I do want to include you and consider your feelings more when I'm planning our scenes. Maybe I can run some of my ideas by you?"

"I'd love to hear them, especially if there is a scene that in-volves a certain ex-boyfriend," Damien jokes.

Raven kisses Damien and says, "I like where this is going."

"Seriously though, what did you have in mind?"

"With Violet, I've been thinking a lot about fisting lately," Raven says with a smirk. "What are your thoughts on the sub-ject?"

Damien holds up one of Raven's hands and makes it into a fist to compare with his own—Raven's is about half the size.

"If she's going to be fisted, it seems a good idea to start with yours. You have my full blessings on that scene."

"Thank you."

"I know just the thing to give you. It's still in the box. My disclaimer is that I've never used it, so you'll have to let me know how it goes."

"I see what you're doing." Raven kisses his cheek. "You've found a clever way to include yourself!"

Confession Booth

Violet has never been so nervous about talking to Raven. Their relationship feels so good, she's afraid to fuck it up. Upon answering the door, Violet blurts, "I have a confession to make."

"Shall we go outside to talk?"

"Good idea." It's a bit windy, but it's still warm. Violet rushes around gathering a throw blanket, sun hats, a couple of pillows, and a pitcher of iced tea. Raven prepares their nest in the partial shade of the trampoline.

"Step into my confession booth," Raven jokes.

Violet takes a big breath then says, "My mistress trained me to start every ritual with an intention, so I want you to know I am only telling you this to create more intimacy."

"I want us to have the kind of relationship I have with Nick, and you have with Damien, where you're able to say anything," Raven says.

"That makes me so happy I could cry." Violet plants a hot kiss on Raven's open mouth. "I don't want to do anything to push you away. I told Damien if you ever tried to break up with me, I wouldn't let you. I'd stalk you. I'd show up at your house, at your work... I'd do whatever it took to get you back."

Raven's laughter melts the ice, a bit.

"Then Damien asked me what I'd do if he ever broke up with me. I told him I would cry my eyes out, between your thighs."

"That a girl." Raven narrows her eyes and removes her rings, rolling up her sleeves. "Can I spank you while you confess?" She doesn't wait for Violet's response before pulling her ass across her lap and pulling up Violet's skirt to expose her rounded buns, separated by a skimpy G-string. Raven warms her hands with light percussive drumming. "Now, tell me a confession that deserves punishment."

Violet gazes into the grass and at the metal base of the trampoline, relieved for the playfulness, but not sure how to proceed without looking Raven in the eyes. Violet decides to start with a small confession and build up to the big one.

"I had sex with Damien this morning and let him cum inside me, knowing you'd smell it if you went down on me."

"You've been a very bad girl indeed. I want details, but first," Raven commands, "I want you to rate how much you enjoyed it on a scale of one to ten."

"I guess about an eight?"

"Count out loud to eight as I punish you." She rubs her hands together and spanks loud and steady.

"One." Slap! On the right cheek. "Two." Slap! On the left cheek. "Three." Slap! On the left . . .

"Count louder, you little cum slut!"

Violet's voice amplifies as Raven escalates in intensity until she finishes the either spank.

"Is there more?" Raven asks.

"Yes Mistress. More spankings please," Violet says, even though her ass is stinging.

"Continue with your confession."

"Well, let's see. I've been having more fantasies about Autumn."

"How many times, since last week?"

"Um . . . too many to count," Violet says in a shaky, small voice.

Raven raises her volume. "You little bitch. If you want spankings without having to count, I'll teach you!" Raven's spanking grew harder and sharper against Violet's bare ass. At the edge of what she can handle, Violet begins to squirm and wiggle.

"Okay, okay," Violet cries, "I can't take anymore."

She sits up and hugs Raven, then explodes with the real confession: "When I first met her, I thought she was sexy and playful, but way too young to take seriously. She was the perfect person for Damien and me to share new experiences with, and she offered a balance for Damien when we have our Fridays. And then, I suddenly realized out of the blue that I'm falling in love with her. I couldn't believe it because I thought she was too young, but that's just a judgment. Love is timeless. So now I'm starting to think of her like my girlfriend. And I find myself wanting to fluid bond with her. But I want to know how that feels to you."

"Well, I don't own you. You don't need to ask my permission," Raven says, but it sounds as if her voice is coming from behind a concrete wall.

"I know. But you're still my queen. I don't want anything to change our dynamic. If it hurts you, I don't need to do it."

"Of course it hurts. The thought of you—and Damien—sharing a lover that's not me, I can't think of anything that could hurt worse, except . . ." Raven trails off, breathing deeply, holding in the tears.

"Except what?" Violet prods, but Raven remains silent.

Violet waits, like a patient puppy at the door whose master commanded her to stay. She knows not to speak.

"Look, you are not my property. As much as I love to pretend you're my bitch and you belong to me, you don't. And in reality, all of our play wouldn't be nearly so hot if I owned you. You're free to love as deep and as wide as you want. That's part of what I love about us."

"Then why are you crying?"

"It just hurts. Don't think just because I'm jealous, I'm not happy for you. I just have to mourn the loss of our honeymoon period."

"That's ridiculous. I'm no less in love with you than the first time we made love."

"Me neither." Raven laughs. "My love for you just keeps growing out of control, like a wildfire."

Violet laughs, which makes Raven laugh. They soften and stare at each other wordlessly.

Raven continues from a more centered place, "Part of the reason we do these slut-shaming scenes is to subvert the idea that having a lot of sex is bad, that sharing ourselves with the world is somehow wrong. We're reconciling this desire to love as widely as we do, despite our cultural programing that says it's dirty and wrong. It's like I'm trying to fuck the programming out of you. I want to cleanse myself of the conditioning so someday I can know what it means to love unconditionally."

Violet notices how conflicted Raven seems as she speaks, and slowly says, "But we're not there yet, are we?"

"Not yet. I wish I knew her better. Maybe then I'd understand what you and Damien see in her. It's easier for me to share my lovers when I know the people I'm sharing them with."

"I'm happy to wait for you to get to know her better," Violet says.

Raven, with apology in her voice, asks, "Maybe just a little time to get used to the idea...like a couple weeks?"

"Of course. She's not in any rush, you'll see, she's like family already."

Raven stands up and leaves Violet on the lawn with no explanation. When she returns, she has a tray of ice, and she takes Violet over her lap to cool and rub her butt, admiring her with sweet kisses and compliments.

"You're such a sweet little bitch."

Blood Slut

All the windows and doors in Violet's house are open, allowing the offshore breeze to cool her skin as she reclines on the living room couch. "Let me massage you," Violet offers.

"You're the one with PMS. I should be massaging you," Raven counters.

"C'mon. It will help my cramps." Violet tugs at Raven's burgundy blouse, trying to remove it without actually exerting any energy.

"Fine," Raven says, stripping out of her half-cup lace bra, exposing her tanned breasts. Violet's hands hone in on Raven's hip flexors.

"I bet if I really wanted, you'd rally to have sex," Raven says.

"Not likely. I didn't even have sex with Damien last night.

When my moon comes this hard, I go into a deep-watery, crampy, dreamy state."

"How did he handle that?"

"You can ask him yourself. He's in the other room."

Raven's body tenses. "He's home? Today?"

"I told him we wouldn't be having sex anyway, so he could work from home." Violet calls out, "Damien! Raven's here!"

Raven rearranges her skirt, but realizes it's pointless—Violet's just lying around in her bra and panties, anyway.

Damien enters casually in his signature undershirt and cargo pants to greet Raven with a warm hug. "Good to see you here, in the flesh."

Raven is instantly flooded and suddenly speechless. "I didn't expect you . . ."

"I don't mean to crash your date," Damien says sensitively. "I just wanted a quick hug."

Raven catches his hand and tugs him onto the couch. "Stay."

"I don't want to be the third wheel."

"You're welcome to drop in with us," Raven reassures him. "I miss you."

"Oh, please," Violet says, rubbing them both simultaneously. "It's so nurturing to have both my beloveds together."

"So, I understand this a historic moment for you. It must be the first time you've actually seen each other without having sex?" Damien digs at them. "Aren't you afraid that means you're losing your edge?"

"Well, I was going to ask you how you handle her when she's out of commission, but I can tell already by your attitude."

"What do you mean? I love her period," Damien says.

Violet jumps in. "It's true. He loves blood more than I do. He even likes drinking it."

Raven mocks him with, "Oooh, I knew you were a feminist, but I had no idea that you were a devotee to the red Goddess."

Violet's laughter encourages Raven to further mock him. "Does it taste better before dinner like an aperitif or is it better after, like a dessert wine?"

Damien plays along. "It's stem cells rich with highly proliferative health benefits."

Violet concedes, "I collect it in the Diva cup you bought me."

"Once you get beyond the odor, which is mostly from iron, it's not so bad. It comes from the womb for the purpose of nourishing new life, so..."

"You don't have to explain. I'm not judging you," Raven says.

"I like to call him my little vampire." Violet kisses him. "I used to water my plants with it, but this is so much better."

Raven kisses Violet and says, "I love the effect you're having on Damien."

"I can't believe you're letting a little menstrual blood get in the way of your sexy time today," Damien says.

"What are you suggesting?" Raven asks.

"If she were my bitch, I'd use it to further humiliate her," Damien suggests.

"What do you mean, if?" Raven quips. "She's always been your bitch. I just get to borrow her from time to time."

A smile slowly spreads over Damien's face. He speaks slowly, "Well, when you put it that way, you could help by pinning her down right here so I could get her blood flowing."

Violet's eyes light up. "You want to double-dom me?"

Raven raises her eyebrow. "Oooh, you like the sound of that, don't you?"

"Oh my God, I would LOVE that!" Violet squeals.

Raven shakes her head and looks at Damien. "You little slut."

"I mean, what makes you think I would want that? I would

really, really hate it!" Violet backs her body against the couch, pretending to resist in slow motion.

Damien leans toward Violet and pins her hips, then commands Raven, "Get her arms!"

Raven crosses Violet's wrists above her head and detains her as Damien rips Violet's panties halfway down at an awkward angle.

Between moans Violet calls out, "Get a towel."

"No! We're going to make you bleed all over yourself you dirty little whore." Raven forces a heavy kiss on Violet's hot mouth. When she looks up, Raven sees Damien is smiling, his fingers already plugged into her thrusting pelvis.

Violet is still struggling. "Slow down. Please, a little slower."

"She says slower," Raven repeats.

"I heard her," Damien says. Raven can't tell if his forceful gestures have slowed, and she has to fight the impulse to protect her little bitch.

"Is she bleeding?" Raven asks.

Damien pulls his thick hand out from between her thighs and licks two fingers. "Not yet." He stuffs them back inside.

Raven says, "When she does, we should write the word *slut* across her chest, like the scarlet letter. We want everyone to know who you really are."

After a number of deep pumps, Damien pulls his fingers out and drags his hand across Violet's left nipple, leaving a shiny trail of pussy juice.

Violet exclaims, "I'm not bleeding yet!" She may be struggling, but she is clearly loving every moment.

"Here, hold her." Raven pins Violet's hands beside her body so that Damien can hold her. "I've got an idea." Raven reaches for her bag and rummages until she finds a tube of lipstick. She returns to find Damien completely on top of Violet. She's struck by a pang of feeling left out. She pushes through the thick delusion to make eye contact with Damien, who nods at her, then she grabs Violet's pretty face and, with her other hand, unrolls the tube of red lipstick. "Hold still you little slut." Raven smears the red across Violet's lips. When she struggles, it ends up streaking across her cheek, toward her chin. "Now look what you've done, you sloppy little whore!"

Damien has picked up his pace. His hand is racing in and out of her wet pussy like a piston. Raven brings the lipstick to Violet's chest, smearing a big scarlet *S* across her left breast. Violet screams, and Raven continues *L . . . U . . . T.*

"Good," Damien says. "Now everyone is going to know you're the town whore."

Violet giggles, "That's a line from Raven's performance."

"Shut up, you little bitch," Raven smirks.

Damien says, "I think you need to sit on her face, to shut her up." Raven considers it for a moment, but doesn't feel confident enough to pull it off.

"Maybe you need to stick your dick in her mouth," Raven counter proposes.

"Maybe," Damien says, "or why don't you show her how it feels to be fisted?"

"Are you telling me what to do?" Raven questions sharply.

Damien backs down. "Just a suggestion."

"Well, I think Vi has had enough for today," Raven says.

Damien's hand goes limp. He searches Raven's face, but she is frozen. After a quick kiss on Violet's chest, Damien slowly pulls out. Violet's first move as a free woman is to wrap her arms around her mistress.

Raven defrosts. She tries to observe the situation objectively, but everything is a blur. A spell has been broken and she's left confused. "I'm sorry."

"It's okay. That was beautiful. It was thrilling to have you both together." Violet turns to squeeze Damien. "My heart is so open right now."

Raven sighs. "I feel like we were out of sync. It was like we kept undermining each other."

Damien places his hand on Raven's thigh. "It's okay, it's all part of the power play."

"But it got ugly for a minute there." Raven shakes her head. Her voice calms as she untangles her feelings with her words. "I just had a sober moment where I realized you are her primary, and I've had to surrender to you like I would a dom, even to date her. Normally I accept that. I don't ever want to overstep my bounds, but somehow in this scene I felt so powerless."

"Is that why you asked to slow it down?" Damien reassures her, "I can understand that."

Violet reaches out to pull them both into a hug, and they lean their heads together to form a pyramid.

"Well, I for one thought you two work amazingly well together, especially since it was our first time."

Damien says, "Violet's opinion is the only one that really matters."

Raven allows herself a smile. "Okay. I'll admit, we are kind of awesome together."

FRIDAY #28

Gone Bananas

Raven wakes up, reaching for her girlfriend's curvaceous body only to find the empty impression left when Nick went for his predawn workout. Tonight will be Violet's first sleepover because Damien is away on his first business trip since he's lived with Violet. Raven's fantasy is to build a giant birdcage in which to keep Violet locked up as a sex slave for the long weekend. In reality, she made an agreement to sleep with Violet for only one night, since Damien is sleeping alone in a strange hotel bed, and Violet felt it was only fair.

When Nick returns, Raven asks for his blessing to spend the night alone with Violet in the playroom.

"I get it. You want your bitch all to yourself; who wouldn't?" Nick acknowledges.

"Thanks for understanding," Raven says, suspecting that

under his dry sense of humor, there's hidden emotion. Is it envy or resentment? She doesn't ask.

"We can all have dinner together," Raven offers. "And for the record, Violet said she didn't feel like playing tonight. She's on her period and inconsolable about Damien's absence and said she just wants to curl up and cry."

Nick shoots her a skeptical look. "And so, I'm supposed to believe you're just going to cuddle?"

"I didn't say that's what I wanted, and I'm taking it as a challenge to cheer her up. I don't know what I'm going to do for her yet."

After lunch, Raven looks for inspiration in her box of toys, but nothing comes to mind. She goes through all her kitchen cabinets and drawers looking for anything kinky: spatulas, wooden spoons, turkey basters, etc.... Then her eyes land on a fresh bunch of bananas resting on top of her fruit bowl and inspiration strikes: she knows what she has to do! Ever since she got Violet's banana love note, Raven could hardly eat a banana without getting wet. One time she posted a suggestive banana meme on Violet's Facebook wall with a list of all of its miraculous health benefits.

Family dinner is a sweet opportunity for Violet to spend time with Mason. Since he's usually at school or in bed during their Friday dates, this is their first real encounter. Violet sits with her legs crossed, watching him eat his pasta. Afterward, Mason makes his mamma proud by showing off his rock collection.

Violet and Nick are still sitting at the table when Raven leaves to tuck Mason in.

Violet giggles. "I don't know how he managed to get the food from the fork into his face."

"Right? Kids don't exactly pop out of the womb with perfect hand-eye coordination. It takes a while to develop." Nick clears the plates. "I'm playing a local gig tonight and have to get my equipment together."

"Can we come listen to you play?"

"The real gig is tomorrow. I'm just feeling out the new venue and performing in their open mic."

"Let me help," Violet says, taking the salad bowl over to the counter. Raven is obviously not a clean-up-as-you-go kind of cook, but Violet knows her way around a kitchen. "Do you have a moment to chat, or do you need to run?" Violet asks casually.

"What did you have in mind?" Nick asks while aiming the sponge for the sink. It's a long shot, but he scores.

"Nothing specific, I just like getting to know you. Raven's always bragging about you to the acting class. She says you're a patron saint of the arts and the primary benefactor of the theater."

"I like to think of myself as a sugar daddy for the Sacred Slut." Nick winks. "It's all just an elaborate plot to get laid."

"She also warned me you have a sick sense of humor."

"Ah, but did she tell you I came up with the name for the theater? I used to joke that if she stayed with me, she'd have to stop being a lesbian activist and start making more sandwiches in the kitchen, 'barefoot and pregnant.'"

Violet giggles, "But seriously, I want to thank you for supporting my relationship with Raven. The other week when Damien was feeling left out, Raven rearranged our relationship so the three of us could play together. It was like a revelation. It was medicine for my soul, and I want to extend you the same courtesy. Not necessarily to have sex, but to include you in our date time. Even tonight if you'd like."

"Thanks, but Raven's been looking forward to finally having you all to herself. Besides, I get Raven tomorrow. Saturdays have become our sacred date night, and I've learned not to fuck with poly scheduling."

"Oh yeah? What are you going to do?"

"We're going out to eat before my performance."

Nick makes a movement to get up, and Violet stops him, placing her hand on his shoulder and blurting, "Do you ever get jealous?"

"No. Not the way she does." Violet stares at him, like a saleswoman who will not stop asking until she gets a customer's credit card, so he continues. "I used to…a little. Mostly, I worried she'd leave me for a woman, but in reality, she doesn't have to leave me, because she can still love women or anyone. She's still very free. Anyhow, I'm so busy with work and Mason that I'm grateful to have Fridays to myself. I look forward to the alone time."

Violet says, "I'll finish in the kitchen, so you can go get ready for your gig."

"You don't have to," Nick says.

Violet slings the dish rag over her shoulder and says, "What else is a bitch for?"

"Well if I had a bitch, housework is the last thing I'd make her do." Nick pulls Violet into a big bear hug.

"I'm glad we had this talk," Violet calls as he leaves.

When Raven returns, the kitchen is spotless, except for a steaming teacup on the table. Violet kisses her queen and says, "It's Egyptian licorice."

"Thanks, sweetie. Mason's sitter is all set up, so we can have total privacy tonight."

The playroom is aglow with candles and flower petals. There is a futon in the center of the room piled high with pillows. In the center of the bedspread is a large banana and two figs laid out like a penis and balls, alongside a vibrator, condoms, and lube.

Violet squeals, "I wondered what you had in mind!"

"Good, healthy lovemaking. It's all natural and totally organic."

"I can't tell you how many times I've fantasized about you fucking me with a banana." She starts to kiss Raven but stops herself. "Before we drop in," she grabs her phone from her little kitty-cat-shaped purse. "Let me check with Damien, since we've never done this before."

Raven is genuinely apologetic. "Oh my God. It didn't occur to me this would be something new."

"So, you just assumed I've had sex with fruit before?" Violet teases. "Is fruit fucking like a thing everyone does and I'm somehow not aware?"

"Tell him I'm sorry."

"It's not a big deal, I have to call him to say good night anyway."

"I'm not attached, obviously, if he's not okay with it for any reason. I'm sure there are a million other things we can do."

"Like curl up like an old married couple and watch lesbian movies together?" Violet says, still teasing.

"Just call him!"

"Okay!" She steps out into the yard, not because she needs privacy, but to give Damien the presence he deserves. Raven sits on the doorstep leaning back on her elbows, pretending to look at the stars, obviously eavesdropping.

"Do you miss me as much as I miss you? How's the conference going? Yes, I'm here with Raven, but I wanted to hear your voice before we go to bed. Of course not. I wanted to ask you something. It's about a possible new experience.... How would you feel if she fucked me with a banana? Yes, it's a real banana, you know, instead of a strap-on. Yes, I'm still bleeding."

She covers the speaker and says to Raven, "He's such a vampire!" Then she listens to the phone again. "Yes, Raven's right here, she says hello..." To Raven, she says, "He says 'Hi.'" Speaking into the phone again, she says, "Okay...are you serious? I will. Thank you. I love you too. Sweet dreams, Lover."

Violet turns off her phone and sits on Raven's lap.

"He said, yes you can fuck me with fruit, as long as you save the bloody banana for him. He wants me to put it in the freezer so I can make him a smoothie when he comes home."

"Wow." Raven thinks about it. "He may be kinkier than I am."

Violet helps Raven stand up. "Yeah, you two are a lot alike."

Raven leads Violet back into the playroom. "Now that we've got permission, it's time to get naked."

Violet whines, "I'm keeping my panties on, for now."

"Fine, a little G-string is not going to stop me," Raven says, preparing the banana. It's about seven inches long, with a healthy curve. "I've got to do something about this little pointy tip, I don't want it to scratch you." She produces safety scissors and snips off the tip.

"If it's organic, we don't need a condom." Violet says, lounging on the futon like a lingerie model.

"I don't want the fructose to mess up your PH balance and give you a yeast infection. Besides, I put condoms on all my sex toys. It's just good practice." Raven holds the banana at her crotch as if it's a girl dick, then uses her teeth to rip a condom open, unrolling it over the fruit.

Violet says in her sweetest voice, "Thank you. Don't forget we have to get my blood on it for Damien."

"Hmmm . . . That's going to be tricky. It's not like he's going to eat the peel. Can we figure that out later? Are you ready?"

"I miss him too much, and I'm on my moon."

Raven gently cups Violet's nipple, and she squeals. "Your body betrays you."

"I'm sorry. You're going to have to force me to surrender to this ridiculous fruit-fucking fetish of yours."

"Good thinking. I'm going to have to restrain you somehow. Let's see . . . I want to pin your arms down." Raven goes back to her toy box and starts sorting through rope.

"As if humiliation with a banana isn't bad enough, you think I'm just going to sit here and wait for you to tie me up?" Violet says.

"Eager little slut, aren't you? Can't even wait for me to find rope. Luckily I have just the trick." She pulls the pillowcase off the nearby pillow and brings Violet's hands behind her back. She stuffs Violet's arms into the case and lays her back, her arms immobilized by the fabric.

"Where did you learn this?" Violet is clearly loving it.

"Nick did it to me on our honeymoon. He took me to China and the second we stepped into our five-star suite in Shanghai, he restrained me with the hotel bedding and licked me until the bellhop came to our door with the luggage. He left me there exposed and helpless while he tipped the bellhop. I was so embarrassed. Nick says the guy craned his neck to catch a glimpse of me on the bed."

"That's hilarious," Violet says.

"Are you comfortable like this?" Raven runs her hands along Violet's shoulders.

"I'd be more comfortable if you were inside me."

"I'm going to warm you up first, that's the fun part. I get to watch you squirm against my vibrator." Raven carefully sets the banana within reach and turns the vibrator on. Violet throws her weight from side to side, but the pillowcase has her pinned. Raven strategically adds her body weight. She moves slowly, up the length of Violet's smooth leg, around her hip, and to her inner thigh. She buzzes down one leg and up the tender side of the other. This ritual helps them both relax. When the vibrator reaches Violet's lace-covered clit, she arches her back and moans. Raven changes the direction of the strokes across her pussy to tease a little before sinking into her crotch. Violet spreads her legs wider, aching for more.

Raven licks two fingers on her free hand and slides them down Violet's panties.

"Please. Mistress, please," Violet whimpers.

Raven flips off the vibrator, grabs her lace waistband, and with a dramatic movement pulls her panties all the way down her body, throwing them across the room. She lifts Violet's bra, exposing her naked breasts, then licks each nipple. After running her tongue across Violet's lips she whispers, "Now are you ready for my big yellow cock?"

"Yes, please."

Raven repositions herself above Violet with the banana between her legs, teasing the outside of her temple by stroking it between her lips, and before she can fully plunge in, she hears a knock at the door.

"It's me," Nick says apologetically, gently opening the door.

"Hold on." Raven seems self-conscious about her position kneeling over Violet's naked body, and she rolls onto the bed.

"Come on in!" Violet calls in a muffled voice.

Nick enters with trepidation.

Raven sets the banana down and asks, "Did you come to kiss us good-bye?"

Nick gives Raven a peck while hovering awkwardly over the naked hostage.

"Actually, I decided not to go tonight."

"Why?" Raven asks.

"I was feeling sort of left out," he admits.

Raven motions for him to sit beside her and simultaneously places a warm palm on Violet's pulsing sex, to both cover and comfort her.

"I started thinking about what Violet said in the kitchen and realized I didn't really feel welcome."

"What do you mean, 'not welcome?'" Raven sounds defensive.

"You're always welcome," Violet says.

Raven gently slaps Violet's pussy and says, "I don't want another word out of you, missy."

"Forgive me." Violet giggles.

"When I thought about how Damien was feeling left out, I realized it wasn't really working for me either. I know you gave him permission to walk in anytime. Part of me wants to know I have that permission too."

"I want you to feel included, but the big difference is that Damien and I have been lovers, whereas, you and Violet have never been sexual, so we will have to slow down."

"I don't want to slow you down."

"We don't mind . . ." Violet says, which causes Raven to playfully pinch her inner thigh, which is still spread open.

"What I told Damien, and the same goes for you, is we're happy to go as slow as we need to so everyone feels included," Raven recites.

Nick whispers, "Thank you."

Raven keeps one hand on Violet as she hugs her husband.

Nick steals a good look at Violet and says, "This scene looks pretty hot."

Raven smirks, "Violet, are you okay if he watches?"

"I'm a hell yes to that," she says. "But no touching."

Raven thinks about it. "We should probably ask Damien if he's okay with Nick being here."

Violet urgently interjects, "Damien's okay with it. I know he'd want everyone to feel included. He'd totally be okay with Nick watching."

"Are you sure?" Nick asks respectfully.

Violet clarifies, "We'll just need to check in with him before any touching."

Nick shakes his head in happy disbelief. "Well, I look forward to having that conversation."

"Make yourself comfortable, darling. We're going to drop back in." Raven flips the vibrator back on.

Nick situates himself on the futon with his legs hanging halfway off. "Did she tell you where she learned the pillowcase trick?"

"Of course, I gave you credit, my love. Now let me get back to business." Raven starts rubbing the length of the banana between Violet's nether lips. "Now, where were we? Do you remember?"

"I don't remember, because I'm feeling a whole new fantasy about being captured by Bonnie and Clyde."

"You mean the criminal superstars who were wild and young and took no hostages?" Raven adds.

"Mmmm-hmmm. Those are the ones." Violet releases her thighs so they naturally fall open again. "Except, I'm a hostage and you two are arguing about what to do with me."

Nick takes this as his cue to improvise. "Don't worry Bonnie, Clyde just wants to watch, this time."

Raven smiles, adds lube to the tip of the banana, and slowly slides it between Violet's lips. Violet comes alive under Raven's undivided attention. Perhaps it's the texture of the banana or the warmth of Nick's gaze, either way, she is instantly on the edge of orgasm.

Raven drives the fruit rhythmically in and out, until her grip becomes compromised. The banana is becoming softer—not wanting to squish it, she supports it with two hands. The more enthusiastic Violet gets with her hips, the more it starts to degrade inside the condom. She continues plunging it in and out until it's nothing but a mushy mess. Violet is so aroused she hardly notices, so Raven keeps fucking her with the limp banana. She supplements the sensation with her thumb on Violet's clit. Loudly moaning, back arching, Violet begs Raven for kisses with her outstretched neck. With hands occupied, Raven lowers herself to Violet's face but loses her balance. The rhythm is broken, but both women become so lost in kissing it doesn't matter. Breathing slows. Big sighs.

Raven lifts her weight off Violet and rolls to one side. She slowly pulls the sad, misshapen banana out. She holds it up for them to admire and they both laugh.

They turn to Nick to share in the laughter, but he has managed to fall asleep. Smiling, Violet says, "I hope the sound of our lovemaking gives him good dreams."

"I loved how you kept going even when your cock went limp. . . ."

Raven kisses her beloved bitch and laughs. "It's not the size of the banana, but the strength of your Kegel muscles that counts. Isn't that how the saying goes?"

Triple Goddess

Raven hates surprises, so Nick learned long ago to ask her what she wants for her birthday. This year, by her request, Nick bought her a session with a local boudoir photographer. Raven excitedly scheduled the photo shoot on Friday as a fun playdate with her bitch. As her birthday crept closer, she felt more generous and offered to include Autumn. She reasoned that it was an opportunity to bond as metamours, and it would immortalize their expanding web of relationships.

"What a poly thing to do!" Violet exclaims, excited by the thought of half-naked photos with both of her girlfriends. When Raven learns Autumn is an experienced model who has her own line of yoga clothing, she immediately regrets her decision.

Raven calls Violet to discuss her second thoughts.

"I've been looking forward to this all week," Violet coaxes. "What's the worst that could happen? Even if it's awkward, I'm sure we'll get some great photos out of it." Then Violet persuades Raven to use retail therapy. "There are few problems that can't be solved by lingerie shopping."

Raven imagines pressing Violet's half-naked body against the dressing room mirror, and agrees to her second stupid appointment for the day.

Violet is wearing the world's shortest skirt as she runs clear across the mall to hug Raven in front of the Lingerie Shoppe. As soon as the manager sees them kissing behind the racks, she sternly reminds them only one person is allowed in the dressing room at a time. Violet musters all of her charm, trying to persuade her to make a powerful exception, to no avail.

"Sounds like she hasn't been laid in years," Violet whispers behind her hand to Raven. The strict guard dog of a manager takes up her post outside the dressing room with arms crossed as she watches Violet model several sets of designer panties. Raven's only solace now is seeing Violet in a silk pair of panties that lace up the backside. Raven orders three pair, for herself, Violet, and Autumn.

Upon their arrival at the photo studio's dressing room, they find that Autumn has already covered the counters with makeup trays, hair products, and jewelry. She undoubtedly has experience in the womanly art of dress up. Violet immediately begins buzzing about with powders, brushes, and pencils. Autumn offers to curl Raven's long brown hair, but Raven declines. When Violet playfully crawls over to Raven's toes, nail polish in hand, Raven can't resist. She looks down at her bitch on all fours, hair in curlers, painting her queen's toes, and smiles. During the twenty minutes it takes to receive her pedicure, Raven asks if they want to set intentions for the shoot.

Raven starts. "The three of us together has me thinking about the symbolism of the trinity, the archetype of the triple

Goddess in Pagan cosmology, represented by the maiden, the mother, and the crone. But I have to admit, I'm not crazy about the idea of being the crone in this configuration, so maybe instead we can focus on the three realms: the Earth, the underworld, and the heavens."

Violet looks up from Raven's toe and says, "Who represents the underworld?"

"Or if you prefer the Hindu lineage, the three aspects of the divine are the generator, operator, and destroyer."

"I resonate with the underworld!" Autumn exclaims.

"Sweet," Raven says. "Violet can be heaven and I'll be Earth—let's see how we can embody those energies during the shoot."

Violet goes next. "Well, my intention is to celebrate having the two of you together. I want our photo shoot to capture the love we have for our whole poly family, including Damien and Nick."

Raven says, "I can align with that."

Violet kisses Raven's finished feet, and both women look at Autumn, who is fidgeting with the clasp on the makeup case. "Um. I don't know. For some reason, I'm more nervous than usual."

Violet tries to encourage Autumn. "But you're practically a professional!"

"At modeling, maybe. But this is boudoir"—Autumn's voice cracks—"with the two of you."

"If it helps," Raven blurts, "I'm nervous too."

Autumn looks at Raven with wide eyes. "Really?"

Violet springs up and says, "Should I ask the cameraman for more time, or should we just rally and do it?"

Raven releases an overdue sigh. "To be honest, I'd be happy to cancel this whole thing."

"Wait. Let me talk to him and see what he can do." Violet leaves the room to bargain with the photographer.

In silence, Raven examines Autumn's face. Her flawless skin is frozen like a little china doll. Raven opens her arms and Autumn rushes in like a child. Her heart is beating as fast as a lost bird. Raven feels the wall, built from judgment and competition, suddenly melt into a puddle around her freshly painted toes. Spontaneous tears stream down Raven's face, and in this moment, she wants nothing more than to make Autumn know she belongs. Raven is flooded by the love she has for Violet and Damien, and she feels it somehow shared by this woman. There is a strange inherent bond that's already been built by loving each other's lovers.

The door swings open and a tall, thin photographer enters carrying a six pack of Budweiser in one hand and a bar of dark chocolates in the other. Violet slips in behind him.

"You all look stunning! I'd love to offer you a fancy bottle of wine, but my next shoot is with a motorcycle model and this beer his treat. I'm going to shoot the biker in the field, so you can hang out for another hour, will that work for you?"

Raven wipes the tears from her eyes. "Thank you. I appreciate the extra time to bond with these Goddesses."

"I don't blame you. I'd invite myself, if I weren't booked today." He sets the beer on a chair and brings both hands to the camera around his neck. "Violet says you don't normally drink, but this is a trick of the trade to help lubricate the nerves."

Violet shuts the door behind him and lowers herself down to the sheepskin rug, gesturing to her girlfriends to join. "So, what did I miss, why are you crying?"

Raven comes down to stroke Violet's leg and says, "It just hit me this is the first time we've spent together."

Autumn pulls a tab off one of the Budweisers. "Who wants one?"

"Gross," Violet says. "That was the stuff Terrance used to drink."

Autumn asks, "Wasn't Terrance the guy you used to babysit for?"

"I still haven't heard the whole story," Raven says, cracking a beer.

Autumn slinks her leg around Violet's lap. "Neither have I."

"Sounds like it's storytime," Raven says as she cuddles in such a way that she can see Violet's face.

Violet hesitates. "Are you sure? It's kind of a buzzkill."

Raven insists, "Exactly, we need a way to drop out of ego and get really naked with each other." Raven lifts her beer and clinks it against Autumn's. "And that is exactly the affect storytelling has on the tribe."

Violet lifts a beer to her nose and says, "Let me smell it." After a long sniff she takes a tiny sip. "Yup. That's the stuff. Babysitting was my first real job, and I was already drinking and partying a lot by then. My employers were really cool college professors, so they kept beer in the fridge and didn't mind if I drank a few on the weekends. I worked with their family for a long time—Allison was like a little sister to me. Sometimes they'd come home late or drunk or they'd drink when they got home, so instead of driving me home, they'd just let me sleep in their guest room, and one or the other would take me back in the morning. Sometimes, Terrance would offer me beer when they'd come back, and we'd all drink together, but the dean would usually tire out early and go to bed, while Terrance and I would stay up drinking."

"Did you have any feelings for him?" Autumn asks while passing around the chocolate.

"Terrance? Ewww. No. He was interesting to talk to because he was so educated, and I thought he was cool because he rode a motorcycle, but I always thought he looked creepy because of his mustache and his round beer belly," Violet says, biting into a square of chocolate and licking her fingers. "Anyway, I remember one time when I got tired, Terrance helped me walk down the hallway. I tried to tell him I could do it myself. I don't remember what happened after that, but I woke up without pants on." Violet rearranges her body so she can look at her two girlfriends, who are reclining on the sheepskin rug, all made up, hanging on her every word.

"The next time they came home and Terrance offered me beer, I told him I didn't want to drink anymore. Especially not Budweiser. It made me nauseous. He said 'Here, take two of these, it will help your stomach get over it.' They were little white pills, and I swigged them down. I didn't know what they were, but I remember feeling too drowsy to drink anymore. I woke up in the guest room, in the middle of the night. Terrance was leaning over me, naked underneath his robe, with his dick sticking out and his hand down my pants. I said 'Terrance what are you doing?!' And he said, 'Oh, I must be in the wrong room.' And I shouted, 'No! Get out of here!'"

Raven comforts Violet with a low voice, "So sorry, honey. What did you do?"

"The next day, when he drove me home, I told him what he did was wrong, and that I wanted to tell his wife. But he said it was an honest mistake and that if I ever told her, she would end their marriage, and it would break the whole family up. So I didn't say anything. I just didn't go back to work for them. But then I started to question myself. Maybe I dreamt the whole thing up? And then I felt guilty for just leaving. And I started to miss hanging out with Allison. So when the dean called to ask what had happened, instead of telling the truth, I just offered to help her find my replacement. I knew a girl in my class who was looking for work. But I got a bad feeling when I heard she quit after only one month.

So I went over to her house to ask her why. She just shook her head and started to cry."

"He molested her too?" Autumn asked.

"I shouldn't have offered her that job. I don't know for sure what he did to her. But I knew what I had to do. I had to tell my story. I started by telling her everything I could remember, but she didn't want to talk about her experience. That's when I knew I had to tell the dean. And I wanted to create the right environment, so I called her and asked if I could come over for dinner sometime when Allison was with her grandmother, so I could talk to her about something. She used to make the best lasagna, and she was always happy to see me. So I came over early to help her set the table, and when Terrance got home, we all sat down and said grace, and then I came right out and told her that Terrance had molested me and my friend. The dean dropped her fork and started crying. Terrance said, 'If you're telling the truth, then what exactly did I do?' I told them every detail I could remember. He looked at his wife and yelled, 'Are you going to believe this bullshit?' She just stared at him. Then he stood up and said, 'I've got to get out of here!' He went upstairs to grab a green backpack and this black mannequin head, then got on his motorcycle and split."

"I'm proud of you for speaking up," Raven says, kissing Violet's shoulder.

"And for telling us," Autumn says.

"I can't believe I hadn't told either of you, till now. I'm not hiding it. It just wasn't relevant."

"I get it," Raven says.

Autumn asks, "What was the mannequin head about?"

"I never figured that out," Violet giggles. "I just remember he had this shiny lacquered head from Pier 1 Imports."

Violet's laughter spreads into uncontrollable chortles and chuckles, like a warm blanket that covers all three of their bodies.

Autumn rubs her hands along both of the other two

women's bare legs and says, "I'm glad we got this time alone without anyone eavesdropping on our conversation."

"I don't know," Raven teases, "I'm sorry the camera guy wasn't here to document this. It would have made an inspired monologue and I would love to direct it."

"Not everything I say is stage worthy."

"Oh, I beg to differ," says Raven.

FRIDAY #30
All-Girl Play Party

Purple is the theme of the party. Not only are there purple fabrics, but purple flowers and purple props placed around the playroom. There is even a purple bundle of rope and a purple dildo displayed on the toy table. Violet is wearing purple boy-shorts under her see-through dress and is kneeling by the stereo tinkering with her playlist. Electronic accordion dubstep blares from the speakers.

At first Raven doesn't notice the music change. She's sitting on a folded futon, studying her index cards. She is wearing a black vest and tight miniskirt. Distracted, she looks up. "What is this?"

"Carnival music," Violet says, tapping hard against her bare thigh to the surreal rhythm.

"We can't play this," Raven declares.

Disappointed, Violet whines, "Why not? It creates a creepy circus-like ambience."

"The answer is in the question. We want women to feel welcome and safe, not stuck on a haunted merry-go-round."

"I'm just trying to help," Violet says. She abruptly turns off the music.

"Look, a lot of these women are going to be nervous, it will be their first time attending something like this."

Violet continues pouting.

"Hey! Come here." Raven taps her lap. Violet approaches, but decides to put her head in Raven's lap instead of her ass.

"What's wrong?"

Violet sighs and says, "I just feel like this whole thing is your event. You just put my name on the invitation, but everyone knows it's your play party. Why'd you even ask me to co-facilitate?"

"Hey, I asked you because you are one of the most empowered, embodied, sexy women I have ever met, and not just in yoga classes either. You are a natural leader. Most of the women coming tonight want what you have. This is our thing. Any bisexual, poly, kinky woman would love to have a relationship like ours. Tonight, we're role modeling sex-positive play for all women. It's like we get to share our Friday playdate with the world!"

Violet seems flattered, but skeptical. "You're just saying that... It's a standard pep talk that you give your performers before they step on stage."

"Look, I thought you wanted reassurance, but I should've asked what you need."

Violet repositions her body. Her legs are crossed as she sits in front of Raven, eyes closed, hand on her heart. "I'm nervous."

"Naturally, there is pressure to perform, but—"

Violet cuts Raven off with, "And I'm irritated!"

"Irritated with me?" Raven asks.

"Yes, and with this whole scene. I just feel like a little bird under your wing."

"You want more freedom, more autonomy?"

Violet cups her face in her hands for a moment. Raven's not sure if she's going to cry, but then Violet lifts her head to say, "I just want to feel like we're equals."

"Equality! Of course. That's what this is about. When we're in scene, you give me your power, your trust, and your submission. We're not doing a scene, we're co-teaching here as equals. . . ."

"But everybody knows it's your party."

"This is our first party together. We'll see how we work together and we can structure it however you want next time. Look, I don't need you to put on a show tonight. If you're irritated, be irritated. This is a come-as-you-are party. We're role modeling authenticity, so just be yourself and let everyone know they're welcome to show up as they are. As for me, I'm anxious too. Mostly I'm anxious about Autumn. I think teaching with you is going to be easy and fun. If it weren't for Autumn. If you didn't have another lover coming, on the same week that you decided to start calling her your girlfriend, I feel we could throw this party with our hands tied behind our backs."

"That's a great image! Maybe we should try that."

"And, if I'm nervous, that means everyone else is probably nervous too, for a million different reasons. So our job is to give them permission to feel, and explore, and play. I propose you lead the toy-sharing protocols and possibly the safer-sex conversation, and I can frame the evening, create the container, and do the closing circle."

"Got it. Strap-ons and safer sex. If I miss something, feel free to mention it."

"Same for you. I know there's an inherent hierarchy because I have more experience, so when it comes to creating the container, I'll be Chef A and you can add seasoning as Chef B. Does that work for you?"

"Yes, my Queen," Violet jests.

"And when it comes to safety and strap-ons, I can play your bitch."

"Ooooh . . . can I do a demo on you?"

"What kind of demo?" Raven's eyebrows shoot up. Violet assumes a begging position. "Um . . . I'm not ready for the strap-on, but maybe with a dental dam. A lot of women have never used a dental dam before and it would be empowering to show them how."

"But I've never used one myself."

"Well then, it's obvious we need a dental dam demo. Should we call Damien to make sure he's okay with it?"

"I have a hall pass for the whole evening. We can do whatever kinky stuff we want, but only until midnight. He's going to pick me up right after closing circle. He even lent us an electric fucking machine. I've got to get it from the car. That would be another fun demo." Violet jumps up so she can run to her car.

"Before you go, there's something I need you to know."

"What?" Violet asks.

"No matter what happens tonight, I have never met a woman who felt more like my equal. With you, I finally feel like I've met my match."

As the doors open, Violet's mood seems to have lifted.

Autumn arrives wearing striped stockings and an adorable festival tutu. As Raven hugs her, she is soothed by the memory of how they bonded at the photo shoot. Raven tells herself Autumn is nervous just like all twenty-eight other women on the guest list. And it's her job to help her belong. The room fills with a diverse range of women with different identities: lesbian, bisexual, trans, poly, pansexual, and other perversions.

During the opening circle Raven takes a poll and is surprised to discover that only about a dozen women use strap-ons. She proudly introduces Violet and sits back to watch her bitch deliver safer-sex guidelines with an impeccable demonstration of how to step into a harness. She is reminded of an airline stewardess performing a safety routine, in the way Violet tightens the straps and positions the dildo for maximum pleasure.

Just as they've almost aced their first event together, Raven remembers they forgot to rehearse the dental dam demo. As soon as Violet mentions the dental dam, Raven takes it as her cue to stand and say, "A dental dam is just like a condom for cunnilingus. There are only three easy things you have to remember. Instead of telling you, I'm going to show you on Violet."

Violet protests, "I thought I was going to do the demo?"

"How can you show them, if you've never done it?" Raven speaks slowly, trying to pacify the misunderstanding. She pulls a chair out and pats the seat. "Go ahead and sit down for me."

Violet presses, with a tight jaw, "Well, if it's so easy, and you're such a good teacher, then you can teach me as I do it."

"Fine. If that's your preference," Raven concedes, trying to short-circuit the crunchy power play.

Violet continues, "Isn't that what we're here for? To give everyone permission to try something new? It doesn't have to be perfect, right?"

"Right." Raven hands the dental dam to Violet, who removes the packaging.

Raven explains, "Dental dams are great if you don't know what someone's STD status is, or someone knows they have HPV and you want to avoid risk of mouth or throat cancer. I've also used them for anilingus. Now, I'm going to sit down and talk Violet through it." Raven sets a towel on the chair cushion, pulls her miniskirt up, slips her lacy black G-string down to her ankles, and steps out, one foot at a time.

Catcalls fill the room.

"Step one: put lube on the side that touches the genitals. Make sure it's water based so it doesn't degrade the latex."

Raven watches Violet struggle with the lube. Raven tries to help by grabbing the dental dam and spreading it above her crotch like a mini trampoline, while Violet squirts out way too much lube.

"Step two: Hold it firmly, from the edges, like this." Raven spreads her legs, and Violet lowers herself onto her knees and slowly places the lubed side against Raven's sex. Raven squeals, "It's cold!"

One of Violet's yoga students blurts out a question from the audience: "I heard you're supposed to wash them first because the powdery stuff can give you a yeast infection."

"Good question, we can talk more about it after the demo," Raven says, trying to maintain control of the room.

Violet chimes, "Dental dams are good if your girl has a yeast infection. Or if you don't want to tell her to take a shower because she smells bad." Nervous laughter from Raven and the audience.

Then, while holding this luby dental dam between Raven's legs, Violet launches into a story. "You know it reminds me of a time when I was in college, I was seeing this guy named Trevor. We had sex in a hotel on a Sunday night and when he came, I assumed he pulled the condom off. He must've thought I pulled it off. It must've slipped during sex."

The audience breaks into uproarious laughter. Violet seems pleased with herself, but Raven is convinced the laughter is at Violet's ridiculous timing. Who tells an inappropriate story when their girlfriend is pantyless in front of an audience, legs spread? Just when Raven thinks it can't get any worse, Violet continues:

"In class the next day, I smelled a foul, fishy odor. I was like, what the hell is that smell? I was sitting in the middle row, so I leaned forward to see if it was the person in front of me. It wasn't. So I leaned back to sniff the person behind me. Nope.

So I smelled the person to my left and right. Nothing. I was hor-rified to find the only other place it could be coming from was between my legs. It was me. So I went into the bathroom and reached my fingers inside and felt a cum-filled condom. I pulled it out and it smelled like a small animal had died and had been festering. I didn't go back to class that day. I was done. It was terrible."

Groans and snickers fill the room, and Raven cuts in: "Thank you for that enlightening story. Can we get on with the demo?"

"You didn't like my story?" Violet teases.

Raven surrenders to the moment. "And for the next act, Violet will demonstrate how to perform oral sex on a woman using a dental dam." She pushes Violet's head down between her legs.

"You'll see that she's holding it in place while using her tongue and lips and chin for sensation. . . . It may take slight-ly more pressure and more presence to transmit sexual energy through the barrier, but it can be an exciting challenge to pen-etrate with your intention. Oh. That's good. Right there...good girl."

Just as Raven starts getting into it, Violet stops and turns to the crowd to say, "And that's how it's done."

Raven removes the dental dam and wipes herself off with a wet wipe, saying, "The last thing to remember is, if you intend to reuse it, remember which side you licked. Never use the other side. If you want personal coaching during the party, just come and get one of us."

Next, Violet holds up a heavy piece of hardware, which looks like a Milwaukee Twelve-Amp Sawzall but has been adapted with a dildo. "Also, Damien loaned me this fucking machine. If you're interested in using this bad boy, please ask. It requires more instruction and serious supervision."

Raven wraps it up with, "That sums up the guided portion of the evening. Now let's get on with the juicy, self-directed, girl-on-girl play until closing circle around midnight!"

Violet is immediately surrounded with women interested in seeing the fucking machine. She asks for a volunteer so she can create a demo in the corner.

Raven scans the room, appreciating the various clusters in varying degrees of sensual connection. Her eyes fall upon Autumn sitting in a meditative pose. Her face is serene and smooth like an angel from the underworld. Raven notices the conflicting impulse to lean in while simultaneously wanting to avoid her. Her higher self takes over. She slowly sits beside Autumn and asks if she can hold her hand.

"Thank you." Autumn nods a little too enthusiastically.

"How are you?"

"It's still so new to me," Autumn says softly.

"I'm not sure which 'it' you're referring to, but the trick is focus and meaning. Where are you directing your focus, and what meaning are you making of it?"

"Violet is so outrageous!"

"Funny, we both have the same focus. Now what about meaning, does her outrageousness empower you or not?"

"I don't know," Autumn admits.

"How about if we focus on an outrageous scene that would really light you up?"

"Well, Violet has been talking about tying me up."

"Oh. She has, has she? Well, what if we both tied you up?"

In that moment a brunette with a wild mop of curls lands in Raven's lap. She's in a tickle war with a blonde with a boyish haircut.

"Mercy! Mercy!" she screams, then she kisses Raven's neck.

Raven pulls out of the kiss and says to Autumn, "Have you met my girlfriend, Jess?"

Jess brushes the curls from her face and flirts, "Yes, we met on solstice. How are you, Autumn?"

Raven interrupts with an inspired idea. "How would you like to be tied up with Autumn?"

"Sounds fun! Let me wrap up my tickle war." She catches the nearby blonde and they sway together as they hug.

Raven says to Autumn, "I'm going to get my ropes and talk with Violet, are you open to us doing naughty things to you while you're tied?"

Autumn smiles and says, "I like the sound of that."

"Okay, I'll do a little negotiation. Stay here."

When Violet wraps up her small group demo of the fucking machine, Raven pulls her aside. "I've got an idea for a scene where we can play as equals. You up for it?"

"It depends. Does it involve dental dams?"

"Definitely not," Raven states.

"Okay then, I'm in."

"How would you like for both of us to double-dom Autumn and Jess with ropes and other toys?"

"Hell yes!" Violet squeals.

With minimal negotiation, they clear a space in the center of the room, laying out a sheet and an array of toys.

Jess and Autumn are placed back to back, blindfolded. They stand with feet wide apart. Their two girlfriends, respectively Raven and Violet, work in tandem as if they share one mind, four arms, and one huge open heart. They weave a complex double harness, which squishes their subs' breasts between ropes, and their arms are bound so they are immobile while being flogged, tickled, and teased. A vibrator is used randomly on the rope, buzzing through the entire arrangement. As a wave of pleasure arises in one woman, the other feels it reverberating in her own body. The Eros generated by this scene is so powerful it resonates throughout the room.

Raven and Violet catch each other's eyes and share knowing nods and reassuring grins. In the beginning, Raven predominately plays with Jess, and Violet attends to Autumn. As Violet gains confidence, she creeps around to pinch Jess's nipples or scratch her thighs, which gives Raven permission to steal a squeeze or a spank on Autumn's tender flesh.

At one point Raven spontaneously grabs Autumn's face and steals her first kiss. It is questionably consensual and decidedly one directional, but it is a first kiss, nonetheless. After what feels like an hour, Raven asks everyone for their final requests before they cocreate a slow, meaningful untying ritual.

Violet keeps both blindfolds on them until the very last moment. She turns the women toward each other and brings all four of their heads together in a final gesture of prayer. "As we give you back the gift of sight, may we be freed from the illusion of separation. May we feel that we're always connected and look through eyes of love."

With a nod, Violet slips Autumn's blindfold off at the same instant Raven removes Jess's. Kisses are shared amongst all four.

During the closing circle, Violet announces that her highlight was getting to tag-team dominate her new girlfriend, Autumn, with Raven's assistance. Upon hearing Violet call Autumn her girlfriend, Raven feels so much love welling in her heart, there is no room for jealousy.

FRIDAY #31

Foursome

Excitement is high. Ever since Damien's return, there've been multiple phone calls, voice messages, and texts in anticipation of this big date. Both couples are in minimal clothing, seated on Damien and Violet's bed. Even though Nick is emotionally comfortable setting intentions before group sex, his muscular body is not physically comfortable sitting cross-legged. Violet adjusts his posture with extra pillows. Once everyone is settled and holding hands, Raven guides them through a few rounds of breathing.

"Thanks for being willing to experiment. My favorite way to start a group scene is to hear everyone's desires, fears, and boundaries."

Damien begins, "As you know, Violet and I have only played with other women. Seeing her with another man feels like a healthy stretch for us." Damien turns to Nick. "Especially you.

Not only because of your experience in poly and group sex, but because you've been so generous in sharing your wife."

Nick jokingly interrupts, "And now you want to repay the favor; thanks, bro."

Violet giggles.

Damien cracks a smile and continues, "Also, it's been a while since Raven and I've made love, and I'd like to rescript the negative trigger that Violet had around us connecting. But I know how quickly sex can bring up old wounds. If anyone gets triggered, I'd rather pause than try to push through. Can we all agree to that? I know I'd enjoy myself more knowing we are all being self-responsible."

"Agreed," Raven says, and Violet nods.

Nick jokes, "Well, you're not likely to trigger me, as long as you use plenty of lube for anal."

"Understood." Damien adds an exaggerated wink.

Nick goes next. "Well, my boundary is no pain. No matter how hot things get, please don't spank or bite me. Which is one of the things I love about group sex—I get to admire Raven being dominant without being the one dominated."

"I can be your surrogate submissive," Violet says, and she fist bumps Nick.

"Seeing my wife in pleasure is my number-one greatest turn-on. I especially love the way she moans when she's taken by another man."

"I have fond memories of you enjoying her sounds," Damien recalls.

Eager to share, Violet says, "My turn?"

"Almost. I don't want anyone to take it personally if I don't get hard. As much as I love group sex, it sometimes brings up performance anxiety, and sometimes it takes me longer to cum than usual, but I know how to work around it."

"Thanks for mentioning it," Damien says.

Violet can't stop grinning. "My heart is so open to every-one. I don't have any boundaries right now, not even if you all wanted to gangbang me without lube."

Raven looks knowingly at Damien and smirks. "That's our little slut."

Violet quickly cradles her boobs and adds, "Oh! Don't forget, my nips are supersensitive, so go easy on my boobies, please."

Raven kisses Violet's hand, takes a deep breath, and begins, "Obviously, the most natural thing for me would be to domi-nate this little bitch. It may even be the best way to get the party started, and when it feels right, I want to drop in with Damien. I feel like our making love would be so healing."

Damien prompts, "And do you have any boundaries?"

"My biggest challenge tonight is feeling free. I don't want to be restrained in any way, including my sense of sight. No restrictions means no ropes or blindfolds on me, but I wouldn't mind tying Violet up. How does that sound?"

"Yes, please. Can we have a group hug first?" Violet giggles with delight.

"Of course!"

They melt into a puddle of arms, legs, and fleshy bodies pressing against one another on the bed. After a few deep sighs, Violet starts to giggle and Raven pulls herself away to fetch a red rope.

Upon returning she commands, "Hold her arms behind her back!"

Both men spring into service as Raven prepares the rope. Damien blindfolds Violet while Nick guides her to her knees at the foot of the bed, giving everyone more space to move around her, tickling and teasing her neck and face as Raven binds her body. After only a few minutes of sensual stroking, she cries, "Stick something inside me already!"

Raven retorts, "Are you trying to top from the bottom? Someone is going to have to stuff something in your mouth and force you to shut up."

Nick looks to Damien for permission. Damien offers a nod of approval, and watches as Nick teases Violet's lips with his soft cock. It looks like he's applying lipstick, at first. With her hands tied behind her, she stretches her lips and tongue out, pleading for more. Raven swiftly threads the rope around Violet's body several times, without disrupting the connection between Violet's mouth and Nick's hardening cock.

When Violet is sufficiently tied, Raven steps around Violet, close to Damien. He grabs her shoulders and kisses her open mouth. She's surprised at how quickly his hot kiss disarms her dominance. She steadies herself against Damien's hips and suddenly remembers she's still holding Violet's ropes. She pauses to hand them off to Nick, who receives them with a knowing nod.

Damien pulls Raven onto the bed to resume their kiss. It feels as if their lips had never separated. It's like Raven is remembering something that was happening before she was born, and though she's been interrupted many times before, it will continue in some alternate dimension for eternity.

Damien's hands work their way down her shoulders to her ass with a firmness that liquifies her. Soon the warmth between her legs overtakes her belly and heart. Her fingers find his erection, hard and cool to the touch. Like marble, he is smooth on the outside, yet firm as a statue. Such a stunning contrast. She traces his shaft with the reverence she'd show for a museum masterpiece. Her fingers lightly adoring Rodin, Bernini, Michelangelo . . . her mind flashes to a series of timeless shapes. It's like she is a muse swimming in a stream of consciousness during the Renaissance.

He whispers, "I want to be inside you."

Raven moans and reaches for a condom the way an artist

would reach for her favored paintbrush. She maintains deep eye contact as he hovers over her, rolls it down his shaft, and aims his cock directly above her yoni. She yearns to close the gap, and is equally eager to savor all of the sensations in between. He presses his fist against her temple doors and slowly slips the head of his cock into her opening. Raven gasps in pleasure, then cringes at the friction. She glances in the direction of the lube on the dresser. He wordlessly understands and licks his hand and strokes himself before entering her a second time.

Ah! Raven sighs as he plunges deeper. The pleasure is far greater than the discomfort. Neither of them wants much movement. Only a slow rocking in the hips as they lose themselves in each other's gaze. Raven is struck by how much she misses him, even now that he is inside her; she longs to be closer. It's not her mind that missed him, or her heart. But her body just can't get close enough. He slides even deeper, confirming that the missing is mutual.

Raven catches a sideways glance at Violet and Nick, who are still engaged in deep oral. Her bitch is in heat, enthusiastically sucking her husband. It's not just sucking, but face-fucking. This pleases her.

Her gaze returns to Damien, who is smiling. So much love in his eyes. A laughter arises from somewhere deep within, then suddenly turns into uncontrollable sobbing. Damien tightens his grip on her shoulders and anchors himself firmly inside her as she convulses with emotion. When the intensity subsides, she simply says, "I missed you."

"I'm right here." He rocks his hips slowly to the rhythm of her sobbing. He can feel the passion concentrated in her pelvis and rolling through her heart. He matches her breath, and surfs every wave of energy streaming from her cervix to her throat. Raven realizes that she and Violet are moaning in unison, but not by each other's hand.

As Raven becomes more cognizant of her surroundings, she feels a warm presence on the bed beside her and Damien.

She turns to find Nick has untied Violet and they are lying beside her on the bed, smiling. Nick finally speaks, "Hey, Damien. Did you break my wife?"

Wiping away the tears, Raven says, "Sorry. It's just been so long."

"It's beautiful. I knew you would cry," Damien says with a satisfied smile.

Everyone here knows that Raven is quick to tears. It's a known quantity, just as Violet is quick to giggles.

"Beautiful," Violet echoes, obviously still in erotic trance herself.

Nick makes an offer. "Since it's a significant first, I thought you might want to witness Violet making love to another man."

Still inside Raven, Damien says, "Thank you."

Raven clears her throat. "Oooh, can I help put Nick's cock inside you?"

Violet squeals, "Yes, please."

All four bodies are as close as possible. Raven reaches across to stroke Nick's cock, which is still wet and hard from Violet's sucking.

"I can't believe how natural this feels," Damien says, leaning across to kiss Violet.

Nick manages to apply a condom and squirt lube into Raven's hand. She strokes Nick to the same steady rhythm of her own hips as she is being penetrated by Damien. Raven plugs Nick's cock into Violet's yoni and delights in the sound of her girlfriend's gasp.

"So beautiful," Damien repeats, admiring his beloved as Nick picks up the rhythm.

"Yes," Violet whispers, throwing her head back in pleasure.

Raven experiences Violet's pleasure from the inside with

Damien's hardening cock. Raven now feels nothing is withheld, not even other lovers. All four beloveds interlocking side by side. It doesn't matter that they have swapped partners. Nobody belongs to anybody. In this moment, everyone belongs to the universe.

ACT IV

RAVEN'S PLAYBOOK

On stage I simply shared who I was, which happens to be a lot of things that a lot of people love to judge and to hate; an ex-prostitute, a pornographer, a witch, a Jew, a lesbian, a feminist, and yes...a performance artist. Interestingly, the people who expressed the most hatred never met me or saw my work.

—ANNIE SPRINKLE

Annie Sprinkle is my mentor because she inspires me to explore the limits of the body, magnitude of the mind, and scope of the soul.

Violet West is my muse because she is the antidote to all the judgment and hate that my art has ever received. When we are together, a new body of revelational work is produced.

Each Friday is an unrepeatable performance for which there is no audience. Perhaps one day, the unscripted scenes from my playbook will find a way onto the stage.

—RAVEN TURNER

FRIDAY #32

Spread-Eagle

I pinned Violet against the futon and positioned my hips between her legs, then spread her legs wide while maintaining a passionate kiss. "How do you feel when I split you open?" I whispered.

"I'm so vulnerable!" she protested, her skirt hiked up to her waist.

I spread her legs farther until her purple lace G-string was totally exposed. "How would you like to be rigged to a spreader bar so you can't close your legs, even if you tried?"

"Do I have a choice?" Violet said, both thrilled and resistant.

"And then I want to stretch your pussy open even wider with my fist," I said, prying Violet's panties down her ankles. I made a show of drawing them to my face and inhaling.

Violet hastily unbuttoned her blouse, revealing a matching

purple bra. The lacy half cup held her round breasts in place as she pulled off her shirt. Then off with the skirt, and finally, with a flick of my fingers, I unbound her boobs.

I felt unbearably blessed to have such a masterpiece in my bed, naked and willing.

Violet's mouth was drawn to my face like a magnet. Her octopus-like limbs reached around my back, trying to peel off my top. But I stopped her—I needed my composure.

I grabbed the duffel bag at the foot of the futon and fumbled around to produce a stainless-steel spreader bar, complete with Velcro wrist and ankle restraints, brand new, still in the original box.

"Oooh . . . it looks like a torture tool," Violet squealed.

"Damien gave it to me weeks ago, so you can relax knowing that he knows all about my little plan."

Truth is, I didn't have much of a plan. I felt a hint of the old familiar imposter syndrome rearing its head. I reminded myself that the success of a scene doesn't depend on toys and gadgets, but the emotional connection. Instead of praying for courage and setting intentions, I decided to blindfold her. I tugged a decorative scarf from my duffel bag and hoped it would obscure my insecurity.

"Are you ready for this?" I asked.

"Ready for anything, my Queen," Violet said, and I felt her body relax under my touch. I planted a gentle kiss on her forehead, throat, heart, belly. . . . I took my time at each chakra.

Violet moaned with each kiss. Whenever the good queen is present, Violet is held in a field of love and trust. But as I approached her nether lips, I could feel the blood lust of the dark queen. I felt torn between the hunger for instant gratification and the sweetness of anticipation.

Then I remembered her flower is a gift, a rare blossom, like an edible fruit that must not be eaten until perfectly ripe. Violet lifted her hips, beckoning her queen to consume her, but I simply sampled with a few sweet nibbles. I didn't dare ruin my appetite.

With a firm grip, I trapped Violet's wrists and dragged her diagonally toward the bedpost where I could restrain her hands. Consciously, Violet knew the cuffs were easy-release Velcro, but I told her to imagine the restraints were iron shackles and she was in a medieval dungeon. Once I fixed her to the bedposts, I pinched her sensitive nipple, and she howled like an animal being drawn out for slaughter. I then administered a slap to each of her inner thighs.

The second set of slaps were delivered simultaneously to both of her stinging thighs. Then I made her wait...so she would be wondering what was coming next. Uncertainty is known to induce a submissive spell.

Then the hungry queen bit her open inner thighs and began plucking at Violet's flower with firm fingers. Violet squirmed at the sensation of teeth, then nails, and eventually yelped when I landed a flat hand on her flower, crushing it.

The dark queen was not seduced by Violet's pleas. I felt eager to humiliate my subject. I turned my attention to the new toy in its long cardboard box. Violet whimpered when she heard me crack into it.

"No whining," I said as the crumpling sounds turned into cold metal clanking. I grabbed Violet's ankles roughly and strapped her to the spreader bar. But her legs only slightly spread—not even as wide as her arms! I fidgeted with the contraption, desperately trying to expand its length, to no avail.

I stood on the futon and lifted the bar toward the sky, carrying Violet's legs with it. Her spine rolled easily into a shoulder stand. I peered at her yoni from above. It seemed so helpless, suspended midair, but not for long. I rolled her back down onto a pillow I positioned under her hips. "I have total access to your flower, you can't close your legs or get away."

"Is this as far as it spreads?" Violet said, speaking my disappointment.

"The damn bar doesn't extend," I growled, "so this is all you get."

"Are you serious?" she whined.

To which I pinched and flicked at the hood of her clit.

"Ow!" She squirmed. "You're being nasty."

"Are you questioning me?"

"Sorry my Queen."

"I'm going to have to spank you for talking back," I said, and I spanked her inner thighs a few times each. Then I stood up. "This will not do! Wait here." I laughed and swung the door open so she could feel the cool outside air against her skin.

"You're just going to leave me like this?" Violet cried.

"Not only am I leaving you naked and unfucked, but I'm leaving the door open so anyone can walk right in. A nosy neighbor could just come in and take advantage of you." Violet froze and remained silent, listening as I left the playroom.

After a minute, I returned with a broom and duct tape from the garage. I brushed the bristles against Violet's side and her nipples immediately puckered. "You are a filthy slut and I'm going to clean you up with this peasant's broom."

She shivered and squealed, and I couldn't tell if she was titillated or irritated. I continued sweeping her legs and toes.

Next, I repositioned the broomstick in place of the small spreader bar and taped her ankles to the wooden dowel.

Violet stiffened at the sound of duct tape ripping as I unrolled it and fastened her feet farther apart. Next I landed a breathy hot kiss on her mouth. "I'm going to miss your lips," I said, holding the big gray roll close to her face. "Take your last deep breath from your mouth, and then breathe only through your nose," I said before spreading the duct tape across Violet's face. "I don't want any more objections from you!"

Still unsatisfied with the distance between her legs, I ripped one of the curtain rods off the wall and let the curtains spill recklessly across the dresser and partially onto the floor. Even though Violet couldn't see or speak, I'm sure she could feel the whole room grow brighter. I unbound her ankle from the broomstick and refastened it to the cold curtain rod. I extended the bar as far as it would go and used the duct tape to hold the adjustable joint. Finally, her legs were split wide.

Her milky thighs were exposed, and her yoni was in full blossom. I stood back to admire my work, and momentarily took pity on my dumb, blind hostage. She was bound, gagged, and deprived of sight, so she couldn't share in the appreciation of this moment. With a sigh, I decided to remove the blindfold.

Violet's pupils took a moment to adjust, but when they did, she had an intense look of adoration toward her captor. I left the duct tape on her face because it pleased me. I asked her if she felt exposed because the window was naked and anyone could walk by and see her completely spread-eagle.

"Mmmm-hmmm." She nodded.

Next, I sat between her legs and ripped open a condom. Then I held my fingers together as if holding a pinch of salt. With my free hand, I rolled the rubber down my fingertips, and stretched it over my knuckles, ending at my wrist. "This is going inside of you," I said, wiggling my fingers as if fitting into a glove.

Violet made a muffled sound.

I applied lube. "You're already sopping wet, but I'm going to use extra lube since you've never been fisted," I said, massaging her wetness with my bare hand.

If Violet wanted to close her legs, the curtain rod wouldn't let her. I could tell by the way her flower was visibly opening that she wanted more. I strummed her clit with my bare fingers. I propped my elbow against my hip bone and held my hand as if it were an enormous erection. I entered her slowly at first with the tips of my fingers. When I felt her soft tissue surrounding my hand as far as I could go, I began a steady rhythm and opened her farther. Little by little I slid deeper, until eventually even my thumb was swallowed by the natural rhythm of her arousal.

Violet was trying to help by rocking her hips, but we stalled out at my knuckles. I leaned forward and kissed Violet's duct tape.

That did nothing for either of us, except make Violet laugh a little.

"I love you, baby," I said, gazing into her eyes.

The fantasy realm dissolved and my heart flooded with love and light. Even though there was still duct tape over her mouth, Violet seemed to be saying it back, *I love you. I love you. I love you,* with every piston of my hand.

Then suddenly, I was in.

My whole hand was inside her.

Violet's eyes grew wide. I'm sure mine were just as large. Our mirror neurons were firing in perfect sync. We were both panting in rhythm, with no separation between us. My hand still dancing in and out, we were two women who felt like one. She'd never let me so deep, and I'd never felt closer.

In a flash, the dark queen was back, feeling deliciously naughty. Violet transformed into an insubordinate little maid-servant seeking punishment for her sins. Violet began moaning, and the duct tape over her mouth worked itself partially free. As if in an act of mercy, the queen leaned in and ripped it off.

"Thank you," is all Violet could say. "Thank you. Thank you. Thank you." I knew she wasn't thanking me about the duct tape, but for the waves of pleasure that streamed through her body.

I received her gratitude and silently returned it with the voice in my head: *Thank you for trusting me. Thank you for being trustworthy. Thank you for letting me in. Thank you for being you.*

Overcome with Eros, energy, and emotion, Violet cried, "I feel full . . . So full."

"You want me to slow down?"

"A little." And Violet said, with foggy eyes, "I love you."

"I know."

"Hug me."

I paused the movement of my wrist and held her with my free arm. Violet tightened around my hand, then suddenly she opened. She felt so vast inside. "Want more?"

"Hold on." She took a big breath, then her whole being relaxed. "No. I'm full." After a few more breaths, she said, "I'm ready for you to pull out."

"Okay, I'm moving slow," I said as I withdrew, holding my free hand at the entrance like a temple guard. Watching over her, ready to respond to her every whim.

"What do you need baby?"

"Cuddles."

No sooner did I unbind Violet's arms, then they were wrapped around me.

The entire queendom disappeared like a dream. All games were gone. Illusions lifted. We were just two naked women, spooning on a queen-sized futon.

FRIDAY #33

Fire Ritual by Raven

The smoke billowed from the cauldron into the blue, cloudless sky as I lit a bundle of sage from the fire and passed it over each sacred object. The altar was made by laying a scarf on the lawn. A candle, a chalice, a feather, and my crystal dildo were arranged in each of the four directions. My ritual knife and rattle were also within reach. Violet stepped out into the backyard and placed a wide-brimmed hat on my head to match the one on hers.

"A ball cap would have been fine." I smiled. "I just needed a little sun protection."

"Are you kidding?" she giggled. "These hats make us look like real witches."

"We *are* real witches . . ." I poked the knife into the cauldron to arrange the kindling. "And this is a real ritual. We don't need warts to prove it. Are you ready?"

"Just one more thing . . ." Violet leaned across the altar to gently kiss my mouth. "Okay. I'm ready now."

"Thanks for the important addition. Now, let's close our eyes and tune in to the place where intentions are born. Deep breath, feeling grateful.

"Breathing into the highest frequency of love we can authentically access, we ask God/Goddess, to support us in transcending the small self so the God force can come through. Let's open by chanting the mantra, Om Ah Hung."

Together with we sounded:

"Ommmmm."

"Ahhhhhhhhhh."

"Hunnnnnnng."

After a moment of silence, I said, "Next I will call upon the seven directions, and after I shake my rattle, you can join me by saying, 'Aho.'"

"Can I get something from the house first?" Violet asked.

"Quick, before I cast the circle, otherwise"—I picked up the ritual knife—"I'll have to cut you a door."

"Oooh, is that what that is for?" She added seductively, "I was hoping you'd use it for something kinky later."

"Go! Do what you need to do," I commanded.

While she was inside, I took a moment to hold the knife to my third eye, and silently thanked the universe for providing this life, this lover, and the mystery of our future together.

Violet tiptoed back with a flute and explained, "I haven't played in a long time."

"Perfect, use your intuition for the perfect time to play." I proceeded to invoke, evoke, invite, and embody each direction.

". . . And finally, to the direction of the center. The ancient keeper of the True Self. We turn inward and invoke all elements, the divine masculine, and the divine feminine, to come to make love within our hearts."

After several breaths, feeling the energy flowing through the central channel, Violet picked up her flute and gingerly, tripping over a few notes at first, began playing with growing devotion. The effect was moving.

When she laid down her instrument, I said, "Truly, beautiful." Then I continued, "Now the magic of transmutation is made manifest with conscious consideration of both light and shadow. Before we offer anything to the Agni, or fire ritual, let's feel into that which we are ready to call into our lives. I'll start."

I held a small symbolic broomstick to my heart, and after a few breaths I spoke: "Although I have a number of old habits and patterns that I'd love to drop into the flames, the one I'm most eager to release is the desire to possess and punish. It's fun to play with those impulses as a way to bring our conditioning to light, but when they don't empower true love, I want to cast them away."

I swept the ritual broom around my aura a few times, then plucked a single straw out, held it above the cauldron, and incanted, "I hereby release the pattern of possessiveness and punishment so I can liberate myself from its temptation." Then I tossed it into the flames to watch it incinerate in a hypnotic dance.

"Aho!" Violet echoed, and she accepted the broom. "Okay. I think what I need to let go of most is the old story that sex is dirty or naughty. I still get this guilty feeling that I'm going to hell, so in order to let myself enjoy it, I feel I have to be tied up and forced. Don't get me wrong, I still want to be tied up and forced, but out of pleasure, not guilt, if that makes sense." I nodded, and she brushed herself in the same fashion, pulled a strand from the broom, and said, "I'm releasing the whole story that sex is somehow not spiritual."

"Aho," we said together.

We gazed into each other's eyes, illuminated from across the cauldron, and she couldn't resist the overwhelming urge to come closer and kiss me. I interrupted with, "Now, as our shadows are brought to light, we can offer libations to the Goddess."

I playfully produced a bottle of wine from my knapsack, as if pulling a rabbit from a magician's hat.

"I thought you didn't drink?" she asked.

"Only a little, in ceremony. But I couldn't pass this up, it's a new label called 'Bitch' wine." I opened the bottle and poured generously onto the ground. "I offer this libation in honor of our ancestors, especially the healers and the witches whose faith went underground."

I positioned the chalice in Violet's hand and told her to "hold steady." I raised the bottle to the sky and dramatically poured a thin ribbon, which overflowed from the full cup and spilled onto the ground.

"I libate to all the circumstances that have conspired to bring us together," I said.

Violet added, "Especially Damien and Nick."

"May you never thirst!" I said, encouraging her to drink. Then I took a sip from the shared cup, and gazed into her eyes.

Violet coughed. "It works for a symbolic offering, but for an aperitif, not so much."

"Don't be a wine snob. Let's make another libation."

Violet raised the cup and said, "I libate to Autumn for sharing our love and sexual healing." She took a swig.

"I libate to our lovemaking," I said before sipping.

She flirted back with, "I libate to more orgasms."

"I second that libation." I put my arm around her.

"I libate to more rituals!"

"Really?" I asked. "You want more?"

"Of course! This is great," Violet said, smiling.

"Be careful what you ask for," I said, and then we shared a moment of reverence. A few breaths to feel the power of the intentions we'd set. Then Violet surprised me with her final libation:

"To the universe for answering our prayers. Especially the ones I was too afraid to ask for . . . like my meeting you."

"Aho!" I affirmed. Then I cupped Violet's face and pulled her lips to mine. Our tongues sealed the magic as my hand found its way to her ponytail, pulling her head back to expose her neck. I growled at her jugular like a feral animal. Soon, we were sniffing at each other, rolling around, biting, licking, stripping each other's clothes off, and feasting from each other's bodies upon the Earth.

Breathless and spent, we collapsed, resting with intertwined limbs until Violet noticed and pointed out, "The fire is going out."

I reached over to the nearly empty bottle and poured it over the embers. "This final libation goes to Agni the god of fire." She sparked and sputtered before fading. "Thank you for taking our prayers to the heavens with your power of transmutation." I looked at Violet and asked, "Anything else, for closure?"

"I'm good."

I placed my hands at my heart center and said, "Thanks to the seven directions. The circle is open but unbroken."

"Aho." Violet's eyes sparkled. "Now what?"

"Traditionally, at the closing of a ceremony, Pagans break bread, but since we've already feasted on each other, we can just rest," I said, pulling my goddess into my arms for a long sweet cuddle.

Suddenly, the sliding door from the house opened and Damien walked out. He was obviously humored by the sight of us lounging by a cauldron. "Look at you two, like arsonists at a crime scene."

"Hi, baby! You just missed our ritual." Violet rose to greet him.

Damien grabbed the rattle and chanted, "Hummina! Hummina!" while playfully skipping around the altar.

Violet laughed, but said, "Don't be nasty. This is serious."

"Serious?" He picked up the wine and rolled his eyes. "Right. I can see that."

I sneered at him. "If I didn't just exhaust myself with your woman, I would take you over my knee."

"What kind of spell did you cast, anyway?" he asked, sitting beside me and kissing my forehead. "Should I be worried?"

"No, but there is something I actually want to talk to you about," I told Damien.

Violet interjected, "What is it?"

I took a moment to pique their interest. "During the ritual, Violet made a powerful declaration, and I got the hint that it might be time for her to meet my mentor."

"Charles Muir?" Damien said.

"Have you met him?" Violet asked.

"Damien studied with him last year." I interlaced my legs with Violet's on top of Damien's. "Which is why he's so good with his hands."

Violet's eyes (and probably her vulva) lit up with excitement. "I want to meet this man!"

"Well, he's coming to town in a few weeks and I think you'd get a lot out of doing the intensive." I smiled at Damien. "You both would."

"Is this because I said I wanted more ritual?" Violet asked.

"Yes, and specifically because you're working on healing the split between sex and spirit. It's a commitment; it's a three-day immersion."

"Charles Muir's teachings are invaluable, Violet. I'd love to go with you, but this is my busiest month," Damien apologized.

"You've got two weeks," I pleaded. "It's not until the Friday after next."

After thinking about it for a moment, Violet said, "So if I went, I'd have to share our Friday date with the whole workshop, and I'd miss my date night with Damien?"

Damien is deadpan: "And what makes you think I'm going to let you enroll my girlfriend in another yoga cult? I've barely finished deprograming her from the last one."

"Because you know I'll bring her back versed in the art of lovemaking. She can come home each night and practice her new skills on you."

"Sold," he declared.

"Really?" Violet could barely contain herself.

"Yeah," he smiled, "Actually, I've been wanting you to meet him."

"I feel so blessed to have both of you in my life." Violet kissed Damien, and then me, and then Damien again. "You are both my teachers, and now I get to drink from to the source!"

FRIDAY #34
Yoga Cult

Violet came straight from her yoga class to my playroom, still wearing a sweaty tank and stretch pants that accentuated her curves. I interrupted our hello kiss when I remembered something I'd been meaning to ask.

"Where did you get the evil idea that sex and spirit were separate in the first place?"

Violet rolls her eyes. "You mean besides my parents both being so religious? Even after I left home to teach at Parvati's yoga studio, I was taught sexual energy is a distraction from enlightenment."

"No wonder you call it a yoga cult," I tease.

"It was a cult! Parvati was fierce. She trained in a particular lineage with a guru, but splintered off to create her own brand, and publicly chastised anyone who strayed from her practice."

I fingered the holes in her top, feeling for the warmth of her skin as our bodies lay entwined on the futon. "How did you ever get mixed up with this dragon lady?"

"I was searching for something. She talked about god-realization. When you're sexually confused, she said, all you have to do is breathe and sublimate. She thought sex leaks life-force energy, which is the fuel needed to reach nirvana."

"That's rich," I laughed. "Are you open to working on this?"

Violet shot me a skeptical smirk. "I've done plenty of therapy, for years after my sexual abuse. It's not very sexy."

"Oh yeah? What was your therapist like?"

"She was a wrinkly old woman with a lopsided face, but an excellent listener."

I smiled suggestively. "You know, there are certain kinds of traumas that can't be healed with talk therapy."

"I've tried primal scream, tapping, and all kinds of somatic healing," Violet defends.

"But some sexual trauma can't be released until we raise the energy to match the intensity in which it was created."

Violet softened with a big breath and said, "Okay. I'm open."

I leaped to the corner to snag a couple of yoga mats and unfurled them side by side in the middle of the playroom. "What was Parvati's yoga room like?"

"It was an old brick building with mirrors on the walls. There was a corridor with two futons in the lobby where people would sit and sip tea. The staff room was behind the front desk. Behind that was a little secret nook for Parvati only."

I tossed a handful of pillows around the mats and motioned for Violet to join me on the floor.

"Okay," I said, "let's play like you're leading a class."

"I feel like the front of the class would be"—Violet pulled one of the mats into position—"here." She sat cross-legged with a straight spine.

"Imagine you're teaching your last class of the day."

Violet giggled with closed eyes. "This is kinky already."

"Deep breath, now," I redirected her. "The class is full. Amongst all the different bodies in the room, there is one man in orange robes. You didn't notice him at first, but now you're sure he's Parvati's guru. He has come to observe your progress. You feel his eyes upon you. You feel a strong desire to impress him. Go ahead and lead the class."

Eager to comply, Violet reached up and began directing an imaginary class. "Elongate your spine and let all your posterior muscles melt down toward the Earth." She moved gracefully into a forward bend.

I took my place behind her, pressed my breasts gently against her back, and whispered into her ear, "He's watching you teach. You feel his gaze on your every move. Your whole body lights up."

Violet continued, "Last two breaths here. Then a gentle counter stretch." She reached back and lifted her pelvis into a reverse plank. "Moving into a twist." Her knees moved one direction while her head turned the opposite.

"His presence is turning you on, but you remember Parvati's words, 'Sex is a temptation.' So you think he might have come here to test you. You go around the room adjusting all the other students, but you don't dare touch his holiness."

Violet rotated her body in the opposite direction.

After her counter pose I directed her, "It's time for Savasana. You guide everyone into their final resting pose so you can finally lay your hands on him. I'm going to be him now, and you're going to prove your devotion." I spread my body out on the opposite mat.

Violet approached my reclining body reverently, placing her hands on my feet as she called out, "Relax your feet. Feet are relaxed. Relax your heels and ankles. Heels and ankles are relaxed. . . ."

"Just touching his holy feet created a bolt of streaming bliss through your body. When you look closer, you can tell he walks around barefoot a lot because he has callouses. Then you see a slight lump around his crotch that is rising under his thin cotton robe. Did your touch arouse him?"

Violet released the light hold on my feet and floated toward my head. I pulled her into a kiss, then a spooning position, so I could continue whispering into her ear as I stuffed my hand into her stretch pants and squeezed her blossoming flower between two fingers.

"When you close the class, everyone floats out of the room, except him. He stays. He says he heard about your sexual confusion from Parvati and has come for a private lesson with you."

Violet moaned.

"You're not sure if he means a lesson from you or for you, but you are happy to comply with whatever he wants. He tells you to lock the doors." Violet's breath became erratic as I worked my fingers into the gateway of her yoni.

"'Do you know why we do Asana?' he asks. He is testing you."

Violet managed to vocalize through her pleasure, "To prepare the body."

"'To prepare the body for what?'"

"For higher . . . unhhh . . . levels of consciousness," she whispered through heavy breathing. "So we can sit longer . . . mmm . . . and resist the fluctuations of mind and the temptations . . . ahhhhh . . . of pleasure."

Secretly, I smiled as my movements became more forceful. "'Correct. We prepare the body so we can give it to God,' he says, "When I sit cross-legged in meditation, I am opening my hips and preparing myself for the Goddess to come sit on my lap. To sit in Yab Yum. Do you know this position?'"

"Of course, it's mother-father pose."

"He asks you to sit on his lap. He wants to give you a special teaching."

I pulled her onto my lap, a position that penetrated the veil between fantasy and reality. Our foreheads came together for one transcendental moment.

I repositioned my fingers deeper inside. "Then you feel the warmth rising from his sex chakra. You feel his cock growing hard and pressing against your yoga pants. You want to grind your ass against him and mount his cock, but you resist."

"Mmm-hmmm."

I imitated the guru's voice through my own arousal, "'Are you ready for your darshan?' he asks. And just when you expect him to force himself inside you . . . he gets up and pushes you onto all fours and directs you to do cat/cow."

I repositioned her sharply and pulled her tank and sports bra up to reveal the smooth white skin on her breasts. Then I positioned her facedown against a pillow and tugged her pants down but left her G-string, moved it aside as I pressed two fingers deeper toward her womb.

"You move slowly. Placing your hands and feet in perfect alignment with your hips and shoulders. He walks behind you and instructs you to pull down your pants. He says he needs to see your anus to know if you're in proper alignment.

"He observes as you slowly wiggle your pants down your hips and step out of them like a striptease, leaving only your G-string. Of course, you both know a mere G-string is not a real barrier. If he wanted to, he could easily pluck it aside and stuff his cock in you." I plunged my fingers in and out to the rhythm of her little moans.

"You can hear him breathing behind you. He walks around to see your face, and you look up to find his rod is at full mast. He positions it right at eye level and he says, 'Now I think you are ready for the most advanced teaching...'" I broke character for a moment and asked, "What's that submissive pose called? The one where you're sitting back on your heels?"

"Vajrasana," she moaned.

"Right, so you sit in Vajrasana, watching as he adjusts his Punjabi pants and pulls up his kurta. His bright red member springs forward, calling out to be touched. You decide this is a test, so you sit obediently waiting for his direction. He puts his blushing penis an inch away from your mouth. 'Do you know why we teach Brahmacharya?'"

"So we don't . . . ahhh . . . squander our sexual . . . mmm . . . energy," Violet said in a breathy moan.

"Correct. Again," I said, pressing firmly on her entire vulva as she shuddered against my hand. "And if you can't see my divinity right now, you are stuck in duality. Do you believe I am God?"

Violet's body convulsed in waves of pleasure as she came on my wrist and screamed, "Yes, Master!"

Afterward, I laid her firmly against the pillow and pulled down my own pants. "Are you ready to surrender to his God Force?" I straddled her face and stuffed my wet clit into her mouth like a cock. She sucked and licked like she was starving.

"Slowly, remember you are kissing God's genitals. He keeps pushing it forward, poking your lips until you take him in fully. Mmmmm yes... Like that." I grabbed at her breasts as I ground against her chin.

My whole body shuddered as I said, "Then he orders you onto all fours again so he can push his cock into your mouth harder until he's fucking your face." She lapped at my yoni with her frenzied tongue, sending pleasure through my body. "Then he asks, 'Are you ready to learn about the seed of life?'"

Violet mumbles against my crotch, "Yes, please Master."

"'That's it,'" I said, feeling the ejaculation rising from my core. "He pulls the head of his cock out, and holds it with his thumb, and takes a deep breath . . . unhhhh . . . he's holding it. . . . You whimper, you want it. But you feel the kundalini rising up both your bodies, then unhhhh . . . He shoots his hot cum on your face and chest." My body shook with a powerful orgasm as her mouth continued to feast on my hot fluids. I broke the suction to dip my fingertips into her mouth, feeling my own juice mixed with her saliva. I dismounted Violet's face and repositioned myself beside her.

"Afterward, he rubs a warm wet hand across your chest, in big circles over your breasts and nipples as he mutters mantras."

I held my hand on her heart as we breathed down from the fantasy dimension, back into our bodies. Reality resumed with tender kisses and caresses.

"How was that?" I asked.

"Strangely disturbing and also deeply arousing. Like a fucked-up, sacrilegious therapy session."

"Yup." I smiled. "That about sums it up."

Tantra Training

Violet's body looked as if it belonged there, lying in the center of the hotel ballroom, on a mat, adorned in a golden robe, surrounded by a circle of students. Charles Muir stood beside her addressing the class. Nick and I sat near her feet, listening to his impassioned address.

"Many women remember their first sacred spot massage as a religious experience, while some describe it as uncomfortable or embarrassing but it's always liberating. Regardless, our role is to practice presence and open a channel for the receiver to move through whatever they need for the highest healing to come through, no matter what comes up.

"In a moment we will begin the demo, but first I want to remind everyone not to think of it as just a demonstration, but as a sacred healing rite deserves your full attention. As Violet heals, so do we. Please hold your questions until after, unless there are any now?"

Nick raises his hand. "Will you be doing a demo for men as well?"

"Thanks for volunteering," Charles teases with a smile. "Fair question. The sacred spot refers to both the G-spot in women and the prostate in men. Now we are focused on the Goddess spot. Your home-play will be to practice with your tantra buddy. We will have a separate ritual where the men get to receive. We will dedicate plenty of time to prepare. So men, you can relax and focus on being of service. Any other questions?"

The room was eager to begin.

"All right. Violet has courageously volunteered for this ritual. We got to know each other during lunch break, and please understand this is not a performance, and I am not here to pleasure her. The impulse to perform or pleasure may arise, and that's fine, but what we are doing is much deeper. When done well, sexual healing can reclaim, reprogram, and reawaken the ultimate gateway to enlightenment. So we begin now with prayer."

Charles arranged himself in a cross-legged position on the bed in front of Violet, who sat up and gestured back when he greeted her with a Namaste.

He ceremoniously produced a little bottle of essential oils and dabbed some on her third eye. "By the power of all that is holy, I call on the ascended Dakinis to dance around and bless us with the deepest possible healing and the widest possible guidance. Amen and Awoman!"

"Do I get to anoint you?" Violet asked.

"If you like," Charles said.

Violet took the bottle and anointed his third eye. "I bow to the God within you."

"Amen and Awoman," they said together.

"And Aho," Violet added.

"Now," Charles spoke to the audience, "we would normally go into a deeper discussion of boundaries, fears, and desires. Since we already covered this at lunch, we are going to skip to intentions. Violet, what would you like to get from this session?"

"Well, I've already done a ton of work on my sexual trauma. For those that don't know, I was molested by a college professor. I feel pretty complete with it. He lost his job for what he did to me and my friend, and who knows how many others he might have molested. At first, I felt bad about telling his wife, and breaking up his family, but I've forgiven myself and feel ready to move on."

Charles nodded. "No matter how much talk therapy you've done, there may still be sexual trauma trapped in the soft tissue of your sacred spot, and this ritual is designed to help you re-sequence it in your body. There is nothing more powerful than orgasmic energy to move stagnant energy."

"That's what I've heard," said Violet, "but honestly, I'm more interested in seeing if you can help my orgasms. I typically cum once and then I'm done. My body just doesn't do multiple orgasms. I wonder if it's the way I'm built, because it has nothing to do with my lovers. Damien and Raven are amazing," she said, looking over at me. "And everyone knows how easy it is for Raven to orgasm. I wonder if it's because her clit is closer to her vaginal opening?"

"Have you ever experienced Amrita?"

"You mean, do I squirt? One time, I had a lover that made me gush all over the bed, but I'm pretty sure that was pee."

Charles smiled. "Perhaps it was Amrita."

"No. I'm pretty sure it was pee. It smelled like pee. That brings up a trigger for me. I'm annoyed with how people in the tantra community think they are more 'evolved' because they can squirt, or make someone squirt. Maybe we're just built differently?"

"Perhaps."

"But if you think you can make me squirt, I'm open to it."

"Amrita looks a lot of different ways for different people. Some people squirt, some sprinkle, some gush or soak. Perhaps, you have Amrita, but just don't know it. I'm not going to try to give you Amrita, or not. The goal of the giver is to have no goals, just intentions. My intention is to be present with whatever arises, without trying to force or hold anything back. Shall we begin?"

"Yes."

"Did you empty your bladder already?"

"Yes, Sir."

"You're welcome to disrobe and lie down. I'm going to begin with a whole-body massage."

He rubbed his hands together and placed one hand on her heart and the other on her abdomen for a moment of silent prayer. He proceeded to massage the length of her body, shoulders, and arms with gentle, slow caresses, occasionally speaking to the room.

"If you are experienced with running energy, you can create a circuit from your heart to your hands and through to the entire chakra system of the receiver. We recommend you honor the whole body for at least a half hour before shifting the focus to the sex center. Take your time before massaging the inner thighs, like I'm doing here. You can offer an external abdominal massage to vibrate the yoni, with no expectation of arousal."

Violet whimpered, "More please."

"When the receiver becomes aroused, there's an energetic prayer field generated around the pelvis—you can feel it, but you want to wait for verbal consent before entering that region. Violet, you're welcome to undulate and sound on your exhalation."

Violet moaned loudly.

"Now, Violet is easy. But sometimes it takes over an hour, or multiple sessions before a woman feels safe and relaxed enough to focus on her yoni. That's okay. There's no rush. How are you doing?"

"Wonderful. I don't need multiple sessions."

"Oh, I heard you," he joked, "you're a one-shot wonder."

Violet giggled.

"Expressing sound is important in this ritual," Charles said to the class. "We want to welcome all kinds of moans, groans, and wails of every variety."

"You've got to give me something to wail about," Violet said.

"Remember, there are one hundred and one different strokes. You want to run the energy from your heart through your hand, especially when your hands are at the doors to her most sacred temple. With devotion and reverence, we feel around the temple garden. Walking clockwise around her mons and into her valley."

More giggling.

"Are you ticklish?" Charles asked.

"I just feel like laughing."

"Use your forefingers and thumb to gently pinch, squeeze, and roll all the way around the outer lips."

Violet kept making playful sounds.

"So after a thorough massage around the outer labia, you want to ask for permission to enter. Violet, may I enter you?"

"Mmm . . ." she moaned.

"I'm not going to enter until you say: 'Yes, I'm inviting you to enter my temple now.'"

Violet exaggerated her invitation by opening her eyes wide and making eye contact. "Yes, I'm inviting you in, already!"

Charles slowly inserted his forefinger and, after a breath, said, "Thank you for the honor of allowing me into your sacred temple."

"The pleasure is all mine," Violet moaned.

He maintained eye contact with her as he rhythmically moved through a variety of strokes with one hand inside and the other outside her yoni.

"You can communicate with simple cues, like: slower, more pressure, less pressure, faster, or pause."

"Whatever you're doing, don't stop," Violet said in a breathy voice.

Charles's speed continued to increase until he said, "And be prepared for emotional release. As I touch different spaces it may trigger memories that evoke grief, fear, or sometimes anger. See, the past, present, and future all coexist inside the yoni."

Violet still seemed to be riding the pleasure.

"Did you have a nickname when you were a little girl? What did your parents call you?"

"Letti," she answered.

"That's adorable. Little Letti. You were so innocent. Did you still use that nickname when you were older—when you were babysitting?"

"Sometimes."

"Let's send some love back to little Letti. I'm going to blast you with a fountain of love. Ready?"

Violet nodded.

"Where are you?" Charles asked.

"I'm right here." Violet giggled.

"I know you are here. But where else?"

Violet seemed frustrated. "You told me to go back to my little girl."

"And how is she doing?"

"She feels loved," she smiled. "I feel so loved by everyone in this room right now."

"Yes. We all love little Letti."

Violet's laughter turned into howls.

"We also respect you too. Your body is your temple. And you don't have to perform for anyone. You are the authority of who is allowed in and who has to leave."

"Don't leave."

"I'm right here. I'm holding your sacred spot, and you feel full. Can you feel your sacred spot swelling with Amrita?"

"I think my bladder is full," Violet said.

"Perhaps. But, perhaps not. You are safe to completely let go. Do you feel safe in your body?"

"Yes."

"I want you to take a really deep breath and retain it for as long as you can. Then, tense your entire body, then emit sound, scream, and completely surrender all control."

"Okay," she said as she inhaled and held.

"Squeeze. Squeeze everything. Squeeze. . . . And let it go. Let it go!"

Violet released with screams, cries, shaking, and all of the primal sounds until she ran out of steam and grew quiet.

"I am sorry. On behalf of all my unconscious brothers who have hurt you, I apologize. You are whole. Do you feel safe in your body, now?"

"Yes. Except I feel like I have to pee."

"I want you to feel safe enough to let it all go."

"Right now? You want me to pee on you?"

"I got you."

Violet released her bladder all over Charles, who simply said, "All right."

Violet giggled. "I'm sorry I got your shirt wet."

He smiled. "I've been blessed."

"I still think it's pee."

"It might be a mixture, but it doesn't matter. It's beautiful. With this nectar from the Goddess, I anoint myself." He rubbed some of the fluid onto his forehead, just as he had done in the beginning. "And I anoint you, and consecrate your healing and your sexual awakening."

Violet giggled. "It's definitely pee."

"Regardless. I'm going to call you the giggle goddess."

"Who me?" She giggled. "Are we done? I feel complete."

"Almost," he said, slowly pulling out. "I need you to rest for a while. Be gentle with yourself. A sexual healing occurs as much in stillness as in arousal."

"Can I rest in my lover's arms?"

Charles motioned to me, "Raven? Come hold her in stillness."

I scooted into the circle to spoon Violet.

"We are going to take a break, to integrate. Get water, go to the bathroom, but don't get distracted. Notice what came up for you during this ritual, and don't expect your ritual is going to look anything like this. Every time sacred spot is performed, it looks completely different."

When Charles came in to check on Violet, I left to get her water, so I didn't hear what they talked about, and when I came back, he left to change his shirt.

"I'm so proud of you," I said. "You gave everyone in the room permission to really go for it."

"How was it for you to watch?" she asked, somewhat self-consciously.

"Stunning. Everyone was touched by your authenticity, several people even cried. Including Nick."

"I felt them, but mostly I felt you," she smiled. "I wish Damien had been here."

I sighed. "Me too. But if he were here, I probably wouldn't have gotten to hold you afterward. Anyway, you'll be back in his arms again tonight. And you get to do the full practice with him—all three rounds. He's very lucky."

She searched my eyes for what was in my heart. "Are you jealous, because Damien did the sacred spot on you last time you were here, together?"

I tried to brush it off, but she was too open, raw, and sensitive to hide anything. "It's not Damien, exactly, it's men in general. They just have a distinct advantage I could never have. I wish I could touch you the way Charles did."

Violet reassured me, "But babe, you totally do."

"It's not the same," I said sharply. "Look at him. He's like an archetype. He embodies the divine masculine, and can help heal everything that is wrong with the patriarchy."

"I don't understand, is this part of your penis envy?" Violet asked with a concerned look.

"It might sound silly, but I feel like if I were a man, I'd be better equipped to heal you. There are still places inside you that I feel I can't reach."

"That is so sweet, but I love you just the way you are, and I wouldn't want you to be any different."

She kissed me, and I laughed to myself. Then I helped her to her feet. "Can you believe we still have two more days and this work will just keep getting deeper?"

"I'm exhausted just thinking about it."

"There are doorways we will cross through this weekend, after which there is no return."

"You make it sound so terminal."

"It is."

FRIDAY #36
Fuck Trauma

"I don't think it's contagious," Violet said, coughing, "but I don't want to take any risks." She lay like an angel in her cotton panties and thin white tank top on her purple cloud of a comforter.

"I understand," I said. I shimmied out of my sweater and pants. "We're almost matching." I pointed to my undershirt and panties. "I don't want to catch your cold, but I'm bummed we didn't get to play last Friday during the workshop, and I'll be away on a family vacation next Friday." I joined her on the bed, nuzzling her neck but avoiding her mouth.

"Why do you have to go on a Disney cruise for Mason's fifth birthday?" she pouted. "Why can't you take him to Chuck E. Cheese or something local?"

"Don't be jealous."

"Hey, if you can be jealous of tantra master Charles Muir, I can be jealous of you going to the Caribbean."

"I wasn't jealous of Charles," I clarified, pulling her closer, "just envious he's in a male body. As a healer, there are certain frequencies I can never fully embody."

Violet turned and cupped my face. "Charles is gifted, I'll admit, but it actually reminded me of how you touch me."

"Really?"

"You can be every bit as masculine as he is," she said, stroking my shoulder. "Do you want me to start calling you *Sir*?"

I laughed and relaxed into the sensations under her busy hands, which made their way between my legs. "You know, Damien said the immune system of the vagina is totally different from the mucosal lining in the mouth, nose, and eyes. Common viruses can't transmit through the genitals, so, technically, I could still go down on you, if you want."

"I've always wondered about that," Violet said.

I pleaded, "Orgasm is the best medicine."

She kissed my neck, and giggled more. "See, you can be a powerful healer too."

"But I don't have the Buddha body or big man-hands like Charles does."

"I can use my imagination."

"Lie down," I commanded. "Let me look at you." I repositioned Violet at the side of the bed with her legs hanging off and pulled her white cotton panties down, but not all the way off.

"Are you going to look at me the way men look at women . . . like meat?" she asked playfully.

"Maybe. Or maybe I'm looking at you like a Butch Daddy looks at his baby girl," I proposed.

"You know, I never really understood why some lesbians like calling their girlfriends 'Daddy,' it's so incestuous. You can be my man, and call me 'baby girl,' but let's leave "Daddy" out of it this time."

"Okay, baby girl." I massaged her inner thighs and asked,

"What if I were a college professor and you were a young sexy schoolgirl?"

"That could be fun." She lay back and closed her eyes. "Imagine I'm in a short pleated skirt and pigtails . . ."

I stroked the soft stubble on her vulva. "And I'm an older professor with a big belly and a mustache . . ."

". . . And I'm sitting in the front row, intentionally not wearing panties, so I can uncross my legs and give you a flirty glimpse at my flower while you're writing on the chalk board."

Her soft, warm flower tempted my first two fingers to slip inside with almost no warning. "Even before I catch a glimpse of your sneaky little yoni, I can smell your pheromones filling the classroom. Like a predator smells his prey. And I know I have to have you."

Violet wiggled her hips and giggled, "Am I your teacher's pet?"

"It's more than that. There is this undeniable attraction between us. It goes beyond the physical, because you're attracted to my mind, and I'm attracted to your innocence and your free spirit. That's why I ask you to come to my house after class." I felt as if her pussy was putting me under a spell. "You're so soft, so young, so irresistible." After a series of deep rhythmic thrusts, I blurted, "I just realized something!"

Through her heavy breathing, Violet opened her eyes and asked, "What?"

"I know what Terrance must've felt like whenever you were babysitting."

Violet shuddered, her eyes rolled back in her head, and I felt her pussy squeeze against my fingers. "Oh, God."

"Is this okay?" I questioned both of us.

"Don't stop," she moaned.

Raven paused. "Are you sure?"

Violet closed her eyes and tilted her head back. "I trust you," she said, "you're a powerful healer."

I resumed thrusting against her undulating pelvis. "I invite you back to my house after class. You didn't wear your panties again today, and you've been giving me glimpses of your yoni all evening. I watch you flaunt your body around the house," I said, surprised by my own arousal. "I can hardly wait for you to sleep so I can watch over you, looking so sweet, just lying there." I positioned my sex hard against her thigh as I continued. "I come over to your side of the bed to tuck you in, and reach into my own pants with one hand while slipping my other hand up your cotton top to grope your perky little titties. And then I see your body undulating, and I take it as a sign that you want more."

Violet pinched her own nipples as I stroked her more firmly.

I centered my face between Violet's thighs and said, "Later, I see your sleeping body, and want more. So I move real slow, and quiet, so as not to wake you as I press my fat fingers inside of you."

I slowly pressed a third finger in, filling her flower.

I found my way to her G-spot, then used my chin against her clit so I could continue speaking. "Then, I start rubbing my bulge against your thigh. I want to have sex so bad, but I don't even know if you're wide enough to accommodate my throbbing cock."

"Oh yes. Yes," she called in ecstasy, shuddering hard against my fingers. "Right there. Yes!"

Her hips bucked against my hand. She shuddered and lay still as the orgasm subsided. With a big exhale, I withdrew my fingers and cupped her vulva.

A strange calm seemed to fill the room, as Violet's breathing slowed. After a while, I said, "That was wild."

"Hold me," she whispered, with outstretched arms.

"Of course." I melted into her chest and she started to cry, little tears at first which turned into the big ugly cry. I was comforting her confused inner child. In my arms was a girl who needed to know she was still lovable. I kissed her forehead, and encouraged her to keep releasing.

"Wow," she said, finally smiling. "I mean. Thank you."

"What are you aware of?" I asked, gently guiding her hair behind her ear.

She sniffled, and spoke slowly. "I wasn't Letti anymore. I was just a girl . . . and you weren't Terrance either. We were archetypes of ourselves playing out these perverted roles. I was every girl who wants to be taken by an older man and you were every man that wrestles with their attraction to youth and innocence. I can't believe how inappropriate it was. How did you know to say all that?"

"Intuition. It just came through."

"Well, I'm so grateful you went with it. That may have been the most healing orgasm I've ever had."

Love Letter

Violet insisted on driving me, Nick, and Mason to the air-
port for the family trip. After kissing me good-bye, she
handed me a sealed envelope and said, "Don't open this until
Friday."

Honoring her instructions to wait wasn't easy. When Friday
came, I found a moment to myself, opened the envelope, and
eagerly read.

Dear Raven,

I miss you already. It may only be a week, but this is
our first Friday apart! Damien asked me how I'd survive
without our weekly playdate. I told him I was going to
wear black and paint my toes and fingernails with black
polish and leave my hair unbrushed and sit in the corner

drinking brandy from the bottle while cutting myself. He said I was being dramatic.

Seriously though, last Friday's fantasy was profound. You took something so wrong and somehow made it into something holy. The idea of older men forcing themselves on me has always been a hot fantasy, but I didn't realize why. Somehow, when you linked it to Terrance, a little space in my heart opened. Even after all these years of therapy, I never saw myself through his eyes until you somehow slipped into his skin. What he did was wrong and inexcusable, but for the first time, I sort of understood him, and that gave me some peace to move past it. It doesn't make what he did right or change the past, but it totally changes my future.

I feel more space under my skin right now.

So here's a little love poem I wrote to let you know, you've pussy whipped me!

Ode to My Queen
She swats me in my special place,
She kisses me gently on the face.
Belts and floggers, spankings galore,
She even calls me her 'little whore.'
Forcefully she tells me what to do,
With wild fantasies that are always new.
Her touch like art, her healing is sweet.
Between my thighs, she creates such heat.
I love my mistress and she loves me.
When we are together, I feel safe and free!

Love,
Your Bitch.

P.S. I admit, at first, I wasn't sure about tantra, and sexual healing, and sex magic, but this shit works.

Fantasyland

66 "I want to take you on a vacation," I said to Violet as we lounged on a sheet in her backyard, both wearing lingerie and holding long-stemmed cocktail glasses.

"It feels like we're on vacation right now," Violet said, looking over at me through her sunglasses. "I mean, every time we're together, you take me somewhere exotic. That fantasy about Terrance really healed something for me. It's like you took me into the past and it somehow rearranged my future."

"I'm so honored that you went there with me. But I'm talking about going away together, for real. Like an overnight retreat, just the two of us."

She giggled, "Like a cruise?"

"No." I rolled my eyes. "I don't want to go on a gas-guzzling boat, I want to go somewhere in nature. Somewhere sexy."

"Take me away in a fantasy."

"I'm talking about somewhere on land," I insist.

"Let's meet in the middle. How about we go to fantasyland?"

I shake my head and raise my glass. "To fantasyland."

She clinked her glass with mine then looked at me seductively. "What kind of magical creatures and wild beasts live in this fantasyland?"

"You would make a very naughty little pixy, adorned in that lacy lingerie." I kissed her soft lips then nibbled at her neck until I remembered. "I haven't seen you in two weeks, I want to catch up before we journey anywhere."

"Did you fantasize about me when you were away?"

"Of course I did. But nothing compares to having you in the flesh."

"Tell me about it," Violet murmured while nuzzling me.

I held her shoulders and looked her in the eyes. "I want to savor this moment, right here with you. As hot as our fantasies are, they take us out of the present."

I gazed into her eyes and took several long breaths, until Violet grew fidgety and broke the silence. "So . . . what toys did you bring today?" She grabbed my bag of tricks and started pulling toys out, arranging them on the sheet.

"I wasn't sure what mood we'd be in, so I brought a little of everything."

"I want you to use them all." She smirked at me, and I gave her a penetrating stare until she continued. "The truth is, when I try not to fantasize, it takes me out of the moment. It's like I'm always fantasizing anyway, so by speaking it out loud, we *are* being present together."

Her circular logic pleased me. I surveyed the arsenal of toys. "Shall we start with the blindfold?"

She wagged her booty and knelt in front of me. "This pixy wants to be tied up and teased!"

"Does she, now?" I handed her the blindfold as I began to tie a few simple starter knots into the black nylon rope. I restrained her wrists as I spoke. "Pixies are curious little tricksters who flit around with their purple dragonfly wings. They are also shy, and they turn invisible and play harmless tricks on other creatures. They can't talk either, they just sigh and giggle and gasp, especially when they're excited. And Violet is always excited by elves."

"Oooh. Elves are hot," Violet interrupted.

I pinned her arms to her sides and wrapped the rope around her chest. "Of course they are. Elves are known for their otherworldly beauty. They live in ancient forests and practice magic and artistry. And there was one particular elf that Violet was most fascinated with."

"I love it. Can we call him Faelyn? Did you know that elves can live up to seven hundred years? That's older than most trees," Violet offers.

"Faelyn, right. So, Faeyln was only eighty-two years old, which apparently means he was still young in elf years. Anyway, one time she was watching him sleeping, and she noticed his cock get so hard, it made a large lump under the sheets." When Violet was fully restrained, I laid her down and lifted the biggest dildo, a dark skinned dong with big bulging veins, and I thumped I thumped against her mons a few times. Then I swiftly pulled her lingerie off.

"So, what did she do?" Violet asked breathlessly.

I traced the dong along the inside of each leg. "She flew close to watch his cock grow. She thought she could even see it pulsing. She was afraid to touch it, but she stared at it so long she became obsessed. Every night after he fell asleep, she would fly out of her little bed and sleep by his bulge."

I teased her clit with the head of the massive cock. "It was an awkward time because Faelyn would have night emissions.

Violet would watch him toss and turn in his sleep, and one time he actually rubbed up against a pillow and squirted everywhere. The smell was intoxicating. It reminded her of the swimming pool. She wanted to taste it, but she wouldn't dare. But she kept creeping around at night."

I continued teasing her with the dong, rubbing it against the outside of her naked pussy. "And then one day, she crawled under the blankets so she could see his naked erection. It was so swollen and thick...she felt a deep ache between her legs, and the sensation was so strong, she nearly fainted."

I plunged the dildo deep inside of her slippery pussy. Her body quivered in excitement.

"Oh, God! Yes . . . it must've looked as big as a tree or a tower to her little body."

"Exactly. So she reached into her little pixy dress and plunged her own fingers inside." I pushed the dildo in as deep as it would go. "It wasn't enough. Her little fingers were too small. She wanted more. So she thought he might not notice it if she just rubbed herself against the side of his erection. She started slowly wrapping her arms around it at first. She felt how warm it was and wished she had big breasts to press against it. Instead, she spread open her legs and came immediately. This made her flutter around the room like she was drunk." Violet moaned and her body squirmed with each stroke of the dildo.

"From then on, she started sleeping with Faelyn. Right alongside his penis, like a body pillow. She got so comfortable with her new home that sometimes she'd forget to become invisible, but Faeyln was a deep sleeper, and never noticed her, until suddenly, one night something terrible happened...."

"What!" Violet exclaimed, aroused and curious.

"Faelyn's den was raided and ransacked by warlocks!"

"Warlocks!?"

"Didn't you know, since the dawn of time, warlocks and pixies have always had a complicated relationship."

"Of course," Violet giggled.

Raven continued slowly, teasing Violet's engorged yoni with deliberate strokes as she spoke. "When the head warlock first heard about the magic of pixies, he started searching Fantasyland for his own little pixy slave.

"When he found Violet, he captured her in a large jug that he used to store mead wine, and took her back to his castle, where he locked her in his quarters. She was terrified. When he got her alone, he looked at her and wondered out loud, 'What were you doing lying with the elf?' She started to shiver. 'What does he use you for?' And this thought gave him a huge erection."

"Oh, God," Violet's body convulsed at this thought.

"The pixie watched it growing in his trousers. And her body betrayed her. She was so small and helpless, but she could feel herself getting wet. So he took her quivering body into his hand and stroked her breasts softly a few times with his dirty thumb. This made her relax a little. Then he unbuttoned his trousers and out sprung his enormous . . ."

"Hold on." Violet's body shook and she moaned, "Hold still. Oh God. Stop." She breathed heavily.

"You good?" I asked, amused and concerned.

"Yeah," she laughed, still panting. "Something about the way you said the word 'trousers' made me cum."

"Trousers, huh?"

"My pussy needs a break."

"You want me to keep it in my trousers?" I teased.

"Hug me. I think I'm ready to come back to the present."

I withdrew the dildo from her swollen yoni and slowly removed her blindfold. "Nothing like a good orgasm to bring you into the moment." I spooned her on the sheet. "What are you feeling?"

"So much love for you and our fantasy world, it feels so timeless, so eternal."

"I know the feeling." I nuzzled against her. "What else is in your heart?"

"Damien is in my heart. I feel so much love for him, and for Autumn too."

FRIDAY #39
Perfect Proposal

I told Violet to meet me at the playhouse because I needed her help on a performance piece I'd been working on. She was so consumed with her big engagement, she almost missed the mascara running down my face.

"What's wrong?"

"Nothing," I snapped. "My higher self is happy for you, for both of you, but my small self is still suffering somehow."

"I love you," Violet said desperately. "You're my queen."

"And I love you," I said as I peeled her arms off me and looked into her eyes. "I love both of you, and the thought of you merging your lives into one makes me feel there is something finally right in the universe. Nobody knows you are meant for each other better than I do. So, it shouldn't burn, but it does. It feels like acid on my skin. I'm sorry, I just need a minute to mourn it. To feel it. And to heal it. But I'm going to need your help."

"How can I help? Tell me what to do. Direct me," Violet said dutifully.

"You know the theater is my church. This is where I come when I need inspiration. I thought we could improv, to help workshop my feelings." I handed her a few pages from my play-book. "I wrote down some lines that hurt the most—if you just read them, we'll see where it takes us."

"Okay," she said. She scanned my writing, moving her lips as she read to herself.

SETTING: The stage is empty except for a bare lightbulb, which hangs from a long cord dangling between two lonely chairs placed center stage, far apart.

VIOLET: Why are you jealous?

RAVEN: My bitch is going to be his bride.

VIOLET: So you wish we were the ones getting married?

RAVEN: It's not that simple.

Impatiently, I interrupt her by pointing to a red X on the second page and saying, "Can we just start from here and do a cold reading? I like to imagine the house is full of allies, and let's just improvise."

Violet scoots her chair in closer to mine, then slowly begins reading.

VIOLET: The view was spectacular. The minute we lifted off, I could barely breathe. We were floating in the clouds. But he didn't propose in the hot air balloon, he waited until after sunset. He blindfolded me, and led me into the backyard where he had made a heart on the lawn with candles and rose petals. Then he got down on one knee with a ring. He told me how honored he is to be with me, and asked if I will spend the rest of my life with him!

RAVEN: What did you say?

VIOLET: "Yes, of course!" I blurted, without even thinking, and then I actually said, "As long as we can still have sex with other people!" Isn't that funny? Then we kissed. We danced under the stars for a while, then he carried me to the bedroom. It was a perfect proposal.

RAVEN: I want to be happy for you.

VIOLET: It's okay to be jealous.

I started sobbing and Violet crawled over to my chair, hugging my legs, listening with her head on my lap.

RAVEN: But I'm already married. Maybe I'm jealous because I'll never be your man. Or because we don't fit together like interlocking puzzle pieces. We can scissor fuck for as long as we want, but there will always be something missing, at least for me. Sometimes I just want to penetrate you with a cock that doesn't detach, or kiss you in public without making a scene. This jealousy goes deep.

Violet speaks without the script now, "Have I ever told you this? I get aroused when I see you cry. Ever since the first night right here in the theater."
She slowly lifted my dress and nuzzled her head between my thighs.

"I don't want to feel this way," I sobbed.

Violet cooed, "I love how human you are."

"I mourn that I can never get you pregnant and be your baby daddy," I said.

"Mourn all you want, I don't mind. As long as you don't mind me doing this."

Violet managed to maneuver her tongue beneath my underwear while I continued a breathy and orgasmic monologue.

"Oh. Well, that does make it a lot easier to mourn, now doesn't it? I just needed to know you're as hot for me as you were before the proposal. Oh, that's good. Technically, you getting married to Damien doesn't change anything between us. Of course, I knew that logically, but my body just needed a little reassurance. Right there. Yes. Reassure me right there. A little slower. That's good. That's it. Yes. And come to think of it, things might change after you're married. It could be kinda kinky. I've always wanted to covet another man's wife."

BLACKOUT.

FRIDAY #40

Prison Bitch

Rounding the last curve in the trail, Violet spotted the cabin we'd rented for the weekend and her body looked visibly relieved. She leaned up against the post on the porch and teased, "Can't you ever stick to the beaten path? I think you enjoy being lost."

I deflected her blame by pointing to the outdoor shower. "Let's rinse off with the natural spring water."

"Should I grab towels?" she asked, lifting her shirt over her head, revealing her bouncy little breasts.

I grabbed for her nipple, but her reflexes were too fast. "No, we can sunbathe on that boulder when we get out."

The shower was made of simple cinder blocks, rusted pipes, and a cement floor that drained into nature.

Violet smelled her own armpits. "I could use a good rinse."

"Let me smell." I sniffed at her like a savage animal tracking its prey.

"Let me go. I reek," she yelled, and she wrestled away.

"Slow down." I held her arms behind her back until she surrendered to my mouth against hers. "I want to savor our alone time. The point of this trip is to take you away from all your usual habits."

"You mean to get me out of my comfort zone?"

"And to get you all to myself for a weekend," I said, caressing her neck and chest.

Violet's eyes twinkled. "You make me sound like a prisoner."

"You're my property now!" My hands gripped at her back as I pressed her sweaty naked breasts against mine.

Violet broke our kiss and said, "I've got an idea. . . ."

But I put my lips right back on hers, refusing to let her speak, holding her by the back of her head. She pulled away and said, "I'm thinking . . . prison scene."

I grabbed her ass hard through her yoga pants and pulled her toward me. "So, what are you in for?"

"I could be showering and you come in and be all territorial and you punish me for using your space."

"Am I a prison guard or another prisoner?"

"I don't know?" She raised her eyebrow seductively. "I've never been to prison. Do the guards shower with the inmates?"

"I could be a convicted criminal who initiates all the new inmates."

"And I could be a drug dealer or prostitute? And you could punish me for being so bad?"

I scanned her sweet face. "No, I like the idea of you being totally innocent. Like maybe you were framed for something you didn't do, or better, you got time for being a peace activist."

"I'm innocent. I swear." She smiled slyly.

"Get in there." I turned her toward the shower and swatted her ass. "Don't wait for me, just let yourself enjoy the water like it's the last guilty pleasure you'll ever get in this damn hellhole."

"Yes, Ma'am."

I disappeared behind the cabin and found a space to watch her take off her shorts and panties. She couldn't see me peeking through the bushes. She stepped into the water, and let it run down her naked body and between her legs. She opened her vulva with her fingers to rinse inside. I tiptoed around, looking for a branch I could use to punish her with.

I snapped it against my knee, breaking it down to the size of a billy club. I smoothed the rough edges by dragging it against the outside of the shower. I took a stance at the entrance and slammed the club against my hand a few times. I didn't say anything at first to intensify the suspense.

Finally I snapped, "What are you doing?"

Violet covered her breasts and crotch, visibly shaken. "I'm, uh, I'm showering."

"Who told you you could use my shower?" I said, slamming the billy club against my hand.

"Nobody was using it," she retorted.

"Well, it's mine." I moved closer. "And so is the rest of this cell block. If you're going to live here, it's going to be on my terms. On your knees, you little cunt." I pressed the club against her shoulder and guided her to the ground. "Start washing my feet."

Kneeling, Violet scrubbed my feet with quick motions.

"Slow down, you little slut," I ordered. "You're not worthy of this job."

"Forgive me," she begged.

"There is no forgiveness here, new girl. Don't think I haven't noticed you, flaunting yourself, like fresh meat. You want me, don't you? I want you to rub your little pussy on my leg like the bitch you are."

She squatted and opened her legs. "Like this?"

"Lean back," I said, looking down at her. "I want to feel the inside of your tight little pussy."

She repositioned herself, opening her lips so her labia pressed against my shin. "This is so degrading."

"Shut up, or I'll stuff my billy club inside you."

She acted shocked. "Is that what you want to do?"

"I said, shut up!" I grabbed her by the ear and pulled her up to her feet and pushed her breasts against the broken wall. "Did you not hear me?"

"Ow!" Violet exclaimed.

"Spread your legs."

She did as I commanded, and I ran the billy club up the inside of her leg.

"Just don't use that club," she begged.

"Stick your ass out," I ordered, pulling it toward me. "Look at that eager little pussy."

I spread her cheeks apart. I struck her right asscheek with the club, just hard enough to make her gasp, and then again, and again, about five times.

"I'm sorry," she cried, "I won't do it again."

"That's right you won't. But I'm going to have to even you out."

I switched to the other side and struck her left cheek, until it was red like the other side. Violet pouted and made a point of rubbing her sore bottom while I turned off the water, which had run cold.

"Are we done?" Violet asked timidly.

"No. You've got to lick me clean."

I pushed her down on her knees and shoved my pussy into her face, and she started licking fast and sloppy as I stroked the billy club.

"You inexperienced little cunt!" I yelled. I placed my knee

between her legs and grabbed her by the hair, making her stand up. "You don't know what you're doing down there. And now I'm going to have to teach you. Get down and spread your legs!"

I pointed to a cinder block for her to sit on with her back against the wall, and opened her feet and legs with the billy club. "Wider," I commanded.

"Just don't use that club thing on me anymore," she pleaded.

"Listen here, you little cunt," I said, pointing it at her face, "you lost all your rights when you were found guilty. Now you're my property."

"Okay, I'll do whatever you say."

"You better." I moved the club down between my legs, holding it like a cock. "Now lick my club."

She bent over to lick and kiss the tip of the club.

"That's better. Now lie back and take it."

I squatted down and shoved two fingers inside of her, ramming them in and out while making circles on her clit with my other fingers. She quivered against my hand, her pussy muscles spasming as she cried out, "Oh, yes, yes, uhhhh . . ." She rode my hand hard, making herself cum. "Right there. Oh, God. Yes."

I licked my fingers and kissed her on the mouth. "Welcome to prison life. I think you're going to like it here."

We ran our hands over each other's wet naked skin. Finally, Violet broke the embrace to dry off on the big rock in the sun.

I looked at her glowing body. "I wanted to tell you I love how pretty you look with little beads of water glistening on your skin, but I didn't want to break character."

"You were very believable. Maybe a little too much," she scoffed.

"What do you mean?"

She got up on one elbow and looked me in the eye. "Are you mad at me? You left me in there for a long time, at first. I was worried you went to go get someone else. And when you came in with that stick, you were so rough. I wondered if you were punishing me for some reason."

"I thought you were into it. You came so fast."

"I was. It just reminded me of the first time you spanked me—remember when you were jealous of Damien, and you took it out on my ass?"

"Am I jealous you're getting married? A little, of course, but I wasn't trying to take it out on you. I was just enjoying the power rush. Did you feel unsafe?"

"A little," she admitted.

"You should've called yellow light."

"I didn't want to stop, you were so into it. I just need a little reassurance."

"That's what yellow light is for...it just means slow down, or check-in." I cupped her face in my hand. "I'm sorry."

"Don't be sorry, it's me." She sighed and lay back down. "I'm still processing the proposal."

"What do you mean, like are you having second thoughts?"

"No. Of course not. I just can't believe I'm getting married. It feels like there's so much happening at once. We started dating Autumn, my pole classes are taking off, I'm transitioning out of teaching yoga, and I need dental work, but I don't know if I should do it before or after the wedding. We haven't decided what kind of wedding we're having or what to do about my parents—they just don't understand my relationship with you, or Autumn."

I stroked her soft skin as I listened.

"I just want to elope. But I can't imagine getting married without you and Autumn there."

A big breeze blew across our bodies and she sighed as if letting all the anxiety blow away with it.

"Is there more?"

"That's it."

"Well, that's a lot. And it's happening all at once. So I understand if it's hard for you to be present with me right now."

"I didn't say I wasn't present. I love being with you, I needed this Goddess retreat to get away from it all!"

I kissed her forehead and cleared my throat. "The truth is, I can't take you away from Damien, or Autumn. It's all just an illusory retreat. I know you're always connected to everyone you love. I know because that's how I am with Nick and Mason."

"Yeah," she sighed. "I miss Damien."

"And I love that about you."

"And when I'm with Damien, I miss you."

"I know, but tonight we get to sleep in each other's arms." I closed my eyes and let the sun embrace me with its warmth.

"Dreamtime is the one place I can go and not be anyone's wife or queen or prison keeper. I just slip off into the void. In the morning, I can choose to be your queen again, if you want. But it's in waking up I remember it's all a big dream."

Engagement Party

"Where can I set the chocolate-covered strawberries?" Nick asked as we entered Violet and Damien's home, carrying a silver dessert tray.

Violet paused her last-minute decorating to greet us with kisses before the other guests arrived. "Looks good, I've got a separate area just for desserts. I plan to make myself into a human platter so everyone can eat off my body."

I raised an eyebrow and said, "You really want random people's lips all over you?"

"Excuse me," she protested. "They're not random people. I've only invited close friends. People from my pole studio, from acting class, and even some from Damien's work, but only the ones who know about our lifestyle. It's going to be an intimate, sexy soiree. Didn't you read the invitation?"

"All I know is this party was planned on a Friday." I swatted her bottom. "As far as I'm concerned, all these people are just here for our weekly playdate."

"Thank you for sharing me tonight." She ran her hand down my arm and squeezed the bag of tricks I carried over my shoulder. "If you want to do another public scene with me, I'm all yours."

"It depends on whether your body is going to be covered in saliva by the time I get you," I replied.

"You first, my Queen. Autumn and I will do our scene afterward."

"What's Autumn doing?" I said, surprised.

"The dessert platter. I invited Autumn to join me."

"But you didn't invite me?" I questioned.

"Because I knew you wouldn't want all the random lips."

I relaxed and said, "That's fair."

Damien entered and hugged his bride-to-be. "People are arriving. Honey, can you get the door?"

"I'll think something up for us to do together," I said as Violet left, then I fell into Damien's outstretched arms.

"I'm so glad you're here," he said.

I narrowed my eyes and said, "Why wouldn't I be?"

Nick gave him a big squeeze and said, "Congratulations!"

"You're looking fit," Damien said, patting Nick's chest.

"It's good to see you being so social," Nick replied.

I teased, "Violet is a good complement to your introversion. Within every couple, one partner is more extroverted and one is less. . . ."

Damien added, "Then there's the ambivert, when both are introverted or extroverted."

I pointed out, "But whenever there are two people, even ambiverts, one person tends to the extroverted pole and the other plays the opposite. It's basic polarity. It's like in power exchange, people can switch from top or bottom, but eventually somebody has to lead the scene. In every marriage, one person tends to become the social organizer."

Nick looked at me. "Who do you think is more social between you and me?"

"That's obvious," I admitted. "I'm really only extroverted when I'm onstage or directing. In settings like this, I get social anxiety."

Nick leaned toward Damien and whispered, "She's only social when she's in control."

"Sounds like you have her pegged," Damien laughed.

Autumn walked through the room, freshly showered and wearing only a towel. Damien held out his arms and she skipped into his embrace.

"Hi love," she said, kissing him. "I'm not ready yet. I've got to costume up."

"Of course, baby."

Nick commented, "Why don't you wear that tonight?"

Autumn blew everyone kisses and pranced off to get dressed.

I turned back to Damien. "As the introvert, I hope you're planning to make a formal toast tonight."

"I don't have anything planned. Isn't that the best man's job?"

Nick clapped and rubbed his hands together. "I've got some new material I could test out on this crowd. I've been working on a bit about Asian lesbian contortionists."

Damien grimaced. "Maybe I better say something, after all. I would like people to think about what partnership means to them but . . ."

I could see his wheels turning, so I made myself comfortable on a bar stool.

" . . . Our partnership is such a new paradigm," he said. "Whenever we go against the standard narrative, we have the obligation of explaining what it means to us, otherwise, people will assume and project the old paradigm. Are you planning to make a toast?"

I shook my head and patted my toy bag. "I'm devising a sexy scene with Violet, but the last thing I want is to steal your thunder."

"No, it's perfect," he said, sounding relieved. "A public scene might be just what we need to further the conversation."

"What if I performed a little ritual and tied the two of you together?"

Damien shook his head vehemently. "Not a chance."

"Just a thought."

Violet entered and reached for Damien. "Darling. People want to see us together. Let's not hide out in the kitchen!"

Before getting whisked away, Damien leaned over and whispered, "You know, we would not be the couple we are today without you." He kissed me on the mouth and put his arm around his bride to be.

I stood in shock for a moment, then decided to prepare the champagne glasses on a platter for the toast. Nick jumped in and grabbed as many glass flutes as he could manage. Autumn waltzed back in wearing a dazzling cocktail dress and offered to carry bottles, and we all entered the living room together.

Violet squealed, "All right, now the party can begin!" She grabbed glasses from Nick's tray and arranged them around the table as I set bottles out.

Nick piped up, "Since you've got everyone's attention, Violet, I'd love to see you do one of your stripteases!"

"Not tonight," Violet giggled, "but I do have an announcement. Damien asked me why I haven't ever danced at a strip club. He said, 'You teach pole dancing, you love talking to strangers, and you are a huge flirt. Stripping seems like the perfect job for you.' And I said I would love to, but my yoga community would judge me. Then I thought, 'Oh, shit! Who's actually doing the judging?'" She laughed at herself. "That would be me!

So I marched my ass straight to the nearest strip club and signed up for amateur night. I'm so excited."

There was an uproar of encouragement from the room, especially Nick, who raised his glass and said, "I'll toast to that!"

"Wait," I interjected. "This is an engagement party, so who wants to toast the lovebirds?"

Violet raised her glass. "I will!"

Autumn said, "You can't toast yourself."

"It's my engagement party, I can do whatever I want." She held her glass up and blew Damien a kiss. "Damien, you are the first person I've been able to share every part of myself with. Whether it's perverted or divine, you encourage me to be the best version of myself."

They kissed while everyone swooned and clapped around them.

"Well, I've got something to say," Nick announced, "because after a decade of being married, I may have learned a thing or two about commitment. Some of you may even remember our seven-year-itch ceremony, which was our version of a poly wedding."

Damien raised his glass. "I was there."

"Right," Nick continued, "This was before we knew Violet. We performed a tantric mahamudra ceremony. We invited everyone we knew, including our parents, and told them they were welcome to attend on the condition they would witness our public consummation." The room had an audible response of surprise. "We had about fifty friends and lovers surrounding us, reading poetry, and throwing flower petals on us as we made love. I will never forget it."

Damien joked, "I doubt anyone else will either."

"Now, my advice to you is to make your ceremony exactly how you want, where you want, and with whom you want. No matter what people say."

"Beautiful, brother," Damien said.

"Who officiated?" Violet asked.

"I did," I chimed in. "Who's doing yours?"

Violet said, "We don't know yet."

Autumn stood up and said, "Can I make a toast?"

"Please," said Damien.

She smiled at the celebrated couple. "I'm working on a poem about both of you."

"Read it!" Nick cheered.

"It's not finished," she went on, "but I have to say, I am honored you've let me into your relationship, so deeply. I feel doubly lucky to be in love with both of you."

She flirtatiously threw herself across their laps and kissed them both.

Violet looked to me. "Raven?"

I pointed at Damien, who shook his head. I asked, "Does that mean you want to go last?" He nodded, so I gave Violet a little squeeze then stood up. "Okay. For those of you who don't know, before I met this Goddess, I had a weekly tantric play-date with Damien for almost a year. Then one day he declared he was ready to find his life partner. That was one of the saddest days of my life, not just because I was afraid of losing him, but because I thought there wasn't a woman in the world who could meet him. I worried he'd spend the rest of his life tragically misunderstood and never find someone who could handle his freaky intellect.

"But then he met Violet. I couldn't believe a woman like her existed. She's a wild, free spirit with an immense amount of love to give. There are few men on Earth who have the kind of security in themselves necessary to hold space for her full expression. And by his love, I've gotten to see her blossom spiritually, sexually, and creatively. She has been good for him as well. He has become more social and open. She not only brings out the pervert in him, but also nurtures his life's purpose. In essence, I can see how these two bring out the best in each other." I looked over to see Violet's eyes brimming with tears. I raised my glass and everyone followed suit. "So here's to a lifelong revolutionary relationship." Glasses clinked and people clapped.

"Beautiful," said Damien.

I sat down, and Violet sat on my lap and covered my mouth with kisses.

Afterward she turned to Damien. "Okay, Honey, I'm ready for your toast now."

He chuckled and said, "I'm not going after that. I want to see your and Raven's performance first."

"Now?" I asked, surprised.

"Why not?" he replied. "This is a party, not a workshop!"

Violet looked at me imploringly. "Oooh, will you tie me up?"

Autumn piped up, "Yes, please. I've been wanting to watch you in action again!"

"If that will please the groom," I said playfully. Then I addressed the room, "Now, this may take a while. I'm going to make a rope harness and then throw Violet around the room a bit. You can talk amongst yourselves while I prep the scene." From my bag of tricks I conjured a silk scarf and nylon ropes.

Damien mused, "Perhaps I can say my toast while you're doing your thing."

"But I don't want to upstage your love declaration," I said.

"We make a good team," he countered. "Think of it like keeping the crowd's attention while I lecture."

"Deal," I said as I slowly peeled Violet's skintight dress off. She spun around in her lacy thong, flaunting her milky bare breasts for everyone to see. I began by running the ropes under her boobs like a bra. Damien waited for the audience to adjust to the exotic scenery before he began to speak.

"A lot of people have been asking what this ceremony means

to us, especially after they hear we're in an open relationship. They ask, why get married at all? Which is an important question. Unlike the majority of society, we don't equate exclusivity with commitment. So, what are we committed to? We are taking a stand for each other's happiness. We actually practice wanting the fullest and richest life experience possible, in every way. So, as Raven wraps Violet's body in a sexy corset right now, I can feel Violet's delight. That in turn delights me." He smiled and watched us while I continued crisscrossing the ropes around her torso, each knot tightening the whole structure.

Damien continued, "We also believe love means seeing each other as we are, both light and shadow, no fantasies or projections, no parts concealed."

I interrupted him for a moment to announce, "On that note, I'm going to blindfold the bride-to-be."

Damien yielded, saying, "Go ahead. So, as we grow and evolve, we do not hold on to outdated visions of each other."

I slowly wrapped the scarf around her face and tied it securely behind her head, which accentuated her red lipstick.

Damien nodded at me and continued, "Love is a verb we consciously practice and a skill we must cultivate. Sadly, most people get married as a gesture of ownership."

On Damien's cue, I decided to handcuff her wrists with black rope.

"Couples are constantly seeking to possess each other, often as a strategy to get their needs met. In fact, most people are so attached to getting something FROM their partner, they don't even think to want FOR their partner. Needing each other is not real love, it's transactional love. True love is when we want for our partners' needs to be met, whether or not we are the ones meeting those needs. Naturally, most people aren't ready for this kind of love, because of our personalities and our programming, so we must go through a process of evolving from the transactional into the unconditional; we must acknowledge our needs and insecurities when they arise along the way. This is the process that Violet and I are committed to learning and sharing together. We are committed to supporting each other's wholeness."

Damien ran his fingers along Violet's exposed skin as he said, "In seeing each other, and knowing ourselves, there is a unique synergy beyond what could be found in either of us separately. So, this commitment is to each other's security as well as to each other's freedom. We are marrying the fullness of who we are now, as well as the potential of who we are becoming!"

Damien ended his heartfelt speech by kissing Violet's lips as I held her ropes and the room watched in silence.

Even after he was done, Violet stretched her lips in his direction, trying to kiss him more. She said, "I love you," when he sat down. The room was too absorbed to applaud.

Nick joked, "That was actually the toast I was going to give, but I didn't want to steal your thunder." There were some chuckles to break the spell.

I adjusted the final touches on Violet's body corset as I said, "If we're done with the toasts, I want to tell you how this scene will go down. I've wrapped Violet in a fairly tight corset."

"It's pretty tight," Violet agreed.

"It's supposed to be," I defended. "It's not only a sexy look, but it also restricts her breathing by constricting her lungs, which manufactures a sensation of breath control. Since she is also blindfolded, she is easily disoriented, and so this will be a kind of internal journey."

In order to demonstrate, I grabbed the handle I'd constructed out of ropes on her corset as I spoke. "This harness is built to distribute her weight in such a way that I can throw her around the room without much effort on my part. Watch this, a little pull in this direction, and she is pulled out of her center. If done right, it should feel like flying."

With my feet firmly in one place, and without letting go of her handle, I slowly shifted Violet's center of gravity around, tossing her to and fro. Violet started off stiff but then surrendered more to the flow. After a few minutes, Violet started to stiffen again.

"Whoa!" she called.

"How do you like that?"

"It's wild."

"I bet you like knowing everyone here is watching your breasts bounce around."

I plucked at her G-string before spinning Violet in a full circle.

"You're all bound up and have nowhere to hide." I spanked one buttcheek and threw her in the opposite direction to spank the other. "How does it feel to have everyone's eyes on your sexy ass?"

"I like it." She giggled.

"She's really flying now," I said, referring to her inner state.

"Whoa . . . it's intense."

I slowed the movement to check on her. "Your breath is a bit shallow but your skin temperature and heart rate are all right." I spun her around and asked, "Want more?"

"Slowly," she said, almost breathless.

I dipped her as if we were swing dancing, then pulled her body back.

"You like that?" I asked.

"I'm feeling woozy," she whispered. "But I'm okay, I think . . ." More heavy breathing. "Actually, no. I'm not. Red. Red Light!"

"I've got you." I immediately scrambled to lay her down and began to loosen her ropes. "I'm untying you. Don't worry."

Damien rushed over to sit by her side as my fingers frantically worked around her chest.

"Uh . . . I . . . I think I'm blacking out," Violet said, going limp in my arms.

Damien took off the blindfold. "Just breathe."

I turned to Nick. "Get my bag! My scissors."

In the next moment they were in my hands, and I was cutting through the rope closest to her ribs. Damien was guiding her through slow yogic breathing. "Slow your exhalation, and relax your jaw." Damien said.

"Can someone get water?" I called out.

Autumn jumped up. "I got it."

"You're doing great," I directed. "You're almost free."

Damien asked, "Can you move your fingers? How do they feel?"

"Okay, I think," she sighed.

"There you are," I said, cutting the last rope at the top.

"I'm sorry," Violet said to Damien as he propped her up.

I held the water to her lips. "No need to apologize."

"I wanted to finish, but I couldn't. I thought I was going to pass out."

"Safety first," Damien reassured her.

Violet looked in my eyes. "But it was a beautiful scene. Really, I loved it. I just got scared."

"I'm so glad you spoke up," I said, relieved.

"Can you tell everyone I'm okay?" she asked.

Nick announced, "She's going to be okay," to concerned friends who were standing by, so they could continue chatting amongst themselves.

Violet lifted her head and added, "Thanks everyone for witnessing me."

Relieved, I said, "I'm sorry I didn't catch it earlier. There was no warning, no yellow light, but it's okay. I'm glad you're okay."

Violet began to gather herself and come fully into her surroundings. "Sorry about your rope."

"It's okay," I said. "It's symbolic. Usually the untying ritual is my favorite part, but this was also significant."

"Yes. It was perfect," Violet echoed from Damien's arms.

ACT V

TRANSCENDENCE

Tran·scend·ence /tran(t)'sendəns/

Noun

1. existence or experience beyond normal limitations

2. often used to describe a spiritual or religious state of moving beyond physical needs and realities

3. the realization that the self is a small part of the greater whole, such as the human race, nature, the universe, etc.

FRIDAY #42

Chakra Meditation

66
. . . And so it is," Raven says, lighting a candle.

"Aho," replies Violet, her hands in prayer position.

Both women sit on Raven's bed, completely naked, facing each other with legs crossed, staring into each other's eyes as if they were looking into the reflection in a mirror.

"Keep breathing," Raven directs, "even if you start feeling aroused."

"What if I'm already there?" Violet giggles.

"Then go deeper," Raven says. "We're starting at the base. Close your eyes and imagine you have roots and the color red is flowing up from the Earth, into the trunk of your being."

Violet peeks through one open eye. "Are you trying to make up for nearly suffocating me last week?"

Raven opens her eyes. "Why would you say that?"

"This whole meditation practice, is it because you feel guilty about being too rough with me?"

Raven shakes her head. "I don't feel guilty, I just want us to attune to each other more."

Violet raises an eyebrow. "By breathing?"

"Are you bored?"

"No. I love doing spiritual practice. I just want to understand the purpose."

"The purpose is whatever we want it to be," Raven sighs. "Do you want to change your intention?"

"Yeah." Violet bites her bottom lip before admitting, "When I said I wanted to be open to accepting anything that comes up, I thought that's what you wanted me to say. But what I really want is to feel the passion between us."

"My passion hasn't gone anywhere," Raven reassures her. "It just seems like every date with you is like skydiving. And sometimes I feel pressure to come up with something better than last week. Just because we're not jumping out of an airplane doesn't mean I'm not hot for you anymore."

"I'm happy to just hang out," Violet responds. "There's no pressure to do anything."

"I know." Raven sighs. "I figure by tuning in to more subtle energies, we can expand our range. When Nick and I make love, it's like playing all eighty-eight keys on the piano. You know how some people only play the high notes and tend to hang out in the ethers, while others rock out with the minor keys . . . ? Well, Nick and I can play the full spectrum and I want that for us too. I don't want to deny our darkness, I want to include it, then transcend it with tantra."

Violet is beaming when she exclaims, "Now that's something I can align with!"

"Why don't you bring your sex chakra on top of mine? Let's breathe the color orange into our sex centers." Raven pats her lap, inviting Violet to come into Yab Yum pose. Violet wraps her legs around Raven's back. Together they undulate, drawing life-force energy into their bodies.

Raven continues guiding Violet: "Now that your sex center is awakened, I want you to open each of your chakras against mine by pressing your sex against my power center, heart, throat, and third eye, progressively. We can run energy for three breaths at each."

"You want me to hump your chakras?" Violet jokes as she scoots back to reposition her yoni into her favorite scissor strad-dle position, connecting their sex centers together for three ex-aggerated breaths. She giggles. "Now, this is what I'm talking about."

"Good." Raven smiles. "I'm going to lie back and I want you to charge your sex center against my power center and breathe the color yellow through to your navel as you undulate against mine."

Violet squats to straddle Raven's waist. She rests her yoni on Raven's stomach and gently rotates her hips for three deep breaths.

"Feels so good. Can I move up to titty fuck you?" Violet flirts.

"Yes, please. My heart is wide open and giving you a big green light."

Violet skillfully slithers up to Raven's chest and undulates around Raven's breasts before directing her sexual energy into Raven's heart and slowing her breath.

Violet is in the flow as she asks, "Now are you ready for me to choke you with my flower?"

"Wait, hand me that pillow." Raven repositions her neck so her throat is more exposed and says, "I'm going to chant and I want you to feel the vibrations from my throat through your yoni, all the way through your central channel. Imagine the color blue."

Violet bends deep into a squat so her yoni is directly against Raven's resonating neck. "Oooh! That's so cool," Violet says as Raven chants a mantra that sends vibrations through Violet's core.

After three hypnotic rounds, Raven asks, "Third eye?"

"I thought you'd never ask."

Violet scoots her yoni toward Raven's forehead but hovers momentarily over Raven's mouth. Raven takes the opportunity to softly kiss her lover's labia, making Violet squeal with delight. Not wanting to get too distracted, Raven pats Violet on the rump, which prompts her to move up.

"With this one," Raven instructs her, "see if you can get your clit lined up with my brow point."

"Maybe you need to coax it out a little more," Violet teases, returning her vulva to Raven's mouth. Raven flicks Violet's clit with her tongue until she feels it bulging from its hood. Reluctantly, Violet repositions herself onto Raven's brow.

"Perfect. Right there," Raven mumbles, still savoring the salty aftertaste of Violet's wet folds. "Now the color is indigo." Raven concentrates all her attention on her third eye and sends it into Violet's womb for the final three full breaths.

Without a word, Violet intuitively pivots her body so her sex is positioned above Raven's crown, and the chakra meditation is completed in silence for three blissful breaths.

Afterward, Violet lays her body alongside Raven's in a silent embrace.

Finally, Raven speaks. "I loved having your yoni essence drip down my crown. It's like you were my muse and that's where you belong. How was it for you?"

"I am so high right now," Violet confesses. "It's funny, every time we do something tantric, I have so much resistance at first, but once we get going, I don't want to stop. I always want more."

Raven kisses her forehead and reflects, "You know, it's not that different from fantasy play, the chakras also exist in the inner subjective realms."

Violet nods. "And it's a lot like skydiving."

Manager's Cut
From *Raven's Playbook*

With a billion items on my to-do list, nothing felt more important than luxuriating half naked in my playroom with my bitch. Between sighs and snuggles, I remembered something I'd been meaning to ask. "So, this is a huge transition in your life, how does it feel?"

"Being engaged?"

"No, stripping. You told me you won the contest on amateur night and they offered you a job. I want details!"

"Oh my God!" Violet's eyes grew wide as she said, "The place is a low-lit, sleazy dive bar. It's so naughty, I love it. The clients are mostly off-duty navy guys, because it's close to the base, but I feel like I'm part of society's underbelly. I get paid to flirt and be as raunchy as I want. And exchanging sexual energy for money has always been a big turn-on for me!"

"And how much will you make?"

"On an average night, they say it's anywhere from two hundred to two thousand."

"Wow!"

"We dance onstage for ones and fives. Then, if a guy wants a lap dance, there's a special area with comfy couches and it's twenty bucks per song. The bouncer stands there like the Secret Service, making sure the clients don't touch us. At the end of the night, we pay them out. I didn't know this, but strip clubs don't pay the dancers. It's the other way around. We pay to dance there. I pay like a ten percent house fee and ten percent for the security, and I tip the DJ too, which in my opinion is a win/win. I am so turned on by having a fat wad of cash at the end of the night."

"If I knew how turned on you'd get, I would've offered to be your sugar mamma."

Violet swooned and pulled me in for a kiss, which suddenly got interrupted with, "Oh! Speaking of mammas, I told my mom."

"No way!" I exclaimed.

"We were lunching at our favorite café. She said, 'I know you must think pole dancing is some radical form of performance art, but why do you need to do it in front of a bunch of drunken sailors? Why don't you find a nice cabaret or burlesque show?' To which I was like, 'First of all, I don't think it's art. I'm in service to the shadow side of humanity. I actually enjoy how raunchy and rebellious it feels. Second of all, those men are fighting for your country.' She sort of frowned and said, 'Okay, I guess there is nothing left to argue. I just hope you're safe.'"

I squeezed Violet's bare butt and said, "You're not the typical stripper though. It's not like you're doing it for money. If you were, that would be okay, I try not to judge any kind of sex work, but I don't think that's all it is. I feel there's a deeper calling here."

Violet admitted, "It's like a personal growth experiment. I

think of it as a laboratory for my self-expression where I get to be in service to lust and greed and the darker side that society has put in the shadow."

I sat up and looked her in the eyes, reflecting. "On the outside, you look like a stripper, but inside, you are an ancient temple dancer. Your dancing reminds people of the ways of the Goddess. The fact you are doing it in some dive bar is more evidence the sacred can exist in the profane."

Violet traced her hands along my face, her eyes brimming with tears, and asked, "Do you mean that?"

"Of course." I nuzzled her neck. "You think I'd just say that to get a lap dance?"

"But I'd dance for you, either way."

"I know, babe. You're easy."

"Because you're my Queen."

Those words struck me in an odd way. I got up and busied myself arranging pillows.

"What is it?" Violet asked.

I spoke in my dominant voice, "I used to think you were mine. That you would do anything to serve me. But I'm starting to see you do it because you love pleasing everybody, not just me. That's what you're made of. It's who you are."

"What are you saying?" Violet asked.

I paused to squeeze her. "I want to love you in such a way that you are totally free to be yourself. I want to love you the way Damien loves you."

"How about you love me the way Raven loves me."

Then it was my turn to swoon and we melted into a passionate kiss. My hand automatically found its way to the nape of her neck and tightened. I pulled her close, and she wrapped her legs around my hips. I pressed my pelvis against the warmth between her legs. I reached beneath the waistband of her panties and spoke in a low tone.

"I can't tell you how many fantasies I've had since you told me you started dancing."

"Tell me."

I offered options: "Do you want to hear my fantasy or your fantasy?"

"Tell me everything." Then she stopped. "Wait. What's the difference?"

I slid my fingers along the folds of her flower as I recalled, "In my fantasy, I show up without you knowing. I'm wearing a suit and tie, so I don't stand out in the audience."

"Are you wearing your fedora?" Violet breathed heavily with her eyes closed.

"Yes. And I watch you onstage flaunting your ass and tits in front of a dozen strange men." Her yoni was already wet and rearing against my hand. "You get down on all fours and slide around the floor in a miniskirt that is smaller than a belt, and high heels. Your dancing bewitches the entire club. Every time you glance at someone, they feel completely penetrated by you. You step off the stage to do lap dances for various men, draping your body over them and tickling them with your hair, then you drag your nails across their crotches to feel their engorged cocks."

"Mmmm . . . You are such a generous lover, sharing me with the room."

"But none of that matters because I know you're my bitch, and you're going home with me."

I grabbed her face and kissed her hard, pushing my thigh into her crotch, feeling her body grind against mine.

"Now, are you ready to hear YOUR fantasy?" I said, with my body above hers. I spread her legs farther apart, and with one hand I spread her flower petals against my own pulsing lips. "You're going to have to beg."

"Please," she whimpered, "pretty please."

"Even though touching the clientele is not allowed by the establishment, you live to push the edges. Whenever the bouncer isn't looking, you reach into a guy's pants or press your camel toe against someone's bare hands." I cupped her yoni hard, pressing firmly against her clit with my palm. "It's like a little game for you to see how much genital contact you can get in one night. And even if the bouncer doesn't notice, what you don't know is that the manager has a video camera. He's watching you."

Violet moaned lightly as my thumb found its way into her opening. "One night after being particularly naughty, you're paying out the bouncers, and one of them says, 'Hey, new girl. The manager wants to see you.' And he leads you to the back office where the manager is sitting behind his desk wearing a tie. He's been busy counting money, but stops to say, 'Come in. Shut the door, I want to show you something.' The first thing you see is a picture of yourself on the security screen and it's frozen on a frame where you are reaching down a client's pants.

"The second thing you notice is that your manager's pants are unbuttoned and he has been molesting himself to your image. You gasp because his cock is still hard. He has a skinny long shaft and it looks so angry!"

Violet's body quivered as I pressed deeper inside, grinding the base of my thumb against her clit. "He grabs your hand and wraps it around his swollen dick, expecting you to finish him off. Then he grabs your face and strokes your cheek, nodding as if to say, *Go down on me*. So you drop to your knees. You lick your lips and start slurping on his angry head. Just when you find a rhythm, the door opens and the bouncer comes in behind you and grabs your hips. You can feel his rough hands pulling your asscheeks open as he unzips and..."

Violet's body seized up, convulsing in pleasure, her muscles tightening and pulsing around my fingers. "Oh, God. Right there." She jerked her legs and arched her back, riding a series of orgasmic waves back to shore. "Hold on."

"Good girl," I said, waiting for her breath to slow down. I gently removed my fingers. "That was so fast."

"So good," she sighed.

"When you first started dancing, I thought I would be this possessive girlfriend, all protective of you, but now it turns me on."

"Yeah, it seems to be going well for everyone. Damien loves it, Autumn is working on a routine to audition next week. How do you feel about us dancing together?"

"I am really getting used to the idea of sharing you with the world."

Dirty Dentist
From Violet's *Book of Shadows*

Smiling is my spiritual practice. I smile even when I don't feel like it. I smile because I want to help people lighten up. Smiling is contagious. When I was sixteen, my dentist suggested I straighten my bite. At the time, I was too rebellious. As I got older, my teeth started to tilt. It's not a big deal, but I was looking at my mom's smile and I notice her teeth are crooked. They didn't used to be that way. I've been thinking it's time to get a retainer. I want something that won't interfere with dancing or my wedding pictures. One of the teachers at my yoga studio brags about her invisible retainer, so I got her dentist's number. After my appointment, I posted this on my Facebook wall:

Violet West
I'm going to do it! Now that the wedding date is set, I've

decided to get invisible retainers. My teeth are going to be straight in about six months. After my first visit with the dentist, I had two interesting revelations:

1) He said I had HUGE teeth. I know bigger is not necessarily better, but I felt strangely proud.

2) When the doctor pulled his slightly bloody glove out of my mouth, I was turned on. I told him that it reminded me of kinky glove play during my moon cycle with my girlfriend.

Comments Raven Turner
This gives me an idea for a new scene this Friday. Be sure to brush your teeth before our date.

I called her immediately to ask what she had in mind. She reminded me that the mouth is a sexual organ. I told her I was nervous about getting a retainer because I had a bad experience at the dentist's office as a kid. She insisted our session would help me to rescript all my past dental traumas.

To play the role, I decided to wear pigtails, no bra, and a flared-out skirt. Raven fawned over my pigtails. She wouldn't stop pulling them and kissing me during our brief boundary- and intention-setting conversation.

When we went into the playroom, it was all set up with a folded futon and pillows in the shape of a big recliner, covered with a sheet. She sat me down, blindfolded me, and told me to imagine I was in a cold, clinical room with certificates on the walls. She thanked me for filling out the new patient form. Then, she said she was going to leave the room to do some quick X-rays on another patient. She laid something heavy on my chest and left.

So I sat there blindfolded, listening for clues of what she was up to. Later I found out she was running around gathering props. She arranged a Dixie cup of mouthwash, toothpicks, and a toothbrush on a metal serving platter beside the makeshift dentist chair. She said she was the dental assistant and told me to imagine a bright lamp overhead and a display of strangely shaped dental tools. She removed the heavy blanket from my chest and said the doctor would be in to see me shortly.

She asked me to open my mouth and stuffed some kind of a utensil in it, then left the room again. It was a little unnerving, but I stayed curious. What was the doctor planning to do to me? When she returned, she snapped her rubber gloves and said, "Hello young lady, I'm Dr. Slinger. You are my last patient for the day. My nurse is off duty—I told her she could leave and lock the door behind her."

"Okay. I—"

"Don't talk, I need your mouth open right now." She put her rubber fingers between my lips and pried them open even more. "For the rest of our session, it's important that your mouth stays open. I understand this is your first visit to see an orthodontist?"

"Uh-hmm. I've seen a dentist before, but not an orthodontist," I slurred.

"Just relax and open wide," the doctor said as she pushed my tongue around with something that felt like a spoon. Then, she removed the utensil and stuffed her dry rubber fingers in my mouth.

"Now that the nurse is gone, we can take as long as we need," she said as she massaged my gums. I realized how rarely that part of my body gets attention. She methodically pressed beneath each tooth and ran her fingers on the inside between my teeth and cheeks. She firmly tugged on each tooth as if testing to see if anything was loose. It was such a strange sensation.

"We enjoy trying new methods around here, especially after hours. I love working on first-timers. That's my specialty, because you have no frame of reference for how this appointment should go."

"What do you mean, we?" I mumble.

"Oh, Dr. Scrivello and myself. He's the one who's going to fix you. He's finishing up with a client in the next room. After I finish prepping you, he'll take over. He's an orthodontist who's working on breakthrough healing methods, but his work is misunderstood. And since he's one of those geniuses who has no social skills, I like to help him prepare the subjects. I apologize if he has no bedside manner, so to speak."

Then the doctor straddled me with a knee firmly in my crotch and asked me to stick out my tongue. She took it with both hands and used long strokes with her thumbs along the sides. I could feel the saliva pooling in my mouth.

"The tongue works so hard, always chewing, sucking, swallowing, breathing, and speaking. It rarely gets a pampering."

Keeping one hand in my mouth, she put the other one up my skirt and rested it on my inner thigh. "We've also discovered that the jaw is connected to the pelvis. If we can get the pelvis to relax, it does wonders for your bite."

She slowly massaged my thighs. I could feel the wetness on her glove from my own mouth. I pressed my head back more and spread my legs.

"That's right. Open wide, I'm going to prepare your pelvis so that Dr. Scrivello can fit his extra-special instrument inside you." I don't remember all the other medical excuses she used to explore underneath my panties, but I kept my mouth open the whole time.

She started out with two deft fingers inside my pussy and two fingers probing my mouth. Next, she put four fingers into my pussy and simultaneously stuffed four inside of my mouth.

I felt like I was falling under the spell of some kind of a

narcotic. I was mesmerized by how she fingered the inside of my cheek by pressing her thumb on the outside of my face.

When I was fully anesthetized, she called another imaginary dentist into the room and told me that his huge cock could heal me if I just relaxed and kept my mouth open. She pulled my panties halfway down, stuffed a massive dildo inside, and just left it there. Then she walked behind my head and cradled it with both hands. She hovered over me and slowly slid her full hand into my mouth until, eventually, she was fisting my face.

Again, she just held me there and told me to breathe through my nose. She had her whole fist in my mouth and a big rubber dong inside me and this went on until I had no choice but to cum. When I started moaning, she eventually removed her hand and her own underwear so she could sit on my face until she came too.

Yours,
Vi.

P.S. This was one of my favorite Fridays ever!

Ping-Pong
From *Raven's Playbook*

I propped myself up on a pile of pillows next to Violet as she worked on my coffee table, which was cluttered with crafting supplies. After adding the final touch to a colorful poster with the words *Our Enchanted Commitment Ceremony* across the top, Violet announced, "I love how the branches of my mind-map look like the wild legs of an octopus."

I held it up like Vanna White and used my flat hand to highlight certain words as I said, "The branches of your mind-map are almost identical to those of a theater production: Venue, Costumes, Invitations, Decorations, Music, Ceremony . . . There's very little difference between ritual and performance art."

"And that's why I'm lucky to have your help!" Violet exclaimed. "I had so much resistance to planning the wedding, I needed you to dominate me into finishing it."

"This is nothing." I grabbed her face and forced a kiss on her open mouth. "The bigger question is what are we doing for your bachelorette party? Typically, I'd say let's hire strippers, but since you're already a stripper, we may have to think of something else."

"Not another thing to plan!"

"The bride doesn't plan her own bachelorette party, silly, that's the maid of honor's job. Leave it to me."

Violet squinted her eyes and said, "I told you, I'm not doing bridesmaids."

"Look, you don't get to say whether or not we're having a bachelorette party. It's happening. But if you behave, you may have some input on what we end up doing. Want me to throw another all-girl play party?"

"We just had one of those. We haven't had a real sex party since Solstice."

"Real?"

"You know what I mean. I'd love to do a mixed gender party. I want to include Damien."

"So you want a bachelor/bachelorette party. How about a fantasy fulfillment party where we play out people's fantasies onstage. Does Damien have a secret fantasy?"

"I've asked him that and he says all his fantasies have been surpassed ever since he started dating me."

"Aww . . . He's such a romantic," I teased. "Nick, on the other hand, has this ongoing fantasy about Asian lesbian contortionists and I've wanted to play it out."

"Where did he get that fetish?"

"Years ago, when he was in Thailand, he went to one of those sex shows where a woman shot a ping-pong ball out of her pussy into the audience. It left quite an impression, and now he won't shut up about it."

"Have you ever tried?" Violet asked.

"Not yet. But . . ." I opened my toy box and retrieved the unopened package of ping-pong balls. "I bought these."

"Wow! They come six to a pack. I'd love to stuff them in and shoot them out like a machine gun."

"Seriously?" I unwrapped the package. "Let me wash them first." I rinsed them in the sink with soap and water, and by the time I got back, Violet was jumping around on the couch like a an adolescent in her bra and panties. I handed her a ball.

Violet held it up to my face and asked, "Will you lubricate it for me?" I licked it once. Then she kissed me hard, and when my face was attached to hers, she slowly stuffed the ball between our mouths and then into mine. I spit it into her hand all slimy, and she said, "Well here goes."

She casually stuffed the ball inside like she was inserting a tampon. Then she scrunched up her face, strained, and said, "Nothing's happening."

I went into coach mode and said, "Breathe deep and relax."

She squatted with her hands in the air, then said, "I think it's stuck."

"Seriously?" I asked as she fished around with her finger.

"I can't reach it."

"How far did you push it up there?" I asked, but her only response was a few grunts and a loud squeal.

"Let me try," I said.

"I think it gets sucked farther in when I try to push it out."

"Do you know how to queef on command?"

Violet looked me in the eye and raised her eyebrow. "No. Can you?"

"Just pull up on your stomach muscles, like this, draw air up there. I used to be insecure about queefing, but then I had a tantra teacher say how powerful it is to bring life force into your womb. It's prana. I'm not embarrassed anymore." I put my hands on my hips and pulled my pelvis floor up as I breathed air in with my yoni. "I imagine this is how they do it in Thailand."

"Cool. Just help me get it out, okay?" she said, her voice edging with worry. I put my finger up inside her, immediately feeling the smoothness of the ball.

"One time," I said, fishing around, "I thought I lost a jade egg up there, but it came out when I sneezed. This is why they make holes in the jade eggs, so you can use a string to pull them out, and why most dildos have flared bases, so they don't get stuck."

"Just get the damn thing out," she exclaimed.

"Relax. I got it," I said, finally breaking the suction and producing the ping-pong ball.

"That was freaky, I don't want to do that again. Don't they say in Thailand, don't try this at home?"

"No, but they do say 'If it's not fun, it's not worth doing.' It's *Sanuk*. That's my favorite Thai saying."

Violet was not satisfied. "I want you to try it now," she pleaded as she pulled at my waistband. I stepped out of my pants and pulled my shirt up over my head, but left my cheetah-print bra on.

"Maybe the lube made it slip in farther. I'm going to stick it in dry." I stuffed the ball just inside the entrance of my tunnel. "Okay, are you ready?"

I took a long, deep breath, and pushed with my stomach muscles, forcing the ball out.

"Oh my God, you did it. You did it!" Violet said in a sing-song tone.

"Well, it didn't exactly shoot out, it was more of a plop."

"Still, it was fantastic! We've got to get this on camera, will you do it again?"

She got her phone and recorded a video of me trying a second time, which was just as anticlimactic as the first attempt.

"It must take a lot of practice to develop the muscle control to get any real distance. And we don't have much time before your party."

"Well, maybe instead of shooting it, you can push it out and I can catch it in my mouth."

"Or better yet, what if you volley it with a ping-pong paddle?"

"Or how about if I put a ping-pong paddle in my pussy and volley it into the audience," Violet proclaimed.

"Awesome! I don't have a paddle, but I do have a hairbrush. We could practice with this." I located a paddle-shaped hairbrush from my bathroom.

"This is going to be epic. We've got to record this!"

"Let me see if Nick's available." I ran half naked to Nick's office and lured him to my room with the opportunity to film the raw rehearsal of our first performance. By the time we returned to the living room, Violet had a condom-covered hairbrush sticking out of her pussy.

"Hi, Nick! Nice suit," Violet said.

"Hey, Vi. Nice hairbrush," he bantered.

"Thanks for filming us," she said, striking an exaggerated pose like a 1950s pinup model.

"Well you know," he said, smiling, "I've been waiting my whole life for a video like this."

"This is just a sneak peek," I said in my director's voice as I stuffed the ping-pong ball inside myself. "We're only doing one take. Nick's on his way to a business meeting."

Violet asked, "How do you want to position me?"

I squatted and waved for Violet to come closer. She dropped all the way down into a backward bridge and scooted the brush toward me like a crab walking on her hands and feet. Eventually, she positioned the hairbrush directly below my yoni.

"Ready?" I said, and I pushed out the ping-pong ball. Violet thrust her hips to swat at the ball, and on her very first try managed to bounce it up and down like a paddle ball expert! We all hollered with excitement.

"Did you catch it on camera?" Violet squealed.

"I think so," Nick exclaimed. "That was awesome!"

"Was it as good as the women in Thailand?" I joked.

"Well now that's hard to say. They had range and aim."

"Just lie to me and tell me I was better," I said, grabbing his phone to watch the video.

"But of course you are much sexier," Nick added. "See for yourself." We crowded around the small screen to watch the replay.

"Oh my God," I winced, "my ass looks huge!"

"It's not exactly your best angle," Violet admitted.

"It's terrible. Erase it!" My directorial impulse kicked in and I handed the phone back to Nick. "I want you to shoot from higher up. Let's imagine the audience is over here..." I directed Nick on exactly where to stand and then I adjusted Violet's position. "This time you're over here. And I'll rearrange so I don't upstage you. And . . . action."

I took a big breath and stuffed the ball inside. I pushed the ball out with a great *plop* and it bounced twice against her paddle. Nick nearly dropped the camera when he raced over trying to catch the ball with his mouth, but missed. We all laughed and gathered around the phone to watch our second attempt.

"This is so much fun!" Violet said, giggling.

"I wish I didn't have to go back to work," Nick said.

"I'm glad you caught our rehearsal." I kissed his cheek.

"I wish I could show it to my sales team at the meeting."

"No. Erase it now." I grabbed the phone, but Violet intercepted.

"No, it's my phone, and my body too, and I want to show Damien," Violet argued.

"Not a chance!" I put my hands on my hips. "It's obscene. I don't want that to fall into the wrong hands."

"Just Damien and Autumn, no one else."

"You promise?"

"I promise."

"I'm trusting you and that's a big deal, coming from me."

"I would never take your trust for granted," she said, kissing me sweetly. "Now what are we going to wear?"

"You could dress like Thai prostitutes," Nick offered, but I ignored him.

"Or we could enter in cute little tennis skirts and sports bras and see-through sports nets around our breasts, like in a burlesque show. We could shimmy out and tease the audience."

"With whistles around our necks." Violet applauded and added, "and wristbands . . . and sports socks . . . This is going to be great!"

"As long as we can get the damn ball to plop out!"

FRIDAY #46
Gentlemen's Club

Violet's new club generally frowns on admitting single women. Most strip clubs try to prevent jealous wives or prostitutes coming and making a scene or competing for business. As such, Raven decides to butch it up. She wears her favorite pin-striped pants with a tailored vest and jacket. As she tucks her hair under her fedora, she looks in the mirror and tries to give off an air that says: *I am only here to watch half-naked chicks dance. I am not a threat to the establishment.*

Raven passes the suspicious bouncer's inspection at the entrance and immediately spots Violet at the far end of the room. She's flaunting hot-pink booty shorts and a matching bikini top as she flirts with a table full of military guys. Even though Raven's eyes are still acclimating to the dim lighting, she can see that Violet is hypnotizing everyone around her. Raven takes a seat in a faux-leather armchair positioned in front of the LED-lit stage. She may look calm, but inside she feels fraudulent. She has always thought strip clubs were degrading to women. She's held a secret judgment about the type of women who call themselves "erotic dancers."

Looking around the room now, it seems to her there are three types of people in the club: dancers, staff, and clientele. The dancers are putting on a big show to hustle money. The staff is there to protect the dancers and maintain order. The clients' intentions are not as clear. Raven suspects they are lost and lonely, hungry for human contact.

Her people-watching reverie is broken the moment Violet appears and draws her into an awkward public hug. She is equally surprised when Violet seizes her by the wrist and drags her through the minefield of tables toward the ladies changing room in back.

"We should be okay in here," Violet says, scoping out the bathroom to make sure they are alone before pressing her mouth to Raven's lips. "I want to be close to you, even just for a moment."

Raven doesn't fully understand all the club rules. She knows dancers are not supposed to bring their lovers to the club, and certainly they are not allowed to make out in the bathroom.

"This place is a trip," Raven says before Violet's lips are sealed against hers again and their two bodies are slammed against a wall of cold metal lockers.

"The fedora suits you," Violet whispers between kisses.

Raven holds Violet by the shoulders to admire her body.

Violet wiggles her bare hips as if wagging her tail. "What do you think?"

She has on more makeup than Raven is accustomed to. "Stunning. I don't want to ruffle you up."

Violet leans toward the mirror to fix her eyeliner. "I know

you prefer the natural look, but it's fun to play dress up." Violet steps into a stall. "Come in here."

Intoxicated by their kiss, Raven has no choice but to follow. Their lips locked, Raven's tension falls away.

"I probably shouldn't give you a private dance, but I will dedicate my next stage set to you."

Raven slides her hand down Violet's shapely hips as she leaves the stall to look in the mirror. Violet re-pins her garter belt. Every move Violet makes is like a dance, whether she's onstage or not.

"When do you go on?" Raven asks.

"Soon." Violet smiles. "You should exit first so they don't see us together."

"Got it. Can I get you a drink?"

"No, silly."

Raven raises an eyebrow, thinking to herself, *I don't usually drink, but tonight I am going to need one.* Then she exits to find a seat at the corner of the bar. Onstage, a hot woman in tall black boots waves her ass around to a Top 40 song.

Raven orders a draft from a waitress in a staff-issued T-shirt who is making her rounds. "Let me know if there's anything else I can get for you." Raven's face widens into a smile in response to the woman's curious stare, and she asks her to break a hundred dollar bill.

"Sure. Are you having a good time?" the waitress asks while making change.

Raven looks up to see a gleam in her eye. Oh God! She's gay. How did Raven misread that? A slow-spreading smile crosses her face. "Better now that you asked." Raven pockets the cash but lingers at the bar before leaving.

When the topless woman finishes dancing, she crawls around the perimeter of the stage collecting bills and thanking the clients before exiting.

As the music changes, Violet steps onstage with her back to the pole. She shrugs one shoulder slowly to the rhythm of the song's prelude. Raven is enraptured. The music picks up, and Violet moves as if the melody were emanating from her bone marrow. The pole is magically transformed into a phallus. Violet's hips move against it the same uncontrollable way as when she's making love. Raven's pelvis responds with sudden wetness. Violet steadies her back against the pole, suggestively biting her lip as she slowly slides her backside to the ground. She spreads her legs wide one at a time. Raven's etheric body is transported onto the stage in front of her priestess. Raven imagines herself standing against the pole, being worshipped by Violet's writhing body.

Violet concludes her dance with a final flurry on the pole that leaves everyone breathless. With a huge and sincere smile, she walks the perimeter of the stage, gazing at each person in the audience as she gathers her cash and holds it to her heart.

Stepping off the stage, Violet goes out of sight into the exclusive area.

Raven makes her way into a corner to stand and watch the lap dances. Voyeurism is participation, she tells herself, as she watches Violet undulate her body over a slack-jawed bald man. Raven feels slightly deviant about her presence being unknown to Violet. The knot in her stomach melts into arousal.

As the song winds down, Violet slows down. She holds her face so close to the man that Raven is surprised he doesn't kiss her. Violet is enjoying this way too much. Raven smiles to herself, thinking, *I'll have to punish her later.*

After several dances, Violet's eyes meet Raven's and widen. Raven returns a stern look and turns her body sharply to leave the area. After a few songs, Violet finds Raven at the bar talking with the waitress.

Upon seeing the strain on Raven's face, Violet asks, "Is everything okay?"

Raven attempts to reassure Violet by saying, "I'll be fine after I see you get proper punishment."

"Oh, goodie. I'm glad you came in, and so you know, you can leave any time you want."

Raven's all worked up from the sexual energy in the air and not ready to call it a night. "I'm not leaving until you do."

"It might be a while."

"I can't trust you here. I will leave when you do and walk you to your car."

"It's a little slow tonight. I'll see if I can get off early." And she flits away in a flash of pink glitter.

Raven's attention returns to the girl behind the bar, who's been eavesdropping while pretending to dry glasses. Raven swallows hard, stuffing down her sadness that she and Violet will be going to their separate homes and sleeping in separate beds with their respective men.

Underneath her yearning for Violet is tender insecurity. It's challenging to see Violet sharing herself with everyone in the club. Raven yearns for the comfort and nurturance she finds between Violet's legs.

After a few short songs, Violet returns and says she'll be ready to go after she pays out the bouncers and management. Raven waits at the bar, coolly watching the bartender with one eye, and tracking Violet with the other.

Violet returns with a duffel bag, and a long coat with fake fur around the collar. "Does this coat make me look like a slut?" Violet asks Raven as they link arms and walk toward the door.

"You are a slut, no matter what you're wearing," Raven quips.

"Fair enough," Violet says as they step into the cool night air. Her little silver Prius is parked in the farthest corner of the well-lit parking lot.

Raven turns to grab Violet's fuzzy lapel and insists, "How about a little makeout session before we part ways?"

"Yes please."

"Open the back door."

Violet pushes the button and Raven opens the door wide.

"Get in. On your back!"

Violet lies down and spreads her legs as wide as she can within the interior of the compact backseat.

Raven carefully climbs into the car and positions herself above Violet. Violet reaches for Raven's face, but Raven resists.

"I want to look at you first...you easy, eager slut. Look how quick you are to spread your legs."

She traces her fingers from Violet's ankle over her soft calf, over the erogenous zone in the back of her knee, to her inner thigh, resting her hand flat and firm there.

"What would you do if I were one of your clients?"

"Depends on which one."

"Oh, really? Did you fancy someone this evening?" Raven traces her thumb along the seam of Violet's lacy panties. She obviously put this fresh new pair on just for Raven. "Uh. There is this one guy, he's quite awkward. He comes in often . . . and always asks for me. I like him."

"Which one? Is he bald?"

"No. The one with curly hair. He's sort of mousey."

Violet peels down her own panties and she starts to undulate as Raven teases her pulsing lips.

"What if he followed you out here?"

"He wouldn't dare. He's too shy."

"Maybe he's just shy in public. What if he saw you leaving, and decided to follow you out to your car and then found you like this?"

"Then you would have to be my bodyguard."

"No. What if I was like, you want to fuck my girlfriend?" Violet seems to feel a flush of humiliation, and starts humping Raven's hand.

"I'd be like, 'She wants you. Let me just spread her legs farther for you.' Or maybe I'd get behind you and hold you down
for him. And he'd get an instant erection . . . I'd tear your panties
off and he'd unzip and his cock would just leap out. I would put
my hand over your mouth, so nobody would hear you scream .
. . and you would definitely scream because I wouldn't let him
do any foreplay before shoving himself inside you. . . ."

Raven slaps Violet's eager pussy a few times. Violet thrusts
her pelvis toward Raven's hand, begging to be filled.

"I'd tear open a condom for him and make him put it on,
but I wouldn't let him touch your pussy, or massage your lips,
the way I'm touching you now, I'd just make him cram himself
up toward your cervix and I would watch you wince, but you'd
just take it. . . ."

Raven plunges two fingers deep inside Violet's soft and eager slit. After a few excited strokes, Raven repositions her own
pussy high on Violet's thigh. She straddles Violet's leg and starts
riding hard, breathing heavy, eagerly thrusting, the same way
she imagines the client would.

"Then, with no regard for you, he'd just use your pussy to
jerk off and collapse on you after he came." Raven lets out a
moan and slows, shifting all her weight onto Violet for a few
still breaths. Without words, both women know Raven is cumming, and they move in unison, savoring the stillness for a few
tender breaths.

"Then I'd tell him to get out of here. He served his purpose.
No cuddles for him."

The lovers giggle as the fantasy slowly dissipates.

"Afterward," Raven continues, "I'd come over and lie on
top of you like this and hold you myself." More breathing. Violet softly caresses Raven's hair. Then Raven notices a subtle
rocking from Violet's pelvis, and starts to meet Violet's movement with long slow strokes.

"So you'd be left here, shocked and breathless, turned on yet abandoned. . . ."

Raven finds a rhythm and lets her hand start to surf it.

"Do you want someone to fill your cunt and finish you off?"

"Yes, please."

Raven looks into Violet's eyes—by the dim glow of the streetlights, she can see the tenderness and trust.

"I love you so much. I want to touch you in that spot no penis can touch. . . ."

Her hand begins a slow and lyrical dance. Violet breathes with a lilting, song-like moan on each exhale. Raven knows Violet's body and plays it confidently like a well worn instrument. This is her favorite song, the final release. And release she does. Violet cums sweetly, shuddering and smiling. Raven's hand stills inside Violet as she holds in silence. They breathe in harmony, parked in the corner of the public parking lot.

Violet states the obvious: "I love you."

"I know," Raven responds warmly.

Slowly, they sort themselves out. "Ready to go home?"

"Yes," Violet says, feeling around for her keys. "I'm so glad you came. . . ."

"Me too," says Raven, smiling at the pun that never gets old.

"See you next Friday?" Violet asks, in a rich tone that says, *I live for Fridays*.

"Let's skip the makeup next time, okay?" Raven advises.

"How about something in nature?" Violet says, rearranging herself into the front seat.

"As long as we can take off our clothes."

"Sounds good." Raven offers a final kiss, shuts the door, and watches Violet drive away.

Wood Nymph
From Violet's *Book of Shadows*

I had no idea dancing would take so much out of me. When I'm on someone's lap or on the dance floor, there's nothing I'd rather be doing. But when I get home, I'm spent. Even though it's only been a couple of nights this week, I told Raven I was sorry to admit that I didn't have the energy to go hiking. "It's like I'm training for a marathon, except I'm running in six-inch heels."

"You don't have to perform for me," Raven reassured me. "Relax; you can even nap if you want."

"But I feel bad about giving all my juice to strangers and not having enough left over to pleasure my woman."

"You're sexy even when you're sleeping." Raven covered my mostly naked body with a billowing sheet.

I closed my heavy eyelids and yawned. "I feel drugged."

"You're just saying that because you want me to take advantage of you." Raven slipped out of her clothes and folded them at the foot of my bed. "You look so innocent lying there, like a princess in a field of poppies."

And then my bedroom seemed to morph into a meadow . . . like a psychedelic spell . . . Raven's hands glided gently over my bare skin like the wind. I melted into the tall grass and watched the sunlight glittering through the leaves. Ferns sprouted up beside my head and curled at the tips. Raven slipped between my legs with her mouth. The soft clouds seemed to be blowing on my flower. Raven pointed out a nearby tree that was dripping with vines and a maze of roots running into the ground. My bedroom became an enchanted forest. The uneven earth was moist and smelled like musk. The lapping of Raven's tongue against my clit sounded like a babbling stream.

Raven lifted her lips and said, "There's someone behind that tree, watching you."

I imagined a huge banyon with ivy spiraling around the base, and I saw something moving in the shadows.

"You're a young wood nymph, with flowers woven into your hair, and you're being watched by the goat-headed god, Pan."

I heard myself giggling, but could barely lift my head. "What's a wood nymph?"

"They are the spirits within the trees." Raven continued fingering my engorging lips in the same rhythm she had been licking, in order to continue weaving the fantasy with her words. "Trees are wise and sedentary beings always growing in the same spot. Each tree is inhabited by a playful wood nymph who likes to dance and play before the sapling fully takes root. Nymphs are stealthy tricksters—they love to explore and interact with animals. If someone sees them they can disappear at will, instantly slipping back into the bark of their tree. They only have a couple of years at most before the bark hardens and they can no longer leave. If Pan sees a wood nymph, he will pounce to deflower her."

"Oh my. I am loving this fantasy."

"Wood nymphs are particularly fun to pluck because they are portals of power. When Pan sticks his dick into a wood nymph, it's like plugging in to another dimension. It's dangerous for a wood nymph; it's intoxicating and draining, so the wood nymphs sometimes defend themselves by turning invisible. Usually, if you spot him first, you can make yourself disappear. But not when you're so sleepy. That's when your defenses are down. Pan knows he can pin down a wood nymph when she's sleepy. Like now—you're aware he's standing behind that tree, spying on you. But you don't notice him tiptoeing around with his cloven feet in the high grass. If you had your wits about you, you would surely notice he's not hung like a goat, but like a huge horse. In fact, when he grows erect, all the blood rushes between his legs and his mind becomes clouded. He becomes obsessed with the conquest. He is more animal than man, ruled by passion. He's lusting after you now with flared nostrils and fiery eyes."

"Oh yeah? And what am I wearing?" I said, testing to see if she saw what I saw.

"Long stockings, of course, and tall boots, which are practical in the woods. But your skin is otherwise naked because you love being massaged by the moss and tickled by the soft bark. And you've got long gloves, cut off at the fingertips, to help you climb trees and pick fruit. You're covered in fern pollen, which glitters in the sunlight. Right now, Pan is staring at your breasts, which are exposed and sparkling in the sunlight."

"Wow." My whole body started trembling. How does she get so deep inside my psyche?

"You know what Pan looks like?"

"Please," I said, and I'm not sure if I was pleading for more details or for her to maintain the rhythm with her curled fingers pressing against my G-spot. Fortunately, she continued both.

"The hair on his head is messy like a bird's nest, but it doesn't hide the thick pointed horns that jut out from above his temples. His hands are wide and humanlike, except his fingernails are black. His hairy legs and ass jut down into hooves like a goat's. His chest is cut with muscles and his waist is trim, which accentuates his growing cock. It's thicker and more menacing than his horns. Look now and you'll see the determination in his green eyes, which mirror the moss in the forest."

I couldn't take it anymore. I heard myself saying: "Oh horny goat head, be with me now."

Instantly, Raven climbed on top of me and stuffed her etheric cock inside me. I felt it filling me, uncomfortably huge at first. Her mythical horn was pushing past my cervix, crowding my innards. She rode me like an out-of-control animal, until our breathing took over. Her eyes rolled back in ecstasy, and then the damndest thing happened. Just as she was cumming . . . I swear, it happened. We both heard it. There was a haunting flute melody playing in the distance.

Yours,
Vi.

P.S. Before Raven left, we reviewed the invitation list for my bachelor/bachelorette party. I told her that Damien loved the private ping-pong pussy video, but worried that the newcomers at the party wouldn't appreciate it as much. She seemed relieved. Then I asked her what she wanted to celebrate on our first "Polyversary." She couldn't believe we've been together for almost a full year, so I showed her the dates in my *Book of Shadows*. She offered to get me jewelry or a homemade dessert, but I told her our relationship wasn't about gifts. I preferred touch and words of appreciation. So she said she'd write me a love declaration. I told her I'd like her to tie me up and gag me before reading it. She agreed, but only because I begged.

Bachelor/ette Party

Autumn lives with her brother, Shawn, and the main hall of their home is filling with friends from varying circles, including actors from the Barefoot and Pregnant Theater, students and teachers from Violet's pole dance studio, and a handful of peace activists from Damien's collective. Nick is seated with his long-distance lover from Japan, Mia. When Raven looks around the room, she realizes her community has become inseparable from Violet's.

A momentary thought lands like a little moth on her shoulder—if she were the one marrying Violet . . . or Damien . . . she would have invited all the same people to her party. This is her soul tribe, and it gives her pleasure to be leading the opening circle. She has a comfortable role to hide behind, instead of having to deal with her conflicting feelings.

Her intention tonight is to take pleasure in other people's

pleasure. It's a spiritual practice. The poly community calls it compersion. But in Buddhism it's known as Mudita: a vicarious happiness that can only come from an established sense of self. Whenever Raven notices jealousy or competition arising in her awareness, she is determined to shift her focus onto Violet and Damien's happiness, instead.

Raven invites the celebrated couple to sit in large thrones, which Autumn decorated just for this occasion. Autumn rushes into Damien's lap to kiss him before the official festivities begin. In that moment, Raven realizes she isn't the only one whose beloveds are getting married. She hadn't considered what it would be like to be in love with both of them without the solace of a primary partner. She glances in Nick's direction and waves. He immediately goes into his role as cowboy, rounding people up and leading them to sit on a circle of pillows in the great room.

Violet watches wide-eyed as a slow stream of guests enter the common room. She meets each person with a reverent smile and brings them into silence once they've all gathered.

"Before Raven starts, I just have to say how moved I am to see everyone." Violet giggles. "I know for many of you, this is your first play party, and a lot of you wouldn't have come if it weren't to celebrate our commitment ceremony. I want to thank you for taking that risk."

"Feels right," Damien says, almost finishing her sentence. "When we decided to have a private ceremony in the woods next week, we knew we would miss our community. We also knew most weddings are so focused on friends and family that they aren't even about the couple anymore. Since our ceremony is designed just for us, this gathering can serve as a backward wedding reception, where we can contextualize our union within the larger ecosystem."

Nick stands up. "We don't have glasses to clink with our forks, but how about we snap our fingers when we want the lovebirds to kiss?" The room erupts in a rainfall of snapping, and Violet and Damien fall into a passionate kiss.

Raven begins, "We will be celebrating these two lovebirds in the most transcendent and transpersonal sense. Naturally, many of you are nervous about getting naked in a room full of freaks. Some of you might be downright terrified, so I'm going to go over the basics of consensual play, so we can all relax and enjoy the magic."

Raven concludes the opening circle by inviting the soon-to-be newlyweds into the center, but Damien objects. "Since we'll have plenty of bonding time when we leave for the ceremony, we discussed connecting separately tonight so we can optimize our time with the community."

"Okay. I stand corrected." Raven improvises, "Let's start with a different icebreaker. Get into small groups for a brief massage with the intention to get out of the mind and into the body and heart. Afterward, it'll be self-directed play followed by a closing circle around midnight."

The room reorganizes into little sensual pods, then it transforms into an adult playground of scantily clad bodies enjoying all kinds of sensual exploration. Raven's first move as party facilitator is to perch on the highest lookout point and watch the moving masterpiece to see if anyone needs support. Violet sneaks up behind the staircase railing where Raven is leaning and kisses her neck.

"Wanna check-in?" Violet whispers.

Raven makes room for Violet to sit beside her and asks, "So how are you feeling?"

"A bit like a butterfly. I just want to go from person to person and spread my love."

"That's beautiful."

"How about you?"

"Well, I'm holding space for quite a few newbies. So, I

thought I'd play the voyeuristic life guard tonight and watch all the gorgeous bodies in motion. I especially enjoy watching my lovers in the midst of pleasure. Nick said his intention was to reconnect with Mia and introduce her to the tribe. It looks like he's doing a pretty good job of it already." Raven points toward Nick, who is in the far corner slowly circling Mia's big breasts with an industrial size spool of saran wrap. Her body is turning into a see-through cocoon.

"That looks fun!" Violet declares.

"And it would be fun for me to watch you play with whomever you want. If you or Damien need anything, I'm here in total service."

"Thank you, for . . . everything," Violet says with a kiss, and flutters away.

As the evening progresses, she witnesses Violet in a number of scenes, lap dances, three-way kisses, spankings, each with different people who have different significance in Violet's life. Meanwhile, Raven practices self-connection with deep breath and prayer. Instead of feeling left out, she puts herself into the other person's shoes. She imagines she is the one enjoying Violet's attention.

The party has a wonderful soundtrack of moans, spanks, and sighs, with chill lounge music as the backdrop. Whenever Raven hears the echo of Violet's giggle, it triggers her into her "compersion practice."

At one point, Raven makes her way to the far corner where Nick is receiving a blow job from Mia. Mia's breasts are pressed tightly against her body with a clear wrap, which exaggerates her cleavage. Raven enters their space slowly and gently reaches down to play with Mia's jet black hair. She starts holding Mia's hair away from her face, revealing her lips wrapped around her husband's erect penis. Raven leans in to kiss Nick with an open mouth. His lips are dry at first from heavy breathing. Then she

drops to her knees to kiss Mia's face for a moment before placing her lips on the other side of Nick's eager cock. Raven and
Mia make eye contact and intuitively maneuver several kisses
across Nick's cock. They take turns slurping his shaft. Raven
notices a pinch of competition and decides to give them some
space. She kisses Mia on the cheek and squeezes her undulating
ass as she crawls away.

Raven moves slowly to the music. It's more like sensual
stretching than dancing. Her peripheral vision is set on Violet,
who is lap dancing for Singh, one of Damien's business associates.

She unbuttons his shirt and then does an impressive hand-
stand to wiggle her crotch in his face, before straddling his surprisingly hairy chest. After her wild, orgasmic display, she manages to strip his button-down shirt off and slip it on herself.
A lacy thong is all Violet has on underneath, and the effect is
stunning.

As Violet locks eyes with Autumn on the couch, Raven
watches. Raven settles back into her staircase perch to watch
Violet crawl across the seat cushions like a hungry predator.
Their mouths meet, and Raven witnesses a foreign language,
created by the uniqueness of their bond. Her stomach aches, but
she reminds herself to stay out of the story. If she didn't know
these women, this would be incredibly hot to watch! Can she
pretend for a moment that Violet is not her bitch?

Raven forces herself not to look away as Violet produces
a strap-on. She pulls it over her hips and begins adjusting the
straps with an ease suggesting she has done it before, a lot.

Violet strokes her erect cock a few times against Autumn's
writhing body, and still dancing, pulls Autumn's panties down.
They slither their bodies around each other like snakes. It's as
if they grew up doing this dance together in a cave where there
was never enough space to move freely. Raven's stomachache
turns into a cramp. There must be a painful belief beneath this

pain: *Autumn fits Violet better than I do.* That's the painful thought, like a steel blade in her side that must be removed.

Raven focuses on the ecstasy on Violet's face as she pins Autumn against the couch and inserts her dick with the help of her left hand. She grabs Autumn's hips and increases the pace. Biting her bottom lip, she scrunches her nose and thrusts passionately.

Raven's arousal draws her closer. She's not interested in including herself, as she doesn't want to interrupt, but she wants to get close enough to imagine it was her. She sits on the adjacent couch and massages her own breasts. She pulls at her nipples and presses them together, which feels good. Would she rather be the one fucking Violet? Or maybe she wants to know what it's like to be inside Autumn?

She sees the beauty of what is happening right now, and realizes it's perfect. There is no need to interfere with reality.

After one brief and beautiful moment, another stabbing pain distracts her. It is a new story. She's concerned about how she must look, gawking at these two women. Are people thinking she's being possessive? Who cares what they think? The truth is, if she looks away, she'll be inauthentic, pretending not to care. Of course she cares. Violet is her beloved. This is not just her bitch, but her soulmate. And here she is, topping another woman, in clear view of everyone. She wants to see it. To feel it. To accept that her beloved is in love with another woman. The energy around her heart and pelvis begins to move. There is arousal, there is admiration, and there is acceptance. And of course, there is love, not just toward Violet, but toward Autumn too. In loving Violet, Raven has grown to love everyone she loves. That's why their love is so enormous.

Autumn is moving toward orgasm—a loud, hot howl grabs the attention of nearly everyone in the room. Violet keeps pumping until Autumn coos: "Slow, baby, slow." They melt into a sweet spoon. And after a minute of watching them cuddle, Raven releases her fixation and allows herself to scan the room.

There is a voluptuous woman flogging her husband in the middle of the room. Nick and Mia are now engaged in a kinky foursome with another couple.

Damien is sitting in the "shallow end," having an intense discussion with a new couple and presumably helping them process their relationship agreements.

Meanwhile, there is a Hungarian man who has tied two women into rope harnesses and is walking them on leashes. Raven knows it's almost time to close the party, and the Hungarian is going to need a little time to unbind them, so she announces there are only twenty minutes left. "Make your last request before closing circle."

Closing circle is Raven's favorite part. It's where the community gathers to share their harvest. Nick makes his way to Raven's side, bringing his sleepy jet-lagged girlfriend along. Violet stays on the couch with Autumn, making room for Damien to sit on the arm. There is a sweet energy in the room. Faces are glowing with post orgasmic smiles. After a brief moment of silent self-connection, Raven speaks slowly, inviting people to share about the magic of the evening.

Damien acknowledges his highlight was how many people were willing to show up for this grand experiment, and he thanks everyone for honoring their boundaries.

Violet agrees and adds how fun it was to dance for Singh, as she seductively unbuttons his shirt and returns it to him by throwing it across the circle.

Autumn admits that an old wound got touched. She felt left out, but was grateful when Violet came and gave her the attention she craved. "Thank you, baby." They kiss.

Raven piggybacks on Autumn's admission by saying, "Thanks for sharing so vulnerably. She is not the only one in the room feeling insecurity, jealousy, competition, or judgment. Whenever people are given permission to shine, our shadows also come out to play. Personally, I moved through a lot of my own ego, and I am still reminding myself the love in this room is bigger than the self-indulgent suffering."

After several more shares, Raven invites Violet and the reluctant groom to the center of the room. "Normally I like to dedicate the orgasmic energy of the night to the healing of the planet and all sentient beings, but tonight, I want to add a prayer for this special union. May their commitment be blessed, may our community grow with them, and may this marriage serve the highest good."

"Aho!"

FRIDAY #49

I Do
From Raven's *Book of Shadows*

I left the stage empty except for a lonely stool beneath a single bulb. I wore all black and set my notes on my duffel bag near the footlights. I imagined the empty house seats filled with an understanding audience. I cleared my throat and began my monologue:

"When someone asks me how I feel about my girlfriend getting married, I see her smile in my mind and I say something pithy like, 'I'm happy for them.' Which is not bullshit—but it's a partial truth. The whole truth is complicated. It's messy.

"I've always had mixed feelings about marriage. As a feminist, I knew marriage was conceived as an exchange of property. A woman was considered a man's possession, legally purchased from her father and bound to serve her husband. So the thought of wearing a white dress, to me, is like waving a white flag of surrender, something I would only do if all hope was lost and my spirit was broken. It's extreme, I know, but in college I minored in women's studies.

"Now look at me: I'm happily married with a husband and child. The layers of irony are not lost on us—in fact, we even named our playhouse the Barefoot and Pregnant Theater Company. I married Nick in part because of his sense of humor, and in part because of the freedom he gave me. Together we reappropriate the meaning of marriage and have a liberated partnership. So clearly, I believe in marriages where people do not succumb to the cultural default, but instead make their own meaning, which is exactly what Violet and Damien are doing, right now, in the redwoods, without me.

"They found an outdoor cathedral in an old-growth forest. With God as their witness, they are making their vows amongst the pines, blue jays, moss, and squirrels. Damn, I wish I were there."

I paused, picked up my journal, and hoped that I could get through this without crying if I just read the lines.

"I wish I could walk her down the aisle and give her away, especially since her real dad does not support open marriage. But she insists on giving herself away, and I respect that, so if I were there, this is what I'd say . . ."

I opened my duffel bag to pull out a hideous, oversized bridesmaid dress. I stepped inside and pulled it up, leaving the back unzipped and the shoulders slightly askew for dramatic effect. Then I cleared my throat and continued reading.

"When I strip off the fantasy, the story, and all the layers of illusion, I see you both, individually and together. You fit. You somehow make this upside-down inside-out world of ours make sense. And as if our world isn't backward enough, open marriage is tough. It's a winding path that doubles back and takes us to unexpected places.

"Although the road is unknown, the two of you are built for

this journey, equipped with complementary skills, and you are not alone. I hereby vow to be there for both of you, mirroring where we came from and helping see where we're going: always in the direction of ever-increasing love. Which, as far out as I can see, has no end."

I curtsied to an imaginary audience then slowly stepped out of the costume.

I reflected, "It's all true. But it's a partial truth. It's probably better I wasn't invited. I would've cried the whole damn time. You know why people cry at weddings? Sure, some people are touched by the beauty, but others are devastated because their deepest dreams have been dashed. When it comes to my bitch, I have unspeakable dreams. And what makes her so precious is that she lets me speak them. So this is what I would NOT have said at her ceremony:

"I wish you were my bride. It's not that I want a public declaration of your devotion. I already have that. Actually, it's because I want to make you my property, like a slave trader buying a servant girl. You bring out the part of me that wants to possess you, to break your free spirit and make you surrender. And the extraordinary thing is . . . you want it too. It's not all the time, but when we role-play, you are right there with me. And when the scene is over, after I've done unthinkable things to you, you go back to him and report every humiliating detail.

"Now that you are married, I will have to borrow you from him. I'll never understand how he finds it in his heart to keep lending you out to me, but for that, I am indebted to him. I am devoted to him. You have managed to find the one man who is not threatened by our darkness, someone whose love is so vast it can hold and heal all of those unspeakable places. And by marrying him, you have made him my master."

CURTAIN.

FRIDAY #50
Rosebud

Violet flings the door open, wearing nothing but a lacy thong. She greets Raven with such enthusiasm that Raven has to pull away to breathe.

"I have so much to share!" Violet says, peeling off Raven's scarf and running her hands over her bare shoulders. "Outside? Inside? Where do you want to be?"

"The bedroom," Raven says, slipping out of her shoes. She sets her duffel bag at the foot of the bed before removing more layers.

Violet follows with a teacup in one hand and her phone in the other. "I got the sweetest pictures!"

"Not yet," Raven says, gently cupping Violet's lace-covered yoni. "I want to feel you first."

"Really?" Violet sets down her stuff and sits beside Raven. "You're usually the one who likes to talk first. And now I'm the one who has so much to share. . . ."

Raven holds Violet's hands and speaks slowly, looking directly into her eyes. "I want to hear the details about your ceremony, I do. I even want to see pictures, but before we go there, I need a favor from you. I want to do a scene. I need to pretend like you are mine. All mine. This may be the last time I ever ask this of you, but it's what I need right now."

"Of course, Baby. You want to steal me from the arms of my husband?"

"No. I want to pretend there is no husband. I want to feel like you belong to me and only me."

"That IS kinky." Violet moves in for a kiss, but then pulls away. "Wait. Do I still dance at the club?"

"You can still be you. I just want you all to myself, just for this moment." Raven finishes taking off her last piece of clothing.

"And how do you plan to do that?" Violet says, seeking direction.

Raven rolls on top of Violet, and hovers above her on all fours. "I want you to give yourself to me in a way you've never given yourself before." Her fingers are plucking on Violet's lacy waistband.

"But I already belong to you," Violet says as she strips down her own panties.

"Not all of you." Raven reaches around to Violet's buttocks, wedging her fingers into her crack.

"Are you talking about . . . my ass?"

Raven looks Violet in the eyes. "Why not?"

"I'm just not into anal."

"But this is for me, not you."

"Oh, really?" Violet says, searching Raven's eyes to understand the game.

"It's like a gift to me; it's the ultimate submission. Trust me?" Raven says, biting her lip and squinting her eyes.

"But I feel like I would have to shave or shit or wash first."

"No. I want you now, just as you are." Raven maneuvers Violet onto her side so she can massage the soft curves of both her back and stomach. She uses long slow strokes, helping Violet relax.

"It feels so dirty."

"It is dirty. You're a dirty girl." Raven's hands begin to work deep into Violet's glute muscles.

"Let me ask you this, what is it about the butthole? I mean I get it's our base chakra and all that, but what's so sexy about the place where poop comes out?"

"If you can drop the social shame for a moment, you'll find it's very pleasurable." Raven warms both hands on the cusp of Violet's bottom as if polishing it. "The root represents a point of singularity beyond the duality of male and female. It unifies all of humanity. And today, I want to focus my love into the deepest darkest part of you."

Violet leaps up to grab supplies. "I have to at least put towels down and you have to use gloves."

"Grab the lube!" Raven shouts between rooms, and more thoughtfully adds, "And I suppose you better grab a dental dam too, so I can lick your anus."

When Violet returns, she spreads a towel across the bed. "Seriously? I've never had a rim job."

"If you can pee on Charles Muir in front of a whole room of people, you can at least let me play with your rosebud."

Once a nest on the bed is properly arranged, Violet sits cross-legged in the middle and takes a deep breath. "Okay, just so you know, anal makes me feel tender and vulnerable. I have a ton of resistance but I want to relax, and let you in." She nods with her hands in Namaste.

"Thank you." Raven bows back and says, "My intention is to heal this possessive impulse of mine. I want to own you and to pretend you are all mine, and then let it all go."

"Okay. This is for today only. I don't want you getting any ideas." Violet nuzzles Raven's neck. "How do you want me?"

"Spread-eagle with lots of lube." Raven playfully pushes Violet facedown on the towels, then positions a pillow under her hips so that her bare ass is lifted toward the sky.

Violet exhales. "I just want to close my eyes and go away."

"You think I'm going to let you lie there and dissociate?"

"Please, Mistress."

"Think again. We need to find a way to make this hot for both of us. How about you tell me a fantasy . . . that way I can be inside your head, as well as your ass."

"Mmmm. Is it okay if I use one of my clients from the club?"

"Are you still attracted to the Ukrainian guy you've been flirting with?"

"Ivan. Oh, God. I can't help it."

"Just relax." Raven scoots in deep between Violet's legs, holding her hips with one hand and fingering around the outside of Violet's anus with her other thumb.

Violet spins a fantasy in order to help herself relax. "Okay, so as you know, Ivan's a regular. He's not a big guy, probably like five-ten, with a shaved head and a thick Eastern European accent. He has this big space between his front teeth, which is the main reason I find him attractive. In Chinese face reading, large gaps in teeth mean instability and violence. I always imagine he's like this dangerous hitman, or a gangster, though he's never been anything but calm and cool around me. He absolutely adores me. He hands me like seven hundred bucks to take care of him for the night. We start off by going to the couches and just talking about all kinds of stuff. He says he likes my face, so I tease him by rubbing my face all over him during his lap dance. Then after a few songs, we start playing this game because he can't touch me. He's working my bra with his mouth and it's a classic cat-and-mouse tease. I slide my breasts over his face. Sometimes I'll use my hair to hide him so he can kiss my nipples, and it turns me on. When it's slow at the club, I can grind on him and I get so close to cumming. I turn around and put my butt in his lap. He gets so frustrated, he grunts out loud, and I can tell he just wants to hold my hips down and . . ."

"Okay, now I want you to drop the fantasy and just feel how your anus is pulling my finger in." Raven lovingly admires Violet's tight little rosebud. She is enlivened by how soft she feels inside, and after her finger is two knuckles deep, she begins to find a rhythm.

"It's so slippery," Violet says, backing her ass up against Raven's hand.

"Yes, now rock your pelvis as you imagine I was the one dropping seven hundred dollars and making you dance only for me. What are you going to do for me, huh?"

"In my fantasy world, we have that same hot chemistry we have now, and you would grab my hips and hold me down against your bulge. You'd force me to grind on you until you couldn't stand it. Then, you'd pull your cock out, spread open my asscheeks, and pull me down onto your cock so I can't wiggle away. Of course, it's uncomfortable having you fill me in the ass. If I really wanted to, I could get away. But since you paid for the time, it's almost like I owe it to you."

Raven notices that Violet has been stroking her clit while she's been fantasizing, and she pushes her hand away. "Have you been touching yourself? You little slut! You're asking for it. You want me to double penetrate you."

Raven slips the thumb from her other hand into Violet's hungry pussy.

"Oh yes! That's a relief."

Raven rearranges Violet's body onto her side again, this time positioning herself so that she can watch the expressions on Violet's face while she works both holes with both hands.

"Mmmm . . ." Although Violet's eyes are closed, there is pleasure on her face as she continues to daydream. "Sometimes you take me in the back room and you don't even wait for me to take my top off. You just come up behind me and tell me to put my hands on the wall by the light switch. Then you slip my panties to the side and fuck me in the ass like you're doing right now. It's like I have no say whatsoever. And you'll reach your arms around, grabbing at my tits and squeezing my nipples while biting on my neck...like I'm just trapped there, up against the wall . . . Oh. Oh, God."

"You ready to drop the fantasy? Look into my eyes."

Violet props herself up so she can feel how deeply connected Raven's dark eyes are to the warm sensations between her legs.

"I want to own you. I want you to feel my fingers working inside you. Loving you right now in the ass and the yoni. I am inside every part of you. There is nothing separating us, no fantasies, and no other lovers. It's just you and me. Can you feel that?"

"Yes . . . It's like you're loving me inside out." Violet rocks harder and faster onto both of Raven's hands.

"Every part of you . . ."

"Oh God, yes!"

"There is no part of you I can't love. Do you get that?"

"Mmm-hmmm." Violet starts to weep.

"Even this part. Especially here."

"I'm yours."

"That's right. Say it again," Raven commands.

"Oh, God. Okay. I'm there." Violet's breathing becomes erratic and she relaxes her entire being onto Raven's hands. Raven's laser focus on Violet doesn't waver through the wild thrusts and heavy breaths, even when she starts convulsing. Finally, Violet lets out a long sigh.

When she surfaces from a deep state of surrender, Violet licks her lips and says, "That was so tender, and slippery. I'm glad I had all these towels." Violet dabs a corner of the towel against her thighs.

Raven gracefully gathers Violet's body close to her in a cuddle. "There was a moment when it felt like a veil lifted."

"Funny. It's like the fantasy fell out from between us."

"I feel more secure now. It was like I needed you to give yourself to me before I could celebrate your wedding."

"I never felt so adored. Like every part of me is lovable."

"Now, I can finally set you free in the fullest sense of the word. I can love you as a free woman, and as Damien's wife."

Raven tenderly kisses Violet's collarbone, then looks her in the eyes and says, "I'm ready now to hear all about it."

Gold Dust

From Violet's *Book of Shadows*

Raven guided me around the back of her house, but instead of leading me into the playroom, she showed me a massage table she'd set up under the great oak.

"I prepared a special treat," Raven said as she untied the spaghetti straps on my cotton top.

After she set my breasts free, I planted my mouth on her face to steady myself as I stepped one leg at a time out of my red jeans.

"What did I do to deserve this?" I asked.

Raven asked, "Want me to count all the reasons you deserve to be adored?"

I stretched my naked body across the table and said, "I'd rather you just show me with your hands." I melted under her long, warm strokes. "Do you have oil?" I asked.

"This is a special kind of massage," she said mysteriously. "I'm just preparing the canvas."

I warned her, "You know I have to dance tonight, so you can't use paint or mark my skin."

"Don't worry and keep your eyes closed," Raven directed.

I couldn't help but peek through the face cradle. I saw her scooping something white from a kitchen bowl. She sprinkled it up my thighs. It felt relaxing, like a white sand beach, except silkier. Like powdered sugar. She swept the substance across my shoulders and kneaded my back the way a baker would roll out a pie on a cutting board covered with flour.

"Mmmmm . . . It's sooooo soft," I said dreamily. Then it started to tickle and I couldn't help but giggle. "I have to know, what is it?"

"Cornstarch."

"Aaahhh." I moaned and undulated as Raven trailed her fingers between my thighs, slowly powdering the ridge where my asscrack turns into my pussy lips. I could feel my skin pucker into little goose bumps. I imagined what my pussy looked like under Raven's ghost-white powdered fingertips. "Will this give me a yeast infection?"

"Well, I don't plan to cram it inside you," she joked.

"I know, but is it non-GMO?"

"Of course, it's organic. It might feel dry, but it's safe. Masters and Johnson used a mixture of cornstarch and water as the ingredients for artificial semen in their studies."

"Artificial semen!"

Raven laughed, "Yeah, in the fifties they used an internal camera to study where the semen goes once it's inside the vagina."

"I love it." I wiggled my powder-white body against the table, wondering where our fantasies might take us this Friday.

"I feel like I'm covered in dry cum, like a sex slave after a bukkake scene," I said suggestively.

"Really? Is that where you're going with this?"

"This is definitely another first. I can't believe it's almost been a full year and we're still having firsts!"

"When you put two perverted minds together, darling, the firsts are unlimited," Raven bragged.

I continued to marvel, "I know that's true of fantasies because they are constantly streaming through us. Firsts are different. There's a limit to things we can actually do, but we just keep finding new frontiers. How many years do you think it'll be before we run out?"

That's when I felt Raven's touch get tense. She said, "I've been wanting to talk about the whole anniversary thing."

I asked as casually as I could, "What's up, babe?"

"I know you and Damien just had a wedding and I want to give it the space it deserves. So I was thinking we could put off our celebration for later."

"Not a chance!" I blurted out louder than I meant to.

"It's not like our relationship started exactly one year ago," Raven argued.

I rolled onto my side, powder flying everywhere, and asked, "When exactly would you say we started?"

Raven sat on the edge of the table and looked me square in the face. "Well, remember the day you massaged me in your backyard . . . ?"

"You mean the day you almost broke up with me?" I asked.

"ALMOST? I was done with you, I had completely given up," Raven announced.

"What I remember is you hosing off and then leaving. You wouldn't even let me pat you dry," I said, feeling rather dry myself, like an old crusty mermaid.

Raven fingered the powder on my back as she spoke. "Right. Well, I remember you wouldn't let go. You fought for us. Then we went to the tide pools and had that whole negotiation with

Damien. I feel like that was the day our relationship really started."

"That's two months later!" I exclaimed. "People don't just
make up anniversaries."

"Why not?" Raven reasoned, "We make up everything else.
We time travel and shape-shift. Our entire relationship is based
on fantasy."

"And love," I jumped in, "our relationship is also based on
informed consent. You can't just make a unilateral decision."

Raven's voice softened. "That day at the beach was when I
had a change of heart—and really devoted myself to you, and
Damien—in the ocean."

I teased, "You know, if you would've just let me wash
you off, you could've had a change of heart under my garden
hose."

I outstretched my arms and pulled her into a sideways hug,
getting white powder all over her top. While she was stripping
it off I said, "Listen, I don't want to minimize that we've been
meeting for a full calendar year. That's a big deal. That's like
what, 52 Fridays?" I said proudly.

"Agreed. It's something special, which is why I want to set
our anniversary apart from your wedding."

"For me, it's like the sun and the moon. You are my queen
and he is, well, he's just Damien. There's no comparison."

"How about July thirteenth? So when it falls on a Friday,
it'll be extra witchy?" she offered, and I could tell she wasn't
going to let it go.

"Fine," I said. "We can change it for next year, but we are
still going to celebrate next week." She squeezed me, and I rolled
over so she could finally massage my front side.

Raven spread the cornstarch around with a feather-like
touch over every inch of this new landscape. She gave extra attention to my nipples.

"Mmmm . . . It's so fine, it's like gold dust," I said, feeling a warmth in my womb.

"It is. It's Mayan gold. That's what the ancients used to call the cornfields."

Raven seemed to massage beyond the surface: deep into my pores, into the subtle spaces inside, into antimatter, into dream-time, where there was a delicious mix of memories. It was like she traveled to a time before we met, like a cellular remembrance from before we were born. An ancient time...

"Do you remember meeting me, before?" Raven asked in a far-off voice.

"Mmmm . . . before what?" My body was convulsing with pleasure.

"Before we wore the skin we're in." Raven stroked danger-ously close to my nipples. "We were temple priestesses, you and I." She walked her fingertips to the crease between my thighs. I looked at the leaves above, wrestling in the wind, then lifted my gaze into the blue sky beyond the trees. I peered at Raven, who was stroking my outer lips, and I noticed the powder beading up against the invisible stubble on my shaved pussy.

Raven continued speaking as if in a trance. "From the out-side, the temple might be mistaken for a forgotten cave. It's a simple mound nestled in the hills. There is nothing remarkable about the hallway that leads inside. It's dimly lit . . ."

We fell into a dream, some of which was spoken aloud, some of it imagined. Or was it remembered?

"The path leads to a dozen rounded doors, each more or-nate than the last. These are private chambers. Inside they are dripping with opulence: colored glass, soft fabrics, elaborate altars. But the doors are locked when occupied, and we hear the muffled moans of seekers wafting out from within the thick earthen walls. You feel called to the last door where a dark priestess stands in the doorway.

"What are those cries?" I asked, confused about what I was hearing.

"'The sounds of war being melted from the warrior and shame being drained from our collective skin,' the dark priestess says, stepping to the side and inviting you through the final open door. Intuitively, you know there is no turning back. You enter. The dark one commands you to disrobe."

"Is it you? Are you the dark priestess?"

"'I can be whomever you want me to be,' the dark priestess says."

My body was writhing under the powder. I opened my eyes and said, "It looks like you, but your face morphs into an old wise woman in one moment and into a little girl in the next."

"So you undress slowly, slipping the straps off each shoulder as you survey the space. There's a canopy hanging over a soft mattress like a weeping willow. A nearby nightstand supports a deep golden urn and several shallow bowls of essential oils glistening by the light of the flickering candelabra. The priestess spreads her scarf over the hand-woven quilt and beckons you to surrender your sky-clad body onto the bed. She reaches for the urn and holds it above your crown, whispering, 'Your mantra here is YES.'

"From the urn, she scoops a full fist of gold dust. The sight of her glowing fingers fills you with desire, which grows as she speaks, her voice echoing through the transformation chamber. . . .

"'This is the answer to every pleasure you seek and every pleasure that has sought you.'"

Raven sprinkled more magic dust over my sensitive skin. I moaned as she massaged deeper. Her hands painted gold over my every curve and crevice. She turned my yoni into a spiraling cyclone of fantasies, where subjective and objective became an indistinguishable flood, a cloudburst that drenched both realms, mixing fantasy with reality, longing with fulfillment, the sacred with the profane, inside and outside. . . .

I was awash with all kinds of sexual longing and a simultaneous sense of satisfaction: beyond the stranger I wished I had kissed, beyond the prison bitch gang bang, beyond the forgiven professor, beyond a lifetime of service as a geisha, beyond the unspeakable, beyond the beyond, into total transcendence....

My breathing brought me back down into this specific time/space reality, where Raven was gently resting on my pelvis and patiently waiting for me to open my eyes.

"What just happened?" I whispered.

"You tell me," Raven said with a smirk.

"I think I just came," I said, astonished. "Were you inside me?"

"No, darling, I wasn't even on your yoni." I looked down to verify that Raven's hands were resting on my torso, but I could have sworn she was inside me.

"Well, that was another first." I sat up, wanting to hug her, but I was a disaster. "You wouldn't believe what I just saw."

"I'm pretty sure I saw it too," she said, dusting the table. "Want to use the outdoor shower?"

"No, I want to use your garden hose."

"Really?" Raven stepped over to the outside wall of the playroom where the hose was coiled. She directed it onto her hands and turned the key. She passed the flowing stream over me. At first, I was shocked by the cold, then sad to see the powder run off my body. I squatted and held it to my crack, rubbing vigorously and then delicately. I fingered my swollen folds before standing up stark naked with rivulets of white water trickling to the grass below. "Can you get my back?"

"Turn around," Raven said, taking the spewing nozzle.

Raven seemed delighted by the beauty of the moment and spontaneously said, "Your cunt is my heart."

I asked what she meant. She said it was the first line of the poem she was writing for our anniversary. I spun around, still covered in streaks of pasty cornstarch, and swiftly kissed her. Waxing poetic myself, I asked if it was about "enchanting gold dust washing down to Earth by the stream of a common garden hose."

"You read my mind," she teased.

Yours,
Vi.

FRIDAY #52

Polyversary
From *Raven's Playbook*

66 I haven't rehearsed it out loud," I warned, scribbling the final lines on an index card. I adjusted the brim of my fedora enough to see Violet stripping down to her polka-dotted lingerie. We were on her bed celebrating our one year anniversary.

"Can I go first?" she asked, crawling toward me seductively.

"What do you mean, go first?" I said, setting my note cards on the nightstand to kiss her.

"I got you a gift and it has the best wrapping ever."

"You did? Where is it?" I asked as she positioned herself in front of me with legs spread, beckoning me inside.

"You want me to use my pen?" I smirked.

She grabbed my black necktie and gently pulled me closer. "No, Sir, I want you to stuff your fingers inside me." She bit her lip. "Slowly."

I moved my hand up her thigh, but she got impatient and grabbed my wrist, pulling it toward her yoni.

"I'd like to hear you beg," I resisted.

"Pretty please?"

I succumbed to her pleading, slipping one finger in at a time. Then I felt something strange. "What is that?"

"Pull it out and see," she said with a smirk.

It felt like fishing around for a ping-pong ball. I was careful not to pinch her as I pulled on the rim of a neatly tied condom. When it emerged, I saw something colorful and mysterious inside.

"Is this my present?" I asked, holding it up to the light.

"Yup," she beamed, proud of her own ingenuity.

"You were right, best wrapping ever." I tore the condom with my teeth, uncovering a tiny gemstone bracelet on an elastic string. "I can't believe it…" I sighed, feeling the energy radiating from them. "Thank you."

"It's made of carnelian and hematite. They're supposed to be good for grounding." She couldn't stop smiling.

"You think I need grounding?"

"It was the only stones small enough to fit inside my special giftwrapping."

I kissed her. "You are unbelievable."

"You're my poet," she cooed.

"My turn?" I asked, climbing over Violet to grab a rope from my bag. First, I fastened her arms to the bedpost above her head. Then, I tied her ankles to her thighs but kept her legs spread wide. I whipped off my necktie and used it to gag her mouth, then I stood back to admire my work.

My bitch was bound and gagged.

"Now don't go anywhere," I mocked as I walked toward the door.

Violet spit the tie out and called after me, "Where are you going?"

I looked over my shoulder and said, "To get Damien."

"Are you serious?" she squealed.

I grabbed her by the face and retied her gag as I explained, "Who else is going to record this?"

Damien dropped what he was doing and didn't hesitate to join us. His eyes grew wide at the sight of his bound bride. He focused the camera on Violet's body and said, "I'm glad I can contribute in some small way to your anniversary."

"You've contributed a ton throughout the entire year," I said.

He nodded then teased, "I figure you may need someone to spot you since last time you tied her up, she nearly passed out."

I grimaced. "You had to bring that up, didn't you?"

"You want me to get the safety scissors?" he joked.

Violet spit the tie out. "I'm fine! Just take the video."

"I told you to keep quiet," I said.

Violet continued, "But, baby, be sure to get a close-up. There, that's all I needed to say."

I rearranged the tie and kissed her through the gag. "You are not to remove this from your mouth again, you understand?"

"I love how you love each other," Damien said warmly.

"I love you both," Violet said through the gag.

"You know," I said, squeezing Damien's thigh, "we wouldn't be having an anniversary without you."

Damien added, ". . . And our love wouldn't be the same without you."

"True," I replied, grabbing the note cards. "And now this poem is for my bitch on our first anniversary. Ready?"

Damien nodded, camera rolling.

"This is my attempt to immortalize the unique world that opened up between us only 52 weeks ago." I straightened my fedora then circled around Violet's body, kissing her neck between lines, pulling her hair and whispering into her ear while reading this poem:

Her cunt is my heart.

She wears the fabric of reality
like black lace hosiery strapped
to her thigh with a garter belt
gifted to her by Lucifer.

When our bodies press together,
her nylon runs and we fall through
a hole in her crotch to another dimension
where unicorns and mermaids
never stop . . . fucking.

Where orchids are talking
and earthworms have eyes.
A limitless universe where nothing
makes sense, except the impulse
to penetrate and ejaculate.

All the flowers become vulvas
whose petals are fleshy and bulging.
Little fluffy bunnies hop by with hard-ons.
She points to a blossom and giggles.
Everything is made wet by her laughter.

She is my oracle. She is my muse.
Every word I write was first formed
in the dreamtime she embodies.
The primal wound of separation
is somehow mended when she
licks her lips.

We need not make love for
the reparation of my madness,
nor share a pillow, nor even a kiss.
Touching or not, we are already one.
For the hole in my heart is shaped
like the hole between her legs.

She is my territory. She is my map.
My hands have memorized her folds and
secret chambers, fingering the mysteries
of the material world until they dissolve,
the moment we cum.
Together or not.

She is my moonlight. She is my soulmate.
Lying in bed as a girl-child, feeling herself
through cotton panties, she dreamt me up.
I marvel now at how, through all the space
between stars, her light managed
to bounce off the sun, and land in my lap.

She is my daughter. I am her Daddy.
In the shape-shifting-time-traveling
field of permission that is birthed by
our meeting, we rewrite the collective
incest wound. Redeeming rapists
and risking eternal damnation.

She is my savior. She is my bitch.
Her fantasies are my spiritual scriptures.
She is the second coming that absolves
the bogus story of original sin.

Our lovemaking is a prayer:
A twisted, fantasy-filled tribute
to the incomprehensible reality
we inhabit.

Our fucking is a rebellion.
Bodies uprising in pleasure
against the systematic shaming of
the source of all life...Woman.
I worship you.

Acknowledgments

To Roxanne DePalma, thank you for the undying encouragement, inspiration, and creative musing. All the words in the world could not express my gratitude for all that you did on every dimension to make this dream a reality.

Deep bow to my agent, Bobby Newman, for vision and persistence through the last five years of publishing this Bitch of a novel!

To my extraordinary publishing team at Cleis Press: thank you Hannah Bennett for being my creative advocate and understanding editor throughout all the last minute changes. And big gratitude to Meghan Kilduff for all your support and flexibility.

Immense gratitude also goes to my entourage of lovers who've supported me throughout the five year journey of cocreating this book:

Michael McClure, Sharmilla Graefer (AKA Red Speckled Orchid of the Amazon), James Schmachtenberger, Summer Athena Fah, Melinda DePalma, Cheri Reeder, Stacy Ellis, Viraja Ma, Mia Mor, Ria Yoshida, Reid Mihalko, Triambika Ma Vive, Jennifer and Jesse Norton, Tahl Gruer and Alix Lowe. Extra special thanks goes to everyone else in the San Diego Super Pod! I wouldn't be who I am if it weren't for your love.

Deep bow to the core members of the International School of Temple Arts, especially Ohad Pele Ezrahi, Baba Dez Nichols, and Bruce Lyon.

Thank you to my Tantra and performance art mentors Charles Muir, Annie Sprinkle PhD, and Beth Stevens PhD.

Thanks to my allies and author assistants: Bryanne Haney, Steven Starr, Jen Moreno, Lurana Donnels O'Malley, Marni

Freedman, and Mary VanMeer (RIP). And special acknowl-edgement to Lilly Penhall for helping edit Act IV into narrative form.

Beta Readers: Josh Zuchowski, Heather Meglasson, Sharmila Grafer, Michael Ellsberg, Jessica Gibson, Howie Morningstar, and my brother-in-law, Christian McClure who also served as our sexy gay cheerleader!

Ultimate thanks to my husband Michael McClure for loving me so freely.

About the Author

Photo: Pien Holdijk

KAMALADEVI McCLURE (KamalaDevi.com) is a mystic, a muse, and a mother whose mission it is to mentor artists and healers and love leaders. She travels the world teaching sexual shamanism for the International School of Temple Arts (ISTA). Her family stars in Showtime's hit docu-series, *Polyamory: Married and Dating*. She's appeared on *Dr. Drew, Tyra Banks* and in the award-winning documentary *Sex Magic*. Founder of PolyPalooza and San Diego Tantra Theater, she is also the author of *Sex Shamans, Don't Drink the Punch, Polyamory Pearls, Sacred Slut Sutras*, and coauthor of *Sacred Sexual Healing*.